THE HOLY fOOL

THE HOLY fOOL

Harold Fickett

CROSSWAY BOOKS · WESTCHESTER, ILLINOIS
A DIVISION OF GOOD NEWS PUBLISHERS

Copyright © 1983 by Harold Fickett
Published by Crossway Books,
a division of Good News Publishers
9825 West Roosevelt Road
Westchester, Illinois 60153

First printing, 1983

Printed in the United States of America

Library of Congress Catalog Card Number 82-73658
ISBN 0-89107 227-6

To Mary

And he said unto me, My grace is sufficient for thee: for my strength is made perfect in weakness.
—II Corinthians 12.9

Part I

Revival Week

Sunday:

Providence

My testimony would have to begin with the revival. I was pastor at the time of the First Baptist Church of Santa Carina, a suburb of ranch houses and Gunite swimming pools in Los Angeles, and I was sitting in my office on the second floor of the educational building, trying to prepare my sermon for that upcoming Sunday, and finding, as usual, that I was unable to concentrate, when I saw a bilious pink bus roll into the Texaco station across the street. Painted on the side of the bus in tall letters tongued with flame was THE HALLELUJAH EXPRESS, and beneath, in script, *Rev. Jenkins Rolling Revival,* and beneath that, in block letters, *"Featuring the Hallelujah Chorus."*

A black man stepped out of the bus, wearing the collar and the black garb—a short-sleeved black shirt—of the Episcopal Church. He hailed the service-station attendant and then turned back toward the bus, and as he did a flash of light from him caught me square in the eyes. He took another step, changing the angle of his body, and I saw a chest-spanning silver cross hanging from a chain around his neck. Young women started to pile off the bus, wearing shimmering dresses or flouncy pants suits, and two of them, walking off toward the ladies room, linked arms and performed several rock 'n' roll gyrations, twitching their behinds and bumping hips. They broke away from each other, and the taller of the two clapped her hands as she bent and swayed at the waist, and then both of them broke out laughing. The Hallelujah Chorus seemed to be having a high old time on the road.

I had to smile at this.

And then the smugness of my attitude—the I-don't-know-about-you-but-I'm-all-right-Jack attitude of evangelical superiority got to me; it was absurd, I knew, and ludicrous, considering the source, and just as suddenly I was furious. But then my anger, which rose out of the frustrations and the accumulated pain of my years in the ministry, began to bump against the scaffolding, as it felt, of that same smugness. A classic depression, a clinician might say; for me, the worst kind of hypocrisy.

For the question came down to this: what was actually going on out there with the Rev. Jenkins and his Rolling Revival? Was the light of holiness and sanctity manifesting itself in forms that some might take for mere entertainment, with a bit of sleight-of-hand or magic thrown in? Was it all flimflam, or was the Lord camping out with those folks?

For my stock-in-trade was hardly any different; and if such a thing as authenticity exists, then I know it's doomed to be buried in either the spangled theatrics of rolling revivals or else in the more sedate shows that I put on every Sunday morning—in all those forms of this world which most often seem, more than anything else, trivial or haphazard. Either nature bears the weight of glory or we have to bear the knowledge that our deepest longings are vanity, because we aren't able to bear up under the weight of it on our own for long.

The question for me had become, Was Christianity true?

I had no way of telling. Not for sure, although at fifty-five I had already devoted thirty years to preaching the gospel, and wished with everything in me to recover the certainty that I had once had.

What's more, circumstances were pressing that question upon me in a way I couldn't sidestep. My ministry for the last ten years had been heading on a pretty precipitous downhill course. Recently, many of my people at First Baptist had made a special point, as I greeted them after the services, of telling me that they were praying for me, and I had been in the pastorate long enough to know that when people start telling you they're praying for you, you're in trouble. Indeed, my ministry seemed to have entered a dark and sodden night of the soul, so to speak, in which I could smell the tar and feathers.

For the past several months I had been so depressed that,

as on this day, when I should have been preparing my messages (our sanitized euphemism for sermons), I often sat locked in a deepening greyness, my mind in limbo, as my brethren at the Texaco station might have it. At such moments of impasse I used to read. Chaucer, Shakespeare, Milton, and the metaphysical poets—authors I learned to love in college. These companionable gentlemen not only supplied me with sermon illustrations, which they did in abundance, but comfort; they helped ease me through that first, early period when I had to admit that my relationship with Constance, my wife, was not nearly what it should be, and wasn't likely to change.

It took a long time for the attendent to fill the bus's gas tank. Even the sanctified life has to operate on real fuel. But at last he signaled to the Rev. Jenkins and the black man took a great wad of bills out of his front pants pocket, wet his thumb, and peeled them off. The women in the Hallelujah Chorus were straggling back toward the vehicle; one's spiked heel had evidently picked up a piece of bubble gum, because she took off her shoe and scraped its heel-tip against the concrete curb supporting the gas pumps. I hadn't noticed until then that most of the women were wearing their hair high (or had on similar wigs), in a spun-cotton style my wife used to call a beehive. The sun, shining down on their heads and on the film of hair-spray which must have held these coiffures in place, seemed at that moment, from out of the wooden darkness of my depression, to adorn them with halos. The effect was so marked that the Lord God Almighty himself, like one of the Church's painters, might have laid on these women a visible sign of their spiritual state.

That was enough for me. I decided then and there that what my church needed was an old-fashioned revival. An Amen! Praise God! Thank-you Jesus! revival. I decided to forget all this agony-of-the-soul nonsense and throw myself into the Lord's service once more. And perhaps, in this renunciation of my doubts and questionings, and of my ambivalent desire to be modest and respectable in order to meet my congregation's expectations of current evangelical fashion, in this plunge into action, the Lord might see fit to place his hand again on my ministry. For I am that minister that you have very likely heard or read about; I am *that* Ted March.

I might never have come up with the idea of the revival, however, if the Hallelujah Chorus hadn't appeared three days after I'd received a letter from an old friend from seminary days, Paul Corwin. Paul had written to tell me that he was staying in San Diego, resting after his latest GO! tour—GO! for Gospel Outreach. Paul took the acronym from the verse that had directed his life: Go ye into all the world and preach the gospel to every creature. Besides its evangelizing efforts, GO! was best known for its world-hunger-relief crusades.

Paul became famous and revered and loved in my sector of Christendom through the promotional films for his ministry. People pictured him as a round-faced, khaki-clad man striding through bleached-out fields in the company of dark-skinned children—at his feet, in his arms, on his shoulders. In his movies, Paul's face is full of the sadness that accompanies compassion; his eyes are small, almost withdrawn, and perhaps would glisten if the film's resolution were better; yet his movements convey a tremendous energy, the sort of brio that politicians try to affect when they roll up their sleeves and go on walking tours of ghettos. Clearly, he is a wonderful man, a pragmatic St. Francis. And from my personal knowledge (and here I speak absolutely without irony) he *was* a wonderful man. In seminary, he and I engaged in a contest to see who could date the most nurses from a nearby college. He won. It was his energy, that brio. It isn't often that we're in the presence of someone who knows how to truly enjoy himself, and Paul had that; he made you believe, through his exuberance, in the goodness of God's creation.

In his letter he said that he might have to remain in the States for some time. He had an unspecified recurring condition, he said, which, although it could be controlled, might become agitated by the rigors of travel and reappear. I knew his "confinement" had prompted the letter. (Paul needed periodic trips on airplanes in the way that I need to play golf.) He wanted to come and preach, he assured me, and since I wouldn't be able to get the revival organized for another month, I knew that in a month's time he would be ready to give me a week of messages that would have my people laughing and crying and reaching deep into their wallets and purses for the Love Offering and charging down the aisles at the Altar Call.

In retrospect, I can see that my motives, subconsciously at least, were mixed. I was well aware that Paul would generate a lot of good will toward me. When the people came to him and bewailed my failings, he would tell them that the local pastor is the foot soldier of Christ's army; that he, Paul Corwin, wouldn't be able to survive in my place for fifteen minutes; that they ought to get down on their knees every night and thank God for their wonderful pastor, and that, come Judgment Day, I would surely receive more laurels than he. And I knew they would buy it, which would give me another year to turn the church around, to get attendance up, get offerings up, and my spirits up, also.

Preparations began. I called Michael Dennis, my young assistant pastor, into my office. Everything about Michael is Southern California: the top layer of his hair bleached out, with honey-blond strands beneath; his speckled-blue, slightly pinched-in eyes above a thin nose, the tip of which is always red and peeling. He has a lop-sided and engaging smile, and a body whose only wear and tear has come about by a lot of volleyball on the beach. Even though there's a kind of sandpiper dim-wittedness to his expression, he's disgustingly handsome. I told him about my plans and asked him to line up the special music. I suggested guest pianists, a trumpet trio, a gospel quartet with a bathysphere bass ("Rocka my soul in the bosom of Abraham"), a women's sextet, the usual complement of folk-rock groups to bring in the teenagers, and perhaps even an oddity like an electric saw virtuoso. (I have a weakness for all this low Baptist culture that is perhaps like the fondness of certain cultured men for vaudeville.) Michael said fan*tas*tic! in that peculiarly Southern California way which paints expanses with the second syllable, thereby expanding the adjective indefinitely, and he went out of the office humming, with his collar-length, thick, bluntly-cut hair bobbing as if in time to some movement of the ocean within him. Michael is so young and blissfully naive in certain respects that he always depresses me, even now (or especially now, considering his interfamilial connections), but on that day I continued undaunted. In certain respects, it's wonderfully numbing to be beyond the age of fifty— on the days when it isn't awful.

I next called Wilomena Sunday (everyone calls her Will), our educational director, and asked her to take charge of publicity. She wondered where she could get accurate biographical information on Paul, in order to write up an article for the local paper. Will is terrific about the details that make for professionalism.

And then I called Cecil Brown, the head of the board of deacons, the ruling body in our church, and "advised him," as we say in committee, that the deacons would probably want to hold a mid-week prayer breakfast with Paul Corwin. He'd get right on it, he said.

I announced two weeks later, at the Sunday morning service, that the revival would begin in two weeks, on Sunday night, and that everyone should pray for revival, in his own life, in the church, and in the lives of friends. The people applauded. That was a strange moment, entirely spontaneous; you seldom hear applause in our churches; even though we claim to be part of the "free" Protestant tradition, we are about as spontaneous in our worship as bedridden shut-ins.

For my own part, lately I had been murmuring my way through my sermons, but that day I preached in my approximation of Billy Graham's voice, the accented words drawn out and sent off with a conviction that seems to swell the excitement of the congregation and detonate in belief among them. Due to lack of preparation, the sermon lacked cogency, but it could have consisted entirely of unrelated syllables—the preacher had his voice back and the people were happy.

I was happy, too. That whole next week I felt that my spiritual aridity, my Sahara drought, had come to an end. The Lord's hand was back on my ministry, I sensed, and plans and events from now on would bear the stamp of providence. Like the Israelites, I was not sure of the reasons for my bondage and aridity, but I had their same hope of deliverance. And if the Hallelujah Chorus was, as the kids say, a bit "funky" to assume the proportions of a celestial omen, I was in no position to insist on a burning bush. I felt my old confidence, like a freshet of deliverance, return and I found myself, in the privacy of my office in the educational building, quoting out loud from the twenty-third Psalm, "The Lord is my Shepherd; I shall not want. He maketh me to lie down in green pastures; he leadeth me beside the still waters. He restoreth my soul . . ."

On the first Sunday of the revival, I sat down to lunch with Constance, my wife, and Benjamin, our twelve-year-old son, in tremendously high spirits—a mood swinger, as you see. My sermon that morning had been the best of the year, which I say in all modesty; it was. The success of it made me bold to ask Constance if I might say grace.

She gave me a quick look, indecipherable if it weren't for our twenty-six years together, from the time I took her out of her Main Line home in Philadelphia into my evangelical underworld. When Constance looks at me in that way I think of the line from the Shakespeare sonnet, which runs, "They are the lords and owners of their faces." Indeed, Constance has an Elizabethan visage; her blonde hair, fetchingly streaked with grey, is swept back from the widow's peak of her regally high forehead; her round eyes, framed by the arched portals of their deep sockets and her prominent cheekbones, are a hard grey. With that diamond glance, full of light yet impenetrable, Constance gave her assent without giving up her sovereignty. This was her table, not the Lord's, and she would remain the demiurge, her look said.

Harsh? Perhaps. I doubt if any pastor's homelife is what it's imagined to be, and mine seems worse. Constance couldn't bear my habit of finding theological significances in the routine. But to my thinking, our French-Provincial table, whose thick wood was aged rather than worn, and the complementing "peasant" decor—rustic sconces, a ceramic tile floor, a wrought-iron screen opening into the living room—all implied a paganism so secure it didn't have to aspire to the elegance Constance had been born into. She would counter that there is nothing inherently godly about Victorian furniture and filigreed silverware on lace tablecloths. And I agree. But in such a setting, because I would have felt more at home, I could have prayed and the family meal have been a communion.

Thus her look said no, even as it said yes. I prayed: Lord bless us and this food to our bodies, and help us to be dedicated to your service. In Christ's name, Amen.

And before I lost the momentum of the morning, I turned to Benjamin and told him about the folk-rock group that would provide special music for that night's revival, and then a few tidbits about Paul Corwin's worldwide travels, leading Ben to expect adventure as much as edification from Paul. I have this weakness with my family of trying to spice up Christianity. And then I said, "If you and your mom were there, we could all go out for some ice cream afterwards, and talk with Paul." As should be clear, I wasn't sure they would come; I never am.

Benjamin turned to Constance and his face was transfigured by the look of a much younger child; besides the pleading in it, there was curiosity, lust for ice cream, but also the hope for a normal family life.

I must explain something about Benjamin. His birth was a mistake—good Lord, what a horrendous euphemism! Constance was in her early forties and we had stopped using birth control when we did have sex, which wasn't often; in fact, it came around about as frequently as national holidays. Menopause seemed much more imminent than conception and yet, like Sarah and Elizabeth, the Lord saw fit to bless her. Her magnificat was an immediate request for an abortion; our marriage was well into its long decline, and she said that she didn't want to raise a child in a divided household, or alone. I said that maybe the child would renew our love, and immediately went out and spent five hundred dollars on baby paraphernalia.

The labor was hard, the passageway having quite forgotten its other traveler, Marianne, ten years before. The baby had a respiratory problem and was in an incubator for the first five days. When the nurse came in with the birth certificate, Constance was sleeping. I asked the nurse to wait before telling her the baby's name and went to the window of the nursery and watched our son, who, through parturition, had been abandoned into a world of light populated by the occasional looming figure of a nurse. Constance wanted the baby to be called Sterling and I had agreed, unthinkingly. But when I stood before the window I knew what Israel must have felt, in his old age, seeing his last-born, and instead I named the baby Benjamin.

Constance now shoved her chair at our luncheon table to one side, flushing, and let her fork fall on her pewter plate so that it rang. I have never in all our married life become accustomed to how fast she can get angry, and maybe never will. "I think it would be very nice if you went with your father, Benjamin," she said, and I saw the cords in her neck drawing taut. "I have promised Marianne that I'd go over tonight and see her new apartment." Marianne was in her early twenties, and at this point had left home and was romping in the surf of the California singles' scene.

I kept trying. "I'd like to see Marianne's apartment, too," I said. "We could all go over there after the ice cream."

"What about *Paul*?" Constance asked, and the scorn she put into this misted those eyes.

"See you," Benjamin said, and hightailed off for his room.

But just before he left, he let me know with a look that he understood how I'd tried to manipulate him, and that he hated me for it; not for the attempt but for being inept.

"What makes me mad," Constance said, as if I didn't know—and I didn't—"is when you say something like, you and your mother, without acknowledging my existence. You might ask me, you know. I'm right here at this table. I'm not an invisible third presence. Ask me!"

"Would you like to go and get some ice cream after the service?"

"You always do this," she said, and stared down at the cloth napkin she was punishing with both hands.

"I know."

"No you don't. You get some project going and then you think things are going to be like they were before. It's your way of courting disaster. I can sense it in the air. I can feel it coming. Why do you *do* this when things are going reasonably well?"

"But they're not. They really aren't, Constance. I'm on my way out at the church. Don't you realize that? What do you imagine people think of a pastor when his own family doesn't support him by attending services?"

"I hate to say it, but *so what*. My work will more than keep us going. It's provided this house for us. You can find something else in the area. We both like it here."

"But you know the ministry is my life, Constance. Well, I mean you are, too, of course. But what would I be if I weren't in the ministry? Anyhow, I'm sure this is going to work out. Paul is *famous*, at least to these people."

"I like Paul. But still, come on, a revival? Next you'll be selling Bibles door to door."

"If that's what it takes."

"Ted, this might sound harsh to you, but you're not a twenty-five-year-old hotshot anymore."

"Experience doesn't count?"

"That's not what I'm saying."

"Oh well, how would you know, anyway. You never come to hear me anymore."

"Ah!" she cried. "The suffering servant!"

"Constance."

"Let's forget it for now," she said. "But if something happens while Paul is here, whatever it is, it's your problem; *you* handle it. This whole business, religion, gets crazier to me every day, and I don't want any part of it. Especially the pain. I don't want to see that suffering servant come crawling toward me on his knees."

"Constance, people can't live like this. You're my wife!"

She got up and threw her napkin into the centerpiece of floating flowers, and at the doorway to the kitchen turned back to me and said, "If I told you what you really are, Ted, you wouldn't be able to sleep."

I sat at the table dumbfounded. Then I thought of the passage in Revelation where God hands each of the blessed a stone with his new name written on it, and I wondered, had I been handed that stone? What did it say?

I met Paul Corwin at the airport. If anyone can appear at home in the modular decor of the Los Angeles International Airport, Paul can. He was dressed in a seersucker suit and looked much thinner than I had remembered him, and therefore taller—I'm six-two and he perhaps an inch shorter—but charged with his old energy, which matched the airport's ambience of hurry and speed. And, of course, his round face, topped by thin strands of blond hair and framed by blossoming sideburns, was familiar, if it looked somehow blurred and less distinct. He greeted me with a bear hug and a clap on the back.

We began talking like seminarians, full of bonhomie, as we went toward the luggage carousel. I persuaded him, in that airport ritual, that he should only worry himself about his briefcase; I'd get the heavier bag. At the carousel, he looked around, and nodded at people he suspected of recognizing him, and twice, from what I saw, they quickly looked away, as if they'd been caught gawking at a lunatic. And for the first time I wondered what the effect on Paul would be if he ever actually had to give up his globe-trotting.

We got to the car and drove off toward his motel in an uncomfortable silence. I kept glancing over at his waxy profile against the freeway traffic, and finally asked him about the status of his health, and his plans, as they stood now. He told me he had contracted typhoid in Malaysia, despite the shots, despite everything, and had gotten so run-down he had almost been unable to fight it off. He still had a touch of it, he admitted, and would have to spend his days in bed, in order to be ready each night.

I asked him if he'd eventually be able to take up his travels with GO! again. *Absolutely,* he said, as if the opposite were unthinkable, or too personal to discuss.

I pressed him for information about GO! but he was strangely reticent to talk about it. His usual manner was to mention whole nations opening up to them, as he dropped the names of prime ministers and heads of state. He was somewhat of a boaster and given to superlatives; his colleagues were "tops in the field" and his programs "second to none." But I could see that he found my questions irritating, which could only mean that his illness had weakened him; besides liking to talk about himself, usually, he was also a man of considerable patience.

I changed the subject to a preacher we were acquainted with, a Brooks in San Diego. "I'm sure Brooks has been after you to preach," I said. "Without supplies, I don't know what he'd do—he just doesn't study."

"I haven't even talked to him," Paul said. He sat up straight. We had been stopped by some crisis in the traffic ahead, with horns going off all around us. Paul placed his hands on his knees as if to steady himself, and turned to me with the attention you might give a schoolboy who needed to be put in his place. "Your sanctuary," he said. "How many people does it seat?"

"Three hundred and fifty," I said.

Paul's eyebrows lifted, expressing partially feigned or real shock.

"With extra chairs," I said, "four hundred."

"From my experience, I'd say there will be at least four hundred and fifty there," he said. "Are your ushers ready for that kind of crowd?"

"We're aware of who you are, Paul. What's gotten into you, anyway? We're friends."

"Oh," he said, and turned to me again, and now I noticed something strange about his left eye. Its underlid began trembling as if to open wider on me—to receive me entirely, or allow me entry into something unspoken. Then he raised his hand and let it fall, and we didn't take this topic any further. But I made a mental note as I pulled away with the moving traffic to contact our family doctor and have him offer his services while Paul was in town.

That first night of the revival turned out to be a beautiful Los Angeles evening—the perfect weather to bring the people out. The hot day had spent itself, and now a cooling wind, which the old poets might have happily called a "zephyr," had come up. The great sky, as Benjamin and I walked from the parking lot into the church, seemed a vast mosaic; its blues still held the ceramic strength, the fire, of that day, and one needed no specific iconography to imagine the Father as Pantocrator in such a heavenly vault. This is the day the Lord hath made, I said to myself, rejoice and be glad in it.

Benjamin and I were a half hour early. We went into the sanctuary to find a seat for him, where I could easily join him after my duties of announcing were finished, and found the place already packed. Paul turned out to be a prophet: in regard to the size of the crowd, that is. The only seats left were in the very first row, right under the pulpit. I left Benjamin there and went to check on Paul, and to get the order of service straight with Michael.

The anteroom, where I located them both, was down a flight of five steps, immediately adjacent to the sanctuary's platform—in the wings, so to speak. It allowed direct and sudden access to the platform, so that the preacher always seemed to materialize out of the clouds or spring straight from an inner sanctum. Paul sat on a metal folding chair, hunched over, his elbows on his knees and his head cupped in somehow prayerful hands. It's a posture I know well from personal experience, and from seeing other preachers adopt it before a service; it seems to ease you through the spiritual bends, when your blood percolates with fear, and you aren't sure whether you'll preach or run, so you sit like that praying that the air bubbles will vanish, or at least not rush to your head all at once, in front of all of those faces. It occurred to me then how that little room had the look of a decompression chamber; the walls form a claustrophobic trapezoid, and the faucet in the sink at the back drips torturously, like a timer going, and, perhaps because the sink itself acts as a sort of vaporizer, the place feels perpetually cold and smells of metallic paint. I didn't bother Paul, except to ask him the title of his sermon. "Eyes to See," he groaned.

I wondered aloud in the direction of Michael where the equipment for the folk-rock group was hiding. He said the group's van had broken down in Palmdale and they wouldn't be able to make it.

"What replacement do you have?"

"I've got an idea," Michael said, for some reason pleased with himself.

"Yes?"

"It will be better if it's a surprise. Just announce that we're going to have an old-fashioned singspiration, with a modern twist."

I wrote that down in my bulletin, wondering about the amount of irony I might put into those words, to cover myself; I dislike surprises. But then my better or craven self came forward, and I asked, "Michael, are you sure you know what you're doing?"

"Pastor," he answered, "this is going to be fan*tas*tic."

So Paul Corwin, Michael, and I walked out onto the platform and sat down in the thronelike chairs behind the podium. And I was struck again by the people. Everywhere. Rinsed blue hair toward the front, the middle of the sanctuary muted by three-piece suits, and young marrieds and their small children at the rear; the balcony, where the choir performs in the mornings, flowered, let's say, with teenagers in multi-colored garb seeming in their tremulous activity a celestially-elevated bouquet. People were even starting to sit in the side aisles, so that the red-carpeted border, which always seemed to me to hedge the congregation in, was hardly visible. And the ushers were setting up folding chairs outside the back door. The eyes of the crowd became the eye of a single creature, a sensation I often suffer, and I could feel their breathing filling the sanctuary with heat.

The service started off in a seemly fashion, although the large crowd did, I must admit, have me gesturing and hollering during the announcements.

Then came Michael with his "idea." He stood before the crowd, so overwhelmingly young and tanned and handsome in his wheat-colored suit that the congregation responded to him with a collective smile. He said, in a voice at once casual and sincere, that he was happy to be worshiping tonight, joining in Christian fellowship with his brothers and sisters in the great tradition of revival meetings. He had heard . . . (he seemed to be faltering) he had heard, that the congregational singing in those old tents sometimes carried for great distances, saving people thirty miles off when the wind was right. (General laughter; no, he knew what he was up to.) And so tonight, he said, he wanted us to join with that encompassing cloud of witnesses, those great saints who have gone before us into the presence of the King, and sing out the joy of our salvation. "Let's lift our voices to heaven," he cried. "So that our souls will follow!"

A fine introduction, I thought, and I enjoyed singing "We Are More Than Conquerors," and "Since Jesus Came Into My Heart." And I was more than ready to get up and introduce Paul, who was looking peakèd, when the modern twist came. Now that you are warmed up, Michael said, and have begun to speak with the Lord, to really speak with him, now is the time to forget our inhibitions and sing the songs we know best, the old choruses of our childhood, our first choral prayers, when our hearts were pure and simple and we knew "Jesus Loves Me." The crowd stirred, the creature unlimbered with coughs, whispers, and laughter that had a catch of surprise.

The organ ran through the familiar chorus, playing it in a high register, a sort of childish falsetto, as introduction. Then we sang

> Jesus loves me
> This, I know
> For the Bible tells me so
> Little ones to him belong
> They are weak but He is strong.

Before the second verse began, Michael invited all of the children in the congregation, eight years and younger, to come up onto the platform, and through the rest of the hymn, the congregation, delighted with the antics of the children—who, of course, waved to their parents, picked their noses and talked to each other in noisy stage whispers—finally did begin to lose their inhibitions; the adults opened up as if their decibels would crack the tomb of age, and they be allowed back into childhood.

Well, Michael, I thought, I've got to hand it to you, this is *inspired*. Paul Corwin would come on now, surrounded by the children, reinforcing the images from his films, and who could say what would happen? I was about ready for us all to be assumed into heaven.

But Michael wasn't finished. He led the congregation in a series of choruses that had accompanying hand motions. The children stayed on the platform to sustain the adults' memories of their youth, and everyone sang "The Foolish Man Built His House Upon the Sand," and we all, in unison and as the lyrics demanded, tapped our fists together to show the building, made a house of fingers, and crossed our hands over one another as if conjuring a deserted strand of beach. Then the rains came down, our fingers fluttered in the air and descended, and the floods came up, and our uplifted palms rose with the water, and the house on the sand went—smash! went our clapping hands.

Michael had released the energy which makes enthusiastic crowds both exhilirating and frightening at the same time. I was not about to announce Paul now, not until the edge was off. And, thanks be to God, Michael came through again. We sang another hand-motion song, "Rolled Away," and then Michael announced "Hal-lay-loo." This chorus called for one half of the congregation to stand and sing-shout, Hal-lay-loo, Hal-lay-loo, Hal-lay-loo, Hal-lay-loo-yah, and then to sit, while the other side of the congregation, rising to its feet, answered, without missing a musical measure, Praise Ye The Lord! The idea, of course, was for one side to shout the other side and, possibly, the roof, down. Fortunately, this last vocalized blow-out exhausted the crowd's crazy energy, and even subdued the children; they sat on their rumps on the edge of the platform with their heads hanging down and probably still buzzing from the blood that had left their faces red.

The congregation couldn't have been better primed for

Paul Corwin's message, and I was quite aware that this wasn't the time for a lengthy introduction. On my way to the pulpit, crossing paths with Michael in his return to his throne, I tried to catch his eye and let him know that he had done so well that whatever personal popularity and loyalty he got from this, I didn't care, I was grateful. But he kept his eyes down, and his hands clasped, a pilgrim on the road to faceless humility. Quickly I stepped in front of him, grabbed him in the collision of an embrace, and while I had his arms pinned and there was no question—in that public setting—of him pushing me away, whispered, "Nice going, son." And, having reestablished our roles through that parental condescension, I stepped to the pulpit.

"Tonight," I cried, to get their attention. "Tonight and for the rest of this revival week we are privileged to have with us the great evangelist and world-hunger-relief minister, Paul Corwin! Paul founded Gospel Outreach, an organization with which most of you are familiar. Gospel Outreach, or GO! now ministers in *sixty-five* countries worldwide. I am sure that Paul's message, 'Eyes to See,' will have a special meaning for us all. And since I know that you can't wait to hear it any more than I can, I'll simply turn the service over to you, Paul. The Lord bless you," I said, as he made his way to the pulpit. I raised and extended my palm. "And make his face to shine upon you." We shook hands—his warm, not cold, as I expected—and then I went down the side stairs and sat with Benjamin. I patted his knee. He turned his head away, embarrassed, at his sensitive age, even to be seen in public with his father (Oh, the mystery of father and son! how we know each other even in our ignorance and solitude!)

An immense vase of flowers was on the communion table below the platform and Paul stood behind the pulpit with his hands gripping its sides—the cruciform posture. His head was cocked beatifically to one side, and all the children were staring at him. The crowd hadn't yet entirely settled, so he waited for the last murmurs and whispers and coughs and shuffling of feet to die down. When it all had, he waited on. I had seen superbly confident preachers employ this tactic before, and I knew that the first words he would speak, the release from this tension— which, I was sure, he would maintain until we were on the edge of our seats—could not fail to be memorable. Paul looked around at the children on the platform, taking a terrible risk that they wouldn't speak first. Yet they didn't. They looked up at him as if they knew this was perhaps the finest event thus far in their lives, as if, later, trying to recall their childhoods, his round face would be their first image of recollection. Still he waited.

I prayed to myself, Dear Lord, let him speak, we can't take this. I looked at my watch. The crowd began to be heard again, at first with a sound as delicate as the onset of rain, but then, like a summer storm, the volume rose and kept going up. The man behind me asked if I shouldn't do something, but I refused to even turn around, suggesting that I had privileged information and knew what to expect; he'd have to wait. "But Ted," he said louder, and I realized it was Jerry Mansfield of the board of deacons. Benjamin grabbed me by the elbow and at his look of anxiety I held up my hand, as if being sworn in by a court, a gesture that means for him to have patience.

Paul peered slightly above the heads of the congregation, as if he saw something there, his expression fixed and contemplative, and slightly pained, so that the skin about his eyes crinkled, and I was sure I saw the tremor in his underlid again. The crowd noise was now at the level of the coastal storms that come in after tidal waves hit Alaska. But then Paul finally moved, his head, at least; he turned it to look at the children, on one side, then the other. The crowd quieted somewhat at this.

Please God! I screamed mentally, *Please! Let him speak!*

Paul Corwin's well-photographed head nodded and his lips pursed as if he had come to a regrettable decision. He took two steps, picked a toddler up from the floor and set him off to one side and, with a path cleared, walked off.

As I leapt up the platform stairs, I heard, above the uproar of the crowd, a great, clanging crash as of Paul Corwin ending his career for good. I ran into the wings and saw him at the bottom of the five steps there, lying in the midst of a nest of steel music stands. Paul had committed a belly flop. He was lying face down. I shakily started descending the steps and saw blood splattered over the floor from what I took to be head wounds.

Then Paul pushed himself up and rolled with a clatter off the music stands. He sat with his legs out in front of him, rubbing a shin that had evidently rammed into one of the stands, and wiped at blood running from his nose, smearing it across his cheek. He looked up at me. I must confess that this awful end to all my efforts had me hepped up something fierce, so that my expression might have made an avenging angel look pacific. Paul started to cry, an ashamed man-melting whimper, and his bloodied face turned a crybaby's pink. Children were suddenly all about us; in fact, I'm sure it was the sight of them, not me, that had started the tears now sliding down Paul Corwin's blood-smeared face.

I shooed the children away and back up the steps toward their mothers, and from the rear of the platform caught the eye of the organist and mimicked playing a trumpet with my hands—an emergency signal for him to render a short and ear-piercing passage of Buxtehude. I stepped up to the pulpit, the Buxtehude finished, and I told everybody to sit down. I pronounced Paul Corwin ill, in my pulpit tones, and requested that an ambulance be called. "Say a prayer for this great man," I said. "Say a prayer and then leave quietly."

Then I nearly ran off the platform, down the steps, and helped Paul into the anteroom decompression chamber, where he could wait for the ambulance and evade the host of solicitous cormorants. In the room on a chair, he continued to cry, but managed to tell me he didn't think anything was broken—he had tripped on only the second-to-last step, he said, being prissily accurate. He didn't need an ambulance.

"*I* do," I said, hoping to stave off the coming wave of questions by keeping matters as dramatic as I could.

I handed Paul a series of wet paper towels for his nose. Finally I couldn't bear it any longer; I asked him what happened. Why had he walked off? He could only lift his hand, repeating his gesture from the car, like a weak familiar of the signal I had made to Benjamin: patience. Then his expression contorted from a muscular spasm, so that in its terrible creasings his face didn't seem to be his. I don't know how I knew—perhaps from hearing his sudden wailing—but I knew my friend had given up any hope for himself, and was crying in my kind of limbo, where the pain of being broken is welcomed at last.

Michael came in. "Is he sick," he asked? "Is it his heart?" There wasn't a smidgen of sympathy in his voice, and I could see that he was still puffed up with his success. He didn't care a hoot about Paul, and for the rest of the evening would be drunkenly inhuman with the power of making a crowd go berserk for the first time in his life.

I was aware of the hazards of focusing my frustration and anger on Michael; I decided to play the whole thing down. "It's not his heart," I said. "Not exactly. He'll be all right."

"Well, what happened?"

"Michael, let it go."

"Look," he said, getting uppity, "you're my boss, pastor, but just this once I'd like to hear an explanation of what's happening. For real, you know? You're going to need my help explaining this."

Oh, the sly rancor that being a subordinate breeds and how it will assert its wormy rights at the wrong time!

I thought that perhaps if I remained cool and gave him a sensational story, the dung he craved, he would go away quiet, satisfied with being in the know. "OK," I said. "But this is strictly confidential, Michael. Paul has a drinking problem." This whopper of a lie came out with such ease that even Paul looked up.

"Ted," he protested.

"Did you know that?" Michael asked.

"I am not stupid." Michael could interpret this as he liked.

"All those years." Michael rolled his eyes up. "I mean, I used to see his films even in Christian Scientist Sunday school. This really blows me away."

"Meaning?"

"His whole operation has been a farce."

"Come *on*, Michael." This judgemental knife of immaturity, which imagines it's parting black and white!

" 'The heart is deceitful above all things,' " he said, " 'and desperately wicked.' "

"Come on, Michael, complete the verse. 'And who can know it?' "

"I don't understand."

"Right," I said. "You don't understand a lot of things." Also open for interpretation.

Michael was getting angry. He said, "I do know that the devil is an angel of light. He is the father and source of all lies! It's pretty clear how that applies in this situation, don't you think?"

It's your attitude that I consider demonic, I should have said. That might have saved me. But even as I lost control, feeling my sight fade away in a swirl of blue, I heard my voice go on:

"You're absolutely wrong! He hasn't had the problem until recently. Anyway, we're all, in our own ways, hypocrites. Does that invalidate all that we do?"

"First Thessalonians, as I'm sure *you* know," he said with that staunch assurance of ill-informed youth, going so far as to lift his chin—the biblical beach boy!—"clearly teaches that wine bibbers will not enter the kingdom of heaven. I guess I'm just stupid enough to take that passage and the rest of the Bible for what it says, Pastor *Ted.*"

Moses hit the rock. I hit Michael Dennis. I here confess this. The accumulated aggravation of my unhappy stint in the service, and the Lord alone knows what else, broke through the surface, and I hit him in the stomach as hard as I could. He fell, or seemed to be lunging at my waist, and in reflex my knee came up and I felt the bone of his nose give as I heard a crackling sound from it.

He started screaming, cupping at the blood pouring into his hands, and staggered a step to the left, to the right, and finally made it over to where he could lean against a wall. He kept crying out from the pain, but was now cursing with a great vehemence.

The ambulance driver arrived at about this point. He had to raise his voice above Michael's screaming. "What happened?" he yelled.

"He fell!" Once you start lying, dishonesty rains down until it becomes a flood.

Michael's protests were queerly amplified by his damaged sinuses. It was impossible to quiet him.

"What about that guy?" the attendant yelled again, turning from Michael to Paul Corwin. "Did he get clipped, too?"

"He's all right! It's this one!"

The attendant led Michael off and then came back to retrieve the once wheat-colored coat he had stripped from him during his cursory examination of Michael's nose. He told me that that nose sure looked real bad, but the young guy would probably turn out just fine, eventually. Kids heal.

When, half an hour later, I hustled Paul Corwin out to my

car, the crowd outside, which had seen Michael being taken away, pressed about us with questions, and several of them kept grabbing at my coat, as if to take me by the lapels. Benjamin was waiting in the car for us—shrewd fellow—and loved the drama of our getaway. Paul kindly collected himself so as not to scare Benjamin, although none of us said anything during the long ride to his motel; and Paul and I barely spoke outside the room before he went in and I heard the scraping of his bolt lock. Privacy. Home safe. I did make him promise to wait for my call the next morning.

As Benjamin and I were driving home, the headlights catching the lane-division reflectors on the freeway, our pathway eerily incandescent, he asked me what had happened. I told him the truth, all of it, or as much of it as I knew, about Paul's typhoid, and how I'd ended up socking Michael. He hung his head at first—how I would abhor any violence in this son of mine, I thought—but then he looked up at the luminous flicker of the reflectors and told me that, for several reasons, he thought things would work out.

"Explain, Benjamin."

"Well, we have faith, don't we?"

With a sideways glance, I caught the glaze of his eyes on me in the dark of the car. "We do. . . But I'm not sure you understand how people will take this."

"People will be praying for you, Dad. I will."

The vibration of the engine was like a rising floor underneath us. For a moment, the correct simplicity of the answers Benjamin had learned from me seemed again as reliable as combustion, the true force which drove the world, however adults might belittle it. I had once asked Benjamin about his conversion experience. He had been nine when he'd come forward during a service I was conducting. "Did you feel guilty?" I asked him, years later. "I was only a kid!" he said. "Mom says you make us all feel guilty about things we shouldn't." It finally came out that he'd felt guilty about stealing Marianne's books. When Marianne turned nineteen, she began a program of sexual liberation with an oddly Presbyterian determination and thoroughness, coupled with a certain erotic-scientism. She purchased every available manual (as far as I would know) of sexual technique, those for the inexperienced, designed to allay fears and bring reasonable pleasure during the first sorties into the meadows of sensual delight, and those for the experienced, designed to allay fears that sexual possibility could be exhausted, containing safe and sane approaches to certain practices—the names of which were sometimes whispered in counselling sessions I've had with fatigued young men. There were marriage guides with soft-focus photography, books of grainy photographs with a minimal text of any socially-redeeming nature, and books which were merely galleries of genitalia, male and female, lest the unwary encounter the unknown.

Benjamin claimed to me that he had taken the books not merely because they were Marianne's—she owned a lot of other things—but because she didn't want him to have them. "They were secret," he said. "I heard her and you fight about them." He said it angered him that he couldn't read the books, or understand what it was that made them "work"; he couldn't put the spell of them together. He kept stealing them, and finally burned them—"In an empty garbage can," he said, "that time part of the roof caught on fire. Mom told the policeman not to tell you. She said it was the kind of thing you'd probably blow all out of proportion." And with this confession, I had seen him heaving his sister's erotica into a garbage can, offering up, like a possessed Levite or, better, Savanarola, the incense of those pornographic lambs to propitiate the bad spirit of Marianne. The serpent remained as cunning as ever, I had thought then, and sensed that Benjamin had performed his ritual betrayal hoping that he, too, might be like the gods, knowing good and evil. Or might at least possess some portion of the willful freedom of Marianne. At any rate, his confession had impressed me at the time with the depth of its spiritual discernment.

At home, we sat in the driveway a moment before going in. Night insects were shrilling at that frequency that driving opens your ears to. I was tired, almost as tired as Paul Corwin must be, I thought, that weary in my bones and my soul, and Benjamin seemed to intercept my thought, because he said, "Dad, what's with Dr. Corwin? He doesn't seem sick, exactly."

How could I begin with my son on this subject that was the daily meat of my meditations? The word "accidie" occurred to me, but it came out of a context even more foreign than typhoid. I finally said, "I believe Paul has reached a crisis in his spiritual life." I felt I needn't add, *I have, too*, and then, in the taut stillness that passed between us, I felt Benjamin receive the weight of this. I thought of forgiveness, which I wasn't sure I deserved and which didn't seem forthcoming; I was truly stunned with unbelief. I had, though, a strange sensation of Benjamin being the apt confessor to my penitent. My silence must have frightened him some, but he remained beside me, and I felt my courage gather to face Constance. I was grateful simply for Benjamin's presence then. I can't say why, exactly. Maybe I suspected that he might be the only one who wouldn't be so harsh on me for my failings, and who, with his discernment and degree of innocence and our blood ties, might be the mortal most nearly competent to serve as my judge.

Monday:

Sin

"What in God's name did you do to that kid?"

Even at nine-thirty in the morning, having spent most of the night in an insomniac vigil, and then being awakened from a dead sleep by the telephone, I could recognize the hectoring voice of my head deacon, Cecil Brown. His is a voice made for oratory, deep, sonorous—like that of a radio announcer's, with an apparent life all its own.

"I've been up half the night and all this morning, talking with people about this thing," Cecil said, not waiting for me to answer. "If you were going to belt him, why didn't you break his jaw, so he couldn't talk? The story is spreading like—"

"Like wildfire," I said.

"I'm trying to help you, mister. The others are after your hide, let me tell you that."

Actually, I knew, he was probably playing both sides, always with his sense of himself as an ecclesiastical power broker. But he might also be a valuable source of information; I said, "I know, Cecil. I just don't know what to say. It happened."

"Oh, man," he said, for once sounding authentically grieved. "Well, if it comes down to a fight, you've got the board of deacons behind you."

A vote of confidence, have mercy.

But, it had happened. The event was there, a rock, a wall— that exitless chamber. It was as blatantly present as the cumbersome fact of my life itself. I promised to call Cecil back.

Even those on the way to their execution or surgery walk nearly as before, and thus I got up and dressed and went out to the kitchen. Constance is an interior decorator and she carries on her work at home, in an asymmetrical addition to the back of our stuccoed house, which is set aside as her office. At this hour she was still in the kitchen, beside the stove, drinking coffee. She said good morning in a breezy way, took another sip, taking in my expression over the rim of her mug, and then she asked me what had happened; I hadn't got up the courage to tell her last night.

"You were right," I said. "I mean, about me and disaster. I can't believe how right you were." And then I told her about Paul, the service, and Michael.

She looked up during my recitation as if praying for patience to deal with a chaotic child—only a mannerism, since to Constance there wasn't anything "up there" but an ozone layer poisoned by hair spray. Then she set those eyes on me. "Tell me," she said. "Will Michael press charges?"

I hadn't thought of that at all.

"The insurance company won't pay for *everything*," she said. "I'm sure of that. He'll probably file a civil suit, at least. He'll want to recover his medical expenses and then some."

I hung my head and scratched the back of my scalp. "I suppose so."

"You'd better call David," she said, in a kind tone of voice, with a faint pulse in it of our life together. David Demetris handled Constance's legal business on a regular basis, and mine, if and when. I like David, which Constance knew, and perhaps it was this liking which helped me identify, now, that diminutive throb through her small speech.

"All right," I said.

She took another sip of her coffee, all business. "Tell him to contact Michael immediately and offer to pay for any medical bills the insurance doesn't cover. Tell him to hint at more, too."

"What should I do at church?"

She suddenly brightened, and her whole attitude shone with the radiance of a liberating thought, her early morning breeziness back; she smiled broadly. The bowed curves of her lips are so perfectly defined and her teeth so heartbreakingly straight that her smile has never ceased to strike me as the epiphany of a god: "she was Diana's child," I often whisper to myself.

"Well?"

"Curse God and die," she said cheerily.

"Come on."

"Resign."

"But we'd have to move again."

"No we wouldn't. I've got my business, which, remember, is much more profitable than being a witch doctor. Oh, I'm sorry. Forget I said that. But you could find something else around here."

"I don't think I could live with something else."

"How have you been living?"

The implications of that question were so vast I said," "Not with something else."

"Maybe not," she said. She put down her mug with the suddenness her anger has. "What I said last night stands," she insisted. "This time you're going to have to go through this alone." She walked over to the swinging kitchen doors and turned back toward me, her hip appealing in profile, her ankles thin— she was always more beautiful to me when just out of reach—and said, "I've got work to do."

I usually take Monday off, like most ministers, and don't for any reason appear at the church. But that day I decided to sneak into the office and see how the battle fared. Was I already thinking of it as a battle then? Perhaps, for I am a true son of Martin Luther, in at least one way; my instincts are assertive, and, as I had so recently demonstrated, when pressed, I am belligerent.

My out-of-the-ordinary office visit had nevertheless been anticipated by my secretary, Donna, a young woman with brown oval eyes and the long thin nose of a Renaissance madonna—a young woman who shows her good looks off to the best effect by eyeliner applied with the steadiest of hands, and who is said (this by other jealous females) to dress well. She had my telephone messages stacked in order of ascending outrage, the last of them a summation: "If that man remains as pastor, you've seen the last of my family and me and my money."

Donna said, "I assume you are not in."

"Completely," was all that came out of my mouth.

So, going through the messages, an electrical tribunal which sang out in chorus for me to recant, I wanted to say with Luther, Here I stand, and add, as did he but in a slightly different tone, God help me. And I began to consider what I would reply. There is more to the mind than intellection, and all my schemes and excuses were met and judged by the spectre of my dead mother, shaking her finger at me and saying, " 'Be sure your sins will find you out.' Numbers thirty-two, verse thirty-three." When I had trespassed as a child, she would stand me in front of her in our kitchen, which smelled of ashes—she was temperamentally unsuited to cleaning stoves—and I would try to explain how my friend had started it, or Dad had said it was OK, and she would simply quote that verse until I acknowledged I had been in the wrong and gave her a full confession.

And there in my office I thought, having understood my mother's reasoning once more, What a magnificent word, "sin." For a moment I was happy, enjoying the radiating satisfactions of that word, "sin," which, for me, captured and comprehended my experience. Although accepting the word entailed pain, the sting of it was curative. For now I felt penitent; I saw the act again, named it as sin, and renounced it before God. There's no use renouncing actions which are only human, provoked, understandable; but renouncing sin, ah, that *works*.

My feeling for the word, *"sin,"* at that moment and the structured course of action I would take at its inspiration—the turning point in this testimony—cannot be explained apart from the story of how I accepted my call to the ministry. Nor can it be understood apart from my relationship to my mother and, through her, to language itself.

For fifteen years my mother had a barren marriage. She prayed for a child, a son, like Hannah and many other women in the Bible. She prayed, presenting her anguish and bewilderment before the Lord. She prayed for fifteen years, and then she finally conceived. She told me she used to laugh at the morning-sickness business of throwing up. The neighbors would ask, How are you getting along? And she'd say, I'm sick as a dog, praise Jesus.

I tried to come into the world, though, the way I've done everything else since: sideways. The doctors had to perform a C-section, and I think they butchered her pretty bad—my father used to talk about her "zipper." She lost a lot of blood and nearly died. They told her to be thankful for modern medicine's ability to save her life. But I was sickly, too, and they weren't sure I was going to make it, and if I died she didn't want to live, she later told me. So first she prayed that God would take her instead of me. Then, when she saw that she was going to live, she promised God that if he let me live, she would dedicate me to his service, as Samuel's parents dedicated him.

"You were God's precious gift to me," she would say. "You were telegraphed straight from heaven." Her voice was deep, even as I hear it now, with a kind of crooning to it.

When I turned seven, we tried to find Eli's temple, the place of this Samuel's service. We used to travel around to hear local preachers and evangelists and missionaries speak. This was in East Texas, where I was born and grew up. My mother would speak seriously after these services, usually at our kitchen table, where she would ply me with ginger snaps, about my reactions. She was looking for some definite leading from the Lord.

We didn't come up with that much. I loved, of course, to hear from her the harrowing tales of Wycliffe Bible translators, stuck in their huts surrounded by pythons while cooly performing one of the greatest intellectual tasks known—that measured and conscientious sifting of Scripture into a new and often unrecorded tongue. That kind of solitary Robinson-Crusoe life appealed to me greatly. It happened, too, that I ended up becoming a pet of our local minister, and my mother persuaded him to begin teaching me Hebrew when I was nine years old. And there was this evangelist, Brother Jimmy Poolster. Brother Jimmy was a preacher, a healer, and he also sold hunting dogs after services. We went to hear him only once, but I was so impressed by the way he laid his hands on the sick and infirm—zapped them, giving them a real hard blow on the forehead with the butt of his hand, after which they fell over, slain in the Spirit—I was so impressed that I got in the line myself. Just to take the carnival ride, I think. I had almost gotten to him, when my mother dragged me out of there and back home. I wanted to talk that night, but there were no ginger snaps; in my mother's estimation, this was not for me. I never minded the bargain she had made with God, because it provided me with a vast and complex faerie land, the future, where I could wander free and forever be at play.

And she was always there to tell me, "You will be God's man. You don't belong to me but to the Lord Jesus. He will lead you into the paths of righteousness for his name's sake. He will keep you. He will raise you up. He will make you a mighty man of valor. A David. A Paul. The Adoniram Judson of our day."

When I was twelve her doctor discovered that she had cancer of the stomach. She suffered for a year from it before the end, the last two months of this in a hospital. I sat with her after school during those last months. I would come up beside her bed and she would take both my hands in hers—the uneasy confusion of a quick, embarrassed kiss, an attempt at our former way of greeting each other. And then toward the last, when she drifted in and out of consciousness, she would keep holding onto my hands, and I to hers, for longer periods of time. The very last day, while she lay in a coma, I took her hands in mine and, strange, she gripped back. Perhaps it was a reflex, but it seemed that the tension in her from fighting the pain passed into our hands and she rested more easily.

Later, in her death-throes—when she was screaming—she became herself for a moment; she opened her eyes, looked at me so that I knew she was lucid and said, "The promise is yours to keep now." I gave her hand a squeeze. She closed her eyes. She died.

I went through adolescence and became my father's son. The change in my loyalties seemed to relieve whatever grief he must have felt at my mother's death; he'd hardly been able to visit her when she was ill. He didn't want his son to turn into a no-account preacher, as he put it; he was a merchant, a middle-class hardware-store owner and he liked things "regular." He did have a religion: a crazy patchwork kind of thing. Whether his beliefs were reasonable or not was beside the point. In this he resembled the Masons. He needed most of all to know that, however bizarre, his notions were a private province and that, like his house and hardware store, he *owned* them.

His faith took the form of rituals which would have looked like ordinary habits to anybody but a son. I knew, though, that his activities as a member of the chamber of commerce, the nude calendar he allowed himself, the blood he gave at regular intervals, his cigars on Saturday nights, the tune-ups he gave our car—all these things were sacred to him. They were his middle way. They were his outpost. They were not to be encroached upon. I knew this because he insisted, as powerfully if not as openly as my mother had, that I should see things *his* way. He wanted me to live a life patterned after his: good works and industry and just enough sin to compensate for life's defects and hardships. That was fine with me. Particularly so at that time, because my father believed in "sowing your wild oats." He had a fierce nostalgia for his own youth and such activity was "part of the bargain," as he also might have said.

The year after I graduated from high school I must have put in about fifty acres of barley, in my cultivated dedication, as it were, chasing girls and drinking at night. I spent the days recovering, supposedly working in his store, but not really, since he was meticulous about his work, which he loved, and kept most of it to himself. He developed a blindness to my late hours, too. He couldn't say outright that he approved of me raising hell, but he often prefaced remarks to me then with our family name. "March," he would say, "you look a little peakèd this morning." And he'd grin. He also took to reminiscing about his life before he met my mother.

I enjoyed myself, well, *considerably*. I ran with a fast crowd. This was in the mid-thirties, and a little spending money made you seem a millionaire. When the weather was warm enough, and even when it wasn't, someone would borrow his dad's car, we'd chip in on a bottle of whiskey, get out some old blankets and round up, as we used to sing, "an armful of girl." The girls were usually from town. Or way outside it. Poor white trash. Actually, they were rich, in their youth and beauty, and some-times (though they had coarse manners and tastes) in what they valued in others. But they weren't aware of this wealth, and so they spent it on us, quickly and lavishly, and we didn't leave them any change. We looked down on them for this, and took advantage of them. What incredible knotheads we were, as if this would prove us fit for life. Hedonism!

Anyway, it was after one of these midsummer night's dreams that my life again took another direction. We were in my dad's car, an old Ford that still had a crank for emergencies, and we were on a country road at four o'clock in the morning. My buddy went to sleep at the wheel and we ran off the side of the road, down a steep incline, and hit the lone oak in a great cow pasture.

I remember how at first I asked myself why someone should be shining lights into my eyes. Then I found myself ten feet beyond the tree we had hit, sitting up and staring into the single headlight that had survived the crash. I tried to move. I felt something in my legs. I looked down at them and saw that they were bent in several places besides my knees, and then I blacked out again.

I couldn't speak when I next awoke, in a hospital. I had a concussion and it had brought about a kind of stroke which robbed me of language. I couldn't read or write. I couldn't even think in words. Whoever I was, was lodged totally in my five senses. They were alive, and set wide open, but there was no "me" to whom they could deliver their messages. I remember staring for hours at the fruit and flowers brought by people to my room. I remember that oranges have pores, an oily surface, a true skin. And the button of a daisy is a field of yellow grasses.

And I remember not being able to name these things and switching my eyes back and forth in anger and boredom and for the sensation of activity going on in my head, which, in some dim way, I remembered as being like what I had known when I had been able to think.

I heard people talk to me. The sounds they made were familiar ones, but they weren't much more meaningful than the random horns which blared in the street outside my window. And I remember the pain, getting up on my legs for the first time in casts, on crutches—how it hit me in the head and knocked me clean out the first three times. Words began to come back, though, and "I" with them. Something popped back into place one morning and suddenly what had been a world of surface assumed depth again; I was back inside my head. I couldn't speak, but made hand signals for a piece of paper. My nurse brought a pencil and pad and the other nurses and some doctors came running. They waited for my first expression, appearing to me like some kind of royal court bleached with anticipation while its queen was being delivered of an heir.

The first words that occurred to me were simple phrases like "oh boy," and "not on your life," besides obscenities, a lot of these. I wanted to sum up the situation for my assembled guests, and then another phrase broke free and floated up from the new spring of my clearing consciousness. Very carefully, with a great deal of effort, I wrote *anathema sit*, from my years of high-school Latin, normal then. I handed the pad to the nurse, who read it, and handed it on to a doctor, looking worried; I'm sure she thought the letters were sheerest nonsense. But then the doctor read it aloud to everyone and explained that the Latin meant "let it be damned" and was the phrase that popes used when condemning heretics, and then he started laughing, seeing the judgment I meant on my state; and soon, they were all laughing, although some of this was at me, of course. I saved up my strength before communicating again.

The next day I wrote, "What happened?" This was to my nurse. She replied, "An accident." I handed her my papal condemnation, underlined twice. Later, I got up the courage to write, "The others?" She looked away and tears started to my eyes. Eventually I learned that my buddy had been killed, that his girl had broken bones but was mending, like me, and that mine had been only bruised. She had been the one who went for help.

I reached a plateau where I could think and write and read and understand everything others said, but still couldn't speak. I think physiologically I was all right by then—new circuits had been rigged up in my brain for all the old functions. Speaking, though, was not a matter of chemistry. I lay there, looking up at the ceiling, hoping and praying the day would end, only to realize that the next one would be the same: the same pain, the same boredom, the same miserable food—everything the same. I hoped it all would end, even though I was sure I'd never leave the hospital.

I understood then why I still couldn't speak. I enjoyed being "dead to the world," because without anything to look forward to do, being awake was a nuisance—my mind speeded up and slowed by fancy—and a torture. I couldn't speak because I basically didn't want to. I found I had a sort of nostalgia for the loss of consciousness I had experienced as a result of the concussion. I wanted to go back, to be *absent* like that again. Sleep was the next best thing. I wasn't suicidal because I had too strong a belief in hell. I wanted to be extinct, not dead.

My dad came by one day, in the late afternoon, and he sat on a chair beside my bed. As he sat there, and time went on, slanting bars of light from the Venetian blinds made him look as if he had on a prison uniform. He hadn't come to see me too often. I wasn't in the kind of shape he found easy to reconcile with his booster philosophy, I assume. This day, however, after much hemming and hawing, he did something I'll always be thankful for; he handed me my mother's old Scofield Bible. "Here, stick-in-the-mud," he said. "Maybe I should have given it to you on your eighteenth birthday, but I wasn't sure you knew I was here. It's your inheritance from her." He crossed his leg over his knee, turning his body sideways to me, and his head bobbed with the stutter that came over him at times of trouble. "Sh, sh, she would have known what to do. Sh, sh—I don't. She would have wanted you to have this, or be with you. She was my—" He broke off. Bars of light lay over his forehead and his eyes, and he held up a hand as if to shade himself from them. In a while he got up slowly and went over and shut the blinds, and after that we had a typical visit—he talking and I scribbling on one of my pads.

The hospital had of course let the Gideons put a Bible in the drawer of my bedside table. I hadn't read it, and hadn't prayed much beyond a few appeals for deliverance, and had quit sending such petitions up when I realized I didn't want God to do anything of the sort; I wanted him to stay strictly out of my life. To invent a creature with a mind of its own seemed to me hideously cruel. How could I pray to a God like that for deliverance? So when I opened my mother's Bible that night it was to read her marginal comments, and nothing else, curious to discover her mind again. I remembered her clearly, and yet something about her presence was already starting to fade. At eighteen, I suspect I felt I could forgive my mother her Christianity, blaming it on her upbringing and the times, and therefore thought my attitude toward God irrelevant, reading her Bible.

I found most of what has guided my reminiscence of her since—those passages of Scripture to which the cracked binding fell open from long use, the India-paper pages yellowed and puckered and rolling up at their edges—passages underlined and underlined again in pencil, in lines ever-so-straight. My mother's passionate care. Nearly all of these passages concerned women and their problems. The stories of barren women were, of course, her special study. And it was from seeing her comment beside the description of Samuel's birth that I understood, once and for all, what had prompted her covenant with God; there, she had written, "Why would God want his gift back?" And later, in a more mature hand, "I know the answer now, praise Jesus."

The more I read my mother's comments, the more of the Bible I had to read, for I could only be in touch with her by understanding what she thought about. It took me two weeks before I worked my way out of the Old Testament and into the New, and another few days before I entered Luke and saw her writing beside the story of Elizabeth and Zechariah. The chapters devoted to the birth of John the Baptist had been underlined and commented upon so extensively that the actual text was difficult to read. In fact, part of the text was written again in the margins by her, with matching asterisks, to show its proper placement. She must have known this by heart. And, next to the well-known passage about the babe leaping in Elizabeth's womb, I found a Jewish star, and later the same star in the back of the Bible, over a poem she had written.

> Now to Father, Son and Holy Ghost
> I give my body as a host
> Of this child whose life is due
> To the providence of God, alleluia.
> John the Baptist leapt in his mother's womb
> Jesus Christ slept in Joseph's tomb
> My baby boy will be born in the spring
> To show again death has no sting.

Her homespun magnificat was my Rosetta stone. I wanted to cease to be at that point, because I found being alive a colossal nuisance, an unending affliction. She seemed to have feared death and to have needed some proof of immortality, which I had provided, whereas I wanted a kind of nirvana, rather than her heaven. I saw the advantages to her side—not simply to escape suffering but to experience bliss—but doubted whether I could feel as she had without the actual experience of giving birth. And then I had a dream. My mother appeared to me as if she had stepped out from behind curtains or a screen, although neither was in evidence; I was delighted and surprised at the magic of her appearance. She raised a hand, and in it held a cross. She said—it was her voice and yet it travelled through me like thunder—she said, "Ye must be born again." She said this five times,

five times exactly (I awoke knowing the number and knowing it
was important), and then she took the cross and used it to open
herself up from her abdomen to down between her legs.

I screamed as if she had cut into me and was awake.

The room was dark, and before my head cleared I thought
I was back home. I looked to my left, for the window, and then
back to the wall at the foot of my bed, where there should be a
gallery of pin-ups. Both were gone. I sat up and my right hand
hit the railing of the hospital bed. I knew where I was, finally,
and wasn't exactly disappointed; being home seemed a kind of
promise, something that would happen soon, if I heeded the
dream. I had always been, even in my father's eyes, an obedient
child, and I found that when I thought of my mother saying, "Ye
must be born again," and considered obeying her, I was as happy
as I had been as her child. I went right back to sleep.

In the morning, I found in my mother's Bible the passage
that she had been quoting in the dream. And I discovered my
own dilemma in Nicodemus's mouth, "How can a man be born
when he is old? Can he enter the second time into his mother's
womb and be born?" Then Jesus's answer: "That which is born
of the flesh is flesh; and that which is born of the Spirit is spirit.
Marvel not that I said unto thee, Ye must be born again. The
wind bloweth where it listeth, and thou hearest the sound thereof,
but canst not tell whence it cometh and whither it goeth: so is
every one that is born of the Spirit."

My mother had brought me into the world in the flesh, and
now seemed to be calling me back in spirit. I had caught the wind
of that Spirit through her and would try to follow her as well as
I was able through her example. I had to experience somehow
what she had at my birth. I buzzed the nurse and wrote on my
pad, "If it's possible, I would like to see five births by Caesarean-
section. Would you ask the doctors?"

The nurse kept smiling at me, by force of will, as she backed
out the door.

For the rest of the day I composed a brief for whoever
would have to make the decision. I recounted reading my mother's
Bible, and how the more I understood her the more I believed
I would be able to speak again. I assured the recipient that my
request reflected not mere curiosity, nor a sick imagination, but
an inkling of how I felt I could be healed. Five, because of the

dream, and so I wouldn't be left with one particular impression of what my mother had gone through, but a general one.

I had never before seen the doctor that my note to the nurse eventually summoned; he sat down by my bed, told me his name, Dr. Ralph Woodson, and said he'd like to know my reasons for wanting to see these births. He sat hunched over, his elbows on his knees, and I figured he must be a head doctor, a psychiatrist— rather a rarity then. He began to explain in a patient voice that it was important for me to write out my reasons for wanting to see the deliveries, and before he was finished, I waved my hand for him to stop. I handed him the brief I'd written out. It seemed to unnerve him that I had anticipated his request. He sat back in his chair and started going through it as if it were an unexpected, detailed bill, breathing through his small nose with his lips pressed tight, a persnickety expression. But I saw that the note got through to him.

I was in a teaching hospital attached to the University of Texas, and one of the operating rooms had a gallery. My leg casts had recently come off, and I had a wheelchair and crutches with which I had been encouraged to travel around the hospital. My request turned out to be simple to grant.

The first time they sent an orderly to get me; after this, they called my nurse and she got me ready. It was about six in the morning when the orderly, a Negro—or black man as we say now—woke me up. The doctors were about to perform a C-section on a woman who had been in labor for almost a whole day, he said. He wheeled me down from my fourth-floor ward to the basement operating rooms, a cheery fellow, whistling "Bye Bye Blackbird"—pausing only long enough to mention that I looked white as a sheet. He dropped me off outside the gallery door, and I swung through on my crutches and took a seat in the second of two rows. There was a hemispherical bank of lights trained on the woman, who looked like a mountain of white cloth—even her legs were covered, split apart, with her feet strapped into a set of stirrups. You could see the woman herself only at her abdomen, where a flap of the cloth was opened to operate, and then her head farther up. The anesthesiologist was at her head, holding a face mask over her, keeping her out. Even so, when the pains came, when the mountain suddenly shifted into a flattened butte, her head rolled from side to side. Then she looked very human, her eyes closed, her face puffy, and her hair matted and wet.

I decided I didn't want to see this after all, and I looked toward the door and noticed a metal pail there. I knew what it was for, or in any case figured they'd rather rinse out one pail than mop the whole floor. I got it over beside me with a crutch, and this gave me the courage to stay, although I was trembling, my teeth were chattering, and I felt I'd have to go to the bathroom.

The surgeon took his place between the woman's legs, the nurses and assisting doctors huddled around, with tables of instruments already rolled into place on both sides of her mountainous whiteness, and the doctor asked the anesthesiologist quite casually how the patient was doing. Evidently, she was doing all right; he took up his scalpel.

The effect on you of watching one person cut into another is at the edge of reason. In fact, when he made that first incision I thought that I had been mistaken, that he was only drawing with a red pin, and then the line sprang into being and became liquid. But when they pried the woman open with a stainless steel retractor, the incision erupted, and blood went everywhere. I found it incredible that they would pull her apart as if dealing with an old valise. Ghoulish. But fascinating.

I thought to myself, How am I feeling? I seemed OK. I saw how quickly they stopped the bleeding by applying clamps, rows of them, lying to either side against the retractor. They sponged up the flowing blood. They waited a moment, the doctors talking among themselves, and then the surgeon stepped around to the side of the woman and another doctor, who carried a large stainless steel bowl, stepped into the surgeon's place. The surgeon made another incision, a horizontal cut into the woman's uterine wall. A tidal wave broke, the membrane's amniotic fluid exploded, dousing the doctor with the bowl and splattering everybody, even the anesthesiologist far up at her head. I had only thought about wounds before in terms of my accident, and fellows I'd seen in fights. This wasn't like that. Not at all.

I grabbed the pail and heaved the little that was in my stomach, and heaved again and again, to no good purpose, really, except that the exertion of it made me feel better a minute later.

When I looked up again, the doctor had his hand and wrist

in the wound. He performed a downward and rotating movement several times, the last time plunging his arm in all the way
up to the elbow and turning it more slowly. Something filled the
horizontal wound and, before I could recognize it, the surgeon
scooped and brought a baby up by the neck, a little girl with a
dark-grey umbilical cord trailing from her mother. He lay the
infant on her mother's chest and cut the cord. Then he picked
her up and gave her a whack on the fanny, which set her to
choking and finally into a scream.

I limped off and wheeled back to my room alone. If it
weren't for my belligerence, or bull-headed nature, I'm sure I
never would have gone back. The next few times I stayed all the
way through, seeing the delivery of the afterbirth, and all the
rest. I want to say that I got used to it, but I never did. I knew
what to expect, and that was all; it wasn't something you could
get used to. And the third time they withdrew the infant, it was
dead. It was fully formed, but still, not even any tension in its
limbs, still and so quiet for so long that I realized nobody was
speaking.

One of the assisting doctors, a young fellow doing his resi-
dency, came up to my room to see me that first afternoon. He
was curious to know what I had or had not gotten from the
experience; the story of the strange boy who wanted to see five
C-sections had spread through the hospital. He brought a surgeon's robe, cap, and mask—old ones that he probably decided
wouldn't be missed, and before he gave them to me (he had them
in a box) he said, "You're one of us now." I put them on immediately, and probably got a bigger kick out of his gift than I should
have, I realize from this distance.

He asked me the inevitable question, and I wrote about my
mother. He asked me the date of my birth, and I wrote 1917 on
my pad. He kept staring at the date for a long time, and then
asked what had happened to my mother. I wrote that she had
died when I was twelve. I had been lucky to have known her at
all, he said; 1917 was an eon away from 1935 in medical history.
And for the first time since the accident, I knew gratitude once
again. When I went to the other births, I wore the robe he gave
me, and carried the cap and mask for good luck.

Eventually, I had seen four deliveries and hadn't yet spoken
a word. I had no idea what my mother discovered in all this; the

miracle of birth struck me as a miracle all right—a miracle of blood and gore, a miracle that our bodies insisted on life in the most degrading of circumstances, and a miracle that women got through it. After my fifth C-section, nothing happened. No inspiration, no words, nothing but a certain sense of relief that it was all over; this was the last time I'd be obligated to turn cold as a corpse in that gallery, then leave nauseated and wrung out, wiping perspiration from my early-morning beard. I was relieved yet dejected as they wheeled the mother off to the recovery room. I was getting up to go when I heard her screaming.

I heard her screaming through a set of double doors and the glass partition on the far wall of the operating room. The doctors took no notice and didn't seem disturbed. I listened to see if she would calm down, but her screams kept up and only grew louder. I waited for what seemed five minutes. Still she screamed and still the doctors paid no attention. I waved and made hand signals. The young doctor looked up at me and nodded, but only in recognition, and finished cleaning up. He waved good-bye to me like a WWI fighter pilot, a two-fingered waggle, and walked out the door with the others to the room where they changed.

The woman kept screaming. I went down on my crutches to see about her, terrified. Perhaps, I thought, she's going to die, perhaps the doctors have written her off. But that didn't seem their mood. I couldn't be sure, and wanted to be reassured by someone. I got to the door and saw printed on it NO ADMITTANCE: STAFF PERSONNEL ONLY. I pulled on my cap and mask, not intending any masquerade but figuring that if anyone were in the recovery room with the woman they'd mind my intrusion less if I didn't come in breathing my germs into her wounds. I didn't understand that there was nothing inherently sterile about my attire, and that I could have passed on an infection with it.

I pushed open the door and the woman's screams seemed to leap and take hold of me, scaring me worse. The orderly who had first wheeled me down stood watching over her. She was on a gurney, her limbs fastened down with leather straps, but still trying to thrash free; convulsive movements went through her body and threw her head around so wildly I was sure she would knock herself out. I went over and looked into her eyes, which were unfocused and confused, like someone with a fever, and fixed somewhere in the distance between us. Accidentally, my hand on the crutch brushed against hers at the side of the gurney, and instantly, instead of simply screaming incoherently, she screamed that she was on fire, that I must give her something to relieve the pain, that she couldn't bear this, that she would die from the heat if I didn't give her anything.

"The after-pains," the orderly said. "She got 'em bad, real bad."

I made the motions of preparing a syringe and plunged it into my arm.

"They can't give her nothin' for a while. She got to get the poison outta her system, fuh they give her some moh."

I looked at him again, wild.

"She gonna be all right, Ted. Long as she yellin', she fine."

Her screaming continued to have a powerful effect on me. The room seemed to tilt upwards and I thought I would lose my balance, with the odds about even as to which way I'd fall. A crutch hit against the gurney and I took hold of the woman's hand by mistake. She grabbed my wrist and squeezed with everything she had. All of her pain was in that grip. I held on to the gurney to keep from falling, and as I did I lost control of my bladder and felt the stinging urine run down my legs. Her pain, as it reduced her to its mouthpiece, now spoke in me. I perceived it as I would a live electrical wire—as immediate as if a sensation of my own. Tears sprang into my eyes. The pain burned through my body. And yet the fire of the pain also cast a light of amazement and awe. I found that I had regained my balance again. I undid her grip and took both her hands in mine. Our joined hands formed a circle of intimacy, and within that circle peace welled up. Her sobs diminished and our holding onto one another changed from something desperate into something neither of us seemed to want to give up.

I don't know how long we were together like that. From the time the orderly ran out and returned to the recovery room with a doctor who gave me a blast of something in the fanny and pried me away from the woman, that much time, but how long that was in minutes I'll never know.

I awoke back in my hospital bed. The young resident had come in and aroused me from my drugged slumber. He made sure I knew where I was and what had happened. Once my eyes remained open, and I had propped myself up on an elbow in bed, he got to his point; he said, "Mrs. Donnelly, the young mother you were with, asked if she could name her baby after the young doctor in the recovery room. That's you, Ted. She wants to name her son after you. Is that all right?"

"Yes," I said. I don't believe I was even surprised that I had spoken. "Yes," I said again. And after that, I could speak normally once more.

I said yes that day to Mrs. Donnelly, to my mother, to my vocation and, in a basic way, to life itself and to God. Now, with my ministry nearly choked off by my own actions, with my witness muted, I needed to say yes again; to embrace the inconsistencies and contradictions of my life, and affirm the presence of the Lord in it all, whether as judge or justifier. But this time that yes could be found, if at all, only in my knowledge of the faith and its language. I was certain that "sin" spoke of my action against Michael as no other word did. If I was able to look at the whole of my life and hear the enunciation of that word once more in the vocabulary of faith, then I might understand it and accept it as enfolded by the Word. Or so my thoughts began to run.

My guardian angel, or whoever it may be who apportions such special graces, gave me the idea of using the revival, going via it, back to the narrow way, if the trail hadn't already been lost forever. I would preach that night on sin, and for the next six nights try to recover the rest of the vocabulary of faith, as God chose to reveal it to me, if he would. I saw I must confess the fullness or emptiness of my experience as a Christian and as a pastor under the aspect of this language. My congregation's revival would be a recapitulation of all their pastor was and knew; it would be my epic poem to them. And for me, I could only pray, it would be my way of beginning again the pilgrimage toward that city, Jerusalem, which had been my goal all these years.

I summoned Donna, my secretary, and told her to get in touch with all the leaders of the church, the staff, the deacons, ushers, Sunday school teachers, women's missionary fellowship members, choir members—everybody—and tell them the revival was still on. Just that and nothing more.

She stared at me not as if I were crazy, but as if I should appear that way but didn't.

After she left, I wrote under the date of my calendar, Monday, August 23, "Sin." I looked out the window. The same intersection was there, with the same Texaco station (minus, of course, the Hallelujah Chorus) on the opposite corner, yet the world in the space of time since had altered, and I thought, *Now it's started. Here we go.*

I made two calls, first to the hospital to see how Michael was. Plastic surgery had been performed on his nose that morning, and he was, in the nurse's trite and (as it turned out) untrue words, "resting comfortably." Then I called Paul Corwin. Before I could say much more than hello, he was begging my forgiveness. He gave me the promise, unsolicited, that he would never preach again, and said he was leaving on a six-thirty flight that evening.

I couldn't let him go like that, I said; what I didn't say was that I wanted some idea of his monsters, perhaps to compare them with mine, so that my dreams, such as the ones last night, wouldn't be solely responsible for giving them their bestial cast. I talked him into having lunch with me.

In the interim, I sat at my desk and thought about my message for that evening. What did I know about sin? I pulled down a concordance from my shelves, and then worked through some verses in my Greek New Testament. I had no trouble with the Greek, because I knew the verses in English by heart, but what did I know experientially about sin? Hitting Michael, there was a start. And another time, when I was in the service, during WWII; but that might give my opponents just the firepower they needed. No, I didn't know whether I had the strength to wield the two-edged sword of that tragicomic anecdote—which wasn't just an anecdote but something I had done, and I sat there considering.

Of course, I'd had my failings like everyone else, but what would my people think if they heard from me about the depths and degradation of actual, low-down *sin*?

My encounters with Paul Corwin, since he had appeared for the revival, had been confusing, and I hoped that our meeting before he left for San Diego would clear things up, although I felt wary as I drove to his motel. Seeing him break down, *abandon* himself to his feelings and fate, I had the intuition that he'd been through something on the foreign front similar to what I'd experienced on the domestic. And if, in his turn, he asked me, What's wrong Ted, what would I answer? *You name it, Paul.*

His motel door opened and he eased out toward the parking lot, into our hazy California afternoon sunlight, wearing dark glasses. I'm sure it was only my reservoir of undifferentiated guilt that made me uneasy about the shades, but I had the feeling as we made our way to the motel coffee shop—a venue we quickly agreed upon; Paul wasn't hungry—that we were two escaped felons. Once there, though, he took the glasses off and laid them casually on the table alongside the sugar dispenser; he had no cloak-and-dagger intentions, as I should have known. His blossoming sideburns were reddish, with flossy white coils woven through them, and the hollows of his eyes, traced across by a multitude of fine wrinkles, were red-brown, as if echoing a theme. I ordered a guacamole burger, with a slice of onion, and coffee, and Paul iced tea. When the waitress left, Paul said, "I want to promise you that I'll never again try to preach. That's finished."

The same apologetic tone again. It left me nothing to get a purchase on. And for a time, we said nothing further. The occasional clash of dishes marked the passage of the slow afternoon in the shadowy interior of the coffee shop, and then I felt a troubling familiar presence—Benjamin?—and sensed that this wouldn't be the confrontation that I had expected.

Our order came, and we mentioned only ketchup and sugar before Paul said, "I've never felt so humiliated, Ted. I hardly know what to think."

"Well, I don't know either," I said, trying to keep the tone light. "What happened? What is it?"

"I stood behind the pulpit," Paul said, and looked out the window as if it were there, "and didn't feel scared—actually, I didn't feel much of anything. Your congregation was waiting, and I didn't have anything to say. My hands were empty." He turned back to me. "It was particularly painful because I've never been a do-nothing Christian. You know that."

"Your head seemed pretty empty, too," I said. This was unkind, but I needed to knock him out of his tendency toward messianic figures.

He gave me the slanted, wry look of, once more, my old friend from seminary. "Ted," he said. "Listen. In 1955 one of GO!'s first full-scale operations sent food and medical supplies to Southwest Africa—the Kalahari Desert. The only people there were Bushmen, of Mongolian descent, and Bakalaharis—dispossessed Bantu. GO! had an old DC-3 transport plane, war surplus, and we used to fly the supplies in, using the desert floor for our runway. The rainy season lasts two months there, usually, but at that point there had hardly been any rain for two years running.

"We used to fly in over the veld, seeing great fires that were burning up the last of the vegetation, and when the smoke cleared we could see the bones of hundreds of wildebeest and antelope. I didn't know much about primitive life then, and couldn't imagine animals surviving in that desert in the first place.

"Well, we had heard that most of the Bakalaharis and their Bushmen servants were encamped at Chukadu, an oasis. The water at Chukadu had dried up, but that was the best place to find a root vegetable, *bi*. *Bi* is their last source of food and water when everything else fails.

"We landed in the bed of a seasonal lake, which by then looked like a salt flat. It was noon and the heat was stunning when we stepped out of the plane. In the distance were three baobab trees, all there was on the horizon—nobody in sight. Our guide had prepared us for a long wait, since these people are suspicious of Europeans. I looked toward the trees and saw the heat spanking across them in waves. The sky was sooty from the fires, but you knew vultures were up there, and then, suddenly, the people appeared—the tall men and then the women in their leather robes called *kaross*. Two hundred people, at the least, spread out in a haphazard way, walking toward us.

"I was exhilirated. I figured we'd be able to give them what we had and be back to make another delivery before the day ended. But the guide was right about them being suspicious; he was from a Bantu tribe the Bakalaharis had been quarreling with. They got it into their heads that the powdered milk we wanted to give them was poison, and that we were after their Bushmen servants.

"I couldn't understand the negotiations with the leader, but just before the Bakalaharis stalked off, one of the women pulled out her lip-plug and stuck her tongue through the hole at us. I got the message. We hung around the plane, however, hoping to negotiate. You could see that everyone there was suffering from malnutrition; the knee joints of some of the kids were like knots in big rope.

"Finally, when the sun was set, and we were about to leave the supplies, so they'd be there the next day, one of the Bushmen mothers brought her child to us. He was about three, but still a toddler, since he'd never had enough calcium for his bones to support his weight. His mouth was cut to pieces and he would have died if we hadn't had plasma along. His mother told the interpreter that she usually kept *tsama*, or dried melon seeds—which are very tasty—in a glass jar that the Europeans had given her when they took her husband away. Those suspicions were well-founded. As it turned out, the baby had broken the jar and tried to eat the glass.

"The doctor on our team, Jim Dorsey, stitched the terrible series of flaps together, making two pieces of the boy's mouth again. Probably from sheer fright, the boy was absolutely silent through the whole process.

"His mother's milk had gone dry, so Jim suggested I fix a bottle. I passed it to Jim with what was probably unnecessary stealth, and the mother watched while Jim fed him. There was a near-crisis with the child after his first swallows; he was so happy to have food he started smiling, and then had to cry out with the pain. His mother went for Jim and the child both but I grabbed her and had the interpreter explain; he told the child not to smile, and the mother repeated, in her way, what he'd said. Jim started the feeding again. The boy lifted his arms above his head and began opening and closing his hands in such an expressive way that his palms became the face of his joy. It was beautiful. A miracle, you know.

"After that, things went fine with the rest of their people. It was amazing in the first place, when you think about it, that they would refuse *anything* liquid. And when they started in on the milk we had, they drank three times what we figured on for their number.

"The sort of story that brings honor to all, wouldn't you say?

GO! built its entire relief network on that kind of thing. But that isn't the end.

"We decided to make a twenty-year retrospective film about GO! We would revisit the areas we had ministered to in our early years, shoot some film, intercut that with the old stuff, and, let's face it, knock out a nostalgic fund-raiser for half the cost of what we ordinarily spent. Probably nobody was aware of this, but we needed a financial boost; the cost of things goes up rather than down, and we'd continued to grow. I got it into my head to find that Bushman baby. I knew I could recognize him, if he were still living, by his scars. But those tribes split up and recombine constantly, and though they might stick to one area, their territory can spread out for several hundred miles. Even so, I wanted to try. I prayed about it, and felt that the Lord wanted me to find that Bushman, too.

"We went out in a jet-powered helicopter, a Sikorsky S-55, which seats eight. It's too well-engineered as a passenger vehicle to carry much food, but it has a bar, and we packed that with orange juice. I might as well mention that it also has a marvelous stereo-tape system, with headphones, to knock out the propeller chop. So there we were, cruising over the desert, sipping orange juice, and listening to Bach.

"At the first encampment where we touched down we found our man right off the bat. A tall Bakalahari, with peppercorn hair shaved close to his head, directed me to him. From my description. I now know most of the dialects, of course. I expected to find the fellow in the usual, flimsy grass hut, but he was off in the open, his elbows on his knees, his head resting in his hands, crouched down, with his dwelling marked out by white sticks. These lay in a little circle around him. He had on a medicine belt and was rocking on his heels to ward off the pain of hunger, a method they have; he was dying of malnutrition. He looked up and I saw the scars. I squatted down and asked him if he remembered me. He looked me over and said his mother had told him, many times, the story about a man like me with a thing that fixed him and a bottle. He stuck his fingers in his mouth and stretched out his lips to make the scars more visible. He couldn't rise, the pain was so bad, but he acted—how else can I say it—*glad*. He was glad to see me. Imagine.

"We gave the tribe what we had, a few rolls and our orange

juice—why hadn't we filled some seats with food, I thought? I insisted on holding the cup for the fellow, to make sure that his Bakalahari masters allowed him a portion. And as I helped him sip the juice, I thought how I had poured my whole life into that scarred mouth. And what good had it done? I'd only saved this man so he could suffer malnutrition all over again.

"A lot of people involved in world hunger say that certain areas of the earth, the Kalahari among them, are so far gone it would be better to write them off—relief measures only prolong the people's suffering. I couldn't accept that. But I saw then that I had done just that. Finding that Bushman turned out to be a miracle I didn't want any part of."

He had finished his confession, it seemed. In the shadowy restaurant I thought of Lazarus, and of Christ raising him from the dead to die a second death. I'd always wondered if Lazarus himself had been as grateful as his sisters.

"After that, I contracted my fever," Paul said. "I never did complete the film. My symptoms are like tertiary typhoid—the non-lethal kind people like Cromwell suffered from off and on throughout their lives—although the doctors can't verify that it really is typhoid. I don't even know if I should call it typhoid anymore, to be honest. I *think* it is. Or hope so. At this point my doctors are starting to comment on the difficulties of my kind of life, of getting my rest and eating properly—obviously, of the consensus that I'm mad. And will soon be anorexic. I told the doctor who asked if I'd been eating properly, when I was in the hospital, that if he looked at my chart he could see I hadn't been eating *at all*. I said that even the *thought* of food disgusted me. He seemed suddenly eager to get out of the room, as if he didn't want to hear an evangelist like Paul Corwin say such things. But I don't have it in me to starve myself; I'll hold my nose and take my filet mignon, when it comes down to it." He put his finger to his nose, where I noticed a delicate bruise.

"You feel betrayed?" I asked.

"I feel like I want to sit down on the ground and rock on my heels. Throw dust on my head, too, so nobody can recognize me."

"Do you know what I think?"

"Just about. We both went to the same seminary."

"You're a peacock, and always have been," I said. "You

have such a sense of self-importance you feel you should be able to change the Lord's ground rules."

"Oh? Well, if I had made a world where people were allowed to starve to death because of an original Fall, I wouldn't undermine the efforts of others who were trying to alleviate that. In fact, the idea of *allowing* starvation strikes me as a lousy idea, under any conditions. It's one thing in a seminary classroom, and quite another in real life."

"Paul!" I cried. "You sound like a *liberal!*"

He looked sideways at me along his nose. "Dirty words will get you nowhere with me," he said.

We both laughed. It was the first real glimmer that I'd had of my old seminary friend.

"And you?" he asked. "You seem to be on the road to becoming a bare-knuckle champion."

"White-knuckle, I'd say. And you'd starve yourself, if you could. Christ only received thirty-nine lashings, so you'll take the fortieth."

"I understand what you're saying, but it doesn't help. I *feel* this. I thought perhaps that if I got up before your people and said the words, said them until they took on their old authority, I'd start believing again. But it was just feeding the man with the scarred mouth again. It's that and nothing more."

"I can't believe that you believe that."

"I don't, really, but I feel it. I'm rich, in a sense, and when you are you don't have to keep up an endless dance to prove to yourself and others that you're young. I could go off and live like Ali Pasha. But I don't believe in that, either. It's just that—" He was staring past me. He paused, and then asked, "What about you? What about your assistant?"

I told him about my plans to continue the revival.

"Well, success!" he said, and lifted and drained his iced tea. And then after a long silence, as he rattled the ice cubes in his empty glass, I knew the matter wasn't settled yet, and maybe couldn't be. I would drive him to the airport and walk him to his plane with my arm around his shoulder, as I expected his would be around mine, in expression of our fraternity—I loved him then not "like" I loved myself but "as" myself. His humanity had been transformed through suffering, for his symptoms might be different from mine, but we definitely had the same disease.

He said finally in a voice undercut, thinned, by futility, "I wanted to help."

And then he opened out his palms to me, the empty palms of a man with nothing to give, or nothing except this defenseless gesture, and I knew the gesture hadn't risen from an excess of pride, nor was he simply trying to save face. It seemed that we were passing the cup of suffering back and forth between us, neither one praying that it would pass from him, and neither one taking it up, although we both well knew that the death of the flesh must be the catalyst of any real change in us. And then, seeing the waitress start toward us across the empty coffee shop, I wanted to turn away and drink the cup's full measure.

"Why are you frowning?" Paul asked. He put a hand on my jacket sleeve. "Ted," he said. "Are you frowning?"

"Beloved," I said, "as I'm sure you know, Paul Corwin, the evangelist who was to conduct this revival, has fallen ill." I stared out from the pulpit. The few people who had bothered to show up acted like drifters, glancing at the ushers and the few deacons present as if the meeting might be a closed session that they needed permission to attend. And the folk-rock group, which had finally showed up, had failed to affect the assembly one bit until the lead guitar player, perhaps in revenge, had embarked upon improvisations during the bridge of one song at such a high pitch that everybody got the expression of having his teeth go into sympathetic vibrations with a dentist's drill—not the most auspicious entry for me into what might be the worst possible course in persuasion that I could have chosen. "But revival," I said, "the renewing of our minds and bodies in the Spirit of the Lord, never depends upon man but on the completed work of Christ. Thus another poor man will preach in Paul's stead. Now I know if you compare my efforts to those we have been anticipating, you're going to be disappointed. But if we all look to Christ and the revival that he alone can bring about, then we can approach the rest of the week with the greatest expectations.

"My subject tonight is sin. That one word, 'sin,' with which I declare, the entire Christian vision begins."

"Like most of my generation when I think of sin I think of

World War Two. Not alone because of the Holocaust, the North African campaign, or because I know the enemy was burned alive by flamethrowers at Guadalcanal. No, I think of World War Two and some stateside mischief which first revealed to me the total depravity of man, myself included, even before Guadalcanal.

"Let me explain. I was lucky to pass the war in a sedentary fashion. Although I ran the mile in high school, the army decided I had flat feet. When I finished my first theological degree and became a Navy chaplain, in 1943, my feet kept me high and dry, stateside. I was assigned to a hospital in San Diego, and had additional, although minor, responsibilites in leading services for the personnel on the base who were headed out to the Pacific theater.

"I am a preacher more than a pastor, I confess, and though I am fascinated by the mind's inner workings, I have never been especially good at counseling. But I was particularly inept at the hospital work I was given to do in the chaplaincy. My mother died when I was young, spending her last months in terrible suffering, and I myself put in time in a hospital recuperating from an automobile accident. These experiences made the suffering of the boys too real and painful for me to cope with.

"As a minister, you have to look at hospital patients with a certain detachment. You cannot relieve pain and give comfort when, after the patient has told you what it is like to hear, under local anesthetic, the bone of a finger crunch as it is amputated, the patient sees that you have clasped your own hands behind you in response. Or, seeing someone who has been blinded, you start to report to him on what you can see out the window. Or, in the presence of a paralytic, you feel compelled to move energetically about the room, hopping from time to time, in order to prove that your legs are still under you and work.

"These three incidents, and others like them, actually occurred when I started work at the Navy hospital. Perverse, you say? When I tried to suppress my behavior, I became obsessed with thoughts of death, and went to see a psychiatrist for the only time in my life. I can't judge the profession as a whole, but that man was a genius: he advised finding other duty.

"I had to convince my commanding officer, the Reverend Captain John B. Tucker, an old Wesleyan Methodist and career officer from Tennessee, that among his charges I was God's chosen for primary, not secondary, preaching and service-conducting responsibilities at the base. Since we were already in the middle of the war, the captain had long before adopted a fellow named Hugh Finley as a surrogate son, and Hugh had garnered this preaching duty, which was one of the better ones.

"In the spirit of Christian love and brotherhood, I went to see Hugh Finley. I described my condition and said that these problems, moreover, had caused serious disturbances in my spiritual life. He might not only be saving me from my distress, I said, but my vocation as well. Please, I said.

"Hugh was homogenized according to the form of the war years: he had slicked-back blond hair, blue eyes, a good jaw, and an expression of intelligent innocence and efficiency. Hugh said he sympathized. He had a similar problem: he couldn't tolerate the smell of human wastes. He wanted to be of help, but he couldn't—maybe another one of the chaplains.

"And that was our interview, short and sweet and, for me, bitter.

"How bitter, I found out later when I discovered, to my horror, that the few preaching responsibilities that I had were taken away, and I had been reassigned exclusively to hospital duty. Captain Tucker rarely visited the hospital and I came to see that Hugh wanted us apart as much as possible, for fear I develop a friendship with the captain.

"Why didn't I simply go and explain the situation to Captain Tucker? you're probably wondering. Well, chaplains, especially stateside chaplains, are always suspected of being cowards hiding behind the cloth. Captain Tucker liked to think differently of his men. In an organizational meeting with us, he recounted an incident when, questioned as to his bravery by another career officer, he had said, 'Any soldier can stand up to the enemy, but only a chaplain tells the Devil himself to blow it out his barracks bags.' You get the point, I'm sure, as I did, about Captain Tucker.

"I had only one recourse, which involved golf, my favorite pastime—as many of you know. Hugh strengthened his status as adopted son by playing golf twice a week with the captain. They had a regular foursome, but I knew there had to come a time when they would need a spot replacement. So, I sent the captain a note saying that I'd love to play with them, anytime they needed a fourth, and went out on the driving range to practice.

"I had played, before I entered seminary, to a competent five handicap. I had heard that one of the captain's ambitions was to straighten out his habitual slice and hit his irons with a high trajectory and a professional right-to-left draw. This precisely describes my iron shots at the time, and I prayed that I could teach the captain to hit his likewise. If I could, I figured I had a chance at his looking kindly on my request for a change in duty.

"In a while, I got my invitation to play. When I met the captain on the practice tee an hour before our match, I saw a man turned out in a straw hat like Sam Snead wore and the voluminously baggy trousers of Lloyd Mangrum. It seemed clear that the captain's true love in life, his real existence, took place on the links—in that dew-washed and clipped green land—the Arden of our middle class. On the course in San Diego the wind would shift, and the air, like some unfathomably huge roller, would break with the smell of brine and seaweed. The captain shook my hand, lifting off his straw hat with his other, and the short-cropped black bristles of his head reminded me of a ball-peen hammer.

"I offered to share the balls in my practice bucket with the good captain and watched as he hit a few. With his stocky body, heavily-muscled arms and considerable paunch, he addressed the ball as a pit dog might its opponent. His knees bent deeply, he cautiously stretched the club out toward the ball, and then quickly, with a great intake of air, he raised the club almost vertically and with the same speed brought it down, always rising on his tiptoes, counterbalancing the power of his downswing. Sometimes he lifted clean off the ground, and usually had to take several little hops after following through to regain his balance.

"The ball, when struck in this manner, did not fade from left to right, or curve directly out to the right; the ball went straight down the fairway fifty yards and then took what seemed to be a ninety-degree right turn. To the captain, and I must admit to me, too, the ball's flight smacked not of aerodynamics but demoniacal caprice.

"I took out my seven iron, and hit several high right-to-left draws toward a makeshift target green about one hundred and forty-five yards away. Soon the captain was watching me. He asked me what club I was hitting, then where I had developed my swing. His expression was that of a child whose whole life seems to depend on receiving the bicycle in the store window for Christmas.

"I gave the captain a lesson, emphasizing that he must *close his stance, swing inside-out* and *throw his hands at the ball* so that his wrists broke sharply. By the end of the lesson I had him hitting the ball with a nice right-to-left tail at the end of each shot.

"The captain and I joined Hugh Finley and another chaplain, a Jesuit named Kelly, on the first tee. For the first three holes, the captain said little, kept hitting his hooks, and walked along beside me, while our companions uttered appropriate exclamations of astonishment and comradely joy.

"As many of you know, I'm competitive. Some of you might put that more strongly. That day I wanted to beat Hugh Finley, an average player, by as many strokes as possible, establishing my worth to the captain when he needed a partner for the local tournaments and, in a sense, announcing my candidacy for sonship.

"At the turn, when we stopped off for a hot dog, the captain left me with the Jesuit, while he and Hugh chuckled together. I wasn't worried about any inside joke, I said to myself.

"On the back nine, the captain and Hugh toured the course in a very odd fashion. Whenever one of them hit his ball into a hazard, far into the rough or into a deep trap, the two went off together, talking in low voices and then breaking into giggles like schoolgirls. At the fifteenth hole, before we hit our drives, the captain called me over. He mumbled something about not wanting the Roman to hear, and then said to Hugh, 'Tell him.'

"Hugh told me a joke. A preacher and a sportswriter were playing a round of golf together. They came up to the first hole. The preacher waggled his driver, brought the club head back, swung at the ball, and topped a drive about seventy-five yards down the fairway and out to the left. He let out his breath and muttered the word 'Boulder.' This happened again and again all through the round; the preacher would hit his shot and immediately say 'Boulder.' After the round was over, the sportswriter thanked the preacher for the game and said he hoped they could get together again sometime. 'There's just one thing,' the sportswriter said. 'Why is it that you say "Boulder" all the time?' 'Because it's the biggest dam I know,' was the preacher's reply.

"This was the first of a series of increasingly ribald stories that Hugh now told me—the same stories he'd been telling the captain all day. The captain stuck around to hear them all again and after the last, which particularly struck his fancy, he was in stitches, repeating the punchline again and again to his own amusement. He was truly 'in stitches' to Hugh Finley, who had him bound hand and foot, and must have known a great quantity of such stories to keep the captain entertained. Beloved, lest I haven't made myself clear: it was filthy stories that had this hold on our captain. I understood that not even a new and golden swing could compete with the desire to step out of the role of authority and piety that the captain had. For however disgraceful such a story sounds in church, we all know that there are many good, respectable men who have a passion for dirty jokes. It's often their way of letting their hair down. And that's exactly what Hugh's stories did for the captain.

"They also dashed my hopes.

"When we arrived at the eighteenth hole, I was so angry I could hardly speak. My temper is one of my own besetting sins. I remember standing on the elevated tee of that last hole, a short par five: the fairway declined from the tee into a swale and then rose toward a hummocklike green. A lake bordered the right side of the hole, and a finger of this lake reached out over the last twenty yards and guarded the entrance to the green. I am sure that I had no eye for the hole's charm, as I see it now; my mind was set on subduing this particular five hundred yards of earth. I swung and slammed the ball two hundred and eighty yards down the fairway, just to the right of center. My companions whistled and cheered, but I didn't crack a smile.

"I walked to my ball with a Prussian arrogance. Hugh Finley had topped his drive. Kelly and the captain were out to the right; the captain had laughed his way back into his old slicing habits. Hugh recovered by hitting a four wood fifty yards beyond my position, to the left side of the fairway, and the captain hooked one over to Hugh's position while Kelly plopped into the lake.

"I waited before hitting my second shot, and here the moment comes; a foursome was putting out on the green, which I thought I could reach in two. As they cleared off, Hugh hit his third, and so did the captain, and Kelly, lying three with the penalty, hit his fourth. Their shots were on the fringes of the green.

"I suspected they assumeed I had taken my second shot, and that's why they had gone ahead out of turn. But I was offended that they hadn't waited for me to play, as was proper, especially since they were slighting the great event of my trying to reach the green in two; and if I birdied, I would post a seventy-three. One remembers some games of golf better than one's anniversary at times, I confess to my own shame.

"They began to stroll up the fairway, the captain and Hugh on the left-hand side, Kelly on the right. I took out my two iron, took up my stance, screamed, Fore! and tore at the ball. My eyes lifted after the thin head of the two iron powered cleanly through the bottom of the stroke, and I saw the ball, like a tracer of warfare, rise slowly toward Hugh Finley's temple and as it reached him lose itself in the saline corona around his blond head. Then he was down, prone, and the sun glinted off the spikes of his shoes.

"I have to admit that in that first instant I felt deeply gratified by what I had done. Then, quickly, I felt guilt and, just as quickly, tried to rationalize. I had hit a slice, more common for me with a long iron, but still against my natural inclinations. But what did that say?

"Besides making the shot when the captain and Hugh were in the way, which was bad enough, I saw that my stance was open, decidedly open, decisively convicting. If only subconsciously, I had opened my stance, intending to slice that ball toward Hugh.

"Then I heard Kelly cheering, and I thought reason had deserted me entirely to hear expressions of shock as cheers. Unless he also had a score against Hugh. But then he called, Great shot! I heard the captain bellow something unintelligible, and I looked back toward him, where he stood as if in attendance on Hugh. The junior officer was still on the ground, but he had propped himself up on one arm and was looking toward the green. In the crosscut checkerboard of grass, the ball rested seven feet from the pin.

"Hugh told me after the round, after I had three-putted from seven feet, that, sensing rather than seeing what was happening, he had fallen, and just as he fell he'd heard the ball's whir as it passed his temple. My playing companions tried to pass off the matter, making jokes about it—but their jokes were as dead as their laughter was. Hugh, however, wasn't, thank God.

"Strangely enough, I got what I thought I had wanted: I became a *de facto* teaching pro for the officers on the base.

"But I'd received a glimpse of myself which changed my view of the world forever. That shot, that stance, and the will which placed my feet and powered my bones and sinews, came from the unexpected revelation I finally arrived at—I hadn't known what I was capable of. But I, the 'I' that resides in my willfulness, the same 'I' which also issues forth in work and progeny, that 'I' demanded its own life. And while I could not live without my instinct for self-preservation, I could not live in peace with that 'I.' For its demands for life became a demand for death. That 'I' demanded that Hugh Finley, in the idyllic landscape of the golf course, having wounded that 'I' more with frustration than his stories, be killed with a two iron.

"The legacy of World War Two, the legacy of my war with Hugh Finley, has been a continuing warfare of personal denial. Having failed in my attempts to execute my own willfulness, I have worked to make that 'I' a prisoner of war. But that 'I' escapes and exposes me as ridiculous, sabotaging my integrity and self-respect—blowing it, in fact, to kingdom come. Hugh lived; I became a walking casualty.

"Now, in the light of recent events, I know what most of you are thinking: Why didn't we find out the man was homicidal before we hired him? The man considers it somehow edifying to get up and tell us about nearly killing someone on the golf course: what kind of person is he?

"I'll get to that question, but first I want you to see the point, for if you think what I'm saying doesn't apply to you, you're not only wrong, you're not Christian in your thinking.

"The Bible tells us that we are shaped in iniquity and in sin are we conceived, in Psalm fifty-one, verse five. We speak of this in theology as original sin. Most of you would say you believe in original sin, the depravity of man, but you don't, really; you believe that there are decent people and then there are scoundrels, and that the two shouldn't have anything to do with one another. But the Bible says that all have sinned and fallen short of the glory of God. Not just a little. The Bible says, in Isaiah sixty-four, that even all our righteousness is as a filthy rag. It's putrid. It's as rotten as it can be. Considerations of taste prevent me from saying exactly how rotten, as implied by this verse."

I paused and thought about using Benjamin's Savanarola experience in an illustration; but I chose a story from the classics.

"An early church father, Augustine, discusses in his *Confessions* the impulse of a baby denied the milk of its mother. The baby reaches out toward the mother, not in babylike innocence but in an adult rage: the baby would strangle its mother at that moment if it had enough strength.

"That same rage is in every one of us whether we like to acknowledge it or not. Jesus Christ tells us that wrath is essentially the same thing as murder, in Matthew five, the early-twenty verses, and John says that whoever hates his brother is a murderer—first John, the fifteenth verse of the third chapter. Every time we get angry with someone what we essentially want to do is kill him. Some of us do a better job containing our anger than others, but as Christians we have to acknowledge that the impulse to murder is within us.

"We can deny this, beloved. We can say that it doesn't apply to us. But then we have to make a hard choice. Because it's obvious that evil exists in this world. And if we are innocent, if original sin does not exist, whose fault is it that evil is abroad in the land? Who's responsible? The scoundrels? *Society*? If we think about it long enough, we'll see there are only two options— us or God. We are responsible or God is responsible, and if God is responsible, then he's a monster. If that's your option, there's no way out, unless you expect to take everything under control yourself soon and do a better job.

"No, as Christians we have to acknowledge that our basic nature is evil. That we are filled with wrath and lust and every vile thing imaginable. That, in fact, we are murderers. This must be admitted, not in order to wallow in guilt, but to have the proper perspective on ourselves. For if Christ took the sins of the whole world upon himself on the cross, that means that we helped put him there. That means that we are culpable not simply for wanting to kill other men but for *wanting to kill God himself!* This is the ultimate meaning of evil, beloved, the ultimate meaning of sin. If we don't have this view of it, there's no hope for change in us, or application of that same death.

"So why, you might think, doesn't God send down his holy fire and destroy us all? Why doesn't he rid the beautiful world that he made of our corruption? Why doesn't he at least strike down unfaithful ministers with suppurating boils? Why does God leave us so often with only the taste of ashes in our mouths to teach us of our misdeeds?

"If you are saying to yourself that the pastor seems to be confusing two issues here, you are correct. There is the theological issue of the nature of man—what sin means to us—and there is the immediate issue of what you all should do about me. For although we acknowledge that we are all sinners, we also make distinctions between people we put in places of responsibility and those we can't trust. Maybe right now you think I should be cast out. Maybe at the least you think I should be fired.

"Well, maybe I should.

"But I ask you to wait, as the Almighty seems to be waiting, until the end of this revival to make your final judgment. I intend to confess to you everything that I know to be true as a Christian and as a pastor; I intend to tell you everything I know about the faith from firsthand experience throughout the course of this week. And then I'll stand before you and you may judge me as you must.

"Amen."

Tuesday:

Justice

Tuesday morning I went to the office, expecting a verdict on my plan to have come in over the straw-poll of the telephone. My message box was empty, however, and there were no telephone slips on my desk, except for one from a newspaperwoman who had called about seeing Paul Corwin. Donna assured me that this was it. I tore up the newspaperwoman's note and went and sat in my office, bewildered. I had no idea where I was with the congregation. I didn't even know where I stood concerning the revival, or what I would preach on that night. The dimensions of things increased in the solitude of my office, and I soon found myself calling Cecil Brown.

Cecil owns a tuxedo-rental business and his shop is so small I felt he was taking his time about coming to the phone. At first he seemed restrained, clumsily evasive, heavy—a sponge obviously soaked with information. I only had to squeeze.

"Cecil," I said, in my forgiving-cordial voice, "I missed you last night."

"Gena and I were with some friends."

"I wanted your reaction on my continuing revival."

There was an empty pause, and he said, "We are going to need more than just your messages, I think, pastor."

I asked him how he knew about my plan, and what he meant by "we." He was, by this time, ready to do just that, as if he felt he'd been sufficiently caught out so that he could excuse himself by saying I'd wrung the information from him.

Through what he told me then and others did later, I have a composite notion of—what shall I call it?—the other or the anti-revival meeting that took place even as I was preaching; I have pieced together how Patti Murphy and her cohorts came to see themselves as vigilantes of the kind I had begun to dread.

Others may not fall in line behind my opinion, but I think of myself as congenial. I like a great many people, and, although I have been hard on Cecil Brown in these pages, it must be remembered that I have spent most of my life working with the Cecil Browns of this world and most of the time have been successful with them—while accomplishing my goals, and making them feel accepted and important. Patti Murphy, however, resides with the half dozen or so people I have—how shall I put this, except to be honest?—instantly hated.

Why? Certainly she is not physically repulsive. Her short hair is helmet-shaped and professionally frosted; her open face, with its bright eyes and upturned nose, retains, at forty, something of the cuteness which must, I imagine, have made her a perky cheerleader in the early fifties. She still walks with the certain spring of one about to depart for the big game. She just might take her old cheerleader outfit down from the closet from time to time, and try it on to recall her youth and her prominence in the school pecking order, and so feel justified when she goes out and acts like a perky lunatic.

Evidently Patti started to organize her meeting within minutes after I had assaulted Michael. She called the Stromms and guaranteed their presence by promising that the Hendersons would be there and, in turn, the Hendersons were secured by promising the attendance of the Stromms. She invited the kind of people who always end up in the middle of a church fight—good-hearted, well-heeled folks, innocents who would never question her advertisement of the meeting as a forum for "those who are concerned about the direction of our church." Really, I cannot imagine what such people go to schismatic conclaves expecting. That Patti had discovered a Northwest Passage to Beulahland?

So they gather. They eat marble cake and they drink coffee out of china cups so thin one can imagine gobbling them up like sugar-hardened meringue. They talk about their jobs and their children and where they have gone or are going on their vacations. Then Patti senses that the refreshment time is going on too long; there is a lack of purpose in the group. She hurriedly talks with Tom Beardsley and Allen Gresham and assigns them roles in the up-coming "discussion." She asks for everyone's attention and says she would like the meeting to start with prayer. All the guests find places to sit or stand about the perimeter of her sunken living room while prayers are offered. She hasn't prompted anyone about the direction of the prayers, and the innocents begin to offer pleas for missionaries and the Sunday school and the sick and even a discerning spirit among those at the meeting. Patti quickly ends this by asking God Almighty "to restore Michael to his full health and strength, and bring him back to us."

Then Tom Beardsley attracts the group's attention by saying loudly to Patti that he has the latest report on Michael's condition. Many side conversations start up as Tom speaks, and versions of my actions are whispered to the few who haven't yet heard, planting the seeds of collective outrage. Allen Gresham, a former head usher, calls up a few of the old tales of my erratic behavior—counseling sessions that have turned into yelling matches, incomprehensible sermons on my off-Sundays, etc.— and wonders if a vacillating manner in the pulpit might not be grounds for a psychiatric examination. Oh, wisdom! Oh, truth!

Allen has committed a *faux pas*, Patti knows. He should not yet have presumed that those at the meeting consider themselves a body capable of taking action. Luckily (for you, Patti), the messenger is just now arriving.

Cecil and several others had earlier told Patti that they thought they should attend Monday's service and Patti, realizing that the impact of the Michael Dennis incident might dissipate, and determined to act quickly—Patti promised to send her brother to Monday's revival meeting, and have him report back afterwards to the group. Patti's brother, Nat, a likable fellow who never took his sister's posturings seriously, tells the group about my plan. He gets that straight, but he garbles the sermon which led up to it, and my sideways or oblique approach appears, in the retelling, sadly confused and disordered.

The innocents start murmuring now, and one of the men, the aforementioned Mr. Stromm, asks Cecil and the others who hold positions of authority whether they think all of this means something; in short, should action be taken?

Cecil, of course, has the kind of mind which finds

conspiracies in trivia—he is a victim of "historical paranoia"; the past has always proved his enemy—and doesn't want to commit himself, yet can't resist speaking. So he holds the floor for five or ten minutes, much to the effect that everything is *ominously* significant, and sits down.

Jerry Mansfield stands up. He looks like an avenging angel; he has mad-hatter red hair and hawk's eyes, over which his brows flare out and up. I must say that even at this remove I do not think of Jerry as a villain. He nailed me, so to speak, to the wall, but he did the hammering with integrity. His accusations, always spoken in a voice leavened with kindness, nailed me because they were as sharp as the truth—perhaps only one version of the truth, but no less penetrating for that. Jerry rises and says, "Sometimes I'm not sure the pastor knows what he's doing anymore. Or why he's doing it. He's either going through some kind of spiritual crisis I can't pretend to understand or he's simply cracking up." He shakes his head, as if these thoughts, long dormant in him, have come to life in speaking them.

The Sundays, Daniel and Will, have arrived late; they've attended the revival meeting and are just now catching the tenor of Patti Murphy's soireé. Will, a lovely and yet mysteriously troubled woman, my educational director, stands and says, "Everybody just stop a minute and look where this is going. I don't think many people here really want to get rid of the pastor, but that's why this meeting has been called. You may find yourselves booting out the pastor before you know what on earth you're doing. I work with him, he's been through a lot, but he's basically a wonderful man who needs our support. Everyone should at least attend the revival and see what he says."

"What about Michael?" someone asks.

Will Sunday once lost her temper, and, rather in the way I struck Michael, accidentally broke her child's wrist. She thinks about this; she says, "All leaders have tempers, and we don't know everything that happened."

Someone else asks about my mental condition.

Will finds herself my spokesman, is angry at this, and thus full of resolve. She begins to debate in earnest, making such fine distinctions—she is wonderfully intelligent—that most of the guests are quickly lost. Side conversations start about how Will's job depends on what she is saying.

Patti sees that the meeting, rather than swelling toward a unanimous cry for my ouster, has become a rancorous debating society in which nothing will be accomplished. The innocents, she knows, will find anything debatable a cause for lethargy. And so Patti, all drama, steps into the middle of the circle, where Will has been fielding questions, kneels beside Will, and opens her arms wide, lifting her appealing face to Will. She says, "I know the deep concern that's in your heart, Mrs. Sunday, and I think if we could just pray together the Lord would surely guide."

Will is properly disgusted by Patti's Joan of Arc impersonation. The innocents are embarrassed, and also attracted, by the peculiarity of a middle class woman on her knees before another. Patti is sincere, they think, and innocents, once they have exhausted their mental resources, always find a mooring in the slime of sincerity. Will sees what is happening and refuses to participate, walking off grandly with her husband.

The innocents are troubled for a moment, but then Patti begins to pray, and other women hitch up their skirts, hold on to their panty hose, and descend to their knees. Men soon join them. The prayers, perhaps through the agency of crisis, become antiphonal. Patti as priest calls out, God save our pastor! And the people answer, God save our pastor! God lead us! she calls. God lead us! God give us your man! God give us your man! God show us your man! God show us your man! God find us your man! And when the calls cease, every person gathered in the circle feels miraculously convinced that I am not God's man.

Before I finished talking on the phone with Cecil, I asked him how in the world he could have cooperated with Patti Murphy's group.

"It isn't her group," he said. "It's called SOP."

"SOP? You mean, standard operating procedure? Or as in a sop to your consciences."

"Save Our Pastor." Then in a hurt voice, he added, "We didn't think of the other meanings."

"I bet."

"Look pastor, we just want what's right, what's just."

And after a backwash of guilt, Cecil's words stood clear: what's just. He hung up. After sin, justice. But even if justice seems to follow sin as one number another, I resisted committing myself to a message on justice. It occurred to me that, handing the knife to my congregation a second time, those members of SOP would be all too willing to use it. More, justice and I have had a long association, and I dread that word as much as I dread the recollection it calls up.

Occasionally I still meet a man who, when I tell him my name, recalls reading about a preacher back in the late forties, somewhere near Chicago, who . . . I bob my head and smile with what I assume is an engaging grimace. I am that preacher. The man looks at me in wonder, as if I might metamorphose into an angel or a demon, depending upon how he remembers the story. And I suppose most such fellows go away and simply report to their wives that I have grown old, lost my hair, and have bulging eyes.

After the war, after my discharge in 1946 and a year as an itinerant pastor for three country churches in Indiana, I was called to the pastorate of a sizable free church, supposedly inter-denominational but decidedly Baptist in its outlook, in Oak Park, Illinois—a posh bedroom community of Chicago. Oak Park is distinguished by its Frank Lloyd Wright homes and its promi-nent figures in organized crime. Ernest Hemingway, who grew up in Oak Park, called it the "city of broad lawns and narrow minds."

I worked hard, studied and preached with great fervor, while at the same time beginning a Th.D. at the University of Chicago Divinity School. But my success in Oak Park was mini-mal, in relation to Constance's, and derivative as well. Her board-ing school manners at tea parties and her Main Line Philadelphia connections went over in a big way with the women of the congregation, who were still avid for "culture" in an up-and-coming Midwestern way. At that point Constance was equally avid that my career progress. And so, at the end of her teas, she used to call me out of the study, on the spur of the moment, and ask if I would mind answering some questions the ladies had on the Bible.

I would sit in our quite comfortable home—filled with oriental rugs and the odd French antique from Constance's dowry, which convinced the ladies of our unfathomable sophistication—dressed in a formally informal cardigan, grey trousers, and ox-blood wing tips. I fielded questions about the Antichrist in refer-ence to Hitler, and heaven in reference to war casualties, and whether the heathen who had not heard the gospel had any hope of salvation. Departing, tendering their farewells at the door to Constance, a woman would always say, "It must be wonderful living with a man who is so *spiritual*." Constance repeated these comments after they were gone, with irony in her voice and a mischievously directed eye, and we laughed together about her spiritual pandering.

The women who attended her teas came regularly to my services, but their husbands did not. And, especially in those days, good lay*men* were the bulwark of a church's strength. Sometimes I visited the husbands, and we would start talking about the war; they respected me for being a chaplain, even if I had been stationed in San Diego, but for many the war was still too present for them to fall back into an easy suburban faith. We made vague promises about getting together for golf and left it at that.

Then a teenager in the church, a fifteen year old boy named Randy Sutter, walked into a drugstore, sat down at the fountain, and ordered a malted. While he was sipping at it, a gangland thug three stools away turned and blew Randy's head off with a revolver.

A preacher is the epic poet of his people, for in telling the old, old story he also tells of present history, besides what has passed and is to come. I went into the pulpit that next Sunday knowing that everyone would expect me to give this event shape; they would expect me to sing its disharmonies until by half-tone modulations we could hear, distantly but distinctly, the music of the spheres, the order and reason of Randy's death. I stood before my congregation without knowing what to say, except that I saw an analogy between this event and the war and hoped to speak to the young men of the town—through the reports of their wives—whom I had not yet reached.

My church in Oak Park looked very much like a high church, Roman or Episcopalian, having been constructed during the days of the gothic revival. The nave before me, denuded of statuary, and not really a nave at all, since there was no transept or side chapels, was very dark; the light from the high windows barely registered the late September day—rain and a whipping wind. The congregation, usually segregated two or three to a pew, by choice, sat in a lump toward the front on my right-hand side. Mrs. Sutter was there in the midst of them, the day's focus.

I felt both a sense of isolation and a paradoxical solidarity. And I started singing of that isolation as a source of power, a fire which would warm us. I said that Christians are an embattled people. That since the days of the Roman Empire the blood of the martyrs has always been the most eloquent statement of Christian commitment. Christ predicted this, but promised, "Blessed are those who are persecuted for my sake, for theirs is the kingdom of heaven." And we are not to be confused, I said, that the days of persecution and martyrdom are over. Although we have given our blood in the past war and in other wars to secure a country founded on Christian principles, still within this country there are those who would shoot down the very finest of our youth, the hope and promise of our future. But let them know, I said, that if we are an embattled people, we are also an army for Christ and his righteousness and justice. Let them know that we take our mission with the mortal seriousness that they take in opposition to it. Let them know that we look to the example of Samuel, who said to Agag, King of the Amalekites, "As thy sword hath made women childless, so shall thy mother be childless among women." And then, I reported, the Scriptures read, "Samuel hewed Agag in pieces before the Lord in Gilgal."

The reference to Samuel, which is from the fifteenth chapter of first Samuel, was inspired in the sense that it suddenly came to mind, but, not knowing much about its mental origin, I didn't know where to go with it, either. So I just left it, ended the sermon there, and closed the service.

I had not made the analogy between the war and Randy's murder as clearly as I had intended. As it turned out, I didn't need to. The story of Samuel and Agag hit home, as it were, and everywhere I went men mentioned it to me and were once again ready to take up arms for a prophetic cause. I was naively happy about all of this, and thought only that now my work with the men in the town would progress.

Actually, to revive a phrase current then, it steamrolled over me. Within two weeks, a group of men came to my office and reported that the judge who would try the case of Randy's murder was controlled by a few of those prominent members of organized crime who lived in Oak Park. They had heard that the killer was related to a man who, through his associates, had paid off the judge and passed down the word to assign a light sentence, which could then be waived through appeal on a technicality. The men who came to me, a large group, under the circumstances—there were about twelve, among them some of those to whom I had made vague promises of golf matches—wanted me to get up in the pulpit and reenact the story of Samuel and Agag, as well as I was able, by demanding the death penalty. I was to focus public attention on the trial, and so force the judge to serve justice rather than Mammon.

I believed in the death penalty then, in the way that a citizen does who answers a pollster's questions; that is, I thought theoretically under certain circumstances, blah, blah, blah. Here, though, was what I took to be a case of vicious, unmotivated, gratuitous malevolence, an act so horrifying that everyone immediately wondered whether the man had been intoxicated, or was sane. Apparently he had killed for sport, or mistaken Randy for somebody else. I had not really known Randy Sutter; when I saw the picture his mother gave the newspapers my own recollected images flickered but never took on the resolution of the photograph. By all reports, he was a nice kid. As they say, an open and shut case, although its very simplicity sealed the motive of the murderer and thus made him an enigma.

Like the pollster's citizen, though, I did not want to become involved. I did not want to start a campaign against organized crime in a town governed by such "prominent figures." I did, however, want to reach the men on that committee, and that is what ultimately made up my mind; there has surely been worse motivation behind many a cause. I counted on my obscurity and the efficacy of bribes to make of my prophetic gesture a symbol of community spirit (an odd usage, yes, but more true than in its usual euphemistic sense) and nothing more.

Yet our age, don't we know it by now, is an age of poetry—not the good poetry of the bard, but the bad poetry of the caption and accompanying photograph: we, too, deal in images but without any depth of imagination, and so the more readily appealing the picture the better. Samuel hewing Agag in pieces appealed, as it turned out, to everybody, almost.

The committee of twelve held, just before the trial was to begin, a public rally, ostensibly about the larger themes of public morality and civic duty (or so went their advertisement of our vigilante activities) while everyone who understood began to call this the meeting about the Sutter trial. The rally chiefly provided a public forum for my Samuel and Agag speech, revised appropriately for the setting of the high school auditorium—essentially Unitarian in its rejection of any ornament save the flag.

The place was packed. I had never preached to so many people, and I savored every instant of the occasion. I was the last speaker; those before me were dour in their concern, and used a language bereft of rhetorical flair, as, they thought, befitted the occasion. But I could sense (how? born preachers simply have this aptitude) that the crowd remained in a festive mood in spite of the councilmen and priests and lawyers and rabbis who were so "seriously concerned."

When it came time, I rose and told a cornball joke, totally unrelated to the Sutter trial, which was appreciated by everybody there. The joke, about the preacher saying "Boulder," did have a tangential relation to public morality, and by this I came back to my subject. On the way, I made several rousing and utterly banal declarations about the recent war, and America, and the founding fathers, and, well, you can imagine. The crowd started interrupting me with applause and then unrestrained cheering. I had preached in enough black churches during my seminary days to develop a rhythm, so that the interruptions, the cheers ringing like so many Amens! and Hallelujahs! lent the speech even greater suspense and then, after its point had been made, a devastating sense of logical inevitability.

By the time I reached the Samuel and Agag illustration, the congregation (for it had become my congregation, unconsciously perhaps, but no matter) was more than with me, and those who had been primed by my first rendition of this began to whisper to the others. I am sure they were saying, here comes the best part, as one would to a friend during the second or third viewing of a favorite movie. And after my Samuel and Agag illustration, I could have pointed a finger and the long knives would have been drawn. But again I simply recounted what Samuel had done and let the image ferment its own brew.

I awoke the next morning to the metamorphosis that almost all public figures, however obscure, experience in our time. There in the Chicago papers was a picture of me with a cryptically phrased caption:

Preacher calls for dismember-
ment of murderer. Story below.

For crying out loud! I thought, and was horrified and bedaz-
zled by the image of brutality I had become in the incredibly
literal mind of the journalist. Indeed, the picture of me showed
a man with a large mouth contorted in so hideous a fashion that
it was apparent I was a dragon. I read the story, hoping for
mitigating words, and found:

> Last night, before a wildly cheering crowd, attending a "public
> rally on morality and civic duty," the Rev. Ted March, pastor of
> Oak Park Free Church, implied that the murderer of Randy
> Sutter should be "Hewed in pieces" as Samuel, the Old Testament
> prophet, dismembered Agag, enemy King of the Amalekites.

Ah! the poetic condensation of the journalist's one sentence
paragraph! "Implied," a weak and misleading verb, was, as the
journalist knew it would be, buried in the midst of all those
clauses, and the machine of that sentence worked not like common prose, by cause and effect, but like poetry, by association.
And I, thereafter, would always be associated with that phrase,
"Hewed in pieces," although the phrase was the chronicler's of
Samuel's life, not mine.

Now, like the man said, I may be dumb, but I am not stupid.
I knew the journalist understood the public's mythic need for
avenging, bloodthirsty gods, for after all we feel more comfortable with deities of that sort than with the Christian God of love;
they are like us, and we always hope we can outwit them. I also
knew that to deny I had said such a thing, or to complain that
I had been misinterpreted, would keep focusing attention on my
brutality rather than on the killer's. My hope lay in redirecting
the public's imagination, so that I might end this as St. George,
if I had begun as his foe. The journalists would probably be as
reluctant to play up the organized crime angle as I had been to
enter the lists at first for that very same reason. But in transform-
ing me into a monster, they had endowed me with the magical
power needed, notoriety, to effect transformations of my own.

After further study of the case, and through the help of a
police officer in the congregation who purloined, with his superi-

or's OK, the photos taken of Randy Sutter after the bullet had blown away most of his face, I asked the news media if I might meet with them. The national wire services attended, as well as our local pharisaical scribes, and I spoke, repeating my Samuel and Agag story, about my righteous indignation brought on by the murder. Then I showed the pictures and put the writers through a recitation of facts memorized from the coroner's report. In that context, Samuel's blade appeared mercifully sharp. Then, off the record, I told about the suspected collusion of the judge with organized crime, and asked them what other recourse I had, as a man who has been ordained to speak the truth. And once more on the record, I insisted that the murderer be given the death penalty. I might appear rabid in the next story, but once sick with the disease of another's madness, my image would be well on its way to recovery.

The next day, the headline in the local paper ran:

Preacher Again Calls For Death

a strangely elliptical phrase, I thought, as if I were among those who, in the last days, call for the rocks to fall on them. But the AP had this:

Preacher Insists On Death Penalty

and the subhead ran

Sources Indicate Killer Has Mob Connections.

The locals were soon forced to follow the nationals' lead.

Constance came into my study a few days later—actually, she ran into my study, grabbed me around the waist, and went down on her knees. She was sobbing so hysterically I was afraid to ask her what the matter was. Then, quite disturbingly, she started kissing me, first my hands, then my face; she kissed me with a certain violence, her lips parting with the force of her attack, so that the edge of her teeth nipped me; she was all over me, as they say. It seemed time to play out my role of the calm, reasoning male of those days and slap her into composure. I didn't do that, though. I simply took her wrists—her hands were at the sides of my head—and made painful manacles of my hands; she cried out from the pain, known and unknown, and let her head fall on my chest.

I was panting. "What's wrong?" I asked. "Tell me, Constance, calm down now, and tell me, please."

"The phone!" she said, in a voice distorted by hysteria. "The phone. A man said, he said, if you preached again, you'd get it 'hot and heavy.'" She looked up at me and then down again, her eyes focusing on some near point, while she concentrated, I suppose, on the meaning of hot and heavy.

And so did I, for the next three weeks, as we continued to receive death threats. The callers, and there were more than one, women as well as men, used phrases like "hot and heavy" "a bellyful of lead," "his life won't be worth a plugged nickel," and variations on "those words will be his last." I list these because of their frightening banality; they seemed to me all the more scary and effective because I could imagine that anyone who thought in such phrases would surely have to rely on violence.

I did the right thing; that is, I immediately called the police. And since they had cooperated before, by loaning me the pictures, they now took a special interest in seeing that I wasn't killed. No questions. A detective moved in with Constance and me, and, to my embarrassment, the force insisted on providing me with an armored truck and driver when I made my forays outside the house, my only ones, to preach.

On Sundays, two detectives sat on the platform with me. During the first service, I saw a rifle trained on me, and shamelessly dove at the detective's feet on my right, thinking he would cover me with his body, which I thought he was supposed to do, wasn't he? He didn't. He picked me up and whispered to me that the rifle belonged to their man in the balcony. The congregation was on its feet, looking all around, and I calmed them by saying I guess I had tripped.

Nothing actually came of the threats, as I'm here to report, except that I became increasingly well-known, which might have made it impossible for my callers to get around to anything definite. At least, during that period, I placed my hopes in this theory.

I was a hero, also, to the men in the community, my erstwhile golfing companions, those on the PMC, which stood for

Public Morality Committee—these committees!—and their friends. Yet, they did not become conventionally pious. Many of them did start attending Sunday services, but the principal change was their eagerness to include me in certain daily and yet ritual activities. In the locker room at the country club, after my round and a shower, often when I was wearing nothing but a towel, they would hail me and insist on my sitting with them in an alcove reserved for poker and highballs.

So I joined their round table, as St. George or Galahad, and held my glass of grapefruit juice high and toasted their health (and secretly uttered a prayer for the well-being of their souls, nothing condescending, not in the least, a prayer of friendship) while they reminisced about the war. One day, one gnomish man reenacted how he had lain on his back and kicked the jammed cockpit of his fighter free as he was just above the altitude needed for the parachute to open; demonstrating, his legs jerked spasmodically, the old terror back in his marrow, and then he came down heavily on the poker table, upsetting the game and everyone's drinks. But no one chided or kidded him about his clumsiness; they all saw that he had been *back* for a moment, had recaptured the stupid tenacity of life, which is our own jammed cockpit of mortality.

Also, those fellows, like my old captain, told ribald stories, and like him complained about their marital problems, mostly through terse allusions: "My hands today"—meaning poker hands—"are about as cold as my wife," or, "We thought about moving, but couldn't get a van big enough to haul Jean." Occasionally a newcomer would look to me, if he knew about my vocation, to see how I reacted to all this. I'll tell you, that male camaraderie smacked to me of the sacred; it was almost a church of sorts, and in ways I presided by simply being there. I was content.

What about the trial? The crooked judge succeeded in having the man extradited to another state and tried there, insisting that because of the publicity the case had received the accused could not receive a fair trial in that community. Unfortunately for the accused, the jury in the neighboring state had no ties to organized crime and saw the facts of the case for what they were; they quickly found the man guilty and served up the Big Juice, the electric hemlock, the chair.

The newspapers gave me a lot of attention after the verdict, asking for my reactions and wondering whether I intended to go after other figures in organized crime. I was Samuel again, but now Samuel as "a prophet of justice and righteousness, the kind of man these times demand." I was invited to appear on local radio shows, columns featured me and my comments, and the invitations to speak from civic groups poured in.

The notoriety turned my head for a while; I even agreed to visit the neighboring state at the time of the execution. Plans for special citizens' committees on crime and the prospect of leaving the local pastorate and becoming another Father Coughlin on radio, a minister to the masses, so to speak, added greatly to my sense of self-importance. A contract with CBS for a biweekly, half-hour show was in the offing.

But I abandoned these plans when I saw that my relationship with the men in the clubhouse had changed. Formerly, during their poker sessions, I had been their innocent, the agent of confession, the unspotted lamb who might carry their burdensome recollections to an altar of forgetfulness. But now I was too much one of them; I had blood on my hands. I had already understood my own depravity from the Hugh Finley episode; what I learned from these men was how my vocation functioned. There was no way, or I did not know the way, to recall what had been lost; our sessions in the poker room, now that the air of forgiveness stopped circulating, became as stifling for the soul as the cigar smoke was for my lungs. I was asked to join them less often, and gradually they stopped coming to church, too.

Other men and women came, though, people I often didn't care for—the sort who find it satisfying to gawk at a well-known public figure and derive pleasure from being associated with their version of a man of power. The church flourished. Although my heart ceased to be in the church's endeavors as before, it flourished like a colony of bacteria.

Was I a man of power? Certainly. However guilty the murderer may have been, once the publicity and notoriety came my way I had quickly quit caring about justice and righteousness and exploited the situation for my own ends; I persecuted a man I didn't know in order to elevate my stature in the community.

I left Oak Park a little more than a year later, out of a feeling of self-disgust, and took the pastorate of an even bigger church in the suburbs of Boston. I remained there for fourteen years, and became, in the words which once heralded my coming as a guest speaker, "a nationally-known church spokesman with the vision of a contemporary prophet and an oratorical manner to match." Nothing much happened in Boston; my ministry was a complete success. And yet, all the time there I felt as if I were Moses in exile after killing the Egyptian, or as if I were Jacob, working double time for the hands of Leah and Rachel, those brides of peace and contentment.

I spent my day of justice as an accused does awaiting the deliberations of an empanelled jury. After eating lunch in a local hamburger joint, and scanning the newspaper, I frittered away most of the afternoon alone in my office. Nothing happened. No one called, no one came by to visit; it was awful.

I finally called Constance, to chat. She was as cheery as she had been since she'd learned of my predicament. She told me to be home at four; I was to help our daughter, Marianne, move a chaise longue we were giving her for her apartment.

I met Marianne in the kitchen, by the chopping table, which stands in the middle of the room. In one hand she held a long cigarette between two fingers, not near the filter like a man but halfway up, and in the other hand a water tumbler filled with what looked like Coke. When she saw me, she put the tumbler down, and brushed loose tresses of her waist-length dark hair back from her face. Rather pleasingly, she resembles both Constance and me; she's tall, like me, big-boned, and has a powerful figure that doesn't suffer when she gains a few pounds; she has Constance's deeply set eyes and her straight nose, though on Marianne these features are larger and bolder, and Marianne's nose slants up just at the tip. Unlike Constance, who has learned to make of her face a mask of classical repose, Marianne's expressions are unrestrained, romantic, volatile, like a coin of love and hate.

She seemed barely old enough to be handling both a cigarette and a drink, and as I stood in the doorway of the kitchen, before we had spoken, my perceptions were not entirely saturated with the knowledge that this young woman was my daughter.

I wondered at her: she was mine and not mine. Of course, I w
and am in love with her, in all of the ways that a father may be
But then in the next moment we spoke and somehow all of that
love folded, as it always does, into the cramped way we have with
each other.

"I've already moved the couch into the living room," she
said.

"I saw it on my way in. Are you ready?"

"Whenever."

The chaise longue or divan was covered with pink satin, but
because of the material's moth-eaten and tattered condition,
Constance had kept a gold, embroidered coverlet over it for so
long that I was surprised to rediscover its true skin. It looked,
really, like a salacious tongue. Marianne and I took it from the
living room and outside into the car. It tipped awkwardly, and
when we finally positioned it in the station wagon, Constance's
car, I was perspiring heavily in the late-afternoon heat.

Marianne lived in the kind of California stucco apartment
building that advertises the virtues of its tennis courts, sauna, and
rec room. It was located on the other side of the Santa Monica
Mountains, which separate the Valley from the Los Angeles
Basin proper. She liked to talk about that side of the city as "my
turf." So we had a twenty minute drive before us—twenty minutes to avoid saying what we had needed to say to one another
for the past six or eight years, and the silence between us in the
car as she drove became more and more uneasy; my thoughts of
what to say seemed frustrated signals to senses that couldn't
engage.

"Mom's told you about John," Marianne finally said.

"No."

"He's staying there, at the apartment. With me."

"You're living together, you mean. You'd better brush up
on your catch-phrases, honey. You'll seem old-fashioned."

"Don't make him feel uncomfortable, please. You were so
good with Jeff."

"I liked Jeff. Did you?"

"Not enough, I guess." She said this not in her deal-with-
father voice, but thoughtfully. In the next moment she might let
down her ill-fitting casualness, which would make things too
difficult for either of us to handle. It seemed simpler to fall in

ith her determination to carry off this task in good style by annoying her.

That's why I said, "If you had loved him, Marianne, you wouldn't have to guess now."

I miscalculated. "But I did," she said, as suddenly angry as her mother, but showing it far more. She pulled out another long cigarette from the pack on the dashboard. "I did love him, but not *enough*."

"I can understand how you can love someone too much, someone that you think you might want to live with; I can't understand not loving that kind of person enough."

"Exactly." She looked over her shoulder and swung the car into the right-hand lane, cutting off a Peugeot. Her response reminded me of myself.

After a while, after we had been cruising long enough to lose any sensation of speed, the roofs of the suburbs filling the valleys on our left and right, the money crop in the field of this city, Marianne said, "I refuse to end up like you and mother. I prefer my kind of mistakes."

"Those are the only kind worth making," I said, trying to be conciliatory.

"Why's life— Why's it so awful?"

"Why do we all hurt each other so much?"

And just for a moment I thought we had arrived at a juncture, a still point. Then she said, "Because of the Fall, right? Sure."

The Fall, which resonates with meaning for me, remains for Marianne part of the oppression of history which her generation believes, rather fervently, can be disregarded and overcome by purposeful indifference. The idea goes, we don't have to be unhappy in the old ways; in fact, we will surely be happier if we refuse to acknowledge certain forms of sorrow. It's a terrific idea on the surface.

We parked the car on the street directly across from Marianne's apartment building, Casa Serra—after the monk who founded most of the California missions. The building's exterior looks like a Hollywood mock-up of a mission church, with a bell tower and stucco textured to resemble adobe, and huge, fake-coffered double doors into which, like a cat entrance, real doors have been hung.

As we struggled with the divan through the facade into the inner courtyard, with its pool and hibiscus bushes, I thought of the old monk trying to convert the Indians, not realizing that he would bring after him a culture so barbarous as to see a mission church as just another apartment building. And then I thought of Marianne, living, as she always had, within a church as a priestess of high apostasy. At the door she said, "You're not going to like him. John. But I do." She looked at me, I suppose in warning, but her expression was for once flat and neutral: implacable, and so, I expected, soberingly truthful.

Meeting my daughter's current lover has never been a moment I relish, but even Marianne's warning, though prophetic, did not prepare me for her paramour. John watched with a gallant poise as we heaved the divan into its final resting place in a bare extra room, furnished until then with only a secretary that had also come from our house. This had been pushed against one wall in the windowless room without calculation, and so we spent several minutes trying to adjust the two pieces to each other.

We finally got around to proper introductions when we emerged back into the brown-carpeted living room. John was tall, slight, with a head of loose curls, the sort of delicate and yet cruel features characteristic of the aesthete, the dandy, the fop. He shook my hand. I noticed his long, stovepipe fingers, rather like mine, and strikingly blue veins over the back of his hands, and figured him to be a drug addict or a TV producer. About the same to me.

But no. It turned out that he worked at Lockheed as an engineer, running simulated windtunnel tests with computers. Marianne, who was working as an executive secretary for an airline administration, left the room to make coffee, and John and I sat on the rattan chairs and tried to find if we could maneuver past one another by acting like buddies. I made mention of the ersatz Tiffany chandelier above the dining room table and the pictures of women in white summer dresses, sitting on lawns at the New Jersey Shore, which Marianne had hung about the room.

"She wants," John said, "the place to have a Gay Nineties feel."

"Just the thing," I said, "with the wall-to-wall carpeting."

He smiled indulgently. Perhaps he thought my sarcasm was intended to win him over by forging an alliance against Marianne's failings, and felt obliged to refuse such an overture. But I was testing to see if he were capable of a love that could comprehend failings. Because if he didn't perceive Marianne's lack of taste, an inherent tendency which her relationship with her mother had exacerbated, he didn't even *know* her very well.

"You're a minister," he said.

I nodded and waited with great interest for what would follow; this would certainly be telling. But he just sat and nodded his head until the superficial mechanics of the remark ran down.

Marianne came back in and sat on the arm of the rattan chair John occupied; she underlined this quite obvious gesture by running her fingers through John's curls. Then she nibbled the back of his neck, and then put an arm around his shoulders, and I had the odd impression that I had hired these two to enact my worst voyeuristic fantasies. Why did I stay? But I did; I wasn't satisfied. I had disliked John immediately and right then felt off-balance; before leaving I wanted to be decided, stable.

Marianne went off to see about the coffee, which resolved me to finish off my interview with this young man. "So," I said, "how's Marianne treating you? You look like you're getting along."

"Our relationship is really nice," he said. "It's probably not so easy for you to understand, Father, but we really do care for each other. Marianne just, oh, I don't know, *makes my day.*"

He looked away, glittering with Napoleonic confidence, entirely assured of his eloquence and the heroism of addressing me in such a man-to-man way, and I cringed. First the boy tells me that sleeping with my daughter is "nice," and then he calls me "Father," showing himself so untutored as not to know the difference between a Catholic priest and a Protestant minister (perhaps he thought me an Episcopalian?), and then he just barely has the taste to prefer an older cliché to the more recent ones. Holy Hannah, Marianne! bring on the drug addicts, the TV producers, bring on the Navy, for pity's sake, but not this one!

Anyway, I knew exactly where I was now, and called to Marianne to forget the coffee, I had to be leaving. But she came out and pressed a mug into my palms, insisting that I stay until she told me her plans for decorating the place. Oh, all right. She resumed her perch on the rattan chair by John, but that was obviously an uncomfortable place to sit. She soon found it necessary to show him where we'd installed the chaise longue, and from the extra room I heard her say that she hadn't really noticed how beautiful the old pink silk was; her mother's taste was so great. I waited for them to return. Soon the door slowly swung more or less closed. I heard the divan creak, complaining of excess weight, and then a volley of laughter. Then there were suppressed whispers and the swishing sounds of rubbing clothes.

I set down my mug, stood up—I would not be a party to this—and walked out before they could come stumbling back in with their eyes unfocused and stupid smiles on their faces. Or whatever. I got into Constance's station wagon and drove back to the church and sat in my office in the educational building, trying to recollect my equilibrium before the service that night. Hedonism.

Behind the podium, I looked out over a crowd that had swelled from the previous evening; the news of what the pastor was up to and the backwash from the SOP conclave had boosted attendance like an undertow boosts the curl of an incoming wave.

"Beloved," I said. "In a telephone conversation this morning, the person on the other end of the line said that, above all else, he was praying that God's justice would prevail in the choices that face this church. An admirable desire and a worthy goal. We all want that, I'm sure. As the prophet Amos said, "But let judgment (or justice) run down as waters, and righteousness as a mighty stream."

"But what is justice? What does it mean to say that our God is a just God?

"In the early sixties, I was pastor of a seven-thousand-member church in Atlanta, one of the more prominent pulpits in the South. At that time, several black leaders of the civil-rights movement called for reparations to be paid by the white churches of America for their role in oppressing the Negro race.

"My congregation's members broke with their usual, polite manner of conversation when this and other racial issues of the day came up; it was almost as if the button which activates a stiletto had been pushed—suddenly they were angry and ready to fight. They felt they had been misrepresented and misunderstood on this issue.

"Knowing how strongly the older members of the congregation felt about this, and that they mistrusted me when I first arrived, because my previous churches had been located in the North, I was quick to point out the hypocritically-veiled segregationism of Northern ghettos whenever anyone engaged me on the subject. I did this more in the spirit of conviviality than anything else; I let it be known that I held the position of a moderate; this problem had taken hundreds of years to develop, I would say, and could not be solved overnight, or even in one generation. In many ways, I was sublimely ignorant of political realities and perhaps intended to stay that way, not wanting to admit that my attitudes might lend weight to the cause of white supremacy. The racists, however, understood this perfectly and took me to their hearts.

"One fine Georgia day in June, with the air-conditioning in my office on full and the branches of the pines beyond my window so still that it made me perspire to look at them, I received a call from a group of men who called themselves the Committee for the Preservation of Civil Rights.

"The leader of the group, a local politician, had a full head of silver hair and wore a canary yellow suit. He had the air of being everyone's best friend, which a lifetime of glad-handing brings with it, and which always seems, to me at least, a chilling substitute for a personality. He had the best of Southern voices, the consonants softened, the vowels wet, the pitch cured by his years in public service. With the other members of the group standing around my desk, this leader said, 'It seems certain coloreds have it in mind to attend services this Sunday. We're not about to have that down here. Not for a while yet, anyway. It's not right for them to talk politics on the Lord's day. We won't allow any commandeering of the platform around here. It's against our church government. It's not right, and we won't have it.'

"The committee members all agreed and picked up the theme, as they spoke in turn: the blacks had no right to interrupt a lawful gathering of Christian people, *no right* to interrupt the reign of law and order with special considerations.

"One very thin man, whose stringy muscles were testimony

to his years of working his farm, said, 'If they want what's coming to them'—and here he almost snickered— 'if they want justice, they have to abide by the laws of the land themselves.' The men all seemed to delight in having the law on their side; they were gleeful.

"At the end of the meeting we put together a contingency plan. If any 'unlawful group' ever (especially that Sunday) tried to take over the platform, a special cadre of ushers would be deputized to deal with them. I would probably spy the group first, and if so, I would flash a signal to call for the doxology. The organ would play, the people would sing, and the blacks would be hauled off, their cries of protest joining the song of praise to the Almighty. Justice?

"I doubted whether anyone would demand reparations from my congregation, but secretly hoped that they would. I believed the committee's insistence on its legal rights to be pharisaical, and found their delight in their manipulative powers sinister. I started to imagine the black leaders' visit, and in my imaginings I saw myself using the situation to demonstrate how loyal the congregation had become to me by stealing the committee's thunder through various strategems. I wasn't quite sure what I was going to do; but I wasn't going to be the committee's lackey. You see me now on both sides.

"When the blacks appeared, for they did indeed, the situation itself proved far more powerful, because it was real, than any stratagems I might have applied in my daydreams. I saw three young black men in the middle aisle walk swiftly past the ushers at the foyer doors. After they had made a decisive thrust down the first third of the aisle, they paused. Perhaps—well, certainly—if they had been dressed as their later compatriots, in leather jackets, battle fatigues, or dashikis, with Cuban shades and Afros that held cake cutters as combs, I would have called for the singing of the doxology. But these men were dressed, as I was, in sharkskin suits and thin black ties. They *looked* like they belonged in my church, except, of course, for their skin. But it was precisely their skin that set them apart, and anyone who stands alone among a hostile crowd draws our sympathy. They continued down the aisle once more, and as they did I could see from their stiff manner and their quick glances how nervous they were. By the time they reached the platform, I wanted to do nothing so much as reassure them.

"I went to the side of the platform, and their spokesman said, 'Pastor, we would like to make an announcement. We will not take long.'

"I nodded, indicating that I understood and that this was fine with me.

"Then we stood together before the people. I clapped my arm around the spokesman and asked the people to listen to the announcement these men wanted to make.

"In the little time it took for me to meet with and to honor the request of the men, I sensed a rigid summoning of the collective will, as if an intruder had walked in on a family fight and best faces were being stonily put on.

"Evidently, the special ushers had a contingency plan of their own in case that Yankee—as I was to be called in the days ahead, although everyone knew I had been born in Austin, Texas— in case that Yankee could not be trusted. After I stepped away from the podium, a man stood up on the left side of the sanctuary, pointed at the organist, cuing him, and scooped and elevated his palms, a gesture for the congregation to stand, which they did. Then the congregation began to file out, from the front pews on back, as if leaving a funeral, with the same solemnity and finality and decorum. They sang the doxology, 'Praise God from Whom all blessings flow,' as they went.

"I sat with the three blacks for a time after the congregation had emptied. It was quiet. The spokesman's eyes were watchful and a bit dreamy at the same time; he looked as if he knew something which always kept him at a certain distance from events. I offered, in a kidding way, to make their announcement before I was fired. He took me seriously and said, 'Buy an overcoat. It'll be cold where you're going.'"

I thought of my Samuel and Agag speech and the events in Oak Park. I thought of my fourteen years in Boston and my desire to be released from the guilt of what I had done in Chicago. But I channeled this to my congregation then in a somewhat different way.

"Until that day in my ministry, beloved, I had thought of myself as a kind of Moses, the judge of right and wrong, the final authority in my church. Until that day I had never quite comprehended how I was more a symbol of my people than their leader. For whatever virtue there may have been in sympathizing with the black leaders and giving them a chance to speak, my motives that day included the vainglory of proving to the committee, the CPCR, that *I* was the kingpin in the church and they had no right telling me what to do. I turned the whole issue into a struggle for power.

"The Lord said, 'Judge not lest ye be judged.' I judged the committee members, and they judged me. The sight of those people, beloved, turning their backs on me has become ever more vivid as time has passed. It's become almost the ensign of my ministry these last ten years. The black man who told me it would be cold where I was going proved to be absolutely correct. For although I ended up taking a pastorate in Tucson, Arizona, one of the hottest places in America, the cold of being judged and cast out from the assembly pursued me and stayed with me there. After Atlanta, it has never been the same; a failed preacher, even among those sympathetic with the cause of his downfall, is a failed preacher. I was fired; I was suspect.

"And I say unto you, beloved, that I deserved it. I deserved it because I hadn't learned yet how God's justice works. I didn't know enough to teach the members of the committee about God's merciful justice, and so avoid the situation I was eventually entrapped in.

"And if we do not learn the lesson of God's merciful justice, beloved, we will all be cast out and shrouded in the darkness of hell. For 'Judge not lest ye be judged' is not only a restriction by which we are to abide, it's also and more pertinently *the way in which condemnation falls on our heads*.

"Let me explain this. I know, beloved, that we are all familiar with the story of Jesus and the Pharisees and the woman caught in adultery. We remember how Jesus wrote upon the ground until the Pharisees left and eventually no one remained to stone the woman for her sin. A preacher I'm acquainted with once delivered a famous sermon in which he speculated that Jesus, knowing all things, inscribed the secret sins of each Pharisee in the dust and it was out of shame that they all departed. What Jesus did was to point out to these men that if the adulterous woman were guilty before the law, then they were, too. And thereby he implicitly asked them this question: Did they want the standards they were applying to her case to apply to their own? Did they want to be judged as they were judging? Before they fulfilled the demands of the law and executed this woman, he asked them to stand in the circle of God's righteousness and contemplate being judged themselves."

I thought of Marianne. So often I'd made her feel condemnation, when I only wanted to say, *Go, and sin no more.*

"If we judge others, beloved, then we must submit to judgment. But if we refuse to judge, then we begin to understand how God's justice operates.

"God's justice is synonymous with mercy. It is standing, as Jesus did, in the place of the woman caught in adultery, and in the place of the rest of us, and himself receiving the judgment we deserve. The sight of Jesus Christ on the cross judges us all. But at the same time it is this judgment that makes mercy possible. We are to follow the Lord's example in submitting to the judgments of others, knowing that by refusing to advocate our own case, we will be represented by our only Mediator and Advocate.

"It is the innocent who have the right to judge. The blacks who spoke that day had every right to judge, for they were the ones who truly had been sinned against; they were the ones who were standing covered by the shadow of Christ in the circle of God's righteousness. God's justice demands that we judge ourselves by how we have treated the innocent, and then become innocent once more, not through power, but through the passive acceptance of others' condemnation.

"In this revival week I submit to your judgment because I am well aware that my only chance resides in finding mercy.

"I've been brief in order to leave before you an even clearer picture of where I stand.

"Amen."

Wednesday:

Grace

The next morning, I had the prayer breakfast to attend, and was up out of bed early. Nothing that had happened in the past few days felt as momentous as having to face those men at that hour, over breakfast, before my queasy stomach and bowels had even begun to have a chance to settle their accounts with gravity. Or, as Martin Luther once said, "What would I not give to get away from a cantankerous congregation and look into the friendly eyes of animals?"

The prayer breakfast met in the social hall below the sanctuary, a cavern with a crude stage at one end for the childrens' Vacation Bible School plays and their parents' antics during Father-and-Son, Mother-and-Daughter, and other, assorted banquets. There were two entrances, a stairway down from the sanctuary foyer, and one directly from the parking lot through the church kitchen. I chose the latter, realizing I would have to put up with Ida, the cook, but hoping to have a chance to assess the mood of the men in the hall through the kitchen serving window.

Ida was at the stove against the far wall, with her back to me, scrambling a heap of bubbling eggs. I went past a stainless-steel-covered table, like an island in the middle of the room, and moved up to the edge of the serving window with my back against the wall, as if I were on the window ledge of a skyscraper. Since I hadn't greeted Ida and had, in fact, counted on her slight hearing impairment to help aid my surreptitious entry, and then stood blatantly eavesdropping, I realized I was hiding.

I was scared. How was I on this day of our Lord to beseech him on behalf of my good laymen, when the longings of their hearts might include a divine attack of cardial thrombosis for me? How was I to mutter even the Lord's Prayer in such a company? Jesus told his disciples not to take thought for what they might say when hailed before magistrates; the Spirit would speak through them. I knew something of this, or thought I did, but ever since I had awakened with the thought of this prayer breakfast, a bouncy gospel tune, usually sung by male quartets, had set the note of my pulse:

> It's me, it's me, it's me, oh Lord
> Standing in the need of prayer.
> Not my brother, not my sister, but it's me, oh Lord
> Standing in the need of prayer.

Some of the voices beyond the window sounded sharp, and others were gruff, deeper as the men talked about the headlines and sports scores, with asides about their families, their words not quite heartfelt and all too clearly only gestures at intimacy—the talk of men who might go on meeting each other for years and never be quite sure of one another's names; or if they trespassed on cordiality that far, would be sure never to ask favors, borrow money, or let any feelings show.

I could hear Cecil Brown clearly, with his baritone voice that resonated and carried like a radio actor's. He was arguing with Jerry Mansfield, whose replies sounded increasingly tinny as his logic became strained. Allen Gresham, the former head usher, joined them, and then Phil Slaughter, whose speech has a syncopated rhythm, completed the foursome, giving body to my prophetic sense of a quartet. As they continued to talk—there seemed to be more in attendance than usual—other voices washed through, but I tried to keep my antennae tuned to those four in particular. There was something about "this being such a mess," Cecil mentioned an "unfortunate public forum"; Allen urged "pressing forward" to Phil's "out in the open," to which there was a chimed "Amen."

And then Ida was in front of me, gripping her spatula, the

halo of her grey hair held in by a hair net, and I saw myself through her eyes—an aging man straining to listen in on others, my mouth probably agape.

"Good morning, pastor," she said, glancing at her spatula like it was a microphone, as if one sleepwalker were about to interview another.

"Good morning, Ida," I said, and tried to smile. "I don't think I'm quite awake yet." I rubbed at my eyes to prove this. "Or that's how I feel. It's going to take your wonderful cooking to get me going, I guess. I see you're scrambling eggs." My stomach went into a bind.

"Yes, and your choice of sausage or bacon on the side! Coffee. And *your* biscuits." At the mention of the biscuits she glanced down, bit her lower lip, and would have been the picture of an abashed schoolgirl if a blush had been able to rise to those grey, powdered cheeks.

These biscuits summed up my relationship with Ida. She called them "my biscuits" because one morning at the prayer breakfast I had left two on my plate. She asked me about it later—she had an eye for who ate what—and not wanting to hurt her feelings I had lied about having a test at the doctor's office later in the day and not being able to eat starch; they'd looked so delicious, I'd said, but then the thought of the test had made it possible to overcome my willful appetite. Actually, I hadn't eaten her biscuits because I'd never cared for them, to put it mildly, and had set a couple on my plate from a childish sense of being polite as I passed the basket. She'd said the biscuits were tricky; she was never sure whether they would come out right; sometimes they were fine on the outside but all doughy inside, and sometimes they burned or got dry. I could indeed attest to that. She'd looked pleased and dismayed, and had said that she'd continue to make the biscuits, especially if they pleased me, because my ministry meant so much to her, and so one lie (as it always goes) had made matters increasingly worse.

And again I was between Ida and the men, lying. I had heard enough from the social hall to understand what I was getting myself into and Ida was wiping one hand furiously over her apron, in a silent plea to get back to her work and let me go out the swinging door. But I wanted a moment more in the kitchen. I told her something like the truth. I said, "Ida, I need some time to think over my remarks for this morning. I know you have a lot to do. Let me just sit on this"—and here I hopped up onto the sideboard—"and you go on. Unless I can help you?"

Ida sang a little chorus of *no*s, waved me away with her spatula, and waddled—amazingly quickly, considering her bulk—back around to the stove and her work, looking back bashfully several times, as if taking mental snapshots of her pastor communing with the Almighty.

My problem was how to pray with these men, or even face them. Various strategies came to mind, but I had to reckon with my own concept of the revival, to own up to everything I had known and experienced as a pastor and *attend to it*. The revival was a small patch of ground, and the purchasing of it had already been done, so I tried to empty myself and walk into that room with only the surveyor's level of my eyes.

And thus I went, casually, praying that I might drop even that affectation, all pretense, and be able simply to see. An unusual number of men were present, close to forty, I'd say, and nearly all were dressed for work in business suits, even though it would be a scalding hot day. The metal tables had been covered with checkered tablecloths and were arranged in a horseshoe; the connecting table was set before the stage, whose proscenium framed the speaker. Cecil and the rest of the boys nodded and smiled at me but looked like they would shy from any move toward conversation, so I went to my usual place at the center of the horseshoe. Ida had put out place cards, which I wondered at until I noticed that the one next to me, written in a flowing script, read *Dr. Paul E. Corwin.*

The men quickly gathered around the table, obeying the instructions of the cards before I had a chance to snatch them up, which left me standing next to a dramatic absence. Several of them helped Ida bring out the platters of eggs, sausage and bacon, the plastic, copper-colored serving pots of coffee, and the napkin-covered baskets of those biscuits. Ida made a point of putting one of the baskets down right in front of me, and then she smiled sweetly and, backing away with her head down, seemed almost to curtsy. I was so nervous, I uncovered the biscuits, and, quite inappropriately, not thinking, put one on my plate. Then Cecil, as if in remonstrance, called the prayer breakfast to order, so that everyone stood in silence behind his chair.

Cecil said in his best rhetorical voice, "Pastor, if you would say grace."

And the phrase struck me as somehow quaint. It would have been more like Cecil to have asked me to return thanks, or to bless this meal, or even, after his ornate and grandoise fashion, to offer the invocation, whereas another man would ask me simply to pray. Say grace? Indeed I would if I were able; I wanted more than anything to say *grace*: the ministrations of that word were exactly what we all needed. After sin and justice, there would have been an end—in the Flood, in Egypt, in the intolerable burdens of the Mosaic law, at that prayer breakfast table—if not for grace. For by grace are we saved through faith, and that not of ourselves; it is the gift of God: not of works, lest any man should boast, to employ Paul's exemplary words to the Ephesians.

"Pastor?" Cecil asked again, interrupting my meditations.

I looked at the men. I needed the grace of their forgiveness. They in turn, having assumed postures of ready-made piety, their heads bowed a respectful degree, their eyes closed and squeezed shut as if warding off sinus headaches, some fingertips gripping noses, a few others unconsciously drumming on the tabletop, needed grace, too. Their weathered looks, their balding crowns and double chins, stooped shoulders, ballooning paunches, moles that might be skin cancers, birthmarks and scars and even the lines about their eyes caused by smiling, their middle-aged flesh that was drawn or sunken and falling back to the earth from whence it came, and most especially those pulsing temples between which they harbored so many illusions, in so many natural and pitiable ways, that none of this was so, all of this needed grace, a gift of new life.

"Dear God," I said, and looked down and saw the biscuit. I picked it up and cupped it in my palm. It was warm, surprisingly heavy, and as hard as stone, and brought to mind Jesus's first temptation in the desert, when Satan invited him, after he had fasted for forty days, to turn rocks into bread. "Man does not live by bread alone," Jesus answered, "but by every word that proceeds out of the mouth of God." And later, at the last supper, he had given his disciples those same words in fuller form, when he said, "This is my body."

"Dear God," I said again, and held the biscuit up to about

chest level, and noticed several men open their eyes to sneak looks at this latest aberration of their wacky leader. And I wanted them to see, because this felt absolutely right. "Dear God," I said for the third time, "your grace is sufficient for us." Then a bouquet of standard phrases came to mind, and with all my will I imposed a period of waiting until they had wilted. "This meal," I said, at last satisfied with the linguistic desert within, "this meal will be nothing if we eat it. Let it be your meal, so that you may transform it into your body. Through Christ we pray, Amen."

In the noise of getting seated, they all looked at one another, waiting for the tip-off of someone's rolling eyes, or a tapping at a skull, to indicate the opinion of what they'd just heard. But preachers, you see, are the keepers of the metaphorical keys, and, after the fashion of Christ with his parables, are allowed to be somewhat hidden in their speech, particularly when praying. So no one made a sign, but I did notice that as the men passed the plates of food, their usual hearty comments were minimal, as if the prayer had left them without much of an appetite. Even so, we ate quickly, and after ten minutes the men were pouring their second or third cups of coffee, easing back in their chairs, and looking around in expectation of the program.

I stood at my place. Cecil tapped his water glass. I hadn't planned on anything except to see clear throughout this, and so hadn't given thought to a program. Yet there I was before them, fulfilling my role, yet without the stuff with which to fill it. I'm tempted to say that as I stood there I felt myself in that dream in which one is onstage and has forgotten his lines. But it wasn't quite like that. I had a sense that each man sitting around that horseshoe was a multiple of his predecessors, the last in a series; and in that row of faces to my right and left I recognized the presence of all the members of boards of trustees, deacons, ushers, and citizens' committees I have ever dealt with. Each was a figure in a mosaic, representative not only of himself but of the multitudes implied by the shimmering background—the golden light which emanates from the past, the background, presses forward in mosaics, doesn't it? That was what I felt, that they were *all* there, at once. They had all returned to question and judge me, and so it was not a matter of lacking a script but of utter spiritual nakedness.

Their judgment, however, remained hidden, and if I was

to *see,* I had to get them to reveal themselves, taciturn and self-protective though they might be. "Men," I said, and this rang funny. "Men, today was to be a special prayer breakfast, since it falls in the middle of this Revival Week. It has turned out to be a more special, or let us say *unusual* revival than any of us expected. Frankly, I've been flying by the seat of my pants ever since Paul Corwin proved to be ill, and haven't had time to prepare to speak this morning. We could just dismiss, and go off to work"—here I suffered my one pang of longing for a re-prieve—"but I'm open to discussing the revival, since certain church members have given me to understand that there's some confusion about the course of events. So, any questions?"

I felt less breezy than this might sound, and the usual lull ensued. I actually worried for a moment that the men wouldn't be as aggressive as their predecessors. Then Jerry Mansfield stood and said, "Pastor, this is hard for me even to ask, but I feel, in all Christian charity, that we as church members need the record set straight. Did you, ah, did you really hurt your assistant, Michael Dennis?"

"Yes," I said, and took a breath, and felt the entry of the calm which often comes after I've started a message on Sunday morning and feel it's going to go all right.

"Pastor," Jerry Mansfield said, bearing down. "Did you do so in anger?"

"Yes," I said, and with the knowledge that I wouldn't be angry now, I felt something distinct from mere relaxation; I was suddenly alert, released, ebullient.

"*Pastor,*" he said, incredulous, and it occurred to me how Jerry has always had trouble relating to the actuality of life. "Did you have any good reason to do so?"

"No," I said, and for a moment was worried that my eupho-ria wasn't simply a matter of confession-is-good-for-the-soul, but might be a dizzying product of my more than healthy mood-swings, and that afterwards I would be paddling up from yet another trough of despondency.

Phil Slaughter said then, "Many of us here, Reverend, have questions, serious questions about, how shall I put it—your com-petency." He waited; they all waited with him.

"So do I," I said.

I looked to my left, to avoid seeing anyone swoon, and saw

Paul Corwin's name card, and recalled the tradition of setting an extra place at the table for the unexpected guest who might turn out to be an angel or Christ. And I thought of Shadrach, Meshach, and Abednego in the fiery furnace, and of Daniel in the lions' den. They had been shielded from certain death by an angelic or Christlike presence. And I realized then the terms of their experience; I would have the same presence beside me as long as I kept telling the truth and made no effort—this was crucial— to protect myself, as they had not.

Cecil Brown now rose and took the floor, as I sensed he'd been wanting to do. "We've been hearing strange stories about you, Pastor—how you sit in your office in the dark, how you've brushed off people who've needed counseling. Maybe you can give us an explanation."

I looked at Cecil, who was obviously agitated, and felt the presence hover. Cecil's face was blotched, with a sparkling of beginning perspiration on it, and I could see that he couldn't take much more of this. Was he on my side, trying to give me a chance to explain myself, or was he trying to back me into a corner? I couldn't tell; I didn't care.

"I hardly know how to begin," I said. "I'm as perplexed as you about the decline of my ministry this past year. I came here hoping to serve God and this church faithfully. When everything seemed to start falling apart, I felt that with a revival . . ." My voice trailed off as I visualized the pink bus pulling again into the Texaco station.

"What about your family life, Reverend?" This was Phil again, zeroing in on my real failing. "We seldom see your wife in church anymore, and keep hearing stories about your daughter. Doesn't the Bible say that a man who can't control his family shouldn't be in the ministry?"

"Yes," I said. "Paul instructs Timothy to choose pastors from among those who are husbands of one wife—at least I qualify there." This feeble attempt at humor fell completely flat. "Choose those who rule their houses well, he says, keeping their children orderly."

"And do you think you've done that?" Phil asked quietly, slipping in the knife.

"No," I said. The euphoria was definitely gone by now, and I could feel depression, haglike, beginning to settle on me and suck at my resolve to remain defenseless. But I fought this off, knowing there would be more, and there was, from Jerry.

"What about your sermons, Pastor?" he asked, and looked genuinely perplexed, with his mad-hatter red hair flaring up as if in further astonishment. "When you first came to us you were so good, prophetic, anyone could see God was speaking through you. Lately, I don't know." He shook his head. "Sometimes it just seems like you're saying the first thing that comes to mind. Or you mumble so much hardly anybody can even hear what you're saying. What gives?"

Jerry was a good-hearted soul, and I was sure he spoke out of genuine concern, not rancor. And though his remarks cut, I had to admit the truth of them; my preaching had deteriorated that badly. I had hoped to regain my form during this revival; but for the moment I refused, still, to mount any defense.

And for the next hour the men and I rehearsed the entire litany of my offenses and inadequacies, as they saw them, while I admitted to them all, yet never once was in fear of being burned. Their reactions to me varied. A few maintained righteous indignation until the end, and were ready, I thought, glancing at their plates at one point, to pick up Ida's biscuits and stone me. One fellow, a young teacher, took a therapeutic approach, and in his questioning encouraged me, as his generation would say, to let it all hang out. Most simply stared at their hands or at the floor in disbelief that such total breakdowns in normalcy were possible.

The last group didn't run off afterwards, as did the hotheads and my therapeutic friend, but they didn't talk to me, either. They hung about looking at the tables and chairs as if these were objects engaged in an animistic masquerade, which might suddenly change into griffins and sphinxes, while I felt that Paul, whom I'd seen off at the airport—how many days ago?—would suddenly turn to me from his empty chair. It seemed we'd all stumbled into a land of mystery, where the presiding presence had led us, and were reluctant to leave.

I had a few civil words with Cecil and then I went out to the kitchen to convey my thanks to Ida for the meal. She said to me: "I heard. I heard it all, Pastor. But they don't know what kind of a man you are."

Back in my office, I laughed for so long at what Ida had said, I started to weep. There I was, sitting in my buttoned leather chair, behind my desk with its family pictures, career memorabilia and executive toys (among them a little pony made of beadlike parts, united by four strings running from its torso through its legs into the base on which it stood, the strings attached to the floating bottom of the base which, when pushed, caused the horse to twitch its head, its tail, bend its legs, slump, and finally collapse altogether)—there in my own world of the mundane and trivial I underwent such a convulsion of emotion I was like an untutored peasant who, seeing an eclipse of the sun, has his understanding of the word blotted out, the earth rolling away from beneath him with the stars, and couldn't name what I felt.

When people say they're not themselves, they mean they don't feel as healthy as they usually do, but I wasn't myself then in a contrary way; it was as if I were the sky in which the eclipse was taking place.

I waited. I calmed down. There was a scattering of memory of moments like this before. Soon I found myself back in my chair but with a heightened awareness of each thing in its specificity—the little pony, Constance's picture in its Plexiglass stand; Ida's grainy biscuit that I'd put in my coat pocket and carried up here and set at the center of my desk, and which I now stared at as I'd stared at fruit and at flowers after the automobile accident that had emptied me of my ability to use language, and of all sense of myself.

Later that morning I received a call from my lawyer, David Demetris. David has perfected his unassailable-lawyer act, from his button-down collars to his gentlemanly reticence (which no jury or client would want to offend, a real weapon), and yet behind this cultivated exterior lies the exuberant spirit of his upbringing. One time I was in his office and he had just finished outlining in a ruthlessly systematic way my tax problems: "You are a minister," he said. "You are not a tax-free charity." We pondered the implications of this in a weighty silence. Then his phone buzzed. He snapped up the receiver, and his features—huge bold eyes, a long nose hooked at the end; broad, thick lips—became instantly merry. "Hel-loh Ma-ma," he said, and answered her questions with flurries of Greek. I was so taken up by his transformation that my tax documents seemed like confetti; here was a man who truly loved his mother.

I usually enjoyed any conversation with David and tried to return his hello that morning with as much spirit as I could muster.

"Ted?" he said. "Something has come up, Ted." And I knew I was in trouble; David never repeats your first name unless you're in trouble, and the more he repeats it the bigger the trouble. "It's simply this, Ted. I've been in touch with all parties about the incident, Ted, per your instructions, and I got a call this morning from a friend in the district attorney's office. Ted, a warrant is probably out by this time for your arrest."

"It's happened," I said, more to myself than David.

"The police should arrive around eleven. Go with them, Ted, and I'll meet you at the station to post your bond."

"You say that like I have a choice in the matter. I'm being arrested, right?"

"Ted, this isn't something to worry about, really. The D.A. has no interest in you. Who wants to prosecute a preacher? We won't get anywhere near a trial. Your case is a nuisance to these people."

I didn't know whether to feel sad, or angry, or relieved. "What is this all about?"

"Mainly a civil suit."

"I didn't realize . . ."

"Yes, it's a real problem. Your assistant, Mr. Dennis, hasn't been receptive to our overtures. I haven't been able to keep him on the phone long enough to explain our intentions. He is acting in a very vindictive manner right now, Ted."

"How much?" I asked.

"There's a great deal of bargaining involved."

"How much?"

"The figure is one hundred thousand."

So Constance's prophecy had come to pass. As Christ said, The children of this world are smarter in the ways of this world. "But I told you," I said partly in reproof, partly in fear, "to promise him I'd pay the bills his insurance doesn't cover."

"And that's what all of this will come to when Mr. Dennis calms down. I'm sure of it."

"Michael should calm down, David. He's probably still in pain now."

"That's it, you see, Ted. The district attorney doesn't want anything to do with you. But Mr. Dennis has insisted that criminal charges be filed. His lawyer, too, is young, like Mr. Dennis, and won't get off the backs of the people over there. It will all come round in the end. What I want you to do, Ted, is just wait in your office for the police. I've asked them to send plainsclothesmen over, although no one has made any promises about that."

"Will they fingerprint me?"

"Well, yes. I've never heard anyone describe that as being painful."

"What about anguish!" My voice rose now in a new anger, climbing into that eclipsed sky; why hadn't I gone to Michael before this, in a spirit of reconciliation? That was my fault and my loss.

"Well," David said. "Let's talk after you're finished at the station, and then maybe you can try to get ahold of the young man. You've worked with him after all, there's a relationship there; once you've talked, the whole thing will probably blow over."

But he's a *minister*, I wanted to say, and realized what that would be saying. "All right," I murmured. "You'll be at the station?"

"I will. Just go along with them and try not to worry."

"Thank you, David. I'm, well, to be frank, I'm afraid. You understand?"

"Of course. See you soon."

I dialed the hospital immediately—wondering whether Michael might not already have been released that morning—and talked to the switchboard operator, who connected me with his room. I didn't recognize at first the voice that came on the line; it sounded delayed, held back, as if it emerged into substantiality only after travelling through the dark passageways of clogged sinuses and then made a loop-the-loop of some new tunnel partially cleared—so duskily muffled it was difficult to make out.

"Where are you?" it asked.

"My office."

"Haven't the police got to you *yet*? Are you hiding or something?

"I'm in my office, Michael."

"I'm calling my lawyer. I'm calling the police again." As the voice rose, it set off high resonances, which made him sound in pain, so that I wanted to reach my hand out to him. "I'm putting you away. You're not a minister, you're out of your mind, you're a maniac, a homicidal maniac! And the world is going to know. You are finished. Check it out."

"But Mi—"

The receiver was slammed down.

I took a deep breath and let it out slowly, feeling my mind head into that realm of the earth rolling away, while my own sinuses ached. The phone rang again, and I wasn't sure I could answer it; Michael had been that convincing. I picked up the receiver. It was Constance. "David just called," she said. Are you all right?"

"Yes. I suppose. I suppose I will be. David says any criminal charges will probably be hard to press."

"That's rather unexpected, isn't it?"

"It is. I imagine I'll recover eventually, though. I hope I will."

"You don't sound yourself. I'm sorry to add anything further, but I've asked the children to be here this afternoon for a family council, like we used to have."

"Today, Constance?"

"Something has come up which must be discussed with everybody. I mean, other than your personal predicament."

"Today?"

"David said you ought to be finished by four, at the latest."

My secretary buzzed, and the button on my other telephone line flashed, indicating she had to speak with me. I told Constance to hang on, and heard from Donna that the police were waiting in my outer office.

"Constance," I said, back on her line, "I'm about to be taken into custody."

"I know."

"What do you mean, you know, Constance? The police are at my *door*."

"David said there would be this formality. Try to be home then, if you can."

"Constance."

She wasn't on the line.

"*Shalom,*" I said, into the silence.

I walked out of my office and greeted the police. They were uniformed officers, not plainclothesmen, a pair of young, athletic dogfaces who kept their hands at their sides as if in readiness to make a grab for me or draw their guns. "I know why you're here," I said. "I'm ready."

"Are you Theodore Lawrence March?" the shorter of the two asked.

"Yes, as I said . . ."

But I was not to be spared the formalities, and I could tell they resented my casual attitude. They made me listen to the reading of my rights in front of my secretary who, I could see, would not get much more done today. They fastened me into handcuffs and walked me out to the parking lot where there was not one but three black-and-white squad cars, all with their flashers spinning, alerting the whole neighborhood to my shame.

I rode down to the station in the backseat, desperate to remain humble, abject, while one officer sat cross-legged beside me. It's quite clear that I have little patience, so I didn't know whether I could go along with them and "try to relax," as David had said, and discovered I was praying so hard not to disgrace myself that I wondered if there wasn't something to Michael's calling me a homicidal maniac.

I was delivered, down dingy corridors, into the hands of an obese desk sergeant. He pointed toward a line of chairs against the opposite wall by a door, and I went over and sat down. The handcuffs had been removed and I rubbed at the red rings, like shadows of them, around my wrists. I wondered when David would arrive, and started to worry that the authorities wouldn't let him into this inner sanctum. I might have been in an emergency room of a hospital; I felt the same sense of an impending answer coming into slow articulation, except that here I was the question, or an uninjured party receiving the treatment.

I tried to adopt my attitude of the morning, hoping merely to see, and, particularly in these circumstances, to see my way back to that hovering presence. I heard a sharp command and looked up to find the corporeal sergeant regarding me. I walked over, looked at the clipboard he stuck before me, and there I was:

name, address, occupation, criminal assault. To complete the
record I gave him my social security number, which he asked for.
He wondered if I wanted to make a phone call, or if I might be
capable of posting bond when the time came. His cheeks glowed
like a cherub's and the mechanics of speaking, merely moving
his lips, caused showers of dimples. I explained what my lawyer
had said to me, or I started to, because at the mention of David's
name he picked up his phone and contacted somebody who was
apparently keeping David waiting. And then I wondered how I
must look in this man's eyes.

After the call, he took me behind a little gate, *bars* to me,
even if they only came to my waist, and I thought of Randy and
his murderer's execution with a poignancy that I never had
before. The sergeant fingerprinted me at a high desk made for
filling out forms while standing; he grabbed my fingers, one by
one, with a rapidity that was something more than efficient,
rolling them from ink over paper. Then he placed me before a
camera, exactly like one at any Motor Vehicle Department and,
without speaking, nudged my feet into place behind a red line
with his own. He hung a placard with a number on it around my
neck, went behind the screen, and gave three short orders I
couldn't make out; indeed, he spoke as if his tongue were as
swollen as the rest of him, as stoutly inert, and so his syllables
wallowed forth from it. He gave what seemed to be an order
again. I still didn't understand, and asked if he'd repeat it, and
he stepped from behind the camera and stared at me as if I
shouldn't be capable of speech, only comprehension, and I had
a glimpse of what it means to be a criminal.

"T-uurrn llefft," he said, and waved his club of an arm as
if shooing a dog. A flash. "Cennn-ter." A flash. "Turn right." A
flash.

He walked off, and I presumed I should follow and was
right; David was waiting for us. I wanted to tell him that the
intuition of primitives is quite correct; the camera can steal your
soul. Walking out of the sergeant's domain, we passed a youth
brought in on some charge, and he looked at me in a way that
made me sense my skin as brittle and dry. I was ashamed, not
guilty—nothing that egotistical—simply ashamed, reduced to
the crispness of a fallen leaf.

David and I went to a coffee shop in the neighborhood and

discussed my case. Michael was still in the hospital, I learned, because he had contracted a slight post-operative infection; his doctors had put him on an antibiotic, he had proven allergic to the drug, and had broken out in a rash from head to foot. David and I considered whether I should wait for Michael to recover before approaching him, but I decided to see him the next day. If he weren't still in pain when I asked for his forgiveness, he might forget the matter, let it drop, and then we would have to resurrect the experience before healing its affliction. "Is it easier to say 'your sins are forgiven' or 'be healed'?" Christ asked, and often did both in the same operation. Michael and I, too, might accomplish something of the sort—he forgiving me, thus altering my presence before him from malignant to benign. I considered the validity of this for a spell.

"Ted," David said, leaning toward me. "I'm not going anywhere in particular, but don't you have an appointment?"

"What's that?"

"I believe Constance mentioned that there was some meeting you had to attend at four. Am I right, Ted?"

At home, sad and scuttled, I saw Constance, Marianne, and Benjamin sitting in the living room, and felt transformed again into husband and father, domestic, my real human self. I sat in my barcalounger, opposite Constance, who was on one arm of the couch, and leaned the chair back through its wooden groan. Marianne looked relaxed on the couch beside Constance, Ben sat on a stool at the fireplace, and the walls around us seemed the mighty fortress of Luther's hymn.

Our family had not staged such a council for years. In fact, Benjamin had never been initiated into the rite, and I realized why this was so; we found with Marianne that these open discussions never came off as advertised. Being a thoughtful nine-year-old, Marianne would listen to Constance and me arguing at the dinner table and then, signaling a judgment to come by plucking out her gum and putting it to rest on the nearest plate, would deliver her verdict. She fully expected me to comply, and I did, most of the time, because she was "daddy's girl" and knew where my nature would take me. For I had acceded in most respects to Constance's will by the time she'd spoken. There was never really any question of there being an open discussion at all; and when Benjamin came along we didn't have the heart to find out how he might affect this process. But we would now.

"We all know," Constance said, taking the tone of a troubled committee head, "about the difficulties your father has been experiencing at work."

Work? I thought. I didn't care for the word.

"And we all have our opinions about the 'why' of these things. But we are not here to talk about that. We are here to come up with a solution."

See, I thought. Pragmatism, thy name is woman!

"What did the cops say, Dad?" Ben asked quickly, excited.

"I asked you to let me speak first, Benjamin," Constance said, being a reasonable parent. "And I did so because I have something of an announcement to make." Constance's left eyebrow arched into an Arabic character, as it does when she has previous, hidden knowledge. "Your father has been offered a job by the seminary from which he was graduated in Philadelphia. He would be a professor teaching homiletics."

"What's that?" Ben asked.

"Preaching, I believe," Constance said. She moved, and sat down in the sofa, beside Marianne, in a deft complement to her formal liturgical manner, apparently finished.

"That's the first I've heard about this," Marianne said, watching me with a sly sympathy.

Ben looked skeptical.

Bright, cheery, verging toward the giddiness of my homicidal mania, I said, "Did you get the phone call *today*, honey?"

"Yesterday," she replied. "My father called. We talked. And I don't know how we got on the subject but we started talking about you when you were in seminary, and daddy mentioned Harold Bullock. Doctor Bullock," she said for the children's sake, "is the president of the seminary."

"Their conversation went like this," I said. "Harold, who can be gushy, said, 'It is *so* nice to hear from you, Constance. How are things going out there in sunny California?' And you said, 'My business is great, Harold; it's not so *seasonal* as it is in the East. But I'm afraid Ted's up against it again; he's just not appreciated.' And Harold said, 'I'm afraid that's the story of so many. At least he's still in the ministry. Can I help in any way now, Constance?' 'Well, we were thinking of moving back to the old haunts, the Main Line. But Ted doesn't know quite what he'd do.' 'Constance,' I can hear old Harold say, 'Constance, we can scout something up here, I'm sure of it.' And you say, 'At the school you mean?' holding him to it. 'I'm not sure,' Harold says. 'I believe he did his thesis on Justin's allegorical reading of the Scriptures. Rather arcane.' 'Couldn't he teach a class on that?' you ask. And Harold says, 'We do have classes in hermeneutics, yes. Of course, your Ted's quite a preacher on his good days, we might use him in that way, too. Our regular positions are filled, of course.' And then you said, 'Oh, he wouldn't need anything full time. If you could just keep him out from under, keep him from getting peckish.' 'We could, I think we could, Constance, I think we could.' "

Constance looked about to stand, a flush in her face from her sudden anger. "That wasn't how it went," she said. Her temper put an ugly crimp in her lower lip, and she crossed her legs as if she might slice me in half by this.

Marianne spoke, for which I was grateful: "Mother, do you really want to move? Your friends are here, your business is here."

"I don't know, honey. Your father and I need some sort of change." Constance set her eyes on me with this last, murmuring admission.

"I don't feel you really want to move, Mom," Marianne said. "You have such appreciative clients."

"What do you care!" Ben exclaimed, in an exaggerated and slurred way. The symbolic power of the fireplace stool hadn't occurred to me before; but then I saw that, with his knees tucked up to his chest, Ben was saying, Look at me, I'm small, I'm still small, and I'm by the hearth where I have a right to stay for a while and you an obligation to uphold that right.

"Ben," I said quietly. "Ben, maybe this is a good idea." It seemed the simplest way of letting him know that there was only one direction this could head.

"The call really wasn't like you've dramatized it," Constance said. "It wasn't. *He* called me, he did, right after I talked to my father. He wanted a contribution. But anyway. I think he said you'd be a 'visiting' professor. You could live with that, couldn't you? And he talked about having a special chair for you, to give the young men the benefit of your practical experience."

I looked at Constance. How I loved her, and how she loved me, and how we could not find a way to make that love *work* —work so our wills would coincide, and become one. In being conciliatory, in approaching me in this way, she had set the reference point that I needed in order to measure the gulf (nay, the abyss) between us. This made me more miserable than ever.

Beautiful, beautiful Constance, who would always be the woman I desired most and would always leave me feeling, as in the moment when I met her, that she would never have me. She was tall and thin and carried herself well, as they used to say, and as we became acquainted she was also set apart from anyone I had ever known or anyone within my circle by an undefined dazzle of gifts which came to be spelled *aristocrat*. And although I realized later that I, a middle-class hardware dealer's son, was affected by the surrounding display which set off my pearl without price, and that my desire for her did after all have in part to do with my ambitions, so that my love for her was not different from any woebegone adolescent's longing for the homecoming queen, I also realized that homecoming queens, and courtly ladies, are goddesses; every harridan standing fat and angry beside her mobile home is a goddess, and we love them without ever feeling worthy of loving them, nor should we. And when Constance returned my love, requited it, I could not and never quite have believed it. I knew the joy of Othello—"If it were now to die, 'twere now to be most happy"—at the one woman I thought would never have me, who now gave me her hand. Yet at any time Constance might retreat into herself, the goddess appear, and I know that goddess's name: Diana.

"I do care, Ben," Marianne said, picking up an earlier thread. "This is my only family."

Constance's face took on her blank look of surprise, and she turned to our daughter. "But dear, I want you to come with us. You must. You'll love Philadelphia. I can do so much for you there."

Marianne as a latter-day debutante, I thought, and har-rumphed. But Marianne said, "I have been thinking about getting married. But the men I know here just aren't into that."

"And Ben, you like the snow, you've always said you do. Think of living where there are real seasons!"

She was rallying them to her cause, trying to marshall their support as openly as I did when I wanted something so badly I cared nothing for style, or honorable, dignified methods. This renunciation of Constance's usual manner cut against her grain; usually, all of her movements were composed, as if she were an artist's model assuming a position, but now she was agitated, balanced on the edge of the couch, crossing and recrossing her legs, and smoothing her dress: she could not be *settled* until the matter had been.

My children waited to see how much I would object, since that's what they do, fathers, they object. But I couldn't, I felt dizzy, suspended again between heaven and earth in that peasant's eclipse, yet on a precipice—one which rose out of the various seismographic dislocations of that day, particularly this sudden willingness on Constance's part to abandon her professional life in California for her old homestead. And perhaps I was merely the blindfolded man who is really all the way down the steps but reaches out for what he feels is surely the last one; you can fall badly that way, too.

"Constance," I said, deciding to be forthright, "I don't know what to say. Would you work back there?"

"Yes. Certainly. I have the necessary contacts. Business ones. I'm not just talking about 'that old gang of mine.' They're quite gone, you know. Or for the most part."

Marianne said, "Dad, I think it's amazing that you have this opportunity. This chance. This *call.*" It was not catastrophe that revived my daughter's faith, I saw, but good fortune. To put it more exactly, she knew how to anticipate the theological argument I would have with myself and tried to prop up a voice on her side in advance. I looked at her to make her feel guilty for this, but she was ahead of me here also and artfully avoided my eyes.

"It is rather like a miracle," Constance said.

This was unprecedented; and the shock of my wife's newfound faith brought me partway back to my ironic senses. "*Like* one," I said. "Give me time to understand Harold's offer for what it is. I don't want to go back there and end up the house cat. But I'm not ruling anything out. OK?"

"Dad, what school would I go to?" Benjamin asked.

A good school, I thought, a better school than those out here.

I realized I wanted the miracle to be for Ben. He so badly needed this move, which might bring Constance and me closer together, if only for the few years he required of us.

He had prompted my first kind words about the plan, and with the uttering of them I had assumed the taxing and perhaps impossible burden of seeing that Benjamin did not suffer for the decision. My son had, as they say, traveled light; through the four moves we had been involved in in his short life, he had learned to make quick friendships but not try to hold onto them; he knew how to ingratiate himself with new teachers without making himself a candidate for fistfights with the local bullies—an easy mixer, Benjamin, his mother's son in that. He still had those skills, and I wasn't worried there. But this was the first crisis in which he would recognize the heralds of our conflicts for exactly what they were, and as our personal problems, with no reference to him. On the threshold of manhood, I did not want to burden him with such an old and continual sorrow. It wasn't in any way a matter of keeping him naive (after Marianne's sex books?), but he was entitled to spring up in the vigor of his youth without the weeds of our advanced age and our growing conflicts to over-shadow him. We were hampering him in this way already, I knew; he lived in dread of his parents. To see it as clearly as I did then hurt.

"Ben," I said, "I think it's better if you don't bother yourself about that yet. I mean, as much as you can, put this whole thing completely out of your mind. I'll tell you by the end of the week."

"When exactly?"

"Sunday."

"For sure?"

"I promise. For sure. I don't want you to worry. You can forget about it until then. It'll be . . . like Christmas. Sort of, at least." I turned and faced the distaff side on the couch. "That's the deal, then, all right? We'll decide by Sunday."

After the council, I went into the room I used for a study, a slim place, with one high, useless window—just large enough for a roll-top desk and a daybed wedged into diagonal corners.

In contrast to the rest of the house, my room looked frowzy, a good place to read letters and fiddle with paper clips. And here my interior theological argument began, in a fashion. I remembered Constance as she was when we became engaged, in my second year of seminary in Philadelphia. Her skirts were long then, and she used to break into a queer stiff-legged trot when we met. She would stop inches before me, and if I didn't take her directly into my arms in a great hug, she would place both hands flat against my chest, looking up, and begin blinking rapidly against the glisten of starting tears. Amazing, that I could carry such memories and still feel so ill at ease in this world.

The first time I ever saw her really break free into a run I was sitting in the seminary-campus coffee shop. She came through the door and sprang past the other tables and chairs, nimble-footed and fast, in a navy-blue suit with wide silk lapels describing a point at the belt around her petite waist. Alligator shoes. A white blouse with pearl earrings, which set off the flashes of color in her grey eyes, each orb a world within my gift of the universe, as the old poets might say.

She didn't give me a peck on the cheek, but sat right down opposite me and told me she had the most *divine* news; I took note of every reassuring nuance from her even then. I hadn't raised the money for my last year, had I? Breathless. I was thinking of dropping out for a term, wasn't I? The denomination sponsoring me was a Baptist one, wasn't it? Yes, yes, yes. Well, she had just come from talking to the dean who said they had just received a full scholarship from an anonymous donor for a seminarian headed for the pastorate as a Baptist. I changed to her side of the booth and sat next to her. I looked out the window. That old building had mullioned windows in the shape of gothic arches. Beyond her was a wintry landscape, snow, classmates bundled in long overcoats, brick buildings beyond that, and suddenly the buildings seemed to blush like terra-cotta in the evening light, filling the wintry world with a silvery-rose suffusion. I turned back to Constance, and the outside light was the light of her pearl earrings, her grey-speckled eyes. I kissed her. We French-kissed for the first time in public, not quite unaware of our surroundings and the more enraptured with ourselves and our love for that, in this confirmation of it and in its daring. The tip of her nose was still cold from the outdoors. She pushed away from the kiss, took off my glasses and smoothed back my hair, then drew me to her again.

Understand, at that time every seminarian had been drilled in God's providential care: how he provided just what was needed, at the last moment and not before, and no more than was needed in order to keep us depending on him and not the riches of this world. A story about a British orphanage had great currency then. The owner and director of the orphanage did not solicit funds to keep it open, but depended completely on God for provisions, clothing, and every other need. One sad winter day the director and his wife and the poor orphans were starving, and there wasn't a crumb in the cupboard. The man could have asked people for help, but preferred to pray, and rose from his prayers to see the driver of a lorry outside the window, next to his broken-down lorry, which happened to be stuffed with food. The driver called up to ask if anyone could use the provisions. Praise God!

Well, that providential story was utterly true, though I somewhat mock it here. It did happen like that for the fellow with the orphanage, but it did not, quite, happen like that for me. I went about for a while at churches where I practiced preaching, giving testimony to this "wonderful evidence of God's gracious care." Everyone ate it up, to use a figure of speech. But the next year I was in the dean's office and felt I couldn't remain forever curious about the donor of my scholarship and rationalized that I would pray—nightly—for my benefactor; and, with my conscience thus appeased by good intentions, I broke into the dean's files. It was my future father-in-law who had given the money, of course. And it wasn't until then that it struck me as odd that Constance should know about the scholarship before I did. I confess here that I did not fulfill my oath of nocturnal supplications.

As I sat in my narrow study, pondering these things in my heart, Constance appeared with a TV tray. She had fixed me a light supper—perfectly undercooked scrambled eggs, rye toast, a sliced orange, and a wedge of gouda cheese. She never proferred such kindnesses to me anymore, except perhaps when a vacation was near. Would moving to Philadelphia truly prove to restore her spirits? Was she right in her intuitions, and was this a glimpse of the tone of life we might expect?

I thanked her. Her hand was within reach and I took it up in mine and kissed her engagement ring. She gave my fingers a squeeze, her manner friendly.

"I think I'll talk about you in my message tonight," I said.

"Don't you dare."

"You've shocked me by your initiative in this."

"You've been shocking me for thirty-five years. And others, many others."

"I wouldn't be allowed to do that as a professor. They'd hang me for moral turpitude."

She said nothing.

"Did you write down Harold's number?" I asked.

She nodded.

I wanted so much to keep her there that I said something honest and foolish. "I don't like your father."

"Daddy is very old and lonely. Why should you feel that way?"

"Because you still say 'Daddy.' "

"It would be a new start."

"In the old place? The family 'manse'."

"Why are you so predictable in this one thing? Can't you just let that go and not be so—I don't know—stereotypical."

"I'll call Harold tomorrow," I said. "He had a crush on you way back when, I realize, so maybe I'll get a different story." I paused; there seemed no movement from her. "Thank you for the supper. I must now to the Good Book."

She pirouetted lightly, and was gone.

Our conversation had the taste of bread, mild yet sustaining, like water and grain, and I thought of how much marriages revolve around food, and of how moments like this one with Constance were as capricious in our house as manna falling, the ravens bringing food to Elijah, and as needed.

Preachers often start or end sermons by quoting from hymns, and one came to mind as a way to start that night: "Grace, grace, God's grace,/ Grace that will pardon and cleanse within." I quoted it, and then said, "Beloved." I was standing at the pulpit before them again. "Yesterday we talked about God's justice and found that we can only understand his right to judge us by understanding the submission in love of Christ to the worst within us all, by confronting Christ on the Cross. The crucifixion speaks of our condemnation, yes, but at precisely the same time it speaks of God's mercy. Tonight we are going to consider God's mercy, his grace, and how it operates within our personal lives. Also, we are going to see whether grace itself, though a free gift, brings with it certain conditions of acceptance.

"When we think of grace we often think of miracles. I'm going to tell you tonight about my experience with miracles, for a number of them taught me everything I know about grace.

"When I was the pastor of a church in Tucson, after my tenure in Atlanta, a dark-skinned woman came into my office for counseling. She had a lovely, distinctly heart-shaped face, with eyes of an Asiatic cast angling up from her high cheekbones. The first time I saw her, her lipstick was smeared—not smudged, but applied as if she were a child playing grown-up.

"I had an oval desk in that office, and I had people, as I had this woman, Kathy Angelo, sit catty-corner with me at the side of the desk. I asked Kathy what she had come about, and she looked down at her patent leather purse. Her gaze wasn't focused on her purse, nor was mine, for against the purse's glossy side were Kathy's gnarled and twisted hands. She caught me looking at them; she wanted me to look and she wanted to catch me, because next she extended her arms and set her cupped hands on the desk. She set her hands before me as if she were a child extending its most beloved toy to the one person who might be able to fix it. I glanced up at her face and noticed then the lines of suffering in her awkwardly-painted lips.

"Kathy said, 'I have arthritis. Soon I won't be able to walk.'

"I asked her about the details of her doctor's diagnosis.

" 'The doctor can take away some of the pain,' she said. Her words were as blunt as a telegram; I'll never forget their urgency. 'But only God can heal me,' she said. 'I have come to find out if you are his instrument.'

"Ordinarily, someone mentioning me being God's instrument of healing might send me to my psychological texts, I admit it. But Kathy didn't make me uneasy the way that someone who seemed slightly unbalanced would; Kathy had the dignity of one who has lived with pain.

"With my next breath, I felt heavy, I felt as heavy as all the world with its pain.

"I put my hands on hers. She flinched at this, but didn't withdraw them. Her knuckles under my hands were as hard and thick as ancient apple trees. I closed my eyes and prayed, 'Oh Lord, where are you? Where are you for Kathy?' And like the prophet, I looked to the wind, and I looked to the earthquake, and to the fire. And then I heard Kathy say, 'Here. He is here.'

"I had been so quickly caught up with this woman and her problem that, hearing her speak, my heart skipped with fear. And, as if I had been submerged in a dream, I hardly knew where I was. I felt foolish and irresponsible. But when I looked up, Kathy had her hands raised in the gesture of Christ granting his children peace. And then she rotated them, back and forth, once, twice; she looked at them as if she had never seen them before. I knew what she was going to say, and then she said it: 'The pain is gone.'

" 'Through Christ our Lord,' I said. 'Amen.'

"After she left my office, the fear of having provided false hope came over me like the seven devils who storm the soul after one has been exorcised. Really, in my heart of hearts I must admit, beloved, I had more faith in the power of her mind to deliver her temporarily from the pain than I did in the Almighty.

"Two days later, though, she telephoned and said she had visited her doctor the day after we'd prayed. The final tests weren't in, but it appeared that the disease had remitted. Not only had its progressiveness stopped, but it appeared to be undergoing a reversal. The physician had been astounded. Over the phone Kathy said, 'Reverend March, my fingers, they're straightening out.' Eventually Kathy's hands looked nearly normal, except for the tip of the left index finger, which remained outsized. This miracle filled me with wonder and awe. Martin Luther has said that the truly fabulous thing about the gospel was not so much that it happened, but that Mary and the disciples and the others who knew Jesus believed it had happened *to them*. That's what I felt, beloved, how strange it was that God had allowed me to be a party to this miracle he had performed.

"In the next week, during my study time, I canvassed Scriptures for every account of miracles by the prophets and Christ and the apostles, and what struck me was their randomness;

Christ healed some people but he did not abolish disease, he did not wave his hand and make it all go away. He was even rather put out with people who insisted on 'signs.' Likewise, the apostles' power to walk out of prison scot-free liberated them only for a time before they were again in the hands of the state. The Lord granted them temporary reprieves to do his work, but he did not save anyone but John from eventual martyrdom, as far as we can surmise. The most telling sequence involved Elijah. Directly after he had humiliated the prophets of Baal by calling down fire to consume the Lord's sacrifice, he found himself hiding in fear for his life from the very people to whom he had just demonstrated so sarcastically and blatantly that he was the Lord's man and that the Lord's power was not to be gainsaid.

"So I tried to keep my enthusiasm for what had happened under wraps. As a general rule, I would have gotten up in the pulpit that very week and hailed the great power of God. But this was downright unusual and I trod lightly.

"But word leaked out. People came to me, and when they were right there in my office describing their ailments and afflictions I did not see how I could refuse to pray for them. Phantasmagorical things kept happening, somewhat humorous things, also. A young man came to me once who had thirty fillings for cavities; his mouth looked like the inside of a boiler. The prognosis foresaw every tooth in his head rotting out before he turned thirty. We prayed. Once a year I still receive homemade picture postcards from him—open-mouthed self-portraits. The inscription on the back is always the same: ' "He breaks the teeth of the wicked . . . and the righteous shall rejoice"—Psalm fifty-eight, verses six and ten. Look pastor, no new cavities!' And he signs his name.

"Not everyone was healed, not by a long shot, and many of the miracles lasted only for a time, or they addressed disorders about which few measurements could be made: anxiety, depression, and familial schisms which needed healing. But I did see things that I hadn't believed possible before. And again, the effect on me was curious; I continued to keep mum. I kept thinking, Why me, Lord? And why now, after all these years in the ministry?

"But back to Kathy Angelo. Until the time of her healing, Kathy Angelo's method of keeping the Sabbath holy had been that of a pilgrim. She had had no church home, as we put it; rather she had the Yellow Pages, her Baedeker to every local shrine. Dating from the time when she had learned of her afflic- tion, she had consulted the Yellow Pages every Saturday for the address of *the* church to which God must be leading her. She did not proceed alphabetically but according to her intuitions, which she hoped would eventually be in accord with the caprice of the Spirit. She crossed off the churches which proved to be utterly without the scent of annointing oil, such as the Unitarians. They were excised after her first talk with a minister of that body. Her visit among those rationalists says more about her, however, than her disappointment in their viewpoint. Kathy was and remained after her healing *immune* to doctrinal theology. She had one criterion for a religion's authenticity: its ability to heal. So her pilgrimage had taken her to the high churches and the low, the Coptics and the Congregationalists, and it had led her through the spectrum of openly heretical sects and free-lance practition- ers as well. She had gone to shrines and tents and small dark rooms over laundries before she came to me.

"When she had been healed she became a fixture at my church in Tucson. The church plant there was modern and well- designed, with a lovely portico at the back of the educational building that gave onto a patio and cactus garden. After the morning service we would have a coffee hour and people would stand around in the shade of the portico—the temperature had often reached ninety by that hour, during the summer of these events—or venture out to the benches in the garden, drinking lemonade or coffee. Kathy was always circulating there, telling her story to someone who had been led by the arm up to her, while people in other groups glanced her way and whispered about her to visiting friends.

"At first, everyone loved Kathy; her candor about her expe- rience was all the more affecting because of her natural timidity; she gave her testimony in a small, piping voice that made of it the vigorous yet fragile song of a swallow. Immensely relieved to be free of pain, utterly grateful, she made others feel that they had been somehow responsible for the miracle, as if they were the adopted parents of an orphan who has returned from school with a perfect report card.

"Then the others who had been healed started to appear in

the patio, telling their tales. Kathy and these further subjects of divine mercy had an immediate rapport and a particular liking for one of their own. This stood out. Their exclamatory greetings rang in the air as they gave one another what were, by suburban standards, lavish hugs and kisses. Every Sunday became a kind of reunion for these people, and during the summer months the atmosphere of spiritual frivolity—I don't use that word lightly— grew and intensified.

"As fall came on, however, a few of the leading church members became indignant." I glanced around at the faces of the present congregation to see if this would have application. "They began to avoid the patio and lingered in the social hall where the punch was served. For a time they didn't admit to themselves that Kathy & Co. made them feel ill at ease; they merely stayed inside the social hall, in spite of how close it was on those still, hot days. The division between the groups became more and more defined and the more I had to shuttle from one group to another in order to chat with everybody, the more I realized the church would rupture and split over these healings.

"Unless, of course, I did something to prevent it. I tried, beloved. I preached a series of messages on the Gifts of the Spirit—the charisma given to believers as listed by the Apostle Paul—which include healing, teaching, speaking in foreign and ecstatic tongues, prayer, and the others. I hoped to educate both parties into a theological understanding of what was going on, since that was the only way I could understand it, and thus turn the sword of division into the ploughshare of community.

"It worked for a while.

"But late in the fall my predecessor at the church came to see me. The Rev. Dr. Arthur McCormack had served at my church in Tucson for thirty-five years before he was pressured into retiring. A strong board of trustees had been elected and they decided the church had had enough of Dr. McCormack, particularly since they wanted to move the church out to the suburbs, and he had been resisting this move for a decade." I paused to let this parallel of church politics sink in. "He turned seventy and they in turn served up an ultimatum; he could retire gracefully with a banquet or he could be kicked out and eat humble pie. McCormack saw the votes were against him, and he chose to be discreet. It hardly sat well with him, however, for in swallowing his pride he had given himself a most literal heart attack.

"All of that had occurred two years before our meeting. He had sent me a letter on my arrival at the church, greeting me, telling me his prayers would be with me, and explaining the circumstances of his recovery from the heart attack in a tone which conveyed his resentment. He hoped I would have better success with 'those rustlers,' his name for the trustees.

"So he came in that day, with a Scotch tam on his head, in a sporty plaid suit and a bow tie. He took off the tam, and I saw why he wore it; his bald old skull looked like a blanched filbert. His manner was, by turns, jaunty and threatening, hearty and gruff. He could not hear very well and asked me to repeat myself. I spoke louder but only succeeded in sounding affected and pompous. Really, he didn't much wish to talk anyway, and only was at ease when he began to deliver the monologue he had prepared for my benefit.

" 'The Gifts of the Spirit,' he said 'are not for our time. The Apostles died; the Gifts ended. Now, if you think different, I suggest you look at First Corinthians, chapter thirteen, verse ten. "But when that which is *perfect* is come, then that which is in *part* shall be done away." *Teleion* is the Greek for perfect; it's an allusion to the canon, March: the New Testament. You see it? The hocus-pocus business has been "done away"; the *partial*, praise Jesus, has given way to the *perfect*. This isn't a news flash, boy; it's been this way since the second century A.D. A *long* time. You don't need me telling you this; you've been to seminary.

" 'But you get some woman in here and maybe she has a twinge of arthritis and you pray with her like you should and she takes aspirin and starts calling you a healer. Oh, I've seen it, I've had it happen to me. Nip it in the bud, fella. Nip it in the bud. She'll run away with you and this church and hurl it into the sea. People have talked with me about this. The minute you turn your back on those people, they're gone, they're off like a herd of elephants. You don't think it can happen, you look at me, you look at where you are, and you don't think it can, but look at me again! I'm you next year.'

"I told Dr. McCormack that I shared some of his views but couldn't deny what was *happening*. I gave him a typescript of my sermons on the Gifts of the Spirit and we parted amicably.

I could count on us remaining on friendly terms, I assumed, only until he'd read the material. The other side had found its leader.

"I was perturbed. I was distraught, beloved. Here I was healing people through no fault of my own, and a good part of my church was about to turn against me. I had been through church splits before and knew the symptoms; the agony was coming on, and, although certain people considered me a healer, I had no remedy for this. Lord in heaven, I thought, what's happening?

"Even in my distress I understood how McCormack's people felt. There were many reasons for their attitude, most of them bad, but not all. They felt put out. Here was Kathy founding her own supernatural enclave, and they felt excluded. And although our wing of the church insists on justification by faith *alone* (as Martin Luther translates Paul, adding that small but overwhelmingly supplementary 'alone'), people are generally known and revered by their contributions, their acts—their *works*, let's face it—within the church. Kathy's group knocked the status rankings cockeyed. And I'm sure these good people knew the resentment of the prodigal son's brother who had worked for so many years and never had the fatted calf slaughtered for him. Why had God chosen Kathy for his anointing and not these good people who had served him so faithfully? I gave the people the correct theological answers to these questions, I felt, but I saw even as I gave them in my sermons on the Gifts that *emotionally* they did not suffice.

"The worst of it, the most disappointing thing for me and the compelling argument of Dr. McCormack's folks, remained Kathy's inability to ground her experience in any kind of consistent theology. She continued her pilgrimage now not geographically, but mentally, with an eclecticism as scattered as the temples she had visited. I tried to counsel her in this, but she found the books I provided slow going and she was not one to plod along; if she needed to journey to Jerusalem, she'd take a jet, not a donkey. During our coffee hour, she would regularly open a shopping bag and display books she had read and thought helpful in the spiritual life. These included *The Tibetan Book of the Dead, Games People Play, The Book of Mormon,* the *I Ching, The Cloud of Unknowing,* Billy Graham's *World Aflame,* Kahil Gibran's *The Prophet,* Betty Friedan's *The Feminine Mystique,* and *Black Elk Speaks.*

"I finally had to invite her to my office and ask her to stop, explaining I had the Gift of Teaching, in capital letters, and she should heed my advice. She agreed. Never have I known a woman so fundamentally, so preternaturally, so unearthly *naive*. She hadn't realized, she said, all the trouble she'd been causing me.

"But she had a favor to ask in return. She and her miraculous compadres had decided to join in a Festival of the Spirit March and Celebration. All the Pentecostal groups in the area had decided to join together and march from downtown to the football stadium of Arizona State and there hold an ecumenical worship service. Might they still go? And would I join them?

"I agreed to go.

"The day of the march came, a beautiful day with the kind of blue Southwestern sky that's so vast it seems to draw you right up into it. Thousands of people assembled in the broad avenue down which we were to march. Barricades were put up at every side street and motorcycle policemen, astride their heavy machines, chatted together in pairs as they watched with interest.

"At the beginning, everyone was confused about how the marchers were to be ordered. Each contingent had its own banner: Zion Temple, First Two Seed in the Spirit Baptist, Church of the Sacred Heart, Church on the Way, St. Alban's Episcopal, The Church of the 91st Psalm. Some thought the groups were to march alphabetically. Attempts by marshalls to arrange the groups in this order proved vain, however, and finally someone out of sight must have taken the initiative, for our congregated mass began to ebb back toward the open lane and away. The banners turned slowly and led us on in haphazard sequence. The signs smacked of medieval heraldry, despite their Day-Glo lettering, and I felt in high spirits, jostling along with my neighbors to our football-stadium Canterbury.

"As we marched I heard the Lord's Prayer drifting back to us as people took it up in song ahead. I recognized what they were singing from the traditional melody, not the words, for most of the impromptu choir sang in ecstatic tongues. Perhaps many members of this congregation have never heard people singing in ecstatic tongues. I hadn't either until that day. The effect of this sort of singing—not the sound itself but the effect it produces in the hearer—is like hearing monks singing plainsong in a

Romanesque cathedral: after a while, the music creates a reso-
nance in the heart, so that the sound seems to be the heretofore
unheard but always present song the soul sings by virtue of its
very existence. It's powerful.

"Now I know that glossolaliacs, the more strident enthusi-
asts of ecstatic tongues, cause a lot of us to climb the walls, and
sometimes there are good reasons for this. But the day of the
march I simply reacted to the ecstatic singing with a kind of
uplifted curiosity (which is about all I know, in this life, of
thanksgiving). I do not speak, pray, prophesy, or sing in ecstatic
tongues, yet I wanted to participate somehow in singing this old
and new song unto the Lord. I wanted to catch the spirit of the
Pentecostal pizazz. So I sang the Lord's Prayer in Aramaic. The
other marchers from our church looked at me strangely, from
which I derived a smug and I thought harmless satisfaction.

"Any time we allow ourselves to feel smug, beloved, we
ought to beware. The members of my congregation in the march
reported my whimsical gesture as if I had been seized with the
spirit like Elijah—who managed in that state, by the way, to
outrun chariots. Two weeks later, the estranged group wanted to
repurchase the old church downtown and move back in, with Dr.
McCormack as pastor. I knew about the group's existence within
hours of their first meeting. We all know that churches are like
small towns when it comes to word getting around.

"Explanations would have been useless. The incident was
a pretext for what the disenchanted members of my congregation wanted to do anyway. The split had been coming for some
time. There were too many people who remembered how comfortable it had been to attend a church not thought of as 'way-
out' by their neighbors.

"I believed, however, that I could prevent the split by
withdrawing. I tried to rein both parties together by letting it be
known I was being 'called' elsewhere. Within sixty days I was
gone, and the search committee started looking for a new pastor.

"But no candidate proved acceptable to both sides, and the
church eventually split anyway."

I watched the congregation. Some of their faces had fallen,
believing the story to be pointless, some looked angry, foreseeing
a point they thought I was going to make and didn't like, and
some remained intent, either leaning forward slightly or sitting
straight up at attention.

"In the New Testament, the friends of a man stricken with the palsy brought him to Jesus. Jesus said to this man, Son, be of good cheer; thy sins be forgiven thee.

"The Pharisees, not believing that Jesus was the Messiah, thought Jesus's comment blasphemous.

"Jesus knew their thoughts and he asked them whether it was easier for him to say that this man's sins were forgiven or to heal him by saying, Arise, and walk. He answered his own question, saying, 'But that ye may know that the Son of man hath power on earth to forgive sins (then saith he to the sick of the palsy), Arise, take up thy bed and go unto thine house.' These passages are found in the ninth chapter of Matthew, verses two through six.

"Beloved, the greatest miracle, the wellspring of grace, is Christ's forgiveness. The Scriptures tell us that he died in order that our sins be forgiven.

"But we have to appropriate that forgiveness. We have to ask for it.

"We all know this, I'm sure. This is the cornerstone of our faith, *as Christ is*. But there's another part of grace and forgiveness that we hardly ever reckon with. Jesus taught his disciples to pray, 'And forgive us as we forgive our debtors.' Like 'judge not, lest ye be judged,' this part of the Lord's Prayer can be taken as a kind of spiritual rule of thumb, a means of reckoning. As the Church, we are the extension of Christ's presence in the world, and he came to grant forgiveness. But how well do we follow his example? Do we actually want God to forgive us as we forgive others?

"My church in Tucson found that *they couldn't forgive someone for being the recipient of God's healing*. There wasn't a chance that healing could come to the church as a whole with that kind of obstinate resistance to grace, with that kind of insistence upon salvation by works. Oh yes, we have our problems with that notion just as the Roman Catholics do.

"During the course of this revival, beloved, let us pray for the first and last work of grace, the miracle of forgiveness, so that God will continue to dwell among us.

"Amen."

Thursday:

Faith

I seemed to be lying on the daybed in my home office. The room was dark. Light, moonlight, a pale corridor from the heavens, fell through the window over the back of my hands. I was happy. I had never been happier. I was young. No, not young; myself, but light. I turned my palms up in the light, and as I did I thought I heard a voice. I waited. I fluttered my fingers in the light, and each finger was itself and also the light, and then each disappeared. And then within the light I saw both hands whole, not simply in three dimensions again, but with a vision that penetrated my palms and curved about every degree of my fingers and rendered as absolute the fingernails, the melonlike knuckles, and the back of the hands with their follicles of hair vivid as sand grasses.

The voice spoke, and I wanted to turn around toward the window but couldn't. Someone was in the room. A figure lay on the bed. His knees were bent slightly and his thighs splayed. I came closer and leaned over him. Naked and hairless, he was an old man, ancient, with his skin stretched taut. At every joint his skeleton had almost worked through his flesh, which had already assumed the milky opacity of bone. He had my face. I had expected this.

I knew there was a glass of water beside the bed and that I was to help him drink the water. The glass in my hand, the glass, my hand, they suited each other. Giving the man the water would be an easy thing to do. I tipped the glass toward his lips, but he wouldn't drink. He shut his mouth tight so that the jawline bulged. I stopped trying to make him drink, and the mouth opened again. His tongue lay in its cavern just off center. I started to tip the glass toward his lips, but once more the mouth closed. I tried again. Several times. He would not drink.

But I knew what to do; I had always known what to do, which surprised me, and yet the voice of intuition was clear, even forceful. It made me glad. I would have stopped and listened to it if I had had time. I dipped my fingers into the water and stroked his forehead. I dipped into the water again and touched his tongue with my index and middle fingers.

Then I watched from a distance as the man who had held the glass, in a movement like pouring water, lay down over the skeletal figure, and then I saw them merge into one person. And although I stood at a distance, I felt the sudden influx of power, the electrical jolt of their union.

I awoke. At some point during the night or morning I had thrown the covers off to one side. Constance was already up; I could hear the raining sound of the shower going, accompanied by the whine it sets off in the pipes. I didn't feel relieved to have migrated from my dream back into day. Something was wrong or would be. I wanted to lie there anesthetized, without a will to stop the dream's operation, which felt like major surgery. And then I was entirely awake. Michael.

North Suburban, like other hospitals, struck me as an empty place. Its terrazzo floors shone under the best flourescent lights, the lobby was decorated with modern, rectilinear furniture that held up well, and Muzak played in the elevators, in the johns and in the gift store, wherever one hoped to be alone. Each patient had his own TV. I decided to warm up for Michael by going first to see Mr. Gibson, a member of the church who suffered from diverticulitis. In his room, he and I kidded each other about growing old and it wasn't long before I knew I'd better get on with the visit to Michael; I couldn't concentrate on what Mr. Gibson was saying.

Michael had a private room, I learned, and I walked in to

find him sitting on his bed, on top of newly made-up sheets. He was dressed. Not simply dressed but, for Michael, dressed up; he wore a navy-blue sportcoat, grey trousers, a striped tie, and cordovan wing tips. I was impressed by the beauty of his shoes. But then I understood—the outfit was a diversion, the shoes a compensation—when I took in the ghastly sight of his nose!

Oh Michael, it must have been painful. Your nose was red and swollen. It started out, as it always had, thin at the bridge between your close-set blue eyes, both of which were blackened, streaks of livid purple among dull violet and jaundiced yellow; but the rest of your nose was surrounded on all sides and nearly inundated by swelling. Your skin had a red patina, too, as if the blood were continuing to rush there, but as our talk went on I realized that this hue was gathered into hivelike clusters and must have been produced by your allergic reaction.

I repented then and there, broken and contrite, wishing that I had received the blow or never been born. It went nearly that deep. Repentance? The sight of you was both more and less than an accusation: this in-turning pressure of judgment brought my hands up in the acknowledgment that I had no authority to wield the sword, and was a living lie in my every action, even this one.

I don't know who first tried to tender speech; I know I greeted you and you said, "Oh, you."

You. No more. In our rivalry you were always one up, and perhaps you had been so sure you would press your advantage that you were hating yourself for being a little weaker in my presence than you'd been in your daydreams.

"I'm about to be released," you said. "Why don't you just leave. People will be coming."

"Good," I said, in that way I have of giving any response to fill the moment, and pulled over a chair and sat down. And immediately wished that I hadn't pulled it quite so close to the bed, which was high, for I had to cant my head way back to look at you and became increasingly aware of my exposed throat. That guilty.

You said, "The police finally arrested you. I heard that."

I was grateful to be accused, and in my role as epic chronicler I told the story of my arrest and booking as if it were the ironic plight of a mutual friend, making a sacrificial victim out of a self that I could talk about without owning up to, a self I hoped you might keep imagining and hating, apart from my concrete presence.

At the end of my story, you said, "But that's not going to be the end of it, you know. My lawyer said you'd try and smooth-talk me out of this. But I'm not going to stop. It'll come to trial and we're going to stick it to you."

"I'm sorry, Michael. I apologize. Forgive me or not as you can."

"You know what they do, man, when you have 'reconstructive rhinoplasty'? They take this hammer, a *big* hammer, and they knock your nose all over your face. You watch it. You're not all the way out, but you're feeling no pain. It doesn't hurt right then. Physically. But you lie on the table thinking about how you must look—like a deformed moron. I was on the table thinking that and I felt silly and started laughing. I'm lying on the table and they've got their instruments up my nostrils and a block in my mouth and the blood is running down my throat so I can't breath and I'm *laughing*. Then you find yourself with bandages instead of a face and you don't feel it's so funny anymore. It hurts then. It hurts a lot. And man"—your eyes wandered and filled with tears—"I still don't know what I'm going to look like. They say I'll look pretty much the same, maybe better, but I still really don't know. It doesn't look like that to me right now. And—you might not think this matters—I don't know *what* you think, but I, I pretty much liked my nose, my *old* nose. I liked it."

I sat still for one of those moments that are as a thousand years to God, and then I got up to leave.

"You're going?"

"I won't bother you anymore."

"Sit down," you said.

I sat down.

"Give me your version. Just give it to me. Why you reacted like that."

"My knee came up in a reflex when you bent over. The punch sprang entirely out of anger. I felt you were judging Paul unfairly."

"It wasn't only that," you said. "Come on. There was a lot more between us than that. You thought I'd won the crowd over. You'd been worried about that for a real long time, and you were afraid it had finally happened. Right?"

"Yes."

"Saul has killed his thousands, but David has killed ten thousands. True?"

"Yes."

"No." You paused as if you, too, were surprised at this. "Check this out. I usually pray before a service, asking the Lord to be with me, calling on him to speak through me, not for my glory but in his service. That stuff. I didn't that night. I thought I'd just go out and do my number on my own and see what happened. Well, you saw what happened."

"Maybe you just discovered what your true intentions were all along."

"All right. I know what you mean, and that's probably the worst part of it," Michael said. "I should have at least gotten a kick out of scoring with the crowd. But I knew I didn't believe in anything that night and I knew Corwin didn't either. I might as well have taken a header into the music stands like he did. Maybe that's what I did, in a way, by reacting like that, calling him a hypocrite. I know I was taking out the pain of doubting I was going through on him. Maybe that's the truth about us: we're sick, we're sadists. Anyway, it's all I can come up with. It's not much, not freaking much."

You stopped speaking, you got off your bed, you slid very slowly off the bed, pouring the liquified metal of your weight into the molds of your legs and feet. You walked over to the window, your weight forward, your steps heavy yet tentative in those new shoes that looked too big for you, as new shoes do on anybody. You cranked open the louvered window, your face a terrible technicolor in the sunlight, and then you cranked it shut again, and turned back to me.

"It may not be much," you said, "but it's enough to make me sure I want to stick it to you even more. I'm going to stop you. What matters is *pain*. You can only understand it if you've gone through what I've gone through and are helpless to do anything about it."

"We're not Saul and David then?"

"This David will kill you in your sleep, Pastor. You wait."

"I'm not so sure about that."

"Why?"

I looked at you for a long time and then decided to go

ᴬrough with what I'd been contemplating. "I'm going to give you the chance, and then we'll see."

"You're not going to plead guilty, are you?"

"To the right charge, yes."

"You didn't come to see me in the hospital to plea-bargain with me. Why did you come here?"

"Remember when I hired you I mentioned getting involved once in a murder case and receiving a lot of attention from the press. You wanted to know what kind of churches I had pastored."

"I remember. Sort of."

I told you again about my Samuel and Agag speech and the press attention and the national radio ministry that I abandoned just as it started to take off. I told you about my Oak Park golfing companions, and how they cooled to me. "But there's a part of the story," I added, "that I never tell. It's a part that I've been trying to forget and that's been dogging me my whole life. My golfing buddies didn't suddenly become clairvoyant readers of souls. They knew what I'm about to tell you."

We heard steps outside in the hallway and thought the nurse was about to come in, but then the steps continued down the hall. This is the story I told you:

The warden of the prison in the state where Randy Sutter's killer was tried invited me, through the newspapers, to the execution. This was, of course, highly irregular, but a minister of the convict's faith was always in attendance, and the idea of my filling that role must have struck the warden, as it struck the press, as a chance for poetic justice. Reporters called me around the clock, it seemed, and asked, in voices that sounded remarkably like the siren song of good copy, whether I would accept the invitation. I misread my friends at the country club; I presumed they expected me to accept. I went in order to insure my credibility with them.

The prison where the execution took place was an isolated building at the center of a bare plain. It looked like the castle of an evil lord, and the very sight of it frightened me. Its design seemed to rise out of a medieval revival of that extended century of nightmare, the nineteenth, with its weighty rectitude and subterranean cruelty; the place resembled the back half of a cathedral, with the bell towers shorn away, so that a lit dome towered above an entrance in the distance. As we drove through the outer gates, I noticed what looked like sightseers. There were about thirty of them, standing beside their automobiles, which were parked along the shoulder of the road as if a funeral procession had pulled over. Headlights trained on us as we turned and made our way toward the prison. They waved. It's terrible the inflated sense of celebrity one can get; I had to restrain myself from waving back.

I still cannot keep from wondering about that warden. Why had he asked me there? What kind of person was he?

We parked on the grounds, and were escorted through the entrance, conscious of sentries up above in towers to the right and left, holding rifles. The passageways of the prison itself smelled, I imagine, like the catacombs of Rome, musty with death. I was searched and had my identification checked several times at pairs of locked gates. One set of guards would check me out and then let me through a set of bars into a free space; then another guard would check me out again before opening his door to me. It was like advancing through a series of locks in a canal. Stage by stage, I slowly made my way into an anteroom around the steel chamber that housed the electric chair. I felt leagues underwater. The chamber looked like the bolted boilerplate of a ship or submarine.

I asked the guard in the anteroom where everyone was. The warden will be along presently, he said. But what about the reporters and the other observers? I asked. He said that to avoid turning executions into a circus, the state had a law limiting the witnesses to five. Finally, a man in a three-piece suit, another with a doctor's bag in hand, a workman in overalls, and Randy Sutter's killer, escorted on either side by two deputies, came in. The condemned man wore powder blue pajamas and slippers which flapped against the floor, a familiar and uncomfortably human sound.

I was there as the condemned man's minister, but I had no idea what to say or do; I had some vain hope that he hadn't been allowed to read the newspapers, and so knew little about my actions against him. As it turned out, I never had a chance to say a word to him. While the deputies took him straight into the inner chamber and strapped him down, the warden, the man in the three-piece suit, instructed me to say the Lord's Prayer. I recited it, watching the condemned man's arms and legs being manacled with leather straps lined with the lethal wiring, and then was silent as the deputy fitted on the leather mask, with its shiny electrodes at the temples.

"Come on in here and pray that again," the warden said in a commanding voice. "I don't believe you quite finished."

I entered the death chamber and began nervously reciting it again, standing by the condemned man but avoiding the movement of his eyes that I could see through slits in the mask. I kept watching the warden. He was stout and balding, with a ring of wispy hair that looked almost like a fright wig. His eyebrows arched high above eyelids that were so fleshy his eyes themselves seemed nearly as small as watermelon seeds. I noticed, too, that his bald head looked as padded as the tip of a big blunt thumb. His whole head looked *engorged* by flesh, which added to my impression of a sinister, grotesque clown. The warden called the governor, or one of his aides, for authorization to go ahead (it was now nearly midnight) and then he ordered his deputies and the workman—who must have been the paid executioner—and the doctor out of the inner chamber. As the last deputy was stepping out, the warden asked to borrow his nightstick, and then the warden slammed the iron door shut.

"Preacher," he said, "you wanted this boy to die?"

I didn't say anything; I was appalled at him and these events.

"You get to kill him, Preacher."

He took out his keys and unlocked the lid of a cupboard-sized electrical box. Two rows of switches with big handles gleamed against a black metal panel. He threw one of the switches, and a great humming and churning like I'd heard only in the hold of a battleship began. Also, a mushroom-cluster of dentistlike lights went on overhead, bathing Randy Sutter's killer in a light which, coming from all angles, eliminated any shadows; he looked as washed out and horrific as an overexposed photograph. And I noticed then that the walls of this inner chamber were covered with flocked wallpaper common to saloons, surrounding the fellow in a queasy, morbid elegance, as if he were already in an expensive coffin. He was screaming now. I hadn't forseen this and was sure there would be a gag, but there wasn't. He kept panting and screaming. I hadn't been so affected by a voice since I stood

beside the young mother in the recovery room after her Caesare-
an delivery.

"The generators," the warden said, referring to the churning noise. "We have to wait for the little red light to go on. Then
it's your show."

And then in your hospital room I leaned back in my chair
and stared out the louvered window you had just cranked open
and closed, and I will tell you now what I was thinking. This
testimony, or whatever you want to call it, is as much for you,
Michael, as for anybody else, and when you had been at that
window before, with bluish stripes of shadow over your hideous-
ly-discolored face, my thoughts had begun in a course I hadn't
at all prepared for in my meditations, in the way that often
happens. I had thought again of my father and of how he had
brought my mother's Bible to me when I had been in the hospital, and of how I was now his age and in a hospital room with
you and, really, in more than a metaphorical sense, was engaged
in the same thing, handing on that same Bible. For we often
embody more than our minds can ever comprehend, and thus the
Word travels from generation to generation. It was a moment of
the sort I would hope someday to share with Benjamin, but his
time would be further ahead, perhaps as he neared manhood, or
so I would have to continue to assume, all things being equal,
and, as we say, God willing. Now there was this area of my
experience that I could never have revealed to my congregation
or, until that future time, even to my own son.

"I didn't have any idea what to do, Michael, how to escape.
I should have acted crazy or started screaming for the others, I
suppose. But I stupidly felt it necessary to try to remain in control
of myself. I fought off nausea and actually gagged up bile I had
to swallow back down. I got light-headed and could feel the
throb of my pulse along the length of my arms.

"The red light went on.

"'You ready, Preacher?' the warden asked. He slapped the
nightstick from his junior officer into his palm. I'm not sure, now,
if he really would have ever used it. But I was convinced of it
then. I was more than terrified, I was *terrorized*. I could hardly
catch my breath.

"And so, with him pointing the stick in the right direction,
instead of fainting or hollering for the others or in any way giving

in, I stepped over to the switch. Standing by it, I could see the condemned man's eyes through the slits go wide with fright. He was silent now. His mouth was working like a fish's and his eyes grew wider as I stood at the panel. Looking at him was like looking at one of those mirror images that keeps repeating itself into infinity; the state of his soul was as unknown to me as the final reckoning of my own, and we seemed to speed away from each other toward that moment.

"How was I to do this, kill a man? The court had declared that his execution would meet the requirements of justice, but how was I to do this thing, conscious of the good and bad—mostly bad—motives that had led me there? To tell the terrible truth, all I wanted to do was get out of that horror chamber as quick as I could.

"The activating switch had a handle that swung it from the copper prongs, up above, down to the deadly ones below: a knife switch. I looked at the warden, who kept raising the deputy's nightstick and letting the weight of it slap into his palm. He pointed. I stared again at the condemned man, and with my mind as dead to any thought as a suicide's at the moment of action, I pulled the switch.

"His back stiffened as if his spine had been fused into metal, the cords in his neck went taut, his head tilted up and his bulging eyes suggested that all the errors of his life and all the horrors that we fear we'll have to see at the end had come to him in one moment. The warden signaled, I threw off the switch, and after the longest of moments, the man slouched.

"The warden went over to him, pressed his fingers against the base of his neck, feeling for a pulse, and then stepped back. 'Again,' he ordered.

"I threw the switch again and smoke rose from the oak chair and the fellow's head. A scent of gunpowder mixed with burnt hair suddenly filled the room. I turned the switch off at the unbearableness of this and looked back at a dead man. His hands, palms-upward on the arms of the chair, had curled into fists, the fingers blackened like monkey paws."

All through the last of the story I hadn't been able to look directly at you, and now I glanced up. I saw that your air of vindictive calculation had left you and you were withdrawn into a tense abstraction—of being thoughtful? of not knowing what to say?

"Someone at the prison, Michael—probably the deputy or perhaps a confidant of his—told the newspapers that I had pulled the switch. The papers kept the story going on page three, four, and five for as long as possible. Official denials were of course issued. I tried to lie my way out of it, too—I literally said I didn't do it—except to my golfing buddies. I made them my jury and they found me guilty.

"Guilty of having blood on my hands. Guilty of pursuing the case for my own advantage and planning to do the same thing all across the country through my radio ministry. Guilty of having extinguished the life of a man made in the image of God without ever thinking about *him* until that warden made me.

"It's not a matter of whether the death penalty should be employed or not. It's a matter, as you said, of our motives as ministers. I wish that the part of me that wants to Lord it over people would have been executed that day in that prison. But it keeps reviving. That's why you're here in this hospital.

"And I agree with you that the pain matters. And that I won't understand how much it matters unless I'm helpless to do anything about it. That's why I told you the story.

"Because if you want to, you can do the thing that will really hurt me the most, you can take the church away from me. For me that's the end. Xerox a few of those old newspaper stories about the execution, and I'll be dead as a doornail.

"But be sure of why you're doing it. And that you'll be able to live with it. That's self-serving in a way on my part, but if you knew what that execution has done to me over the years, you'd know I'm also thinking of your interests."

"Get out of here," you said. "I don't know if I can handle this." You refused to look at me. "Get out of here."

"Michael."

"Telling me that story might be the cruelest thing about this whole scene. Or the sickest. I have to think about that."

"I only want to add that I don't think you've really lost your faith. You're just seeing how human, as well as divine, the whole business is. That shows growth."

"And I'm supposed to grow some more now and forgive you?"

"The growth shows in your attitude. You have a more realistic view of what it's like living in the real world."

"I understood we were supposed to keep our thoughts on things above."

"But it's life in this world that we're responsible to the Lord for. I don't believe you could construe any of Jesus's teaching to mean 'deceive thyself.' "

Still you refused to look at me. "Let up, will you?" you said. "I have people coming. Leave."

I got into the elevator and rode up to see another member of my congregation. She was on the cancer patient floor. The elevator doors glided back and, getting off, turning the first corner, I saw the floor's conference room through its large viewing window, which, with its seminar table, might have been a college classroom, a quiet place of disinterested inquiry and speculation. It was not. Every time I went by, when on hospital visits, I couldn't keep myself from reading its bulletin-board calendar, fixed to the door, of upcoming events: Thursday 7 PM Film "It Happened To Me" 9:30 Group Therapy/Discussion Session. Friday 7 PM Film "Dying" 9:00 Discussion with Dr. Frandle. Topic: "How To Talk About It With The Ones You Love."

As I passed by the open doors of the semi-private rooms, I saw, as I had lately, a woman standing with a pillow under an arm. An ash-blond, with Scandinavian good looks.

I stopped at the nurses' station and inquired about the woman I wanted to visit, Frances Cushing, an old lady from East Texas. She had cancer of the bladder, and the day before had undergone surgery in which radium needles were implanted in her bladder. She wouldn't be able to move until their work was done, and I didn't know if she could receive visitors yet.

I asked a nurse, who grabbed up a metal folder and returned it to its place in such short order it seemed she had scanned the contents of its chart for only the space of a camera flash, and then spun around and sent one of the other nurses off, before turning back to me, and saying, "Yes, Frances. We're all very encouraged about her. She has a few tough days ahead of her, lying in that one position. You understand these cases?" I nodded. "Fine. Her nurse is attending to her right now. You can go in in a minute." She turned in comradely attention to one of her co-workers, and while I stood there, no one paying me the slightest attention, I thought how officious and secure these nurses seemed in their procedures, how similar it all was to the military, down to the coarse affection implied.

I wandered over to room 1206. The attending nurse passed me on her way out, saw that I was going in, and said, "Be careful. It's dark in there."

And it was. I couldn't see for a moment as my eyes adjusted to the semidarkness, and I called out, as someone does when, unbidden, he has crossed the threshold of an open home, expecting that his host hasn't heard his knock: "Frances?"

"Brother March."

"Yes."

"You wait there a minute. Then you'll see your way clear. Isn't this a sight? An old lady tucked into bed like a little bitty baby! Come on over here. I can't come to you."

I could see now by the light which filtered in from the window, in spite of the drapes, that they had sculpted a trough on the bed where Frances lay, packing her in on either side with rolled pillows so tight that her form underneath a top sheet, with the toes sticking straight up at the ceiling, reminded me of a mummy. Yet her head and neck, surrounded, too, by a horse collar of pillows, gave another impression; not closed in upon itself and quiet but open and telling, even in the semidarkness. Her Roman nose seemed the gnomon of a sundial, and her bluish hair in disarray on the pillows around her head resembled the dial's corona of rays.

I turned at the side of the bed and leaned way over so that she could see my face at least once during our talk. "How are you?" I asked, hovering.

"How do I look?" she asked, and her eyes weren't open with fear but half-closed with sly mischief. "It looks to me like I'm in the hospital. How does it look to you?"

I stood back up, pulled a chair over beside her bed and sat down. "About like that."

"They told me not to move," she said. "I can't move for three days. Can't move nothin', not my legs, not my arms, not my head. They said if I did, it would be painful. And after what they've done to me already, I believe them. I do. Anyway, I'm real glad to see you."

"I'm glad I'm here."

" 'Oh, say but I'm glad,' as the song goes. Did you know I used to play the organ for my church in Lufkin. I did. It was the old kind you had to pump with your feet. It was just like me now. Old."

I didn't know what to say to that.

"I'll tell you something if you promise not to tell."

"I promise."

"People think it's hard staying so still for three days. It's not. Not here, anyway. When I get restless I hit the button of this gadget, and the nurse comes runnin' with a shot that sends me into wonderland. I'm taking drugs, Pastor."

"Frances!"

"Why, the first time I thought I was on the train to glory. But I woke up right here, plump in this bed, and they told me—like they said they would before the operation—they told me I couldn't move. You know what I told that nurse. Guess. I bet you can't. I told that nurse that 'in my Father's house are many mansions.' And that pretty soon I'll get to move as much as I like and without Mr. Bekins. Amen?"

"What's your hurry?"

There was an awkward silence.

"Well I am real glad to see you even if I can't even turn my head to see you *good*. When I told that nurse about my Father's house she thought I was daffy. It's good to have my preacher here. You are a fine preacher. I've heard a lot of them, you know. You're fine. Fine.

"Do you know that I love you, brother March? Do you know that? You see, you can say these things when you're an old lady in a hospital bed on drugs who can't move for three whole days in a way you can't when you're just you. I'm glad to say it. But I mean to tell you that I'd love you even if you weren't so wonderful in the pulpit. 'Because he first loved us.' Amen?"

"Amen. Frances, I don't want to tire you."

"Tire me? Brother, you simply have no idea what kind of energy you got lying in a bed for three days hardly blinking. I mean *no* idea. I'll let you run along when you get bored, don't worry."

"I didn't mean that, Frances."

"I know what you meant." She paused. "Here's a question

that will keep your interest up, I believe. It's been keeping mine, I'll tell you. Why you think God did this to me, brother? Put me in this bed and told me not to move? Why you think?"

I was silent.

"That's a hard question, now, isn't it? 'Not for the sin of his parents, or his parents' parents, but that the kingdom of God might be made manifest.' That's what Jesus said the only time someone asked him. A good answer, don't you think?"

"Yes."

"Yes? Pshaw! Brother March, it wasn't a good answer, it was Jesus. King of kings and Lord of lords. Praise his name."

"It was indeed, Frances."

"But now I'm asking you for the second time. Why am I lying here with deadly poison needles killing the cancer I got eatin' at my insides?"

I waited for her to go on.

"A smart preacher like you don't know? I'm going to write a letter to the denomination. Sending out a preacher who doesn't know the answer to the easiest question in the world. Come on, brother, take a guess. You don't have to worry yourself none, this question's got as many lives as a cat. You can't kill it."

"I'm not sure I can give you an answer."

"You can at least try. Come on, now. *Think.* I have to lie here for three days thinking about it. You can think about it three minutes."

I thought hard for what she took to be three minutes.

"Time," she said. "Well, you fail. But I'm going to tell you the answer so you won't fail next time. Here it is. It's God's will, brother. Just that. It's his will. We're talking about God. God. God doesn't get *surprised.* He knows, he's God. 'In whom we live and breathe and have our being.' God is God."

"But he doesn't want you to be sick," I said.

"That's not what I said, brother. I said it's his will, not his pleasure. 'For God sent his son into the world not to condemn the world, but that the world through him might be saved.' You know what happened to the Son, I imagine, and that was the Father's will, too."

"It's a hard gospel you're preaching, Frances."

"But it's not a long-winded one. I am getting a little tired. You can go in a minute. But before you do, pray with me, all right?"

"Of course."

"And I don't want any of your doubting-Thomas prayers, either. You pray that I get healed and right quick. And you believe that I will be healed. You claim the promises. None of us are worthy of them. But if you pray, I'll be healed. You call upon His name and you remember that God is God. You pray now."

All the time she lectured me I could hear in her voice the quickness of fear wedded with the certitude of faith, its mocking arrogance. And now that she asked the same of me, speaking swathed and bound in what might at any moment prove to be her winding sheet, I was ashamed of myself. If I could not follow her up Jacob's ladder, the least I was able to do was look on in admiration. I prayed.

David Demetris called that afternoon. The preliminary hearing of my case, with him representing me, had not gone well. Michael had scrawled a note from his hospital bed, which the district attorney's office had handed along, insisting that justice be served and the case prosecuted. A report on Michael's condition from his surgeon and the attending physicians stated that the break had been a multiple fracture and the surgeon had had a difficult time extracting bits of fragmented cartilage and bone before he could even begin reconstructing the nose itself. David had argued that I hadn't kneed Michael, so much as Michael's face had fallen and struck my knee. The judge wasn't buying. He had become exercised, David said, about David's representation of my sterling character; crime was crime, the judge said, and he wasn't one of those on the bench who went soft on white collar, or in this case, clerical collar, criminals.

He'd allowed us, earlier, to post a modest bail.

The revival crowds had been building, and that night the sanctuary was nearly as packed as it had been for Paul Corwin. There was a better mood among them than earlier in the week, and they seemed to fall in love with the tenor soloist Michael had engaged, Johnny Johanson. He was a Swede with a clear voice, a singer who didn't fake his way through the high and low passages with vibrato but hit every note squarely, and at the same time had the offhand knack of phrasing essential to a really good singer. Somehow in public performance he sounded as genuine and likeable as the person you might overhear in the car beside you at the stoplight—belting one out to the band on the radio in one of the best voices you've ever heard. Johnny had also perfected the art of the big finish, and the crowd was happily quiet when he handed over the service to me.

I thanked him, prayed, and began my message a little unsure of where I would go. "Beloved," I said, "last night I told you of a woman named Kathy Angelo, her miraculous healing by God, and the split that this charismatic phenomenon and others caused in my church in Tucson. But my ministry to and my association with Kathy continued for a while. There's a Part Two, if you like, to her story.

"When Kathy heard the news about my resignation she was upset, to say the least. I had expected this and I wondered, given her abiding theological naivete, what would become of her church life. We had a last interview in my office. As the conversation seemed about to end, she unclasped her purse and took out her checkbook. The check she wrote out and handed to me was for twenty thousand and no one-hundredths dollars.

"The amount stunned me. Was she rich? I had never considered whether she might be rich. Was she? Kathy asked me if I could get by on this for the next few months. I told her I couldn't accept the money and gave her back her check.

" 'We must do something,' she said. 'After all I'm responsible.' Before I could contradict her, she asked, 'Do you play golf? Would you play golf with my husband?' She said it in such a way that I could not discount that she meant as his hired companion, *for a living.* I replied as casually as possible that I loved golf, that I'd love to, but I didn't quite understand why she seemed to be attaching so much importance to a golf match.

" 'The time is dark,' Kathy said. 'The time is very dark, but we know it will be light.' She stood up, gave my hand a squeeze in both of hers, and left the office.

"One's first meeting with the husband of a woman one has seen miraculously healed must be a rare event in anyone's life; that day proved to be memorable to me for other reasons as well.

"When I arrived at the first tee of the Tucson National Country Club at eight on the morning of our match, the weather, for a late fall day, was hot—eighty degrees and climbing. A man was waiting there in a Toro golfcart, and my golf bag was beside his in the back of the stubby vehicle. From a short distance he looked flashy and powerful. He wore silver-rimmed royal-blue sunglasses. His wavy hair, combed back from his low forehead, was being blown back by a hot wind; he was big-shouldered, his arms were heavily-muscled, and he had a powerful build. The vee of his open collar drew attention to a silver medallion he wore. He wanted me to call him Duke, and I insisted he call me Ted, not Reverend.

"At our turn to go off the first tee, the Duke commented on how the heat had burned up the fairways. 'We'll get a lot of roll out there today,' he said. 'That's OK by me, this monster can take the snap out of your shorts.' He waggled his driver, and then took a fierce swing, the shaft of the club whistling through the air. 'Go ahead,' he said to me, 'step up there, Ted, and pop one. Show us the way.'

"We hit our drives and took off. We found we were both players of long standing, and this opened us up to one another. The Duke was a remarkable fellow. He talked about his background with an ease that suggested he was only reminding his listener of what that listener already knew. In my case, this was true in part, as I'll explain directly. In his twenties the Duke had been a professional boxer, and had even gone for a shot at the middleweight crown. In that fight, after having been pummeled for eight rounds, he had thrown a desperate overhand; it landed, and he managed to stay on his feet while the referee counted his opponent out. He left the ring and got into an ambulance to spend the night of his greatest victory in the hospital. Internal injuries. Smart enough to know how lucky he had been, he bowed out when the promoters offered him a shot at the title. He said, 'I wasn't meant to be the King.' In one newspaper story about his retirement from the ring, a reporter had christened him 'The Everlasting Duke,' and I remembered that, since I had been an avid reader of the sports section since I was a boy.

"I could see how his Italian features had been roughed up and thus softened, where the clumsy gloves of his opponents had smudged the lines of his eyebrows and depressed his nose at its

bridge. And when we took off our shirts on the eleventh hole—
they were wringing wet with perspiration—I saw that the mus-
culature he had developed as a boxer had sagged but not entirely
left him. Toward the end of the day, he told me how grateful he
was to me for helping Kathy. Her illness had 'fouled up everything,' he said. The Duke owned health spas, hot spring oases, in
Arizona and the southernmost parts of California. His method of
running the business had been, in part, to spend fortnights at
each of these resorts, going over the year with his managers,
while Kathy swam, sunned, and tried to discover if the guests
were satisfied, from what she overheard. The Duke and Kathy
then had dinner together every evening. It had been a wonderful
life, the Duke said, but Kathy's affliction had nearly put an end
to it. 'I don't see how she coped with the pain,' the Duke said.
'And, of course, you don't want your wife on display in a wheelchair at a health spa.'

"After a full day of golf, thirty-six holes, we joined my wife,
Constance, and Kathy in the club's dining room. I was famished.
We sat down at a table by a great picture window overlooking
the eighteenth green and fairway. The kids who caddied were
finishing up their evening of nine holes, and I remembered a
summer I had spent toting bags, how my shoulders had ached,
and how it didn't seem that long ago—the promise of those days
we can always recapture.

"We talked casually, the Duke and I grabbing up peanuts
from a bowlful he had requested, crazed for salt after hours in
the sun. My wife let the Duke run on about his boxing days, and
I thought that a good sign; ordinarily she likes to redirect a
conversation at the mention of athletics. It occured to me how
much I wanted Constance to like the Duke, and that was odd
because, after all, I thought of this as a valedictory and not an
inaugural dinner. But somewhere out on the course, I now thought,
as I turned and saw that the light had faded so that I had to peer
toward the eighteenth green through my own reflection, the
Duke and I had become friends. Our steaks came. As I was
savoring my first bite, Kathy asked if the Duke had talked over
their plan with me.

" 'Reverend,' the Duke said, 'since the healing Kathy and
I have tried to figure out a way of thanking you. We were in a
hell of a jam, and then you came along. Everything turned out

aces for us, but lousy for you. And you a man of the cloth, and everything. I couldn't figure how that all fit in, not until I saw the connection.'

" 'Don't hint,' Kathy said, 'tell him!'

"The Duke grinned—a dazzle of goldwork about his front teeth. 'I own health spas, right?' he said. 'And you,' he said, 'you help people get healthy again. I think we ought to team up. I think it's a natural. You can change my life like you've changed Kathy's. And you and Constance can forget your money worries from now on. I want you to help me shape up these spas into Christian resorts.'

" 'Christian conference grounds,' said Kathy.

" 'Right,' said the Duke, 'like camps, except for adults. You will be—what did you want to call him?'

" 'Camp Father,' Kathy said, and I almost groaned.

" 'Only if you like,' said the Duke. 'Any title you want, it's yours. You'll handle the speakers and set up the schedule. I'll run the business end.'

"We talked about the plan for the rest of that night. I came to understand how Kathy could have written out a check for twenty thousand dollars. The Duke's holdings were extensive. He was a one-man conglomerate. Anything seemed possible with all that money at one's disposal. So on that night, and in the following days, I thought of the Keswick Convention, the National Camp Meeting Association, and the Holy Spirit conferences at the turn of the century. Conference grounds, within the evangelical and fundamentalist movements, beloved, have not traditionally been places where mom and dad merely dump their kids for two weeks and take a breather. Conference grounds have served as convention centers, and out of these conventions have come the agendas for whole decades.

"After my years in the ministry, I thought I knew the lay of the land in the evangelical world pretty well, and one of my concerns was that we always seemed to raise up the wrong kind of leaders—celebrities who were asked to be spiritual giants within weeks after their conversion, and who often became so appalled by the way in which the church exploited them that they turned back on their commitments. And another group, the hugely popular ministers and teachers, who often sold such a simplistic and at the same time rigid gospel that, while they were able to live off the fears of the masses, they made the church look ridiculous in the eyes of intellectuals and mass-media commentators. I dreamed of using the Duke's health-spa empire to raise up a whole new generation of Christian leaders; to sponsor serious theological debate; and, in sum, to hoist the evangelical church out of its own mental slump and help it, once again, to address the real problems of the day. For in many ways, beloved, our wing of the church is still committed to an agenda that those turn-of-the-century conference grounds came up with. We still need some kind of organization, along the lines that I was dreaming of then, to put us back on the track. We're far into the twentieth century now, needless to say.

"Well, then, the conference-ground ministry with the Duke and Kathy lay before me, and its scope expanded day by day in my thinking. Certain traits of the Duke gave me misgivings, however. About his Christian commitment he would only say, 'Sure, it's tough to believe that stuff when you're growing up. But when you're married to a walking miracle you have to think again, right?' Any further inquiries he dodged by saying, 'Religion is your end, Reverend.'

"I was also troubled by discussions we had about his end: money. We were in disagreement over whether the conference grounds should be set up as a nonprofit organization. The Duke didn't think so, and made general statements on the advantages of a free-market economy. He liked the carrot on a stick idea of capitalism. 'It keeps everybody off their behinds and on their toes,' he said. '*Motive-ation*, that's what it comes down to.' I talked about the motivations of charity as opposed to those of profit; everyone involved should see working at the conference grounds as a ministry.

" 'We're talking Chicano busboys here, not angels,' he said.

" 'I'm talking about human souls, whether they're Chicano, black, Italian, or Anglo-Saxon.'

"The Duke respected my ability to argue. He admired my punch of throwing in Italians with other ethnic groups, and waited for me to follow up with a compromise offer. That was the way the Duke's mind worked; business had taught him to see discussion as bargaining. There were no non-negotiable items in his world, and the idea that there were in mine proved difficult for him to accept. He believed, fundamentally, in the mutuality of Americanism and Christianity, in an alliance of social Darwinism and predestined election, as if the pugilist's rulebook, set down by the Marquis of Queensberry, must have had a section on tussling with angels.

"Finally he saw that I would not be moved. We agreed, therefore, to let a lawyer establish the Duke's spa kingdom as a nonprofit institution. I was allowed to direct the lawyer to refer to Forest Home in California as a model construct. The Duke insisted that we allow ourselves to draw immodest salaries; my income would quintuple. Our venture would officially begin when the lawyer had completed the work to our mutual satisfaction.

"The day when we would read the final plans arrived. I was to meet the Duke in his downtown office about five o'clock, and then the Angelos and the Marchs would go off to dinner. But before that, after lunch, I was to help the public relations firm in charge of our publicity tape an announcement about "Living Waters Retreat Centers." Kathy had come up with the name. I disliked it; it sounded too much like the pseudo-Indian names of YMCA camps, but I hadn't been able to think of anything better. That morning I prepared a one minute speech I hoped the firm would approve of.

"Kathy was at the studio when I arrived, which surprised me. The slight young man who represented the company surprised me even more by showing me from the waiting room of the building into a TV studio—I was thinking in terms of radio. We stood in the shadows behind the three cameras and looked toward the stage area, with its blue blackdrop lit by an arsenel of Fresnel lights. Pythonlike cables slithered over the floor as the cameramen did a slow dance with their heavy partners, rehearsing the movement of their shots. Two boom mikes hung out over the stage like traffic lights suspended above an intersection. I had been in a TV studio a few times before, taping those Sunday morning programs on local stations that nobody watches. Still, I felt the thrill that TV studios inspire in visitors; the feeling that this complex of technology, trained as it is on a shockingly small space, must be devoted to something impossibly worthy; that all this light, the blinding white Fresnels, must illumine only things and beings which are perfect, celestial, those capable of being at home in this heaven of scrutiny.

"The slight young man instructed Kathy to come and stand on an X in the stage area. She put her hand to her chest and laughed nervously. A young woman brought me a simple academic robe, the kind I wear for marriages and funerals, and I donned it. I was asked by the young man to stand on a small stool which someone had placed upstage of Kathy and to her left.

"When I was in my position, the slight young man said 'Look happy and inviting. You're inviting your best friend to come visit you, and you'll just be tremendously pleased if he does. No, Kathy, don't wave. That's it, smile. Run the tape! Reverend, not sincere, but *fun*. It's going to be *wonderful* if your best friend will come see you. Everyone will have *such fun. Fun! Reverend, Fun!*

"Over the loudspeakers, I heard Kathy's pre-recorded voice, saying approximately, 'I lived in pain from arthritis, until the day when a man of God prayed and laid his hands on mine. Now I want the world to know and benefit from my divine instrument of miraculous healing, the Reverend Ted March. So my husband and I have devoted our personal fortune to establishing centers of healing where all may come and experience the amazing power of God. Come this summer to a Living Waters Retreat Center where the streams of living water will minister to all in need. Write today for a free brochure. Reverend March and I will be there to greet you.'

"I had stopped having *fun* the second I heard Kathy's voice. I turned and asked her what she knew about the commercial.

"'I told the Duke you might not like it,' she said. 'But he said it would get people to come. It would get *streams* of them. Please don't be angry with me.'

"I love Kathy to this day and I assured her that I wasn't angry with her. But the Duke was another matter. I went over to the slight young man and told him to dismiss everyone and go home. He said that he had been hired to do a job. I told him he had certainly done one. Adios.

"I went directly to see the Duke. I was angry and hurt. I despaired of our mission, although I did allow myself the wan hope that the Duke's crude methods signified nothing more than simplemindedness. If I realized that Kathy would remain theologically naive, perhaps I should also accept and forgive the Duke's vulgarity. You see, beloved, I wanted very much for the enterprise to succeed. And I hoped it still might, as I drove toward our late-afternoon parley, if only I could convince him to become a silent partner, completely removed from the operation.

"The Duke had his office at the top of one of Tucson's handful of skyscrapers, the Home Federal Tower. I took an elevator up to the twenty-seventh floor and went into his suite of offices at the end of the hall. I announced myself to the girl at the desk—an attractive young woman in poolside attire, lavender teardrop shades, a T-shirt, and shorts. I looked down at her sandal-clad feet beneath her glass desk top and saw goose bumps over her legs from the air conditioning. She appraised me with a skeptical eye—I looked like anything but a health nut. And then cheered up when she realized who I was. She graced me with a smile and called my name in to the Duke in his inner office, and then asked me to wait a moment; the Duke, she said, would be right out.

"I waited for much more than a moment. The girl rubbed her hands together and then hugged them between her thighs. It was freezing in there for her, and I realized the Duke must have insisted on her sun-worshipping uniform. After a good twenty minutes had passed, she said, as if apologizing, 'Well, he's with his lawyer now.'

"I was at the door and through it before the girl could stop me. We appeared before the Duke together, she just behind, with her hands on my shoulders.

" 'That's all right, Susan,' the Duke said. 'I was just about to call for my impatient friend.' The girl backed away and closed the door. 'Harvey,' the Duke said to his lawyer, 'I want you to meet my minister the Pastor Reverend Ted March. Harvey is our counsel, Ted. He's put together quite a package for us.'

"We shook hands. Harvey looked like an old boy out of an Eastern prep school, in his madras shirt and khaki trousers. We all sat down, the Duke behind his kidney-shaped, smoked-glass desk, Harvey and I before him. There were photographs on the walls of the Duke in his boxing days, and a whole series of him in front of his resorts, the places becoming larger and more outlandishly Moroccan as the Duke physically aged.

" 'Lookit, Teddy,' he said. 'What you're going to hear won't be what you expected. I've been thinking. If we went with your ideas I'd have to practically retire. I'm not ready for that. It's my money, you see, and I want to keep it working for me and you and yours. Harvey and I have come up with a plan that will make everybody happy. Go ahead, Harvey, lay it out for the man.'

"Harvey informed me that the spas were to be turned into franchises owned and operated by 'spa ministers' who would function within the corporate structure of Living Waters Retreat Centers. My job would be to set up the model programs which every other spa minister would be obliged to copy, maintaining the 'continuity and consistency of the product.' I would help the corporation find other spa ministers who would be willing to buy in, and be capable of performing a miracle now and then, to keep the company's image intact. For these services I would own twenty percent of the corporation—without investing a penny, Harvey emphasized in a threatening voice—the other eighty percent being held by the Duke. And I would own the first Living Waters Retreat Center outright, if I agreed to run the place as a corporate franchise as long as it proved profitable. I would also hold the title of president, while the Duke would be the chairman of the board.

"Then at length Harvey explained the market studies he had commissioned and went into details on how the corporation could expect to do better than break even the first year—very unusual for any business venture, he said—and how much money, loads of it, would come in afterward. 'It knocked me over when I found out how many religious sick people there are,' he said. 'This thing looks like big business; big, big business.' What he and the Duke had in mind was a marriage of Lourdes and McDonalds. Miracles to go.

"The Duke dismissed Harvey, thanking him grandly as he shooed him toward the door and out. Then the Duke walked around me to his desk, but instead of sitting down he stood at the window, which occupied all of one wall. He asked me to come over and stand beside him. He clapped an arm around my shoulder. I could smell his cologne. He gestured with his arm toward the city and the desert beyond. 'Look where you are,' he said. From that height the city appeared huddled about our skyscraper, resting in its shadow. The desert and the mountains beyond, diminished by the sprawl of housing about the town, looked like a papier-mâché representation of a man-made world. 'You don't

get here,' the Duke said, 'by thinking straight. You don't command a view like this and the respect of everybody down there
by being timid. I've quit sparring with you, Teddy. I'm giving
you one hell of a chance and I expect you to grab it.'

"As he had in the last round of his last fight, the Duke had
come on hoping to land an overhead blow. I was scared. My legs
trembled and made the weight of the Duke's arm around me
seem insupportable. He didn't move or say another word. The
heaviness of his clasp increased, as if the longer he gripped me
like that the greater his hold over me became. I finally understood the Duke and his mercurial attractiveness. His was the
force of desire, the power of time and circumstances to intimi-
date us and make us exchange our principles for what seems like
security. He was offering granary bins for God's manna. And for
an instant I was tempted—the blow of temptation exploded
against my defenses—and in that wingbeat of the fallen angel
I came to know the majesty of Satan."

I thought of Michael, and of how I hoped he had heard
something of the depths of human temptations we face in the
ministry.

"But then, in that same moment of my greatest temptation,
ever, I saw with absolute clarity how giving in to the Duke would
be to deny my ministry, and turn my back on Christ. What the
Duke offered was a life free from life's usual limitations. Faced
with the same temptations, but with the stakes of the whole
world at issue, our Lord declined by submitting to the weakness
and poverty of the flesh, by refusing to use his glory for his own
benefit. He beat the devil by refusing to take up the challenge,
by not being enticed into a fight. And I also wanted to show the
Duke that, unlike his master, he remained a man, made in the
image of God, a person for whom Christ died. I said, 'No deal,'
and then I hugged him as if he were a dear Christian brother.
And, though I didn't know quite why at the time, I turned and
kissed him on the mouth.

"The Duke wrenched himself away from me in horror. *A
minister!* his look seemed to say. His foot twisted, or perhaps he
tripped over the leg of his chair. He fell backward and hit his
head on the side of his desk going down. He howled in pain and
called me a pervert, a deviate, a *sicko*, and said he never wanted
to see me again. He was cussing me out roundly as I left his office.

"Beloved," I intoned, "sometimes we think of Christianity as if it were a money-back guarantee, as if it's supposed to exempt us from the temptations of life, or make preachers into ready-made saints and laymen into people who will know nothing in this life but health and wealth. We are tempted to think that there are two lands in which people dwell, the land of the Lord's anointed and that of the world. Beloved, there may be a difference in citizenship, *but the geography of the place is exactly the same!* The issue is not whether you're going to be put in the fire with Shadrach, Meshach, and Abednego, or put in the lion's den with Daniel, or walk through the valley of the shadow of death. Beloved, the only question is, Are you going to meet the Lord there! You are in the fire, you are in the lion's den, you are in that valley of despair. But it is precisely in these locations that Jesus Christ can be found. Not floating above in the clouds, not yet. Right now he's still here among us in his church and in the person of the Holy Spirit.

"The Duke's offer was tempting. Not having money scares us all, and so even though what the Duke wanted me to do was fairly outlandish, believe me, it was tempting.

"But there are far more difficult temptations. Today I talked with a woman who has cancer of the bladder. Yesterday she had an operation in which her surgeon implanted radium needles in her bladder, hoping that the radiation given off by these needles, which would probably kill a normal person, would instead kill the cancer in this woman's bladder. Some of you know this woman and some of you don't. I'm not going to mention her name in order to protect her privacy. But I'm here to tell you that she's one of the greatest saints I've ever met. This woman cannot move a muscle for the next day and one half. If she does, she might dislodge one of the needles and die as a result. She has had to keep still now for two days already. And you know what this woman told me today? You know what she said? She said it was the Lord's will that she was there. Not that she's sick; he takes no delight in our afflictions and oppresions. But she meant that even in this fallen world the Lord can use evil itself as a means by which he comes to us. He can use disease. He can use poverty. He can use despair. He can use these things in the same way that the doctors can use radium, a form of death, to overcome death.

"For that's exactly what Jesus did! He died and we must die

with him in our daily humiliations and sufferings in order that we might live with him in glory!

"This woman told me to pray for her. She said, 'You pray that I get healed and you believe that I will be be healed. Claim the promises. None of us are worthy of them. But you call upon his name and you remember that God is God.'

"If you recall, beloved, that's nearly the exact same thing that the centurion said to Jesus. He said that he knew Christ was perfectly capable of healing his daughter, that the Lord had but to 'speak the word only.' Christ granted the centurion's request. And he added, 'I have not seen such faith, no, not in Israel.'

"Faith . . . Faith is our subject tonight, for it holds within it all that I have said and more, much, much more.

"The Scriptures say that faith is the substance of things hoped for, the evidence of things unseen. It's not a guarantee, nor an exemption from the common run of human experience. Faith is all about healing, but not necesarily about the healing of this or that disease. These are only signs that there is hope for each of us that one day we will be healed, absolutely healed, of sin and its effects, and transformed into the perfect and supernatural creatures God made us to be. Now we barely have glimpses of these creatures, or see them through a glass, darkly. They are more astonishing than archangels!

"Faith determines not so much what we experience but whether we recognize the Lord in our experience. It's our profession that yea, though I walk through the valley of the shadow of death, *Thou* art with me!

"We are wrong to assume and we are foolish to rely on being sheltered and comforted in that valley in the various types of health spas, the false Christian way stations, that we often trust in instead of Christ. We can only rely on Christ's knowledge of and his loving submission to the worst in this world, the power of evil itself. We can only rely on the kiss of Christ in turning his cheek to the devil—that the power of this love is greater than Satan's hate—and on the apparent defeat of the Lord in this world that has brought us the victory we know now, and will know fully in the next.

"Amen."

Friday:

Hope

Friday, and I had a funeral to preach. At my desk at home, my feet up, rubbing two paper clips together, I thought about the impending graveside service, but couldn't see how I would say what was in my heart. It was not that the fellow, Walt Winters, about whom I would deliver the eulogy, was a scoundrel. The reverse. No, contemplating the eulogy of Walt Winters I had a maddeningly foreshortened perspective, as I did when as a boy I had run out of money at the penny arcade and could only stare into the darkened viewer of the crank-operated movie.

Walt had been a carpenter, a good one. He built cabinets, and at get-togethers among church members he would gravitate toward the kitchen and its woodwork. He would reach out and close and open the doors with a patient hand, slowly, diagnostically. By chance, I caught him opening cabinets the first time we met and then made it a habit of watching him repeat this secretive, furtive gesture. He was like a grandfather, full once more of hope, taking another look in the bassinet, only to see that his daughter's child was as ugly as ever. And then he would walk away, back out into the living room, and drink his coffee with the others.

We always greeted each other warmly. He left the impression of a tall man, since he kept his back straight, and his erectness was emphasized by a rigidly at-attention grey crew cut. I would say hello in his hearty way right back to him, which seemed to betoken that one day we would get together and *talk* for the one time that would be needed to find out why our ready, fellow-feeling was there.

I was usually engaged with someone else, but would keep watching Walt out of the corner of my eye, noticing again that he had a nice way of just standing in a crowded living room with a cup of coffee by himself, not embarrassed, not hurt, not looking as if he felt anything because no one was speaking with him, just standing there, drinking his coffee, keeping his saucer at belt level in one hand while he raised and lowered the cup with the other. And I always thought, *now*, go over there and talk with him. But I never managed to break away before someone else came up and spoke with Walt. Why?

He had died suddenly, of a virus that attacked his heart. Perhaps I could use the disease as the underlying metaphor of my confessional remarks. I swung forward and put the paper clips aside.

The line of cars formed in the church parking lot and we drove out slowly, as if grief had made us too fragile for the usual jolts of the road. I was behind the family's car, which followed the hearse, and I could see in my rearview mirror the caravan stretching back two or three blocks. This was one of the biggest funerals I had ever conducted at the church. Everything had gone well, so far, if you can say that about a funeral, but I still had to speak personally, if publicly, to the family during the graveside service.

Walt was to be buried at one of the "cemetery parks" of Los Angeles, not Forest Lawn, but another place like it up in the Hollywood Hills. This cemetery was designed to look like the estate of a French baron, with a Chateau mortuary at the center of its grounds. The lawns were landscaped to take advantage of the rolling land; areas seemed to compose themselves into the private valleys and clearings of an illusory forest, the favored picnic haunts of the ancestral family. The flat tombstones gleamed like so many coins thrown on the grass for children to hunt, as if here death was the final happy elevation to the aristocracy.

I parked and accompanied the widow, Dorothy, up to the site, a place on high ground by a line of trees, where the coffin was duly carried up by the pallbearers and laid on the mechanical bier. The scent of the flowers, which were set up on stands, blew in the desultory wind of that unusually humid day. Dorothy had on a flat hat, with a veil, and she stood beside me quietly until the nearly seventy-five people who ringed the grave had all been assembled. Then she stepped away, separating herself from me by several degrees in the circle to indicate, I supposed, that she was ready to be addressed.

I prayed. Then I read from the Psalms, concluding with verses from the twenty-seventh:

> The Lord is my light and my salvation; whom shall I fear? The Lord is the strength of my life; of whom shall I be afraid? One thing have I desired of the Lord, that will I seek after; that I may dwell in the house of the Lord all the days of my life, to behold the beauty of the Lord, and to inquire in his temple.

And I read from the Gospel of John, chapter fourteen:

> Jesus said, Let not your heart be troubled; ye believe in God, believe also in me. In my Father's house are many mansions: if it were not so, I would have told you. I go to prepare a place for you. And if I go and prepare a place for you, I will come again, and receive you unto myself; that where I am, there ye may be also.

"All his working life Walt Winters was a carpenter," I said, my voice winging up from the midst of our blackbird flock. "He was known as an old-fashioned craftsman, and people valued his work. Some of you at one time or another have come up to me and spoken of his kitchen cabinets in tones of awe. These were his masterpieces.

"I've heard others, when they were debating whether to employ Walt, complain of his slow work habits. I hope you don't mind me mentioning this, Dorothy. It says a lot about the man. Walt wasn't going to rush, and he wasn't going to be rushed. He didn't make as much money as he might have because of this. But I'm sure it bothered Walt much less than it would other men. He wanted to do every job *right*. He cared that the work be done correctly, with great skill and attention to every detail, even when those hiring him didn't. He cared about the work itself. He was a man of great personal integrity.

"Now, we all know that God loves us equally. He loves every one of us unconditionally and absolutely. You can't be more loved than God loves you. But we also know that he doesn't love us all in the same way; Jesus treated his disciples differently, according to who they were as individuals. John wasn't Peter. Peter wasn't John. And Jesus loved each one for the person he had created each to be.

"We know, too, that Jesus was trained and worked as a carpenter. We can picture Jesus with Walt as he did his work, watching Walt perform many of the same actions our Lord had during his earthly life. He must have taken a special pride in Walt's love of the wood He had created. And we can think of Christ receiving the resinous scent of the shavings as Walt's gift of frankincense to him. As Martin Luther said, the cobbler praises God when he makes a good pair of shoes.

"God created man in his own image. The Creator made us all creators—gardeners, carpenters, and householders. We were and are not asked to perform our work as slaves, which would make work only drudgery, for God created work itself as a means of knowing and loving him, a way of enjoying his love and recognizing our likeness to Him. And that's why the Psalmist wished 'to dwell in the house of the Lord.' This is 'the one thing he will seek after,' or require. David had built his own home. He knew the joys of doing that, as many of us do. And so, when he speaks of his longing to know God absolutely, he hopes and expects that experience to be like the happiness his own home has brought him.

"What the Psalmist asks of God, Jesus promises. He says to us, yes, the pleasure you take in your humble dwellings will be magnified many times over when you are with me; you will not live in mere houses but in heavenly mansions.

"Notice that Jesus was speaking to his disciples here, those followers who were about to experience persecutions that would deny many of them even the humble joys of this life. He was speaking to those who would remain faithful to him, to those who build their lives on the foundation of his death and resurrection. Jesus was speaking to those who would make of their lives a dwelling, a cabinet or a house strong enough to weather the natural and supernatural devastations of this life.

"Walt was this kind of disciple. In doing his God-given work, he made not only cabinets but a life that was a cabinet filled with service to God; he made of himself a tabernacle in which the light of the Lord burned brightly. If we grieve today, if we are in pain because we have lost Walt's presence among us, we can take comfort in the sure knowledge that Jesus has granted David's request, that those of us who follow him will live forever with him, and that Walt knows these things now as we never can in this life."

I looked out over the cemetery. The sloping lawn fell away toward the baronial mortuary, whose red-roofed turrets at each corner were dreamily distant in the smoggy and humid day. I was sure they were nonfunctional—architectural icing. Walt would not have approved. His big Adam's apple would have bobbed swallowing this down. I had been sad, but then I thought of how relieved Walt must have been to be quit of this. No more kitchens with badly-made cabinets! In my sudden joy it seemed that like doves or homing pigeons we might all arise and, with a great explosion of wings, fly home to Jesus. I nearly laughed out loud.

I put my head down and my hand over my mouth, but my sides shook as if they would put off the encumbrance of flesh. I tried to suppress my mirth, but I noticed that people had their faces screwed up, looking at me, nevertheless. And so, when I was sufficiently calm, I quickly ended the service with a prayer.

What happens after a graveside service is never predictable. Members of the family linger for widely-differing amounts of time—all the way from running off to camping out. It's hard to know what they need or expect. But nothing in my experience compared to what happened then. After my prayer, the widow took the few steps to the coffin, reached out and laid her hand on it, long enough for the sensation of its temperature to register and fade, and then she moved away, walking faster as she left our circle and went up to the hill to where the car for her was parked. I shook hands with several people, who muttered appropriate remarks about Walt, as I was attempting to do.

Then Patti Murphy stood before me. She looked angry. Her short frosted hair was like the helmet of a Trojan warrior. Her mouth was puckered slightly, as if she were about to spit out a bit of meat which had been lodged between two teeth and worrying her all day. She didn't stand still; she shifted her weight from one hip to another, quickly, with a little hop, so that when she landed she gave a kick at the ground as she got her foot under her. Viscerally, I must have remembered my boyhood fights, for my arms tensed as if I wanted to give her a good push, or maybe topple her over while she was in midair, between hops. I thought, This is a woman, March, control yourself. We had not exchanged a word yet, but already this pint-sized Amazon had me going.

"Hello, Patti," I said.

"Hello," she said.

Two glancing blows, no points scored.

"You were close to Walt and Dorothy, weren't you?" I asked, trying to be conciliatory.

"I sure was. That's why I can't understand how you can have the gall to get up and speak about him like that. As if you were his friend. You hardly ever said hello to the man. I don't think I saw you talk to him for more than two minutes running in your life."

Many things sharpen human faculties: greed, caffeine, a lust for power, anxiety, but surpassing these by far is hate. You can count on those who hate you to know precisely where your weaknesses are.

I tried to disarm her with honesty. "I thought a lot about that today, Patti. Everyone grieves Walt's death for his own reasons. I guess not knowing him is mine."

"Walt Winters had one more good point that you didn't mention." she said. "You couldn't have, because you never took the trouble to know him. But the thing about Walt was, he didn't make so much money, as you said, because of the way he did his work. You got that right. But Walt died a rich man. Tell me how you think he did that."

"He was rich in many things—friends, his family, work."

She looked at me as if I were the original dumb bunny— that rabbity, hare-brained, bucktoothed nerd. "Preachers never know when to quit, especially you," she said, and suddenly the hard tanned mask of her face broke at every age line, and her eyes began to tear. "I'm not talking about friendship now! I'm talking money! Walt was rich! But you didn't know that, did you? You never took the time to find out!" She screamed all this out, which promptly attracted everyone's attention, and I saw gatherings of two and three move toward us to compose a crowd again.

"I didn't know."

"Of course not. How could you? But I'll tell you the reason, although it's too late to help poor Walt's cause any. The reason is that Walt knew how to invest his money. He was brilliant at it, as a matter of fact. He had the Midas touch. What do you think about that?"

I must here confess that I'm only human, and the first thought that went through my mind was whether Walt had left any money to the church in his will.

"I'm surprised," I said.

"Well, here's something that should shock you, if you have any decency left at all. The one thing that Walt really wanted these last few years, his last wish, was to become a deacon at the church. You and those snobs thought he was just a carpenter, what could he know. He could have bought out everybody on your board of deacons from petty cash." Having delivered her revelation, Patti calmed down a bit and settled her weight on both feet; she wiped away her tears, sniffled, and looked up at me with eyes that were distant with memory as well as focussed with accusation, each like the sun that day—hot, and yet shedding a light softened by the heavy atmosphere.

I was bothered about Walt, but thinking more right then of my history with Patti. Her husband, Ray, had died within the first months of my ministry at the church. He had been killed in a commercial accident; he was a building contractor, and had been sipping coffee at a work site when a truck, delivering steel, had careened onto the grounds and crushed him against a stack of cement blocks.

Patti insisted that Ray's funeral not be an occasion for mourning but a "time of testimony to the resurrection power of Jesus Christ." A program for the service was printed, to which Patti and other members of the family contributed capsule autobiographies, giving the outlines of how Jesus had transformed their "miserable" lives. Patti had me preach an evangelistic message, and she insisted that we give an altar call at the end. No one came forward, though, and I suspect that walking down the aisle might have felt too much like volunteering to get into the coffin with Ray. It surely disappointed Patti.

After the service, she gave a buffet lunch for her relatives and friends. She changed from her mourning weeds into a lime green cocktail dress. Lime, with her frosted hair. She greeted the men with comradely hugs and the women with cheek smooches, and told everyone how good it was to see them again; she took people by the arm and made introductions, and whenever she went off to answer the door, urged everyone to eat his fill. And later, as she moved among the clusters of people, her usual athletic walk took on the precarious character of a ballet dancer walking on her toes. We might have been attending a wedding reception given by a youngish mother rather than a funeral. Her behavior disturbed me, to say the least, and I went over and asked if we could speak privately.

"Now?" she asked, like a child stalling on his parent.

"It's about the arrangements." A poetic lie.

She led me into the house's master bedroom and closed the door behind us, in a manner that almost suggested that we were a happily-married couple, stealing away from our party for a few moments. She asked me to sit on the bed, which transformed my impression into a full-fledged condition of anxiety. I don't like to sit on other people's beds. But I obliged her for a moment or two before again standing up. She was still at the door, her face aglow with hysterical bliss and her eyes, unseeing, blinded by what she must have experienced as prophetic ecstasy, as if in her somnambulism she had recognized someone's hallucinatory face. Marianne used to use a word to describe people in Patti's condition that I still like: bonkers.

Patti needed to mourn, I knew. Her overcompensation and the overdone triumph of the funeral service made it clear to me that she was mad at God for taking Ray. She had to admit to her feelings before the healing process of mourning could begin. I didn't know Patti that well then, and I wasn't sure whether she could handle what I was about to do. I also knew that I didn't like her very much, which made me question my motives; but in the main I was trying to save her from the depression that she was headed for if I didn't do something soon. "Patti," I said, "before we talk about the arrangements, I have a couple of questions. Things which, as your pastor, it would be helpful for me to know."

"Anything, Pastor," she said, and sat down in the chair at

what must have been her writing desk. "You've been so consider-
ate and wonderful."

"Patti, did you love Ray?"

"Very much," she said, concerned.

"I mean, what was your life together like?"

"We had fifteen of the most wonderful years ever. Many
women live for much longer with their husbands, but they're
never really happy with them. I was. I'm so thankful to the Lord
for every minute of those fifteen years.

"Fifteen years of marriage. I'm surprised, then, that, you're
not sad."

"But Pastor, I know my Redeemer liveth. All those things
you said; Ray is with the Lord. We know that."

"I know, Patti," I said, in a way that might have seemed
peremptory or rushed. "But *we* are here. You don't have Ray
here anymore, with you. Not ever again. I would think that
would make you sad. I would think you would miss him."

"Pastor!" she said, outraged and hurt. Her unlined expression of bliss was broken now, her eyelids heavy, her cheeks
beginning to give with her grief.

"I think you are sad, Patti. I think you are sad and angry
about Ray's death. I would be."

"Pastor," she said again, this time as if calling for help.

"I mean, think about the way he died, a truck running him
down, driven by a man in his own employ. Goodness."

"Stop it," she said, pleading. "Why are you saying these
things?"

"Then there's the whole concept of God's part in it, Patti.
Why would God take him away from you like that? Look at you.
What are you going to do now, a woman who hasn't thought
about anything but her husband and family for the last fifteen
years. Ray left you some money, but it won't last forever. You're
in a pickle. You've got to raise the kids and somehow keep the
family together. You're really in no shape to get along without
Ray. What are you going to do without him? Doesn't the sover-
eign God of the universe know these things?"

I was looking straight at her as I went on, and yet she
reached back and threw the letter opener at me with such a quick
backhanded movement that I didn't have time to shield my head
with my forearm. I watched the instrument fly past to my left;

it had been heaved, not thrown, and it did not rotate end-over-end but revolved through a horizontal axis before it hit the wall.

Patti was on her feet. Horrified at what she had done, afraid of herself, enraged at me, she stood with her arms slightly out from her sides, shaking and unsteady on her feet, crying, taking great intakes of breath to sustain each astonished sob. Wanting to run, I imagine, but blocked by her guests, she was reduced to the experience of childhood terror, in which parents have adopted the bullying mask of the world. She looked at me, and said, "You . . . you." Then she looked down. She held one hand to her head, the thumb and middle finger at either temple, and I suspected that all her phantoms had taken off their celestial costumes and were standing naked.

A woman was calling from beyond the door. "Pastor? Patti? Are you all right?" The other guests, or at least some of them, were with the questioning woman; I could hear their shuffling movements as they maneuvered in the hall.

I was at the door when Patti spoke again, and for the last time that day to me. Her eyes were focused again, keen. "I hope," she said, "the Lord comes fifteen minutes before you're saved."

That was the most sinister way in which I'd ever heard anyone tell another person to go to hell, but as I made explanations for Patti, I was glad that she had rallied enough to see me as a villain. She had started to feel the pain, and I believed that eventually, after she had gotten through most of the grieving she had to do, she would see that I had only started her down a road she had to travel anyway, and the sooner the better. But there wasn't enough forgiveness in Patti for the matter to be resolved in such an expected way, and from the time she had counted me among the damned, I grew, in her eyes, in favor and stature with the Adversary.

So even as we stood at Walt Winter's graveside, we were back in Patti's bedroom again, except that she had attracted a chorus of onlookers, who now stood about us, wondering what was going on. She became aware of their presence, too, and changed her tone. "No, I don't think it's a matter of decency with you, Pastor. I hate to say this, but I saw you laughing after the message. We all did. What are we to think, Pastor? What can we think. We love you in the Lord, but how can we support you in your present position, if you can't uphold us spiritually? Think how Dorothy must have felt. It's a matter of basic mental competency." She paused, and smiled a sweet, pathetic, condescending smile.

"Patti," I said, "you've never gotten over Ray's death. That's why you're doing this now. You and I know that. Don't compound the problem," I said, raising my voice, and meeting the eyes of several in the chorus, "by misrepresenting me to your friends. No one mentally incompetent could have spoken as I did today."

"Pastor," she said, "We're going to get you help, even if you can't admit that you need that help."

"What do you mean?"

"You are destroying yourself, Ted. There's a special meeting of the board of deacons tonight and my committee is going to propose that we give you the time you need to get help."

"You mean a sabbatical?"

"Well, no. The sheep need a shepherd and how can we know if you'll ever be ready to come back?"

"You're trying to get me fired. Why don't you say it after me, one time: *fieurrdt*. So you won't confuse the deacons. They're not well versed in spiritual obscenities, Patti."

She turned to the chorus, shrugged her shoulders as if to say, what can anybody do, walked to the side of her friend, Maggie Cook, and then turned and left with her.

I had avoided any violence and had even avoided screaming. I had avoided sarcasm, until the last. But I had not avoided this special session of the board of deacons at which SOP would propose my dismissal. I had not avoided the steel-laden truck which had turned onto my own turf and was now headed straight for me.

I went back to my office at the church to do a bit of thinking in the dark. Oh, the sweet dark. I sang Negro spirituals to myself down in the dark bowels of self-pity. I had about had it. I still cared, but I did not believe that I could counter SOP's efforts. It wasn't merely a matter of politics, of convincing people Patti was a hysterical woman on a two-year, vindictive jag. The worse thing about lies is that they can have more force than truth even when the truth is known, if they appeal enough to the imagination, as Patti's falsehoods did. And so the situation would have to be changed; my little world needed redeeming. But I, didn't I know it, was no savior. "And if Christ has not risen, we of all men are most miserable," says the Apostle Paul. On that day the Lord's power seemed to me to have been buried afresh.

But I had the word for the day: hope. The contrary of everything I knew and felt then, hope loomed up before me with a death-cackle for a laugh. Tomorrow's word trotted out, too: charity. Faith, hope, and charity. Sin, justice, grace, faith, hope, and charity. Except for Sunday, the typology was complete, but whereas my nouns had filled me with confidence before, I now saw the string of them as a frail line of defense—a spider's web for a sailor's rigging.

I did not go home for dinner. In fact, I fell asleep there in my office—I was walking into another depression, into the arms of despair, where I have slept up to fifteen hours a day in the past—and woke up to find I had only twenty minutes to prepare for that night's service. I went to the private washroom attached to my office, and as I washed my face I remembered the times I have had elective surgery; a nurse always woke me and asked me to go to the bathroom and prepare myself for surgery. I did what she said, shivering, not because the hospital was truly cold early in the morning, but because you shiver when you wake up scared. And now I performed those same, simple tasks of washing up with the oddest sensation. I was preparing for a crucial appointment, and felt all of those hospital moments present in my private washroom. Before, the doctors had at least in a cursory way explained their procedures to me; on this occasion, however, I didn't know exactly how I would be cut up.

In my condition a sermon on hope could only be a perfunctory exercise. And it was.

I met with the board right after. We assembled in the fellowship hall below the sanctuary, the site of the prayer breakfast. For deacons' meetings, though, one of the folding cafeteria tables was set up on the stage, and when the sergeant-at-arms drew the curtain, we were in session. A standard amount of joking had to accompany this purely ceremonial closeting, for the men (no women admitted to *that* crowd) liked to think of themselves as protean figures, fine fellows with nothing to hide. Board meetings were often called following church functions: the men had to come anyway, for example, to the Father-and-Son banquet, right? These piggy-back arrangements were tolerated, but since the kitchen was just off the hall, there was the noise of clean-up crews to contend with, and board members found themselves shouting things at one another which properly should have been whispered, if voiced at all. The curtain had been drawn one night to act as a barrier against this. Somebody said something about the Great Wall of China, and that, shortened to The Great Wall, remained the curtain's name.

The Great Wall screened us on this night from Patti Murphy and other members of SOP, who sat in the banquet hall like onlookers waiting for the lights to dim before the execution. Or perhaps we were at a different stage in the proceedings; maybe they would be called as witnesses. I hoped not, as I took my place at the table, and saw the sergeant-at-arms pull his last pull at the curtain's drawstring. The space this left us in—the men on either side of the table touched the curtain or the rear wall if they rocked back in their chairs—felt unusually cramped. Perspiration broke out over me and my hands felt cold. It was as if a magician had placed me inside this box to disappear. Perhaps though, the box—more tall than wide—might be more properly called a casket, since a magician's assistant does return.

But did I want to return? Could I even carry on with Patti and the rest?

I looked at the men, hoping to divine what they wanted. Their expressions were placid, their eyes quiet, not timid or embarrassed; they were comfortable on this stage: for them it had scope, as if The Great Wall opened wide to the world. They were going to be just and fair and reasonable, and even spiritual; moreover, they were going to get to do something *important*. They looked pompous in the security of their predestined lines. If I had sensed anxiety, seen averted eyes, weak smiles, and the rest, I might have had a chance to persuade. None of that. Oh Lord, I thought, this is going to hurt.

Cecil asked Jerry Mansfield to lead in prayer. "Most

precious heavenly Father," he said. "You alone know the human heart. You alone will hold us accountable at the last. We thank you for this, because we know you understand us perfectly and therefore will judge us correctly. But Father, as frail as we are, we must sometimes make decisions. Give us wisdom then in these matters before us. We ask it in Jesus' name, Amen."

Oh Lord.

"Pastor," Cecil said. "Mrs. Murphy and others, many others, have urged members of this board to get from you an accounting, an explanation, for your recent behavior, and to discuss with you, in this review, whether God wants you to continue your ministry among us." He paused, put a hand under his chin, and pinched and stroked its bullfrog girth—that valuable voicebox. "Do you have any definite leading in this regard?"

"What do they say I've done?" I asked.

Rich Taylor, the sergeant-at-arms, a big man who even at forty-five struck one as having the build of a fullback—with large, round eyes, a Roman nose, and thick lips—a modern-day centurion, said, "We don't want those"—and here he lowered his voice—"people around. We didn't invite them."

Cecil said, "Of course not. You must believe us, Pastor. You're not on trial here."

"Just for my information, then, what are those people doing out there?"

"Patti asked if she might organize a prayer chain. People will be here all night to pray specifically for you."

"Wonderful."

"How," Cecil appealed, "was I to tell the woman she wasn't to pray?"

"All right, Cecil," Peter Henderson said. Peter was a small compact little man whose nose looked like a slightly impacted bullet. "Let's get to the issues."

"I have my agenda prepared," Cecil said, in a tone of fastidious rancor. "Now if you would, Pastor, please tell us your sense of God's direction in this."

"I don't mean to be impious, Cecil, but you fellows called the meeting. You're the one holding the agenda, Cecil."

"And the first item on it calls for you to make a statement."

"Let's move on to the second item, then."

"You have nothing to say in your defense?" Allen Gresham asked.

"Not unless I'm on trial."

"Pastor, why be like that?" Jerry Mansfield asked, pained.

"Because, Jerry, I've been called before my own board of deacons and asked to justify my recent actions and defend my performance as your pastor. This at the instigation of a vigilante committee. And I come in here and Cecil asks me to speak of the 'Lord's direction.' As if that had anything to do with it. What hogwash."

"I agree," Rich Taylor said, suddenly all worked up. "Allen called me and said we'd have to ask for your resignation tonight. Why? What's going on here?"

A number of men, including Cecil and Jerry, scowled at Allen, giving themselves away as co-conspirators.

"I said," Allen said, "that recent events seem to demand we do something. Now, if the pastor can explain. Well, then." And his small hands drummed on the table in a frightened percussive arpeggio.

" 'Recent events,' " Rich Taylor said, dubiously, my ally.

Peter Henderson, in a slow, insulting voice, said, as if correcting Rich, "He put Michael in the hospital."

Because of his build, Rich had probably had to counter taunts and insinuations about his intelligence all his life. "I know that," he said quickly. "But perhaps the pastor can explain." He looked at me.

"I was angry," I said.

Rich kept looking at me, and as he realized this was all I could say, his eyes left off searching mine, retreated, focused again, but from the vantage point of home ground, at a continent's remove now.

"Everyone gets angry," I said, still trying. "You were angry with Allen."

He put his index finger to the side of his Roman nose. I wouldn't have cared for the equation, either.

"We are missing what's crucial here," Jerry said. "It *is* a spiritual matter. This incident," he said, his reedy voice beginning to strain like a clarinet played by a novice—*in*cident! "This incident is only the most dramatic example of a more basic problem."

"Which is?" I asked.

"Tonight." He swallowed. He found it difficult to speak; the words would not sound, as if trapped. His face was shading toward a range of violet. He reared his head back and forward again as if, in his role as avenging angel, he had to emerge from clouds to deliver his verdict. "It's you!" he cried at last. "It's you! You asked us at the beginning of the week to judge you by this revival. Tonight you delivered a message on hope. It was bleak." His voice broke on "bleak," so he repeated it. "We don't know what's wrong. We would like to help. Believe me. At times you have such understanding."

I looked around the table. "You want me to resign?" They stared down adamantly. "I'm not sure what's wrong," I said. "I appreciate what Jerry's said. I want to keep on being a pastor. My ministry," and here I stopped, trying to control my emotions. "Forgive me. Or be patient a little longer. Let me finish the revival. Just let me finish that. I'll announce my resignation Sunday evening, after the final revival service."

What had it been? Farce, chicanery, or a twisted passion play? Before I left the meeting that night, as a few pitiful statements of thanksgiving for my ministry were made for the record, I looked up at the curtain hiding all this from the eyes of man. Its material was not plush or heavy; it was made out of light synthetic stuff; flame retardant gave its black surface a metallic sheen, which the red, blue, and yellow striplights illuminated—halloween colors that reminded me of carnivals with their freaks. Where was I? That curtain would open soon, and I'd walk back out of this, but I wondered if I would ever be able to speak reasonably again. I was not simply without a script now but without words. Oh, I would hear people speak to me and might reply but the words would sound in my ears and feel on my tongue as they had over that stretch when I was in the hospital, as meaningless intrusions on the world's silence. The book of nature would be closed to me: that curtain drawn.

At home I found Constance in our room, propped up in bed, reading *Architectural Digest*. She was in a blue flannel nightgown but—piquant detail—with her large pearl earrings still on, her hair perfect, while the TV opposite the bed projected its pictures toward her, unattended. I switched the set off as I crossed the room. I stood before my dresser, placing my cufflinks, wrist-watch, and keys in the tray where they rested each night.

"Hi," she said.

"Hi," I said, working my belt out of the trouser loops.

"How did it go?"

"The service or the board meeting?"

"So it was bad." She paused. "I wouldn't ask you to talk about it, normally, but since we have the decision to make, please tell me."

I turned around to face her; she was good, I thought, at being strong in the face of adversity, when the trouble fitted in with her plans. Like my deacons, happy in a predetermined course of action, her ability to remain calm sprang out of felicity; she could be felicitous when all was within her bounds. Her look was as undisturbed yet as bountiful as the surface of a well and I was near death from thirst. I reminded myself that even water can be poisoned, and I should not, as the rejected men from Gideon's army, drink unaware of the enemy.

But who was to say there was a battle to be fought? Not me, not that night. And was she my enemy?

I went over and sat on the edge of the bed. I took Constance's hands in mine.

"This has happened before," she said.

"Someone called you?"

"This has happened before. I've seen it in your face before, your cheeks giving down to that wounded mouth, the cleft in your chin so deep." She reached up and traced a line along my jaw, from my sideburn to the tip of my chin. She squeezed the two halves of the cleft together. "I'd like to mother you now. But I'm glad when you look this way that it's a man, not a boy, who's been hurt."

She embraced me. We held one another for a long time. She kissed me before we again drew apart.

"Oh, I need you," I said. "You'd make a wonderful preacher's wife."

"Really."

"Yes."

"Well, I think you'd make a fine decorator's husband."

"Don't say that. Don't make it a matter of sides just now."

"But Ted."

"Get ready to see the little boy," I said, and walked back over to the dresser.

"Daddy, my father, understands. He does. You two have different backgrounds but you do have your *pride* in common. After all, he had to retire and sell the business."

"I'm to retire."

"Don't be that way. You know what I mean. That's willful, and it *is* childish."

"He lives on the wealth he accumulated from that sale. What am I to live on? What can I get from this sale?"

"You have a choice still?"

"No."

"Good."

"*Good*," I said, mimicking her smug voice.

"I will not let this be my problem. Not this time!"

"See the woman and her comfort."

"I think we've arrived at the point where I won't be able to sleep with you in this room," she said, her face crimson, her earrings roseate.

"I was the one fired tonight. I think *you* should sleep in the guest room." I started to enjoy this; a child is not responsible.

"This is my house."

"House? The whole world's yours. The devil seems to have given you a mortgage."

"Please leave."

"Thank you for your permission," I said. (I'm not good at fighting; I can't fight fair and only the most beautiful arias can justify such theatrics.)

Benjamin came out of his room at the lower end of the hall, his hair mussed, his pajama bottoms riding high and twisted to one side. He must have been tossing in bed, listening; his face was pale and his eyes looked canceled with half-circles of ink. He was startled, either by the light or my presence—the latter, probably, since he didn't blink or squint but kept his eyes open like a hare caught by hypnotic headlights. "Benjamin," I said.

He came back to himself, and asked his question in a grouchy voice: "Why can't you guys stop it?" From his tone, he might have gone on to say," So I can get some sleep," but he let the question serve for now and evermore.

I didn't answer, but went to him and attempted to turn him, my hands on his shoulders, back toward his room.

He resisted. "I have to go."

I waited for him to come back from the bathroom, seated on his single and rather small bed. The only light was from the hall. There was little to see in his room anyway: Constance would put up a racing car or baseball poster occasionally, and Ben would promptly take it down; he kept the walls blank—insults to our touted image of a family.

He came back in, taking mincing steps, his shoulders hunched, his toes pinched inward, the walk of a humiliated domestic servant. I tucked him into bed, and he rolled away from me without a word.

I couldn't have this. I got into bed beside him. I looped my arm over his side and chest and hugged him to me. He slid all in one piece, his legs remaining in a tucked position as his back with its pointed shoulder blades met and rested against my chest; his body, the carapace of a sea-creature, was quite beautiful, yet cold and as if uninhabited. How long had it been since we had lain in the same bed? Long enough for our mutual fear to make the bedclothes feel cold and damp. He was too old for me to comfort him in this way, too aware of me as the force which had thrown him up on this uncongenial shore of my difficult marriage. His ribcage underneath my forearm rose and fell irregularly. I didn't dare move. I could only hope that sleep would make him forgetful, and that he might sail back into the depths of his relative innocence.

Soon, happily, his breathing became more regular. A harsh scent, salt and sulfur, rose from his body, and then he began to radiate heat. I put my hand on his downside shoulder and hugged him even closer. His flesh was now as spongy as bread. He smelled like Benjamin again, his own scent drawing me into his life as it never would again; henceforth, only lovers would know him in this way. As a parent, I was permitted this one last time to lie by him, he not as yet having completed the second gestation period of childhood, in which the more important separation of flesh from flesh occurs. He was almost in possession of his own soul, however, or so one must presume; at the age of accountability—lovely and terrifying thought. Simply to get into bed with him again and hold him wouldn't be possible.

In our last communion as father and son, then, we sacrificed our life together. I could only hope that I had taught him enough of my faith so that on the appointed day this death and our earthly deaths would be swallowed up in victory. But, oh, when I thought of all the pain in our family caused by my ministry I wondered how he could possibly grow up to regard the faith with love and accept it for himself; it was far more likely he would be morose, or hate both it and me. How many times would I have lost him then? And how could there be a heaven for me?

I whispered, "I love you, Ben."

He breathed out a *hhhmmmmm* in response, a sign he had heard if not understood.

I waited until he went completely to sleep, and then I got out of his bed and went into the living room.

I did not turn on a light, but sat on the couch and looked toward where the glass doors opened onto the back yard. The moon must have been full; it was lighter outside than in, which made the doors appear to be the opening of a cave or tomb.

Well, if my fancy had grown morbid that day, there had certainly been enough deaths to justify it. The death of Walt Winters before I had befriended him, the death of my ministry at the church, in part brought on by the death of my relationship with Patti Murphy on the day of her husband's funeral; the death of fighting with Constance, the death of my example to Marianne and Benjamin—in sum, the death of the hope that should be within me.

I prayed as Martha had, asking why Christ could not have intervened before the death of Lazarus. Why did you wait, O Lord? The thing that struck me about all the deaths I had known that day was how *unnecessary* they were. For that is death, isn't it, the end of meaning? Perhaps Christ would yet arrive and say, Lazarus, come forth! Wherever I went until that time, I would be knocking around a tomb this quietly deserted and this vast.

Saturday:

Love

Constance and I hid our fights from Benjamin as best we could—not too well, which my crawling into bed with my son the previous night had proved. Still, we did not want him to walk sleepy-eyed into the living room on the mornings after and find me sleeping on the couch. Family policy required that I slip back into our bedroom before he awoke, at the prompting of his interior clock, with its Swiss accuracy, at precisely seven.

I opened our bedroom door slowly, trying to gauge the speed of its swing, pushing it fast enough for it not to creak, but slowly enough for it not to bind with the jamb and start vibrating, in which case it emitted a series of "wa" sounds, like an old ceiling fan starting up. Constance was lying on her side with her back to me.

I put my shoes in my closet, hung up my tie and the jacket of my suit, which I'd slept in, and took the three steps over to my dresser, where I laid my shirt after I had folded it. Slipping out of my trousers, the clink of coins in my pocket sounded like muffled bells, and I had to dig my toes into the deep carpet to keep my steps from resounding, remembering some sound like this from before. I cocked my head and listened. There is something about the early morning, perhaps only the rebirth of our senses, that creates an atmosphere of silence into which sounds blossom and take residence in the world; so that moving about the room, attempting not to wake Constance, it was as if I were cluttering the place with solid objects, destroying the empty world of repose with *things*.

I got into bed at last and Constance turned over and asked me, in a wide awake voice, the time. Then she laughed.

I took her into my arms, something I might have done without a second thought years ago but which now took mental preparation. We looked at each other, two strangers on a busy sidewalk who have collided. My impulse to take her into my arms had been the reflexive memory of my love for her, which long ago had descended from my brain into every nerve. The great host of these nerves, a choir mighty in numbers and strengths, had sung out for her, in praise of her, in need of her. Her look changed into an ironical smirk, a what-do-you-think-you're-doing expression, which my mental preparations helped to ease.

I kissed her on the cheek.

"What time is it?" she asked again.

"Five."

I didn't ask why she hadn't been asleep. She probably had been, but Constance slept as lightly as a soldier who must keep his rifle by his bedside. A child of this world's preparation?

Her expression changed again: her eyes turned slightly inward, the two fingernail wrinkles between her eyebrows indenting.

I kissed her again, gently brushing her lips.

She embraced me in return and laid her head against mine, her chin nuzzling into my neck.

"I think we might move," I said.

She did not pull back but kept her head next to mine, whispering into my ear, "Back home? To Philadelphia?"

"Yes."

"You want to?"

"If I can find work. Anything at all."

"You're sure?"

"I've been thinking about it all night."

I hadn't answered her directly and she waited for me to continue, as if noting my evasion. Her next words were soft, but they were intended to be persuasive, if indirectly. "It's not an easy decision for me, either. I'd practically have to start over in the business."

"No, don't move," I said. "Keep your head there."

"You understand what I'm saying, Ted? We've had so much trouble, being of two minds in the past. I'd like to feel that we have a chance of it not being that way this time."

"I want to keep holding you. Hold on to you." She didn't reply. "How much?" I asked. "Thhiiiiiisssss much," I said, giving her a great squeeze.

"Ted,"she said, and laughed. "Ow. You'll hurt me. Enough now." She laughed again.

"Do I love you enough?" I asked, being serious.

"Much more than enough." She leaned back away from me, propping herself up on an elbow. "But you've loved your work more. Has that changed?"

"Does it have to?"

"Think of how people treat you. And look what it's done, turned you into a person who has to take out his frustrations in violence. I'm sorry, but that's the truth."

"No more than me—sorry, that is."

"Don't be self-indulgent. You've been above that."

"I was thinking about Michael. Again. Tell me how I'm supposed to stop loving my work."

"I didn't say that. I didn't ask that of you. Never. Have I?"

"Not directly."

"How can you say that? I've let you drag me all over the country, and I never took it to mean that you didn't love me."

"You have taken it to mean that I love my work more than you."

"Don't you?"

"I hope it's God I love and not my work."

"That's not what you just said."

"It's hard keeping them straight. My habitual sin. Forgive me."

"We're going to move then?"

"Is that how you interpret that?"

"What?"

"That the move will be my penance for the past?"

"*Ted.*"

"*Let it*, Constance." I reached out, pressing down with the back of my hand against the mattress and sliding this hand under her, so that I held her in both arms. "Let it." I kissed her and kissed her again, and then started to make love to her. It had been so long. She was light and soft in my arms, and my body ceased to be anything other than desire moving to meet its end. Its only sadness, its only joy, was that she, its bread, became its hunger: my appetite for her could never be satisfied, nor did I wish it to be.

She twisted away, turning her face to one side, pushing me away with both hands on my chest. "Ted, I'm sorry. I can't help thinking. You know how I am. That makes it impossible for me. Please understand. It's just too soon."

"I do."

And I did understand, but my body, of course, did not. I sat up and put my legs over the side of the bed, my back to her, and waited through the withering silence. I couldn't stand looking at her; she bore the contours of my desire's perfect match.

Finally, she scooted over to me, raised up, put her hand on my shoulder, kissed my neck, and said, "The shower's yours. Hot or cold."

Why couldn't Constance trust me? Throughout this account I have shown us at odds, but our skirmishes in that past week had been only the dueling of intelligence and counter-intelligence before a major military operation: we had met on every front but the true site—reconciliation.

Jealousy lay at the heart of the matter. The kind which this story speaks of in its essence, a jealousy which shows us to be impossibly more than animals, possessed of longings with divine ambitions. Jesus asked, "Is it not written in your law, I said, ye are gods?"

As I've written earlier, I worked for fourteen years at a church outside Boston. I always recall the suburb where we lived as it appeared in springtime; every tree and plant wore a green that made me believe I had never seen the color before. Many in my congregation devoted themselves to gardening, and I, too, came to enjoy the pastime. The toil involved—weeding and pruning and watering—rather than being laborious, served as a pretext for noting and appreciating the changes which each day brought into the life of our garden. I went out to look at the roses in the same way in which I eagerly awaited the final tally of attendance figures for the Sunday school on Monday mornings. In many ways, especially when compared to the spiritual high-jinks at my other churches, my pastorate was characterized by the peacefulness of the landscape itself. Those old oak and maple trees, stone fences, and clapboard houses mark what I've known of Shakespeare's green worlds: his Illyrias and Ardens and Belmonts.

But the bard would have found a certain portion of my ministry there wanting, for in it the physic of nature was poisoned by the corruption of the city and the deceitfulness of the heart. We seemed to be in Eden just after the Lord God pronounced his judgment of Eve, which included the curious clause "henceforth, thy desire shall be to thy husband." In the garden, evidently, Eve loved God as Adam did. But the Lord condemned her to loving her husband first; and certainly women have been suffering the affliction of their husbands ever since.

The wanting portion of my ministry appeared in the person of Amanda Trilling, who joined my suburban Boston church. She and her husband, Charles, had moved to the area from Philadelphia; I was given to understand that Charles had been lured away by a computer firm. I had been at my Illyrian church about five years then. Shaking hands at the back door after the eleven o'clock Sunday worship service, I met the couple for the first time. I always devoted a bit of extra attention to newcomers, asking them how they had heard of the church, and if they had any children, and exactly where their new home was located.

Instead of receiving my solicitude in the embarrassed and noncommital way of most folks, Amanda couldn't get enough of it. "I want to confess something to you," she said. "From the way you preached, well, I misjudged you. I thought you might be hard to talk to. You don't usually find someone who's obviously such a strong leader and someone you feel close to right away. Well, I've found that in you. You're absolutely wonderful. You must be terribly close to God. I bet you pray without ceasing. That's the kind of thing that's awfully hard for most of us to understand, but I can see it in your eyes, you know the deepest secrets, don't you?"

Her husband had drifted away by this time, and although I took a step toward him and called his name and started to extend my hand to say good-bye, he walked away without looking back, and his name was lost in the onrush of Amanda's words. I was forced to concentrate again on whatever it was she was saying. "I'm so relieved. I'll have to tell you some time about our church life in Philadelphia. Boy. The things that happened to us there. But this isn't the time or the place, is it? It never seems to be, does it? Isn't that just one of the most intolerable things about life? But when you preach it's like the soul of the whole congregation fills your words and we can all go home feeling like at long last we've been understood. That's exactly the way a preacher should be, but from the ones I've met. . ."

She went on. And on. Trying to conclude this and my later conversations with Amanda was like trying to swim beyond the breakwater on a day of heavy surf; there was always a good chance that one would be upended, borne along, and nearly suffocated.

About Constance's height (to speak explicitly of her), Amanda had dark hair which fell about her shoulders and ended in wispy tresses curling every which way. Her eyes popped out at you, as if she were opening them wide while saying "boo" to a child, but since they remained that way all the time they were genuinely unsettling. Her empress glasses emphasized this, magnifying the eyeballs themselves and decking them with black cat-wings which, although heavy, did not completely obscure her thick black eyebrows. She had a large mouth, and when she smiled the corners of it pulled back to expose several teeth behind the canines; to be fair, her teeth, white as chalk and perfectly straight, stood the exposure. Her chin looked like an inverted pyramid with it's apex lopped off, and this abrupt termination made me aware of her face's otherwise rectangular shape. Thus her long bangs and cat glasses, probably. Small breasted and broad hipped, she was deep in the haunches and somewhat squat, like a wing-backed chair. She favored loose fitting smocks, usually in a dark shade of blue or red, and was wearing one of wine-colored velveteen the first day we met.

Obviously, she made quite an impression on me—Amanda impressed everyone, and in a way which encouraged them to avoid her. To be frank, I had a nut on my hands.

Rather, Constance and I had a nut on our hands. Because the next Sunday, before the worship service began, Amanda introduced herself to Constance and sat down beside her in one of the front pews. Constance always sat up front, on purpose, still caring, at this time, that my work prospered. She hadn't reckoned, though, that anyone would sit beside her Sunday after Sunday, as Amanda did.

Amanda used the time before and after services and sometimes right in the midst of things—during the offering, for example—to ask Constance about me. Her questions first attempted to fill in my biography. She wasn't content, however, with a résumé of what pastorates I had held or even an account of my schooling, but delved into my parentage and upbringing. She also asked Constance how we met, how I had been on dates, and wanted to know especially whether I had been, in her own words, "a good kisser."

Her questions did not become as intimate as this might imply. Amanda had the heart of a young girl in many ways. She was also an omnivore of information concerning me; she prized Constance's telling her whether I ate the portion on my dinner plate that I liked the most first, or last, as much as she did on how well I "made out." We did not understand why she would find such details pertinent until later.

It goes without saying that Constance did not encourage Amanda. Constance did a fair impression of the Medusa, turning on Amanda her most outraged and baleful looks, but the herculean strength of Amanda's curiosity prevailed. Soon I started receiving letters from her. I include a selection from them here to document the course of our relationship in Amanda's imagination.

Dear Reverend March:

Do you know how wonderful you are? I've been coming to your church for two months (Constance and I have gotten to be such good friends!) and I've never heard a speaker so wise. Almost every Sunday now I listen to your sermons and wonder how you can know exactly what I need to hear. Thank you.

I wish I could repay you somehow. But I know a man of God like you doesn't want what other men do. Well, I won't cry (boo hoo), I'll be strong for both our sakes.

But if you ever need my help, *for any reason at all*, please call. (466-9935)

Devotedly,

Amanda

Dear Pastor:

I had to write after this morning's service. I must warn you about something. When you walk to the side of the pulpit, plant your feet apart and point to the heavens, your long legs look sinfully powerful. It's thrilling! But I'm afraid it's indecent. Have pity on us women! Have pity on Amanda!

This isn't criticism. It's not. It's simply a piece of advice that will help you avoid certain situations. Perhaps we could discuss this in your study?

A weaker sister,

Amanda

Dear Pastor:

Do you often get letters from the ladies in your church? Do they tell you the secret things that are in their hearts, while they pretend to look for the key? How do you know us so well? You've found your way into our hearts and are knocking, knocking, knocking.

Sometimes late at night I can hear my heart beating and the sound it makes is you rapping your knuckles on my chamber door.

Yours in charity,

Amanda

Dear Reverend March:

I made up a poem about you. I don't think Constance will mind. No one could ever love you like she does.

Ted be nimble
Amanda be quick
Tie yourselves up
With a burning wick.

Love in the heavens
Love in the dells
Love that lights
the darkness of hell.

Wish I may
Wish I might
Wish to be
that light's own wife.

Tonight I don't have to rely on wishes, for it's Wednesday and I'll see you at prayer meeting.

Until then,

Amanda

Dear Rev:

How big is your imagination? Sometimes I imagine things you wouldn't believe.

Picture a feast in ancient Rome. I would be one of the Christians, tied to a stake and about to be set on fire to light the festivities. But you would turn a favorable eye on me and ask me if I'd like to dance for the guests and for my life. I come down and put the rest of your harem to shame. Caesar wants me for himself and offers me half his kingdom. But I ask only to remain your slave. Forevermore. Picture that.

Picture, picture on the wall, who is the fairest of them all? Me? No, Constance.

Come to Rome with me, cheri. Oops, wrong language. I will always be yours,

Amo,
Amas,
Amat,

Amanda

Dear Teddy Bear:

I want to take you out from my closet and play with you. I want to hold you in my arms until we drift off to sleep. And in my dream you will come to life. I will kiss you, and you will not be a teddy bear at all but the prince. And when you kiss me in the dream, we will awake, and find ourselves in each other's arms. Naked.

I don't even know how much hair you have on your body. Could you find a way to reveal this to me, because I like men without much body hair. But if you truly are a burly old hairy bear, I'll cope.

Love you muchly,

Amanda

Dearest Ted:

Thank you so much for preaching last Sunday on the woman caught in adultery. I know that was for me. I caught the Morse code flashing from your eyes. Boy, never a truer word was spoken than when the Lord said that only those without sin should cast the first stone. So, go ahead. Cast the first stone. Hurl it. Hurt me. I can take it.

But please don't take your love from me.

A penitent slave,

Amanda

Dear Ted:

What do you think of oysters? Vitamin E. I was hoping you would think of Vitamin E. That's *all* I think about these days. It's like having a jingle in my head that I can't get rid of. Vitamin E, Vitamin E, Vitamin E. Do you take it?

Do you think this could be an inspiration from God to found a community based upon the consumption of this essential life-enhancing chemical?

Ha. Caught you. Amanda isn't as crazy as you think she is. She's just crazy about you.

Amanda

My One and Only:

I've been thinking about our love affair, and I've decided we should keep things Platonic. Ours is a fairy tale romance, and as soon as we touched each other it would be midnight. What do you think? Should we?

Perhaps I'm losing heart, my love, but how can I go on like this without some encouragement? You are too good for me. Too spiritual. Sometimes I think you hardly touch the ground when you walk. But still, your feet must get dusty sometimes, and couldn't I be the one to wash your feet with my tears and dry them with my hair?

You can have anything you want anytime,

Amanda

On Sunday Amanda, as usual, sat beside Constance. From my vantage point on the podium I could see that Amanda's locks had been cut and set in the same style Constance wore, the hair brushed straight back and curled under just above the shoulders. The appearance of two such hairdos side by side made them look from a distance like the same wig in two different shades, silver blond and mahogany, on styrofoam heads in a beauty shop window. I hardly dared to imagine their individual selves and faces.

In the next weeks Amanda conformed her image more and more to Constance's. I have never had much faith in the premise of most cosmetics—that art can largely compensate for nature's deficiencies—but I confess that Amanda was able to turn herself into a facsimile of Constance. After her hair change, she discarded her cat glasses and took to wearing contacts. These not only changed the color of her eyes from brown to grey, but they also clouded the manic intensity of her eyes and lent her something of Constance's placidity. Next, she threw out her blue and purple smock wardrobe and started to wear the traditional cocktail dresses Constance has always favored. She must have purchased these in sizes for women with Constance's slim figure as well, for at first her broad bottom filled the dresses so that one could see the impression of her girdle beneath. A diet, however, reduced the girth of her bottom and thighs until she weighed no more than her model. She could not, of course, do anything about her large mouth, but I swear she found a way to darken her teeth to the rear of her canines so that even her smile was closer to Constance's. And as a final touch she shaved and shaped her eyebrows to thin and abruptly-attenuated lines. When we thought she had stopped, she dyed her hair. Still, her eyes could never be the deep-set and perfectly-round sort which distinguished my Diana. Thank heavens, indeed.

Unaccountably to me, Constance, at first nonplussed by Amanda's metamorphosis, gradually became sympathetic to her. Constance was certainly not in any sense flattered by Amanda's mimicry. Nonetheless, she tried to convince me that Amanda was harmless and needed someone who would take the time to understand her. She insisted that I let the situation be, and we stopped discussing it.

I did not let the matter go, however. I called Amanda's husband, Charles, and arranged for a meeting over lunch, and we sat down together at a good restaurant, an old colonial mansion with three or four tables in every low-ceilinged room—a place that served the best pecan rolls I have ever tasted.

After we ordered, I asked if Charles knew that his wife had been writing me letters. With another man I might have been afraid to bring up the idea that his wife was carrying on an imaginary love affair with me—another man might have wondered how imaginary the affair really was. But not Charles. There was something *stricken* about him. A short man with a body one could imagine becoming arthritic, Charles had thin yet coarse black hair; combed to one side, it rested above his high forehead like an overhanging roof. His small, weak eyes peeped out at me as, I imagine, a baby ostrich's might, through gold-tinted horn-rimmed glasses. Perhaps, though, his skin, which always appeared oily and tacky from sweat, was chiefly responsible for his harried look.

With the topic introduced, he took off his glasses, shut his eyes, and rubbed his temples with thumb and forefinger, the gesture of a man who has been through this before. The waitress served our entrees, and we ate and he talked. Two years after their marriage, I learned, Amanda's impersonations began. She had always been high strung, Charles said—"a fritzy circuit"— but after their marriage she had become strangely lifeless, complaining constantly of running a fever. Their family doctor took

Charles aside and asked him if there were any reason why Amanda might be depressed.

Charles didn't know, but he thought she had seen marriage as the be-all and end-all to her problems. But life just wasn't like that, he said. He was no Galahad—she always brought up that sort of story—and, though he tried, he simply couldn't be what his wife wanted. Yet, he still believed that she loved him. Two years after their marriage, Amanda improved. He thought she had found some way to reconcile herself to married life. And she had. Her "play-acting."

An administrator from a local college—they were living in Pittsburgh at the time—came to tell him that Amanda was impersonating a faculty member. She spent her days walking about the halls of the classroom buildings, in the library, and the faculty lounge, striking up conversations with people. She had gotten away with her act—it was a big campus—until she tried to pose as the teacher of a class on the first day of a new semester. The real professor called security.

"A cry for help, the doctor called it," Charles said. "But you know how doctors are, all patience and understanding and then they lay it on you. He wanted me to commit her." Charles left off speaking for a minute, took off his glasses, and sat blinking and sweating. "It's hard for anybody to believe this," he said, repositioning his glasses, "but I love my wife. How can any doctor, I don't care how smart, know better than me how to take care of her, huh? Maybe I've just been selfish, I don't know. I'm telling you she is as good a wife and mother as any. At home, Amanda treats me—well, she makes me feel loved."

I suspected that she did, and during his recitation I'd made a few pastoral remarks, much like a doctor, I supposed, and like the doctor had felt that Amanda should be hospitalized. But I had waited to "lay it on him" and was glad that I hadn't; perhaps Charles did know best. I certainly couldn't dispute his devotion to her.

He said, "We move when she begins to cause real trouble. Like now. Moving always shakes her out of whatever fantasy life she's living in. She acts perfectly normal for a while, sometimes for a long time. It depends on how long it takes her to find a more attractive life than hers—I think that's how it works. You know, I don't read much, I never have. I got through my humanities courses in college by taking careful notes on the professor's lectures and then memorizing them. Amanda's interest in all that, though, has made me think sometimes that I'd like to build a tower and keep her locked up in it. Then I'd be the most fascinating person she knew."

He tried to smile, he looked down, took off his glasses, extracted a handkerchief from his breast pocket, and cleaned the glasses as if, with effort, he could make them serve as his crystal ball. Vitamin E, I for some reason foolishly thought.

He said, "We'll go away. That's the best thing for us. I'm sorry Amanda has caused you all this trouble. We'll go away."

I told him I thought perhaps his wife did not need to be hospitalized; she might simply find a competent psychiatrist. Did they have the money for this type of treatment?

"I've been thinking about finding a good shrink myself," he said. "Look, I'll talk to her, I really will, after we move." He glanced up at me through those lenses, and I could see it was useless to insist or even suggest that they not move. Like even the gentlest of animals (for his face made me think of an opossum just then), he would fight if pressed.

"Please," he said. "I'm only asking you to give me time to find another job."

I imagined what his résumé must have looked like and pitied him. I assured him that I had only wanted to discuss the matter and that any course of action he might take was his concern. He said it had been good "to get my feedback," the first time I ever heard that expression, which fixed it forever in my mind as ludicrous, and we parted. For the time, he'd said, they would refrain from attending my services.

Shortly afterward, I received the first of a new series of letters. Amanda in these took to writing me as if she were Constance. And all the information she had extracted from Constance about our relationship contributed to her new and unnerving tactic.

My own Ted:
        Are you surprised that your wife should write to you? It may be highly unusual, I know, but I do have a clear purpose in mind.

Remember during your seminary days how we used to correspond? I have kept your love letters from those happy times, and I was rereading them just the other day. Oh, Ted, how we loved one another back then! But more important, how we *told* each other of our love. I believe we still have the same passionate lust and love for each other as we used to, but we do not express it as we did then. That's why I'm writing you this letter. I want us to write love letters to each other again, so that we can speak what's on our minds, in our hearts, and tell of the blood in other places.

We have been married now for almost fifteen years. I know the defeats you have suffered. I know how much it hurt you to lose your hair and develop that paunch. You are vain, my darling. But you are my darling still.

Each night when I crawl into bed with you I feel like a bride again. Well, not really like a bride, like that time during our engagement. Remember?

Please respond in kind and be the playful lover you are when we next meet.

Your own,

Constance

Dear Ted:

I thought your letter to me killing, simply killing. You do go on, and that's the way I like it. On and on and on.

Sometimes I feel slightly abashed at the way I look these days. But I have given birth to our children and, I think, must be forgiven my sagging derriere. And each time you come to me again I do feel reborn in your love. I feel once again the debutante I was when we first met. So come to me often, for no one likes to feel old.

Perhaps the thing which keeps our love from reigning with Anthony and Cleopatra and the Prince of Wales and Mrs. Simpson is my deep allegiance to my father. I cannot help myself in this, any more than you would be able to help yourself if your mother were still alive today. But darling, don't you realize that if I had not learned to love through my relationship with Daddy, I could not possibly be the wife I am to you. And think,

he taught me only so much and no more. You taught me all
the more.

Teach me more tonight.

Until then,

Constance

Amanda had many of Constance's favorite expressions down:
"highly unusual," "respond in kind" and "slightly abashed."
"Killing, simply killing" must have come from an old MGM
comedy with Cary Grant. But then Amanda was still so present
in the letters, also, with her interrogatory openings and free-
association departures from decorum.

They upset me so terribly at the time that I took them to
Constance. I wanted her to be aware of how Amanda's fantasy
was developing, and I wanted her to stop giving this woman any
more information about our private lives. Did Amanda really
know about that time during our engagement? I thought this
must be a lucky guess, and I never discussed it with Constance.

She found the letters no cause for concern. I tried to make
her promise not to feed the woman's imagination anymore, but
she made light of the matter and said that I was upset because
the letters had hit home. This was of a piece with Constance's
new attitude toward Amanda, because at some point during the
whole affair Constance began to enjoy the haughty flamboyance
of Amanda's masquerade, and looked upon her, I thought, as a
kind of living puppet or twin doll.

Then about two months after my lunch with Charles, he
and Amanda came to church and announced after the morning
worship service, at the back door where I had encountered them
for the first time, that they were moving to Florida. Before
Amanda could envelop me in conversation, Charles hauled her
off, his arm gripped tight around her shoulders, and then looked
back and gave me an ill-disguised high sign.

After they moved, however, another letter came.

Dear Ted:

What is love? Is it the thistle blown in secret through the
night?

Is it the suffering and pain I feel, now that we have parted? Is that why the Bible speaks of "becoming one flesh," because absence does not make the heart grow fonder, it breaks the heart? But why is it that we often only know we are in love through negative emotions? Anger, rivalry, and jealousy?

Sometimes I do not think I have, as you might say, the gift of loving. I wonder whether people have a talent for being in love and letting love make them happy. I have never felt "in love" for any length of time, and I'm brought up short when something, perhaps a woman you glance at in the street, makes me aware of how possessive I am.

It is hot here in Florida. They say a sultry climate stimulates some people. Not me.

I miss you. I have been missing you for a longer time than you'll ever know.

Pining with the loblolleys,

Constance

This letter disturbed me for a number of reasons, the most obvious of which was that the cure of moving had not worked. How long would Amanda go on harboring her fantasy? And what exertions on Constance's and my part to disabuse her of it might be required in the future? I also detected a change of voice in the letter which I did not know how to account for. The penchant for interrogatory sentences remained, along with the juvenile suggestiveness, but this letter had a more serious tone, and I was afraid that Amanda might be on the verge of entirely losing touch with reality.

The next letter, though, allayed some of my anxieties.

Dear put-upon pastor:

Who loves you more, Constance or Amanda?

I have been both so I know the answer to that question.

Yes, I am back to being Amanda. I leave you to Constance, and, although I'm sure you'll be relieved, I wonder if you won't regret the loss of Amanda's love. She, after all, never asked for anything in return.

Ted and Constance
sitting in a tree
k-i-s-s
i-n-g

First came love,
then came marriage
then came God
in a church-drawn carriage

Ted invoked Him,
Constance prayed to Ted
but nothing happened
in their big, wide bed.

Ted's on a limb
Constance is, too.
Amanda about sawed
their house in two.

Sorry, sorry,
she quickly said.
Something is funny
in my crazy head.

Loved each other once,
Now love each other twice
And be content with
your first wife.

That's probably the last poem I'll ever write. It takes love to inspire me, and love may be finished with me, as I am with you, as my poem shows.

So now that we aren't lovers anymore, I will ask one little favor. My husband and I are returning to Boston next week—he'll be doing a consulting job for his old firm. I'd like to see you in your office on Tuesday at two o'clock in the afternoon. I know you do counseling at that time, and perhaps you'll have to rearrange your schedule a bit, but please be waiting for me. I only want to say good-bye and give you something.

As before, until then,

Amanda

I debated whether to keep the appointment with Amanda or hide—I could have my secretary explain to her that I had been called to someone's deathbed. But I was curious. I wanted to see if she had actually abandoned her fantasy. Would she still be making herself up and dressing like Constance? The possibilities of her appearance intrigued me. Never before, however, had I spoken with Amanda in private and if, to satisfy my curiosity, I let her in, I did not know how I would get her out.

Then I thought of the button under my desk. I used it to signal my secretary to come in for dictation or other instructions. This button might be useful if Amanda went on and on, as she surely would: I would arrange with my secretary that when I pressed it she was to come in and tell me I was needed at the fictional deathbed.

Amanda's visit made me extremely anxious, and when my secretary brought her in at two on the dot, I was so upset I could hardly bring myself to look at her. She sat down on the couch and put out her hand as if about to pat the cushion and ask me to sit next to her, while I mentally upbraided myself for not having the couch removed for her visit. Putting my feet up on my desk, tilting far back in my reclinerlike office chair, I meant to suggest that I couldn't be more comfortable than where I was.

I took a quick glance and saw that she was apparently undergoing another metamorphosis: her hair remained à la Constance, but she had reverted to her empress glasses, these with darkened lenses, and not the flaring upturns encrusted with rhinestones. It was a bright but wintry fall day, and she wore a coat with a fox-tail collar, which she did not bother to take off (and I was certainly not going to come within the proximity necessary to help her to), and then she spoke in a voice which was nothing but colored exhalations. She had laryngitis.

I was overjoyed.

"I'm sorry," she said, in her hoarse whisper. "I wanted so much to talk with you." She tried to clear her throat and rasped out, "I'll give you my present and then I'd better go."

I said, still not really looking at her, how unfortunate it was that she had lost her voice, and how, in light of her illness, it was generous of her to be here.

"No, no," she whispered. She turned to look in her bag, and then turned back to me again. "Close your eyes now. Please. It's a surprise."

I did not care to close my eyes, but ostensibly I played along. I hit the button, though, just in case.

Then I heard her moving about. "Keep them closed, shut tight," she whispered. I heard her walking over to me, around the desk. I pivoted a quarter turn in my chair to face her and, unable to trust her any longer, opened my eyes and saw, at the instant that she sat herself on my knees, facing me, that she had unbuttoned her coat and was naked beneath it.

"Constance," I said.

The secretary knocked and came in. She had opened the door purposefully, but now it closed even faster behind her.

"Constance," I said again, in wonder. For it was not Amanda, nor Amanda playing Constance, but the real Constance, my wife, who had been playing Amanda supposedly playing Constance.

Right, it *was* Constance.

"Just hold me," she said.

I did, closely in my arms. She started kissing my ear. I kissed her throat in return. She put her hands to the back of my neck and lifted my lips to hers. She kissed me deeply and as if with a will not to let up. I ran my hands over her back, and then, even as she drew me into a closer embrace, placed my hands lightly at her waist and did nothing more than passively submit to her kisses. Her passion subsided. I tried to hold her again, but in a comforting way, and at this she gave me one last squeeze and stood back up.

Why had I not responded? Certainly I was upset and confused by Constance's strange behavior. But it was something else, something I couldn't identify until I knew more about the motives behind her Amanda charade. Constance buttoned her coat, walked back to the couch, and sat down again. "Do you want to talk about this?" I asked.

She now beckoned to me again to sit on the couch, extending a hand and drawing me to her, and a light shone in her, as if I were seeing the full moon through high, flying clouds. I sat and she pressed and kneaded my hands with her thumbs.

"We don't have to talk if you don't want to," I said.

She squeezed my hands harder. "You never noticed the postmarks on those last two letters you received from Amanda? Look again. I wrote them."

"I thought I detected something about the style. I should have guessed."

"Amanda. I detested her at first, but she kept after me until I saw a certain charm in her craziness. Even if it was only in her imagination, she loved you *completely*, in a way I felt you had kept me from doing. But you didn't respond to her at all, and she kept on. Why couldn't I? All she wanted was to be in my place. I ended up envying her. I wanted to become the part of Amanda that loved you so fanatically."

I tried to hold her again.

"No, wait, I want you to understand something, Ted. I've been bored. Or complacent. Or both. Anyway, at some point I started caring more for others and the opinion I thought they should have of me than for you. I've retreated into the role of the 'society woman' that my mother drilled into me. And I hate myself for it. I'm not sure what I was trying to do today. But you must understand that writing those letters helped. So today I became what I wanted to be. Amanda. It doesn't really make sense, does it?" She paused with a catch of the kind that it seemed Amanda's craziness should have caused in Amanda herself. "Hold me now, please. Hold me."

We embraced.

Much later, months after the incident, as the problems continued in our marriage, I began to understand why I hadn't accepted Constance's "gift," or been able to respond to her passion as she might have liked. It wasn't just shock or obstinacy on my part. Somehow I had known that Constance was trying to revivify our marriage with the water of her love, but she had sought to do it profanely: by displacing God, her rival for my affections, with the secular Amanda—a washout. If she could only for a moment loosen my attachment to God, then she could rebuild our marriage on the basis of human love alone (or so she must have reasoned) which for her was a much more congenial foundation. Amanda was to be the fulcrum to accomplish this. Constance was asking me to love her before all others, including God, and I couldn't do that. Not that human love isn't a wonderful accomplishment. But if it is to find its proper expression, it must body forth the love of the soul for God; if it's self-sufficient, it becomes destructive, as any sexuality that believes it is self-sufficient does. So, I reasoned, I found myself rejecting the openness of Constance's offer. This was surely the point at which those machinations of mental preparation, and my ensuing reserve, had begun.

Which wasn't all, to carry this through. Constance was also trying to rekindle the romance of our marriage, which had faded along with the fading promise of my career. In Amanda she saw a kind of purity of devotion to me that she had once had, and she thought that perhaps if she *became* Amanda, she could recapture it. Strangely, this had worked. For the brief moment when we embraced, before I stopped responding, I had felt a longing in Constance that had been absent in her since the first years of our marriage. Perhaps if I had simply been a husband, we would have rushed ahead and sorted out the metaphysics later. But I had been me, I had lost that opportunity, I had even sinned against our marriage by rebuffing her and insisting that my allegiance first be to God and afterward to her. To speak of the woe that is in marriage.

To speak of the woe that is in marriage, later that day I had a wedding to perform. The young husband and bride were so much in love that when, in counseling, I had asked them about their problems, they had pivoted toward one another on my couch, their knees swinging shut like two sides of a gate, and then, instantly reassured by glancing at one another, had looked back with disbelief at me, the evil naysayer. Couples like this cannot believe that the categories of their vows include contraries; for better, for richer, in health, are all they hear.

I was sitting in my church study after the service, thinking about these things, and the whole matter of love, the day's word, when I received a call from my daughter, Marianne.

"Dad," she said, "how's it going?"

"Till death do us part," I said.

"What?"

"Nothing. What's on your mind."

"I called to find out how you're doing, that's all. So tell me. What's up? What are you going to preach on tonight?"

"Love," I said. And added, "You're maneuvering, Marianne. You never ask me about my work unless you want something."

"Why are you in such a bad mood?"

"Tell me why you called."

"Love," she said.

"Love?"

"Or the lack of it. John moved out." A pause. "Aren't you going to say anything?"

"I'm glad. I didn't like him." I had almost forgotten his name.

"No sympathy? There are a lot of fish in the sea?"

"Where you're concerned, Marianne, there are far too many fish in the sea."

"*Thanks a lot.*" I heard the pain in her voice register. "I would be really angry with you right now, I should be, but I have to admit I'm kind of relieved myself. We weren't getting along."

"Now that's news to me."

"What do you mean?" Another pause. "OK, yeah, I'm sorry about what happened with the divan. But I was really pissed at you that day."

"Oh?"

"Yeah, for being you. For being my father who makes it difficult for me to make a relationship work."

"I'm a deterrent? I find that far-fetched."

"I don't know why I talk to you. I get on the phone and you start calling me a slut. It's very mean. Apologize."

"I apologize. Cross my heart. Whatever the circumstances, you're still my daughter, you know that."

"I really am bummed out about it, though. I cannot believe I fall for these insensitive jerks. Why do I?"

"I don't know." I was an insensitive jerk once, I was tempted to say.

"I want somebody strong, you know, and then I end up with these *children*. Little boys chasing girls on the playground, that's all it is with them. I find them, and I play tag. Maybe I should go to see a psychiatrist or a psychologist, one of those guys. What do you think?"

"I don't know."

"What I really called about was your move with Mother

back to Philadelphia. I called her about John and she told me. We were thinking I might move back with you. Stay a while in your new place until I can find a job and an apartment."

"If we go, you can certainly come too."

'Mom said you were going, for sure."

"Well, we are, I guess."

"So, it's OK?"

"I would miss you terribly if you didn't."

"I'm so old, Dad. I'm twenty-two. I shouldn't be depending on you this way. You think you're too easy on me? That I might be more grown up if you let me fall on my face and didn't pick me up?"

"I think that sometimes, yes."

"I do too. Don't stop though."

"All right. As you like it."

"Oh, Mom wants you to bring her meat order home from the butcher. I told her I wouldn't forget."

"Fine. If she calls again, tell her I got the message. Bye."

"Listen, dad, I love you. You know that, don't you?"

"Yes."

"Bye."

"Bye."

I had been thinking only a few moments of Marianne's state when I received another call, this one from my father-in-law.

"Ted, how are you?" he asked.

"Well enough," I said. And there, in that exchange, our relationship had already declared itself; he knew very well how I was. Passing the time of day about my state, as in a psychiatric ward, was a test, since nothing between us had single, simple meanings.

"Constance tells me I'm to have the good fortune of seeing you move back to the Main Line."

"Yes, we might do that."

"She wants, she says, to have the privilege of taking care of me. I don't need her to do that. She'll get in the staff's way. I don't want you to disrupt your lives for me in this way, Ted."

"Oh no." Your life has nothing to do with it, I almost said.

"Because I'm strong enough and I have my wits about me."

"Of course."

"I cannot say these things to Constance. I need your help in this matter with my only child."

He had protested once too many times, and I finally heard him and understood; Constance had fretted about his health for the last decade, since her mother had died, and now it was deteriorating. Suddenly, I realized, our long warfare might end; whoever had been my enemy may have died, and I might climb out of my trench and walk about his territory to see what had become of him.

"If we move, it will be pure selfishness on our part."

"Good. But why say 'if.' I thought Constance said you were decided about the matter."

"Provisionally."

"Well, I won't ask what the provisions are."

"My finding work. Why shouldn't I tell you? We're too old, Dick, to have such good manners."

"It's when you're old, Ted, that you see their value, when the body puts you back in the undignified position of a child."

"How sick are you? Please tell me."

"As I've said, not that unwell. I was speaking of small things, minor indignities. You know."

"Hold on a minute, will you?" My secretary had come in the door. In a stage whisper she told me that Jerry Mansfield had come to see me and was waiting in the outer office. I whispered back that he should come in when I was off the phone, in a minute or two. "Sorry, my secretary had to give me a message."

"That's all I have on my mind anyway. When do you think you'll be moving?"

"I may be free to start the process quite soon. But I'll need at least a month to wind up my affairs here."

"Perhaps we can all celebrate my birthday together later this year. I'll look forward to that. It's good, you know, to have things to look forward to. Keeps one going."

"I understand. Well, we'll be in touch. And I'll keep Constance from fretting over you as much as possible. I give you my word."

"I would appreciate that."

I thought he might have hung up, since he had a habit of

letting a conversation drift off while slowly replacing the receiver, rather than ending with a formal good-bye. But his voice came on once more: "Ted, you know we haven't been in accord on every family decision, but I want you to know that you can come back here without any misgivings on that score. I give you my *word* that I'll keep the hell out of your lives. I'm not up to interfering, and I never should have, I admit that."

"Thank you Dick. I appreciate that. We'll be in touch."

"Yes." And he drifted off, which a click and the dial tone confirmed after a few seconds.

Jerry came in and I stepped from behind my desk and shook his hand with a sense of conflict, of barely concealed tension, and our greetings ended as if we were both trying to think ahead to the next thing to say. I asked him to have a seat on the couch at the far end of my study, where the walls were covered with books, ordered and arranged on the built-in shelves by the Dewey Decimal System. I sat down in my rocker beside him.

"So what do you have to tell me?" I asked.

He looked down at this folded hands for a long time. "Pastor," he said, and raised his eyes to mine. "Pastor, I'm sure this whole matter has been worse on you than on anybody. But I want you to know that some of us have suffered with you. I helped bring you to this church, Ted, and I had great expectations for your ministry. Maybe that was a large part of the problem—we all expected too much. But I'm saying that this hasn't been easy for any of us. I haven't slept very well this past week. I've been tormented by this situation."

He hadn't slept, I could see; his milky complexion, with its ancient red freckles, had taken on a kind of translucence, the sheen of fish scales. He had ruddy pouches under his eyes. "Jerry," I said, "I understand that. And I appreciate it. If everyone had your integrity, a lot of things would have been different."

"Thank you. But what I want to say, the reason I came, in spite of what I said yesterday, is that this doesn't have to happen. I don't want to see you resign. There's only one thing I can't reconcile in my mind, Ted. It's not hitting Michael. We've all been angry enough at times to do just about anything. There but for the grace of God, right? But what I can't understand, what I don't know for sure, is whether *you still love the people*. All things are possible in love. It would take an uncommon saintliness, I know, to love and forgive Patti Murphy, but if you want to, if you are willing to try, I'll break my back to get this thing reversed. Can you?" He looked at me, his eyebrows forming an asymmetrical wedge, since one was stronger than its mate, his peregrine eyes watching.

"I don't know, Jerry. I really don't. The problems have built up until it's hard not to think of myself and my family first. What you're asking doesn't seem humanly possible."

"But with God all things are," he said.

"Yes. But you want an answer and I'm not sure I can give one. If I were to stay, I could only pray for a special grace. You see, this is my job. You know how much a man feels about his work. I would be much better off, the people of this church would be better off, if I didn't take that so seriously. At least Michael would." And I tried to smile.

"I suppose I can't ask for anything more than that. But isn't there something you can give me to fight for you with?"

"I promised the board I would resign. The way the timing is set up, I don't see how it's possible for me to renege."

"I think I can get a quorum together after the service. If I could, what would you say?"

"I don't know. I don't."

He stood up, and so did I. He looked so uncomfortable that I had to say something. "Jerry, I have adjusted to situations worse than this. I can again. You have not wronged me in any way. As the church used to say, Go in peace."

The tension about his eyes and mouth seemed to dissipate. And then the corners of his lips drew back, not in a smile, but a closed, distended line, a seal, as if I, a discourteous guest, had refused the meal he had set before me. He shook his head. "I will pray for a miracle," he said. "God has his hand on you, I just know it."

I said, "There are times when I wish he had a lighter touch."

Then he did smile, and shook his head once, and left.

I sat back down at my desk and saw by my wristwatch that

it was a few minutes past three o'clock. I tried to think of what
I might say at that evening's service. What were the exigencies
of charity in my own life? How could I speak of them?

"Thou shalt love the Lord thy God with all they heart, and
with all thy soul and with all thy strength, and with all thy mind;
and thy neighbor as thyself." The Old and New Testaments,
both, right there. "These things I command you, that ye love one
another." The Church. I heard these verses as if they were the
taunts of enemies, humiliating gibes which accused me of being
inept. The Scriptures read like a single long plea to please love.
Love! Love! Love! Nothing could be more obvious. But when I
considered how to go about enacting that commandment, I was
frustrated to the point of giving up. My life seemed like that
word game which consists of a crosshatch of letters that look at
first as if they are arranged randomly, but on closer inspection
reveal vertical, horizontal, and diagonal groupings which compose words. So, the demands of love lay before me, but I could
not see how they spelled out my course of action: I was frozen
within random configurations.

To Constance that morning I had said that I loved God, not
my work, before her—or to say it honestly, *more* than her. But
how did I express my love for God? Through my work. The past
week I had tried to hold on to my job, to find out whether I still
understood God enough to love him, and had failed to. Did I still
love him, then? Jerry had asked if I loved the people enough to
forgive the ones who had vilified me. The difficulty of the second
commandment, loving our neighbors, makes clear whether we
are fulfilling the first, loving God, as forgiving those who trespass
against us reveals what it means for God to forgive. Which put
everything into a cocked hat. I did not love my neighbor as
myself. I was unworthy of being the shepherd of my church.

Did I love God?

I did love Constance and Marianne and Benjamin, and I
might even come to love my father-in-law, or at least take pity
on him as he faced death. Perhaps I had opposed my love for God
with love for my wife because I, like Constance in the Amanda
affair, saw the attraction of the fantasy—the power to love whole-
heartedly without receiving a rebuff. Which would mean that
God was simply not there. But not necessarily, for "the Lord
chastens whom he loves." The faith has always had its escape
clauses.

"God is love."

As usual, I knew I must start all over again at the very first lesson. And then I knew what I would do. Whether I would once again interpret my life in terms of the great nouns of the faith, or discover what I knew in Constance's arms, at the center of our family, through charity, or simply content myself with the immediate poetry of the flesh and all things human—love as the refraction of glory in the sensuous and sensual, or merely the sound and the light show of a biological wizard—whatever the state, I knew where I would find the satisfactions left to me.

I asked my secretary, Donna, to come in, and told her I was canceling that night's revival meeting.

She asked me if I was unwell.

I said no, I simply didn't see any point in holding the service.

She looked unexpectedly downcast at this; I asked her why.

"I was coming tonight."

"You were? You never come to special services."

"This week I've felt closer to you," she said. And I saw in her sudden timidity, her slightly bowed head and closed-in shoulders, that she meant it.

I thanked her. I asked her to post a notice of the cancellation on the back door to the sanctuary, on the side entrance, and on the way in through the educational building.

Before she left my office to do this, she said, "Don't change. You're you." And then she turned and was off.

There it was, love: brief, muted, awkward, and overwhelming. Who can fathom it? I went home to try.

I found Constance in her office. She was working at her tilting drawing table, under a light clamped to its side which, with its armlike skeleton, could be adjusted into an infinity of positions, and was now shining directly on the sketch she was making. She rotated in a semicircle on her drawing chair to face me, and I took the seat she uses when she's at her butcher-block desk. Her room at the back of the house, joining and extending the roofline of the second story, has a slanting ceiling extraordinarily high at the inside wall. Which gave her office the feel of those paintings in which St. Jerome labors away at the Vulgate in palatial quarters, an expansion of an intimate task in terms of its grand effects.

"You're home early," she said.

"For good," I said.

"What?"

"I think so. I'm pretty sure."

"You want to move, then."

"If I'm not locked up."

"You are *not* going to be locked up. David said there was no question of that."

"Well, then, we'll move."

Constance capped her rapidograph pen and put it on the stand at the side of her desk with its companions. She looked pleased, but in the way of someone whose victory has come too long after the time when it would have been sweet, or past the point of having energy left to celebrate.

"Are you going to announce it at the service this evening?"

"I've canceled the service."

"You did?"

"Yes."

"What was to have been the day's word?"

"Love."

"Oh."

"It made up my mind. I love you and Marianne and Benjamin. I don't know about anything else."

She got off her chair and came over to me. I stood and we embraced, holding each other, not speaking, not kissing and without the least caress, just holding each other. Finally she said, "Marianne's coming over. I'll make dinner for us all."

Constance, Marianne, Benjamin, and I assembled around the table, all spruced up, Constance in one of her classic cocktail dresses—an elegant shirt-dress in black, set off by her pearl earrings and necklace. Marianne had on a peasant blouse with red and orange embroidery around the bodice which, even without any cinch at its waist, made one conscious of her capacious breasts. Benjamin had put on a blue dress shirt with a button-down collar, tucked into his usual corduroys. And I had gotten out of my sharkskin suit coat, stripped off my tie and donned a plum-colored silk smoking jacket that Constance had given me three Christmases past—I had even tried on the cravat that went with it, but thought I looked ridiculous enough in the jacket, and stuffed the cravat back in its drawer.

Why we had dressed up wasn't clear. Constance must have talked Ben into it, and presumably telephoned Marianne after our talk, suggesting that any showiness might help cheer me up. I took my cue from Constance, when I saw her black dress laid out on the bed as she took her shower. Around the table, standing by our places as Marianne brought in the last of the dishes, we looked like a family on the first full day of its vacation; a bit better, our color higher as if from the mildest and most flattering case of sunburn; and more alert, our senses hungering after experience. In my smoking jacket, I took the pleasure anyone feels in playing a new role, with the sense of farce at finding in the role the true lineaments of one's character.

We sat down and Constance asked quickly if I wouldn't like to pray. I did. Constance had prepared one of my favorite dishes, veal saltimbocca, cutlets topped with proscuitto ham, and the whole covered with melted cheese. She had brought out a good bottle of her wine, a beaujolais, and I surprised everyone by asking if I might join Constance and Marianne in drinking a glass. Of course, then Benjamin wanted some, too, and we allowed him a thimbleful.

"A toast," Constance said. "Here's to my husband, Ted, who has never looked as young or as handsome as he does tonight." Marianne and Benjamin looked at their mother in disbelief, but she drank her toast and turned to me with bright eyes and her chin held high. My offspring finally followed her lead.

"A toast," I said. And Ben immediately demanded more wine. We tipped a little into his glass. "A toast," I said again, "to my wife, Constance, your mother, who is the fountain of youth."

We drank to her.

"A toast," Marianne said, and Constance and I smiled at each other, a little afraid of what she might say. "To my parents." Ben interrupted her, asking for more wine. We replenished his supply. "To my parents, who have endured the longest adolescence ever recorded—mine."

We laughed and drank and Ben clamored for more wine. We told him that he'd had enough, but he insisted on making *his* toast, so we relented. "I toast Marianne," he said, "who taught me about sex." With our laughter, Ben turned crimson, but I could see that he was pleased with himself, and now nearly grown up.

Later, propped up in bed, I was reading one of Constance's magazines—looking at the pretty models, really—when she walked out of the bathroom in a gossamer robe which concealed, I knew, a matching negligee. She got into bed next to me, propped up her pillow and sat there without taking a magazine or her current mystery novel from her night table, her arms folded. Dressing for the occasion had always been her sign that she wanted me to make love to her. After that morning, however, I wasn't sure.

"Do you want me to make love to you?" Sometimes you simply have to say it, I had learned.

"I don't know. I'd like you to kiss me."

I complied with her wishes. "Anything else?" I asked. She grabbed me under the arms and bit my ear, which did not lead to out-and-out rapture.

"Ted, will you be happy there, in Philadelphia?"

"I can't say. I've been unhappy for so long I sometimes think I never was happy. I know I was, but I can't remember it."

"In old books they use that phrase for sex: 'she made him happy.' "

"A lot to ask," I said.

"Yes," she said.

"I liked being with the kids tonight. We haven't had a time like that with the family since—well, who knows?"

"Ben is getting to be a stitch. Girls call him now, did you know that? One especially, Cheryl, though she gives other names, but I know her voice."

"Really?"

"Yes. He's confused by it, I think. Girls grow up faster."

"Until what age?" I asked.

"Death."

"Is that right?"

"Most girls, or women do." She paused, then said , "Years ago, Ted, before we left Boston, I thought time was slowing you down. I thought you were getting on an even keel like everybody else."

"Perhaps Marianne and I are two of a kind, from adolescence to senility with no stops in between." I waited for her response, but none came.

We sat for a moment or two.

"I'm so tired of having to think about things," she said.

"What?"

"I don't think it's going to work tonight, either."

"Oh."

"Do you mind if I go to sleep now? Or do you want to talk?"

"Go ahead and turn out the light. If I can't sleep, I'll go out to the living room and read."

I lay for some time in the darkness, with her back to me; she had curled on her side after switching off the bedtable lamp. After a while, I reached out and touched the valley of her waist and the steep incline of her hip. She did not stir.

I slipped out of bed. But before continuing into the living room, I turned back to look at her. She must have been sound asleep, for, turned on her side, she lay on her arm in a way that made it look as if it were growing out of her head, a posture that would have made anyone who had not left her body to the care of sleep uncomfortable.

About to end the day as I had begun it, keeping a vigil in our living room, but still pausing for another moment at the door, I wondered why I shouldn't be beside Constance, enjoying the end of sorrow that this night had promised. What fires burned on the hills, or what did I expect to appear? Perhaps my love for Constance kept me up, since it had never been fully satisfied or quenched. Perhaps she and she alone was the altar on the holy hill to which I must deliver myself up for a sacrifice. Hadn't I done this already? Spurned the Lord as a false lover, and taken up with this fetching deity?

As I write this, these words seem harsh, extreme, and make me uneasy, as if hubris really can be so committed. Without the words, that was what I felt, this uneasiness. Instead of going into the living room, I turned and knelt down at my side of the bed. I prayed that Constance would understand the whole matter of this account, somehow, and that eventually I would, too. A gripping pain streaked across my chest, and I was breathless with fear, until a quiver under my cupped hand, my heart, began to reassure me. I sweated and plunged into what I did best; I prayed.

Sunday:

Redemption

With my hands on the sides of the pulpit, gripping it in the bicycle position, as we spoke of it in seminary, and the people before me, falling away and then rising like a gulf to be traversed, I was about to deliver my farewell sermon on the Sunday evening at the end of revival week. Constance and Marianne and Benjamin sat together in one of the back pews on the right side. Patti Murphy was down front, among her SOP coterie. Across the main aisle from her were Cecil and Jerry and several other board members, not with their wives—I could pick their wives out from the crowd in other locations—but together, prepared to act in concert.

I stood in silence for a long time before beginning. I looked at the sky-blue ceiling, then down again at the people, a mosaic of faces, divided into quadrants by the blood-red carpet runners in the aisles. The building, the mahogany pews and the stained glass windows of the twelve apostles, six to a side, these things, this place, felt like home. Then I heard the crowd murmuring, and at first I mistook their whispers for anxiety about my ability to preach, but after turning to neighbors for confirmation, they were looking toward the front, on their left—my right. There I saw Michael Dennis, entering through a door from the educational building, take a seat in a front pew. He looked better; the swelling had gone down so that his nose looked merely as if he might have a severe head cold. As it happened, his timing made it seem that I had been explicitly waiting for him, and perhaps I had been.

"My message this evening, beloved," I said, my voice low but gathering with urgency, "is entitled, 'Pilgrimages.'

"Picture Moses, if you will: He is one hundred and twenty years old. He's an old, old Semite, with a hooked nose and spittle at the corners of his mouth. He wears a cloak that he has been sweating inside for more than forty years while the Israelites and he have been nomads. He's got two fellows on either side, who are there to help him toil up to the very top of Pisgah, at the summit of Mount Nebo. He needs their help, his limbs are brittle and arthritic—he hasn't felt anything but pain in his left hip for thirty years; but he doesn't want the aid of these Boy Scouts. He supports himself on his staff, the same one that became a serpent when he threw it down before Pharoah. The same one he hit the rock with, twice, and because of which he has to climb this blamed mountain instead of being carried into the Promised Land with pomp and circumstance.

"It takes a long time, beloved, for Moses to reach the line where the desert becomes a mountain forest and a longer time still until he climbs higher than the tree line. It takes longer, in fact, than absolutely necessary, because Moses knows he is going to die once he finishes climbing and so he takes his own sweet time. Wouldn't we all?

"He finally arrives, though, at the summit, and turns his eyes toward the Promised Land. What does he see?

"What does any man or woman see? All of life is a journey. A pilgrimage. And each moment is an arrival and a departure.

"We have all journeyed to this place tonight. To this time in our lives. To the top of our own Mount Nebos, if you like. What does each of us see?

"The Scriptures are silent about what happened to Moses on that final mountain. People usually assume that Moses had a look at the Promised Land, like a tourist at the Grand Canyon, and died happy. Others feel that Moses didn't die a natural death at all but was assumed into heaven like Enoch. The Scriptures report he was buried in the valley of Moab, and that the archangel Michael disputed with Satan over his body. But the Israelites never found his grave, a strange circumstance in the lives of a people who carried Joseph's bones with them when they left Egypt five generations after his death.

"I ask you tonight to consider the possibility that Moses fell into one last prophetic ecstasy. In his final vision this side of death he saw the tribes of Israel inhabit most of the Promised Land. Not all of it. Quickly he sees the Israelites take up with the gods of other peoples. The gods of the Amalekites, Hittites, Jebusites, Amorites, and Canaanites. They have been expressly commanded to exterminate these people and their totemic or physical gods, but they don't. They fail.

"Israel's kings become a necessary evil. Saul and David and Solomon rise up before Moses. He envies their power, and perhaps regrets not being more ambitious, as he had been instructed to be in the house of Pharoah. Next he sees the Northern and Southern tribes at war, trying to foist their leader on the other. This does not surprise Moses. He has had a lifetime of trouble keeping the peace in the Tent of the Presence. Finally, inevitably, comes the Babylonian captivity. The dream of the Promised Land vanishes and so does Moses' vision.

"Moses looks out over Canaan once more and sees he has led the Israelites . . . *Where?* Nowhere but back to Egypt. For they, the Israelites, *are* Egypt—they are carrying it with them wherever they go. Moses cannot believe that the Lord would do this to him, and in an utter rage he cries out to Jehovah and laments the futility of his long and arduous life. This was the extent of what it had all been about? The anxiety and pain and suffering and death? (So much death!) The Exodus nothing more than a change of venue? He can't believe it. And in the midst of giving the Lord a good piece of his mind, Moses dies, and the Lord and he settle things later."

I paused long enough for the people to understand I had made my point about Moses.

"Look at your own life, now, beloved. Your mother bore you in pain and grief. She changed your soiled diapers, kissed the bandage she put over your skinned knee, and wiped away your tears. She was proud of you when you graduated from grammar school and high school and perhaps very proud indeed when you made it through college. She treasured the cups you won in speech contests, the medals for races and the pins for becoming a cheerleader, or if you didn't win any of these and weren't singled out in this way, she made you understand you were important. It wasn't the end of the world.

"She saw you married and have children in your turn and she doted on such magnificent progeny.

"But now her strength has waned. She can no longer care for herself. And when you go to visit her the nurses are condescending in a way that robs her of her dignity. And perhaps during the most lucid moment of your talk with her—for the past has become a random file, its only order the before and after, suggested by whatever piece of information memory has picked out for the moment—during that moment when her eyes clear and she becomes aware of sitting in a wheelchair, she looks at you and says,'Why, you're fifty years old, aren't you?'

"And as you have seen your own body more and more conform to the decaying images of your parents, your father's early stoop, your mother's stringy calves, your father's poor eyesight, your mother's high blood pressure, you know surely that unless a terminal disease or sudden violence intervenes you will find yourself in that wheelchair with one eye on your prosperous son or daughter, and the other on death. And before your mother you weep, a child once more, as does she, once again your mother."

High up in the pulpit, I felt all the power returning, as if I were a kite sailing in the wind of the Spirit, or as if, like Samson, I had found in my extremity the man I had been created to be. I would sing it all out once more, high and low and rough and soft and dark and light, and bitter and sweet as it might be.

"Not just each of us, beloved, but everyone together is making this journey and this pilgrimage! We have come out of prehistory into history, learning how to store grain as well as knowledge. We have known our golden ages and our dark ones. We have seen great rulers: Pericles, Alexander, Charlemagne, Elizabeth, Victoria, and Elizabeth again. Philosophers like Socrates, Plato, Aristotle, Augustine, Aquinas, and Locke have taught us to love wisdom. The poets, Homer, Virgil, Dante, Shakespeare, Milton, and Wordsworth, have celebrated and decried life. As have the musicians, Bach, Beethoven, Chopin, and the artists, Praxiteles, Leonardo, Michelangelo, Vermeer, Picasso. The scientists have learned about creation. The discoveries of men like Harvey, Pasteur, Roentgen, and Salk have made our lives more secure and comfortable. And we know all of this because of the historians: Thucydides, Livy, Bede, Caedmon, Gibbon.

"But although we mark history with names and dates,

history has been, in the main, the story of people like you and me. Laborers, tradesmen, farmers, clergy, soldiers, bankers, and civil servants—all childen growing old as we sit in that wheelchair watching our own children grow old.

"Together, the great and the little, we have built civilization after civilization, the one conquering the other and in turn being conquered, clearing and building and being leveled again. They were as real as we are. Pathetic and noble by turns. Loving and hating.

"And here at the present summit of history we can see it all being wiped out. Immolated in a celestial firestorm, in the splitting of a very few and, up until this century, undetectable atoms.

"It is not given to man to know the times and their seasons; the end may come soon, and it may not. Yet the Bible long ago announced what we cannot avoid envisioning. 'And they (the devil and his forces) went up on the breadth of the earth, and compassed the camp of the saints about, and the beloved city: and fire came down from God out of heaven and devoured them.'

"History is a synonym for extinction.

"Let me say it again: *history is a synonym for extinction.* Our continuing life in the memories of others, in their genes, in the work that we have done and its consequences—these are merely fond notions. Nothing can take the chill out of the grave. Nothing. Though it isn't ultimately victorious, nothing can take the chill out of it. Nothing.

"Moses, and we and our fellows in all ages must suffer death, both the death of the body and the spiritual death of seeing our work come to nothing.

"But hear O Israel!" I cried out. "Our only hope, our only mediator and advocate is Jesus Christ.

"Born of a young girl in a stable with the sweet stench of hay and dung in the air, Jesus Christ cried out in our midst. Yes, angels announced his appearance to Mary and Joseph and to the shepherds. But Jesus Christ took his first breath in this world and screamed from the pain of it like any other baby, and that annunciation, of God accepting the pain entailed in being human, was by far the more important.

"He grew to be an adult, and, as he did, learned the

common human lessons. He longed for what he could not have, he was cheated and made to look a fool, he lay through long nights of nausea and fever. He watched his parents sin. He saw people he loved die.

"When he entered upon his public ministry his brothers thought he was crazy and his home town laughed at him. His own mother seems to have questioned whether wandering about the countryside and taking up with a bunch of fishermen had anything to do with what the angel—had it really been an angel?—had told her.

"The people were fickle. One day everybody wanted to make him their king, and the next day they were ready to stone him. They liked his baiting of the religious authorities, but they were afraid he had an impractical streak. He couldn't seem to get it through his head that now was the time to liberate the people from the tyranny of Rome. He wept and lamented the inconstancy of Jerusalem when he should have been organizing. Even his closest disciples had a temporal notion of what he should be about; they quarreled about who should be his right-hand man. They wanted him to crush their enemies.

"At the end of his ministry, with its miraculous and noble and frustrating events, Jesus came into Jerusalem to celebrate the Passover. He must have smiled ironically when he heard the multitudes hailing him and crying, *Hosanna!* It would be only a few days before even the stout and redoubtable Peter denied knowing him, and a few more hours after that when he would be executed as a criminal.

"As his death approached, Jesus must have thought about it more and more. He thought about it in the way you and I might anticipate open-heart surgery. We would know that the surgeon was going to cut us open with a knife from below the neck to our navel. We would know that our flesh would have to be pried apart so that the doctors would have room to operate. We would know that our ribcage would have to be cut down the center with a high-speed circular saw and broken open with a tool like a jack and that finally our heart would be placed on a table outside our bodies and repaired while our life was sustained by a machine. As these things occurred, we would be anesthetized, but unless we died on the table, we would return to our senses and know *all too well* what had been done. Jesus looked forward to his crucifixion in much the same way, except that he knew he would not be anesthetized; he knew that it would be necessary for him to refuse any relief that was offered.

"Why else do you think he prayed in Gethsemene, sweating drops of blood? From his first breath he had known the pain of this life, and he went to his crucifixion in the awful knowledge of what it would be like, in detail, to the blackness of the end.

"Still there was one surprise. It was the worst news that anybody has ever had.

"Scourged so that his back looked as if it had been slashed with razor blades. Crowned with a diadem of inch-long thorns so that his vision of the world in those last hours was tinted with blood. Spat upon, made to carry his cross until he dropped from exhaustion. Nailed to it through his hands and feet. Every muscle in his body starting to cramp. His lungs beginning to fail—he had to push up with his legs from the peg through his feet to inhale, every breath an agony that only delayed a more terrible pain. In this unimaginable state, Jesus Christ was stunned with a knowledge more horrible than any pain that the flesh is capable of. He cried out, *Eli, Eli, lama sabachthani!* My God, My God, why has thou forsaken me? And it was at that moment, when the Son was abandoned by the Father, when the Godhead received into itself the full measure of this world's condemnation, that Jesus Christ proclaimed *the first credo of every Christian.* For I say unto you, beloved, that until we have faith which calls upon God precisely when God is silent, we have not the faith of Jesus Christ. Through our Lord, the Godhead received the knowledge and judgment of hell and death, which is to die eternally aware of being abandoned by God. That was what Jesus Christ knew in that all-encompassing instant on the cross. It is no more than the fate of man and mankind, and no less."

I took several deep breaths. I heard my next words, like the forerunners of an unseen yet advancing army, already out into the air.

"But be of good cheer! As the Apostle Paul writes in the fifteenth chapter of first Corinthians: 'If in this life only (that is to say, not in the life beyond the grave) we have hope in Christ, we are of all men most miserable. But now is Christ risen from the dead, and become the firstfruits of them that sleep . . . For as in Adam all die, even so in Christ shall all be made alive.'

"Because we have a certain hope in Jesus Christ, we must not betray him by our unwillingness to die with him in his uncertainty. And when we are uncertain, we must claim, in our own agonies and passions, that he *is* our God, *my* God. As the Apostle writes: 'For now we see through a glass darkly; but then face to face: now I know in part; but then shall I know even as I am known.'

"Even so, come Lord Jesus. Amen."

The words left off their march. And suddenly I knew—as if I had been rendered nearly insensible by the difficulties of my own journey and had then, returning to my senses, become aware of having had in my ears for several minutes the sound of a stream and had indeed entered a cool and shady wood where I might refresh myself—I apprehended all at once that I had penetrated an utterly changed landscape. My words had created a camp, finally, the circle in which God's center is everywhere and his circumference nowhere. I saw each face in my congregation, and they were pellucid raindrops on a pane of God's house, each drop a globe in which the whole of the house was mirrored, and each drop a pearl, not finally an ephemeral gift of nature, but a permanent adornment of God's dwelling. And in that instant I dare to say that he gave me the eyes to see the souls in my congregation as he sees them at all times in his eternity: Michael in his need for recognition and Patti in her abhorrence of death and Cecil in his fear of ignorance and Jerry in his adoration of the normal and Constance in her prideful self-sufficiency and Marianne in her devotion to human love alone and Benjamin in his desire for control over his own life.

I was another Legion, inhabited by every one of these devils. And I knew that God's hatred of all of this was simply his desire to deliver us from the pain we had mistaken for life: his judgment was his love. Even in eclipse, however, the sun of God was to be seen in the transfigured faces of his people: the light was there; God was present as he had been in the pillar of fire before the Israelites.

People told me later that I stood before them weeping for what seemed minutes. I only remember the joy and that at some point I realized it was time for me to announce my resignation.

I decided not to. There were very good reasons why I should, and I couldn't muster anything like an argument to the contrary—except that God had set me on this holy hill, in the clement atmosphere of his grace, and I was *his* now as I never had been before, and he could do with me what he would. No, I did not make this gesture for my people. Curiously, at the end it had little to do with them at all. I let my silence stand as a sign that it was up to him and him alone where we journeyed from here on out. I had become a pilgrim.

So I gathered up my courage and asked Cecil and Jerry to come up onto the platform. The congregation whispered together, the sound of it like an orchestra tuning up in its oceanic mass and spumes of sound. I turned aside from the pulpit and huddled with the men. They were frightened, their faces drawn and bloodless.

"I'm not going to resign," I whispered.

"Do you have anything to say in your defense?" Jerry asked hopefully.

"The sermon was all."

Jerry turned aside.

"We have a contingency plan," Cecil said, his stage whisper touchingly dramatic and political and comic.

"You want to take over the service, then?" I asked, guessing what my fate was to be in all of this weighty hesitation.

Cecil replied, "Yes, but you stay right here on the platform with us."

Jerry and I took seats to the right of the lectern. Cecil went to the pulpit and asked all those who were not members of the church to please leave. A few people, all of them members, got up and left, probably innocent of the moment's occasion. Then Cecil explained that the board had asked me to resign, and I had not complied. Therefore, they felt compelled to put the issue to a vote of the entire church membership. Not wanting to prejudice the proceedings, the board would not make any statement as to its actions, but would simply invite anyone who desired to do so to speak to the issue before the vote.

Cecil recognized Patti Murphy. She stood and turned around to face the greater body of the congregation.

"This church," she said, her voice tremulous, probably from fear of public speaking, but tremulous in a way that made her words stand out with a shaky bravery, "this church, ever since my husband died, has been my whole life. It, you, all my friends, are my life. Most of you know that I have helped organize several discussion groups to speak to this very issue facing us. I did that because I felt—and our discussions have confirmed my feelings—that we have laid a burden on our pastor's heart and soul too difficult for him to bear. His lapses and failures are due to our own poor lack of faith and our failure to support him in prayer. I and those who have attended these discussions have spent many hours in prayer about his situation. We kept a vigil as the deacons met to consider their course of action. We have, more and more I'm afraid, been convicted that we have alienated this man to such an extent that, although God will and has forgiven us, his mercy would take Reverend March to another place. I don't mean it that way. I mean, another location where his gifts could be more fully used."

Patti then turned and faced me. "Pastor, I of all people regret that it has come to this. Especially with you, you who helped me so much in my time of grief. But where the Lord is, there is unity, and we have been divided too long." She turned back to the congregation but, after a moment's hesitation, seemed to decide to say no more and sat down.

Allen Gresham, the short former head usher who favored bright plaids like the jacket he had on that night, was up. "I'm not the spiritual person Patti is," he said. "And so I won't try to talk that way. But it seems to me that it's kind of like baseball. When a team is going rotten, it's usually the fault of the players. But you can't get rid of all the players, so you try to start over and change your luck by getting a new manager." He paused. "That's about it. A new manager." He sat down.

Mrs. Sunday, my educational director, stood up and said. "I can't believe this! You listen to Reverend March preach a sermon like that and then you get up and talk about him as if he were a shell of a man or some poor baseball manager. *Come on.* What have you got against him? Let's at least hear it, and then maybe we can find a means of reconciliation." She sat down and turned to look at me. I thanked her with a nod and a smile.

Her speech stopped the outpouring of sentiment for a time. Then Phil Slaughter was recognized.

"I'm for Mrs. Sunday," he said. "Let's come clean. Exactly what kind of a man are we dealing with here? Some of you may vaguely remember a young pastor in Oak Park, Illinois, about twenty-five years ago, who gained national notoriety by leading a movement to make sure a local murderer got the death penalty. Without his involvement, the man would have probably never been executed. A couple of the newspaper accounts even suggested that the pastor himself pulled the switch. I, for one, would like to know the truth of the matter. *Reverend?*"

A nervous silence spread through the congregation. I looked at Michael Dennis. He was slouched over with his elbows on his knees and his face, crimson, held in his hands. Patti Murphy appeared, for the first time since our confrontation in her bedroom, confused and disoriented. When I had told Michael this story in the hospital, I knew there was a chance he might use it against me. But I thought he would have the courage to first confront me directly about it; I was disappointed in him.

The congregation was waiting for my response. Although Phil had told the story very sketchily, leaving out everything that would soften the picture of me as a bloodthirsty tyrant, what could I say that would change anything? The brute conclusion of the matter overwhelmed any other consideration.

I rose and said, "Yes."

After that, all hell, as they say, broke loose.

Michael Dennis jumped up and shouted at Patti Murphy, "I told you to keep that strictly to yourself!"

"I did!" Patti shouted back. "I don't know how—"

"She didn't tell me!" Phil claimed. "After Reverend March told us that he had almost killed a man with a golf ball, I began thinking; if this guy can do a thing like that, what else is he capable of? So I did a little research and discovered your capital punishment thing."

"Are you saying you're against capital punishment?" someone shouted from the rear of the congregation.

"Of course he is!" another man shouted back, "Who in his right mind wouldn't be?"

"What about deterrence?" the first man called out. "We can't let these guys think they can get away with hacking up student nurses and murdering whole families!"

"Only God has the power over life and death!" another voice called.

"Hold it, everybody!" Cecil bellowed. He stroked his bull-frog double chin several times, his substitute for a wise old man pulling at his beard. "We're not here to debate capital punishment. We're here to determine if Reverend March is fit to be our pastor. Before we vote, does anyone have anything *of relevance* to add?"

Michael Dennis rose. His new nose, puffy face, and dark-circled eyes were the most dramatic, if not the most telling, testimony against me yet. "I've had a lot of time to think while I've been in the hospital these past few days." Michael said. "I was furious when it first happened. The pain . . ." He gestured as with vague laziness; he was having trouble organizing his thoughts. Had the general disorder of the meeting made its way into his brain, short-circuiting connections? Or was he confused at a deeper level—his skewed visage an emblem of his spiritual equilibrium having been equally knocked about? I couldn't tell.

He began again. "I don't know for sure what you should do about the pastor. He's made me aware of some things about myself that I'd never seen before." He paused and looked down. "I don't know what I'm going to do myself . . ." His diminishing voice here stopped. I thought he must be referring to the court actions but couldn't tell what the others made of this and hoped he would clear it up. He kept standing and looking down, however, and didn't speak.

"That's the kind of man we ought to have for our pastor!" a deacon shouted, rising at the other side of the auditorium and pointing at Michael. "He's still suffering, we can all see that, and yet he's beginning to forgive his enemy. He may be young but I don't think we've seen anything like his spiritual maturity from his boss!"

Michael held up both hands and waved them back and forth, half-blessing and half-urging the man to quiet down, it seemed. Then, slowly, Michael sat back down. I could see, although the others couldn't, how unhappy the entire scene made him.

A man rose and told everybody how I had insisted upon a Sunday school teaching program published by a denomination that had released its clergy from their obligation to believe in the Virgin Birth. Another mentioned how I had cut him dead in the street when he was with some business associates who were on their way to a coffee shop where I might have witnessed to them. A woman said I had laughed at her when she told me of her concern for the teenagers who spent their time in worship services holding hands. Another told of how impatient I had been with him when he called one night needing to talk over a morally perplexing decision he had to make in his business.

While these accusations were going on, from the time the dark secret of the execution had been revealed, I had been watching the reactions of Constance and Marianne and Benjamin. They looked like stoical members of a family at a state funeral, the children imitating their mother, whose face was blanched and her eyes lifted in an abstracted air that left you wondering whether she was in shock and daydreaming her way through the ceremony, or was utterly aware of her horrifying circumstances and the only way she could get through it was by counting off each second in her head with the knowledge that eventually the seconds must end.

And as the accusations accumulated without any further testimony on my behalf, Constance and my children prepared to leave. Marianne and Benjamin went out before her, and she turned back for a moment, standing at the very rear of the church, in the middle of the aisle, looking at me with a completely changed expression, beseeching me to come with them then and there, her body beseeching this, her brows knit, her hands folded. With the sea of my congregation between us, our places at that moment were an iconography of our life together: she at home in this world and I willfully stranded somewhere, perhaps still voyaging, but perhaps simply stranded on an island of calumny and foolishness. She seemed to observe me as one does a ship or an airplane about to depart, with a concentration so alert to any movement that the craft appears to break away before it actually does. Still she waited.

I prayed for an understanding of what to do, and decided that I must remain faithful to that moment of vision before my congregation, even though, seeing Constance waiting for me, the joy of the experience was replaced with cold and wearying duty.

She turned, and once out in the night broke into the stiff-legged trot that it seemed I hadn't seen since my seminary days, catching up with Marianne and Benjamin.

When Cecil was ready to take the vote, I went up to my office and waited there for the tally. I felt strangely light and free, as a condemned man might feel, I suppose, before he begins contemplating the entry of worms into his coffin. Also, ridiculously, I remembered with a disproportionate shame the time I had run for class president, in my junior year in high school and had lost. They announced the results at a school assembly, and I sensed that my friends around me leaned away when the principal read the other fellow's name. I thought of the judgment and the Lamb's Book of Life, and understood the terror that that particular scene has inspired through the ages. I looked at the little pony and at Constance's picture in its Plexiglass stand on my desk, sensing the upswing of another, seismic dislocation, when Jerry at last knocked and came in. He stood with the vote count in his hand as if it were his hat.

"How long will you give me to clear out," I asked, without any preliminary discussion or even greeting.

"Oh," He looked surprised at my mildness. "A week, two weeks, three."

"Was it close?"

"No."

"Has everyone gone home?"

"About."

"Thanks."

"Thanks?" His peregrine eyes took in my posture in the church's chair. He put a hand to his mouth, as if about to mention something he'd forgotten, but then didn't speak. I had a sudden sense that at that moment he had seen himself not as the avenging angel, as I'd been seeing him, but as Judas. He turned and left.

"Dear Jesus Christ," I prayed. "Behold the handmaid of the Lord; be it unto me according to thy word."

Part II

The Last Days

Tribulation

In the days after the end of the revival and my ministry in the church, Constance and I acted as if my firing were something we had been through before and knew how to deal with. I had lost other churches, of course; cleaned out offices in Atlanta and Tucson and holed up at home until I found another sanctum. But in going back on my promise to resign, in double-crossing Constance, I had forfeited the Philadelphia dream and the possibility of reconciliation with her.

This assumption underlay everything we said to one another in those next several days but, like the greater portion of the truth, it was never spoken of in so many words. We kept our voices low and talked sensibly about what tasks I should perform that day; when I would pack the books in my office, and where in the house we would store them, and so forth, until I exhausted the last remnants of my former employment. Then Constance began to speculate aloud about her "options," while I, disenfranchised, could only look on and murmur replies as needed, and watch and wait for her to decide on a definite course of action. Oh, those terrible conversations, so mature and sensible, when what I wanted to do was say the right thing, or scream at her. But no.

Ten days after my final Sunday at the church, after returning home from a lunch meeting with David, my lawyer, I found the house quiet and abandoned, with the air of desertion floating through the doorways. At first, I was simply, if keenly, exasperated. Constance's gesture seemed unreal, and I half expected her to return smiling—her only form of apology. Then I saw the note on her bedside table. I didn't snatch it up right away but walked through the house, visiting the corridors and rooms, and letting their emptiness enter my heart.

Then I came back and sat on the edge of the bed and read this:

Dear Ted,

Ben and I are on a plane to Philadelphia. I apologize for leaving in this way, but then you have rarely consulted me about your decisions. No, that's not what I want to say. Frankly, I didn't have the courage to leave otherwise.

Ben fought me, and I had to tell him we had agreed on this. Please support me. I will have an easier time being both mother and father if you look like the villian. It would seem the kind of sacrifice you're good at.

You see, I'm bitter, and I'll just end here before I say anything else. Give us some time, a week or so, and then you may call Ben at Daddy's.

C

I don't know how long I sat there. My arms felt numb and elongated—bare coastlines pounded senseless by an Arctic sea—and I wondered if I would ever move again into the animate world of impossible choices of this goddess, my Diana, or would remain this frozen waste.

It had grown dark outside before I stirred. I walked into the living room, sat down on the couch, and found myself relapsing into my wooden state—the depression that had brought on the revival that had brought on the rest. I did, however, awake from the dream of the usual to see my surroundings as a storybook of Constance's abilities and tastes: the dining room to my left with its French-Provincial table, the pastel colors in the living room, especially the soft peach carpet, and the painting above the stereo cabinet, with its complementary and contrasting electric blues and vinous purples—all of this, my home, spoke to me as Scripture used to speak to me, and said, *You don't belong.* I had been Constance's suitor, only, and now that she was gone my presence here in her house was an intrusion.

The doorbell rang. I didn't expect to answer it. But as I went toward the door I found myself feeling glad not only at the possibility of seeing someone but strangely pleased, relieved, actually, not to be so near paralysis.

It was Marianne.

I asked her in, and said that no one else was home.

"I know," she said. "I know. That's why I came over."

I embraced her. I felt what I had always felt holding my daughter, what a bigger woman she was than Constance, how the allure of her patchouli oil eluded me, and her habit of keeping her body fitted to mine disturbed me, and how I liked the way she would give my arm a comradely squeeze above the elbow. And then I felt my family through her and realized that what made our embrace different now was that she was the last member of the family left for me to hold. I began to cry with great galloping sobs that made it difficult to catch my breath.

"Maybe you should lie down on the couch, Dad," she said. "Want to?"

Forgive me, it felt like a temptation. I sat on the couch with my head in my hands and wept. She sat beside me for a long time, her arm around my shoulders, and then stood up, leaned over, and looked into my eyes like a doctor or a parent. "You're not in any physical pain?"

I shook my head.

"That's the truth?"

I nodded.

"I'll get you a compress anyway."

Her response was so much her mother's—which sent a ray of light down into the sorrow, making it easier to bear even while defining it more sharply.

She brought the damp washcloth and placed it on my head and placed my hand over it in a firm way that meant I was to hold it there. Sitting down by me, she rubbed my shoulders and kept asking me at intervals if I was all right. At last I choked out that I wasn't having a heart attack, and this seemed to keep her content to stay beside me and let me cry.

I became more calm, gradually. I wiped my eyes with the cloth, handed it back to her and told her, really, I was fine now.

She hugged me again, pulling me toward her with those strong arms looped under my own, pressing her head into the hollow of my neck. My returning tears were almost pleasurable, for I felt that they were now under control. I stood and walked across the room to the sliding doors and looked out to the pool and the hibiscus bushes beyond the deck. It helped to be able to stand there and look at our backyard in the tranquil night. I had always had the sense that I could slide back these doors and step out into my beginnings. I decided that I would spend more time in the backyard, and allow the vegetation and the water and the sun and soaking heat help to effect the healing that I needed.

"Have you eaten?" Marianne asked. Her need to check on me like a nurse seemed to overcome her patience.

I shook my head.

"What would you like?"

"Nothing now. I'm not hungry."

"You have to eat."

"Not now."

"But I came over to cook for you."

"Marianne," I said, and turned slowly around. "You know you can't cook."

"*Can too*," she said, imitating a brat.

"What then?"

"I'll fix you some eggs."

"It's late. I don't want eggs."

"A hamburger, then. Steak. I could go out for burritos. Just tell me what you want."

"I don't know what's in there. Anyway, I'll cook."

"Forget it," she said, and marched out to the kitchen.

I heard the suction, the kiss, of the refrigerator being opened, and then cabinets complaining on their dry hinges, then the clatter of plates. The noise of life. I turned again to the backyard. The cupboard next, and the chime of stainless-steel serving bowls. Glasses and pots and pans were shoved about in the porcelain sink, the gritty scrape registering in my back teeth. The racket died away after a while and then the kettle began to whistle. A moment later a crash came, the splashy sound of glass breaking and the *tss* of something hot. Marianne screamed. She had been hurt, I could tell.

I rushed in and found her bent over, holding one wrist down

at her thighs, her eyes closed tight; she took a breath and held it against the pain, rocking with it. Our filter coffee system had tumbled from the top of the stove, smashing the glass coffee pot and spilling grounds and the half-brewed coffee all over the front of the stove, down the floor and nearly over to the sink. I jumped to turn on the cold water, led Marianne to the sink, and plunged her scalded hand and wrist into the water.

She kept breathing hard and saying, "Oh, Daddy, I'm sorry . . . I'm sorry . . . I don't know what happened."

I got some paper towels and started to clean up the mess.

"No!" she screamed at me. "I'll do that. Dad, I said I'll do it!"

"Marianne."

"I can't handle this!" she screamed. She looked back down at her wrist and started crying.

I went over and put my arm lightly around her. "Can I at least get you some ointment?"

She looked up at me, and made a swipe at wiping away her tears with her good hand. "*No.* I'll be fine. I'm going to be fine. I'm going to clean up. And then I'm going to cook. It doesn't hurt that much. I'm . . . It's everything, you know."

"Thank you," I said. She didn't understand. "For screwing up. At least there are *some* things you can count on in this life."

"Dad," she said, as if scandalized. And then we both laughed "Is this really happening to our family?"

"It's not supposed to, is it?"

"Ben needs you still. I told her that."

"Let's not get into reporting conversations."

"OK. But what I meant was *I* still need you."

I gave her another hug. "Good. I need you." And what I meant to say was that she had, in the strictest sense, restored my soul, for on that night I would have been as lost and diffuse as that peasant's galaxy if Marianne hadn't been there to hold me and name me as her father.

Later, after we had cleaned up together, we sat down to a dinner of tuna-fish sandwiches and potato chips at the breakfast table in the kitchen. The fare increased my sense of exile from the blessed state of the routine, but its picnicky elements helped buck me up. Under the flourescent lighting in the kitchen, Marianne looked older: her mascara and powder had caked, lost their artful bond with her complexion, and the highlights at her cheek-bones looked too definite, as if they were welts or blaze marks. Even so, when she tilted her head to one side and curled the ends of her waist-length hair around and around her index finger, I was astonished at the number of young men who had dumped her.

We began to eat, and for several minutes didn't talk, hearing the domestic whine of the refrigerator and beyond that a silence which should have contained Constance and Ben.

An instant before I would have spoken, Marianne said, "Do you have any plans, Dad?"

"Not beyond the trial."

"I thought that was just a bluff."

"My lawyer tells me not to worry, but he also wants me to stay in town."

We took bites of our tuna-fish sandwiches and I found myself wishing that between Marianne and me the details of the case could be avoided.

"What's he like, Michael Dennis?"

"You've met Michael."

"Sure I've met him, but I don't understand why he wants to put you in jail. You've already lost your job."

"I hurt him pretty badly. He suffered while he was in the hospital. I visited him and saw that for myself."

She looked down, and the color in her cheeks became mottled—spots of an anxious pallor. "He was good looking," she said, keeping her gaze directed downwards.

"You needn't worry," I said. "His new nose will make him more of an Adonis than ever. A little too perfect, that's all." I watched her struggling to hide the satisfaction she took in this news, maintaining her same demure expression but with her hue of vitality returning—a clear sky, and the waters became clear once more for the young. "What about you?" I asked. "You were going to move with your mother."

"With the *family*. And maybe I'll go later, but I won't go like I'm in some spy picture. Which is what I don't understand. I mean, what changed? You were getting together on this, I thought, and then when I asked Mom what happened, she did her classic, 'It's-all-too-hopelessly-complicated.' But I pressed her and she said something about the difficulties of arranging these things, and stretched her neck like she does when she's lying. So what I'm asking is, what happened?"

"I tried to stay at the church. I fought, after I'd promised to turn tail and run."

"Yeah, you did. I know you did. Why?"

"I guess I value being a minister more than anything else."

"More than mother. And Ben and Me. That was the choice?"

"Your mother thought so. And in a way she's right." Marianne leaned back in her chair and held her chin in the manner of a businessman considering an alternate point of view. She wanted to look as if she could consider this proposition in a mature and imperial way. Nothing, of course, could be more threatening to one's daughter, whatever age she's reached, than having to reconcile her parents. I tried to buffer the truth. "It's the faith, Marianne. I value my life and my family, and the rest of this world, because I love God. If I lost that, I'd lose everything else."

"Like the verse about being willing to leave father and mother for Christ's sake."

"Yes, but I'm not a cultist. Not in that sense. You have to see, also, that following Christ should make you love your family even more in the end."

"Mother's too down-to-earth for that. But she's *always* been that way. So what's different now? Why couldn't you go on together?"

"I was cheating on her."

"You were?" Marianne said, dumbstruck. "You know, I once heard about this crazy lady in Boston who was after you."

"No, I've never touched another woman." The truth needed saying now, and although I hardly expected to fathom it that night, I tried: "Our situation is similar to what I said to you about loving too much that day. It's that and it's what it's made me into."

"Which is?"

"A failure, and a violent failure on top of that. Your mother really wants to save me, and I haven't let her."

"But you're so right together. I've never told you this, but I always thought you two were more interesting than any of my friends' parents while I was growing up."

"It's pleasing to me that you think that. But we haven't

done much together lately except fight. And by lately I mean the last decade."

"What can you expect of me, then? You're always getting on me about breaking up with guys, aren't you?"

"We want you to be happy."

"Well, Mother says I'm looking for a father figure in a man, so I must be doomed."

The conversation had suddenly switched directions, back toward Marianne, and that suited me fine. "That's what's known as a truism; it's so universal it isn't of any real value."

"Yes, it is. Like Gary, he was perfect, good looking, kind—a *dentist*, for godsakes. But his life didn't *mean* anything to him. He didn't really know what he wanted, or else he didn't want anything in particular. And I'm like that, I don't know what I want out of life, really, so why should it bother me? But it does. And everybody I meet and get into a relationship with is that way. And I end up hating them all. It's crazy. It's driving me right out of my *brain*. But there it is, and it's all your fault." She flashed me a coy smile.

"What are you going to do about the apartment now that John's moved out? Have you decided?"

"I had it in mind to bring that up, if you were stable enough."

"What do you mean?"

"You're all alone in this house. I have an apartment I don't really need."

"Oh, yes, *please*. Come live here. I . . . I would be grateful. Believe me, I would."

"Great!"

We thought about this a moment more and all the ways that it wouldn't be so congenial came to my mind, as I'm sure they came to hers. But to be frank, I was afraid of living alone after so many years, after all the habits of marriage, and I let Marianne's be the last word on the subject. *Great.*

Several weeks later, the trial, such as it was, took place. My lawyer David Demetris and I met the guard at the door and he showed us into the courtroom. There we waited at our table before the empty bench, in front of a small theatre of seats for spectators, all of which were also empty. David had taken me through the whole process that had brought us here, assuring me along the way that each step was our last, so I considered myself justified in doubting his assurance that my own passion play would end with the briefest of days in court. Nevertheless, as I sat waiting for the other participants to appear, I was buoyed up by the thought that the matter wasn't important enough for them to be punctual.

The bailiff arrived at last and spoke with us briefly, to make sure of our identities—that I was March as in *The People* v. *March*. Then he went to get the court reporter, who was lingering outside over a cup of coffee. After another twenty minutes, the prosecuting attorney arrived; he evidently had been the one holding things up, for soon the judge emerged from his chambers wearing the kind of robe I did for weddings.

The bailiff announced the presence of his honor, J. Packard Lamb, of the thirty-second district court in the state of California, while the prosecutor, across from us, riffled through his file of notes. The judge had the misfortune of being a dead ringer for his barnyard surname: actually, he looked more like a ram, his head blocklike, his eyes small—close-set and wet—and a long but lambishly flattened nose.

I turned to the prosecutor, praying that physiognomy would prove an old wives' tale, or that in my adversary's appearance I would find reason for hope. The prosecutor was tall and very thin—a miler in college, I would bet; he would not let up. He looked as if he still enjoyed the health of his days in training, and the only sign of his having aged was that his hair had thinned and in shape become a skullcap. I saw only concern in his face, as he continued to thumb through his notes.

The judge took his seat, the bailiff read the indictment: one count of felonious assault. He continued on with the history of the case, noting that I had pled not guilty and waived my right to a jury trial at the arraignment. The judge then asked the prosecutor to present his case.

The long-distance runner stood, but kept looking at his folder. When he spoke, his voice broke immediately, and he coughed to cover this. He then explained that he had taken over the case from someone on vacation, and either his office had lost the file, as he believed, or, as one of their secretaries had reported to him, the original prosecutor had understood that the case would never come to trail and so hadn't prepared for it. He had gone through the instructions and information given him by the other lawyer, but all he had been able to discover of relevance was the phone number of the alleged victim, Michael Dennis. He had been unable to reach the young man at this number. The arresting officers knew nothing more than what the charge contained. The prosecutor asked, rather weakly, whether the trial might be rescheduled.

David jumped to his feet and said very rapidly, with Greek inflections stealing their way into his voice, "Your honor, the state obviously has no real interest in prosecuting this case. I ask that a mistrial be declared and the charge dismissed."

The judge, David, and I looked back to the prosecutor as one. He looked steadfastly at his notes, but I could see his neck coloring pink, with speckles of crimson in razor-burn patches—so striking a reaction that it summoned up thoughts of chameleons.

"The prosecution seems to have no objection to the motion," the judge said. "Nor should it, considering the position it finds itself in."

The judge looked back to David and me. "Before I act on the defense's motion, I would like, with your permission, counselor, to ask the defendant a few questions." David did not reply directly but sat still, his arms folded across his chest, scowling. "Assault is a serious offense," the judge said. "It's unusual to see a clergyman before the court on such a charge." He spoke in the halting manner of someone simultaneously explaining himself and probing for secrets. "I will not require your client to be sworn in," he said, his voice growing testy, "but I want some information on why this man is before me, so I have a better sense of how to rule on counsel's motion."

I saw no harm in satisfying Judge Lamb, especially if it would get me out of his court in short order. Without a word to David, I said, "Your honor, I'll tell you what you want to know." David exhaled as if he would blow us out to sea.

The judge looked at David and sniffed. "The court appreciates your willingness to cooperate. If you would tell us what happened, then, in your own words."

And then I realized that in such a court anything could

happen and wished I'd kept my mouth shut. But I went ahead and told the story anyway, while David hummed from time to time, not loud enough for the judge to hear but with enough volume to register his exasperation with me, and perhaps suggest a toning down. The judge leaned forward and ducked his head lightly, hunching his shoulders. He seemed to find my position as a clergyman the spice in the story, for he gave out little grunts of recognition when I alluded to the pressures I was under due to my position. I hoped his sympathies were aligning along the analogous position he occupied in the public sphere. I couldn't tell, though. I made sure to emphasize that breaking Michael's nose was an accident caused by uncontrollable reflexes.

At the end of my story, he sat back and was about, I thought, to give me some advice, one man to another.

But at that moment someone behind me called out that he insisted on testifying. I looked back and saw Paul Corwin, dressed in the slightly military khaki fatigues that he had often worn in the films on his missionary work. His nose was beet red—whether from excitement or sunburn or booze, I couldn't tell. I sensed at once that Paul possessed again something of his old crusading zeal.

The judge said, mostly to me, "This man couldn't be Michael Dennis, could he?"

"No," I said.

"Of course not," he said, reconsidering. "Michael Dennis is a young man. Who is he, then?"

"The evangelist who broke down the first night of that revival I organized."

"I've come out" Paul boomed, "to serve as a character witness and to give this court an option which will serve the state's interests far better than incarcerating Reverend March."

David gave me a murderous look which expressed, exactly, what I felt toward Paul right then. Paul came forward and sat down beside me at our table. He gave my leg two great pats, and, as they say, exuded confidence—filled the atmosphere around us with it like an octopus surrounds itself with its own getaway cloud. I was sure he wasn't drinking, not yet. Or not now.

"We are not hearing testimony, exactly," the judge told him. "But the court would be interested in why you've come."

David looked toward the ceiling and puffed out his cheeks

and then exhaled mightily once more. Paul stood and began to pace before the bench in his cinematic style. Did he indeed view all the world as his stage? "Your honor," he said, "I am president and founder of an organization called Gospel Outreach. We are primarily a hunger-relief ministry. In the last twenty years we have channeled nearly half a billion dollars into about seventy countries worldwide. In other words, I have spent my life, your honor, as a man of peace, a minister of mercy, feeding the hungry multitudes and caring for orphans. Perhaps you have heard of our organization. We've received commendations from heads of state all over the globe. And our own government works very closely with us in distributing aid to impoverished nations. I'm honored to say that I've met and talked personally with the last four presidents of this country. One of them used to ask me to Camp David for weekends, incidentally. A beautiful, beautiful place. Every American should be happy that our leaders can find rest and solace there.

"But the point I'm trying to make your honor is that certainly if anyone is a man of peace, I am. I abhor violence. I have seen what devastation the evil in the heart of man has brought down on innocent people all over the world. I wouldn't be here today if I thought that my testimony in behalf of the Reverend Ted March would be inconsistent in any way with the testimony of my life.

"Reverend March and I have been friends for more than twenty-five years. There isn't a man in the ministry who is closer to me, and I'm happy to say it. That's why, when I heard that Ted and his congregation were unable to resolve their differences— which I must take responsibility for in part—I started inquiring to see what opportunities the denomination might offer Ted, a man who has served our church so well for so long. I went to Ted's house today to tell him that the denomination wants him to become its chaplain at the university medical center here in Los Angeles.

"His daughter, Marianne, whom I love as one of my own, told me about these proceedings, and I rushed here to suggest that, although the facts are against Ted, and might suggest to the overly imaginative some psychological problem, nothing could be further from the truth. The facts, plain as they seem to be, do not justify depriving this community of Ted's gifts. The denomination and I believe in the value of those gifts, and we ask the court, we plead, for mercy. Why not allow Ted, your honor, perhaps on the basis of probation, to pay for his crime by doing good works, by ministering to the sick and the suffering. Why, indeed, your honor, should the state insist on punishing a mild infraction of the law when the principals involved have forgiven each other and are now back on the closest of terms?"

"Wait a minute," I said. "What are you talking about, Paul?" The judge was shaking his head as if dazed.

"Michael."

"Michael?"

"He and Marianne are back at your house now waiting for the verdict."

"Your honor," David said, "would you please rule on my motion. I have a lunch appointment, and I'd like to go eat."

"Yes, all right. The case shall be dismissed on the grounds of insufficient evidence, etc., etc. You can fill in the rest of that, can't you?" he asked, looking at the court reporter. The man nodded yes. "The court thanks this witness for coming, and apologizes to the accused for any unnecessary anxiety these proceedings may have caused him." To Paul, he said, "About this job offer; will Reverend March have to work for you, Mr. Corwin?"

"No, he will be under the home-missions board."

"Well then, I recommend—let's call it my 'sentence' just among us—that you take the position, Mr. March, until you find something better." The judge gave a little tap with his gavel, stood and walked out with a lightness of step that had me seeing him abandoning himself to a mountainous field, *gamboling.*

With no cheers from spectators, no flashing cameras, the end of my trial left me with an irate lawyer and a confused friend. I pacified David by thanking him again and again. And then I went out to lunch with Paul. We ate at a good restaurant a short walk from the courthouse, a place where the lights are kept low, the tables spread with white linen and set with china and heavy cutlery, and warm rolls come to the table as a matter of course. Paul took one and buttered it as I told him how he'd nearly wire-rigged my day in court. He laughed at himself. He said he was feeling his old self and wanted me to see that he could still speak in public. "The forum inspired mostly rhetoric, and once I got going, I couldn't stop." He also got me to say I didn't mind, by insisting on his concern, his good intentions, and his ignorance of the situation. Anyway, I was free.

I asked him as soon as I was able about Michael being at the house with Marianne, phrasing the question into a statement, in order to disguise how shocked I was by this.

"Are they interested in one another?" he asked.

"Marianne usually seems interested, but it's hard for me to tell when she's serious. Did they look that way to you?"

"He was just there, but it seemed rather cozy, given the circumstances."

He had now eaten one roll and begun another, and saw me notice this.

"I'm eating again. On my way back, I think. I even want to go back out to the field, although that would probably finish me off." He put down the bread. "It's a crazy religion, Christianity. Not that you can't make a strong apology for it, but you know what I mean? The sociologists think it makes sense to let certain areas of the world starve, but it's the kind of sense I'm glad God doesn't make. Maybe I'm getting to be a mystic. I think we have to do what we're commanded to do and leave it up to God to orchestrate things. He's not interested in sacrifice, or theological hair-splitting; he wants obedience. I bet the music the angels sing isn't like the old hymns; I bet it's got a syncopated beat and some harmonies that would send you and me up the walls, like a fingernail scraping a blackboard. What do you think?"

"Maybe."

"Anyway, I'm better. The night I collapsed, I started feeling better right away. I had to be crushed. It got something out of my system, I think. I knew then that I'd been through the worst and I stopped being afraid. Our talk in that coffee shop helped."

"I'm glad."

"Are you all right? You don't seem that shaken by all you've been through. But you're not quite yourself, either."

"I lost Constance and Ben; they went back to Philadelphia."

"You don't mean she's filed for a divorce?"

"I doubt that she will, unless she finds somebody else she'd like to marry. You could say she has grounds of desertion."

"Marianne's at home with you, though."

"Yes."

"Look, take this job. It's about time the denomination took care of its walking wounded. Sorry. I mean, you've been making hospital calls your whole life; it's in your vision to see the world that way. This is something you know and can do without having a congregation to deal with all over again, at least at the start."

"I've always hated visitation, to tell you the truth. That whole part of the ministry terrifies me."

"Oh. Well, there will be other things."

"No. I might take it. Maybe I should. It was the judge's 'sentence' after all."

"I'll tell the board to find you something else. I have some pull there. Forget about it."

"No. I'm serious. In fact, it makes a lot of sense. You're not the only one who thinks Gabriel could be the original for Satchmo. There's definitely a whole lot of shakin' goin' on."

I had the presence of mind to excuse myself, later, in order to call home, while Paul waited to catch the waitress's eye. I wanted to rush back and question Marianne about Michael, but needed to have him out of the house, so the phoning in of my good news would serve this purpose. We spoke briefly—I wanted her to relay this on to Constance and I was at a pay phone, after all. I thought she sounded purely and simply relieved, except that the conversation lapsed when I told her I was out to lunch with Paul, and she didn't mention that he'd been to the house, or ask any of the expected questions about his health. Because she didn't confess anything to me, I assumed that Marianne must have been hoping Paul had kept Michael's presence a secret.

Again, I saw Paul off at the airport, and this time we parted as brothers.

At home, Marianne and I whooped it up for the first few minutes, hugging and exclaiming and carrying on like I had been let out of jail, which I guess I had been in a way. We sat down in the living room together while I told her in detail about what we came to call my "mistrial." Towards the end, I mentioned Michael having been seen with her that morning.

Talk about throwing water on the fire! Part of Marianne's joy at my escaping conviction was in the way in which it must have made us seem equals, or me an outlaw who had gotten away with it—her dominant mode of thought about herself. Now that she was suddenly back on trial, her rationale tried to preserve us as Bonnie and Clyde.

"You must have just about lost it when you heard that," she said, and tried to laugh.

"I didn't know what to make of it. I still don't."

"I did it for you," she said, instantly serious. "I went to see Michael one evening of that first week after Mom left. Somebody had to talk him out of pressing charges, and besides David, who else was there? And it worked."

"He didn't drop the charges, though." I was a stickler on this, having worked with The Law.

"He as good as dropped the charges. Look, he had forced the district attorney's office to go through with indicting you and bringing you to trial. They didn't want any part of it, they said it was a waste of their time. And when he finally decided he didn't want you to go to jail, or have a record, he was too embarrassed to go back to them. I made him promise, though, that if the trial came up, and the jury was being selected and all that, he would come forward and call the whole thing off."

"But Marianne, there wasn't going to be a jury. The whole matter could have been decided today by the judge."

"Really? We thought we had some time. Anyway, it worked out. And Michael did move out of his place for the last couple of weeks so no one could find him. You said that pretty much squelched the whole thing."

"Well, that did help, but I wish you had let me know about this before. I could have used the sleep I've been missing."

"I wasn't sure how you'd feel about my going around with Michael."

"You're dating?"

"That first night when I went over there—what can I say, we hit it off."

"He can be a charming young man."

"You hired him, right? He keeps getting better at being

charming. Really, I'm not sure I understand how he got you so uptight."

"Please, don't take his side. Not this evening."

"I'm just trying to explain why I find him attractive."

"He is good looking."

"Yeah, he is, but it's so much more than that. He's, I hate to say it, but he's like you. He has what he calls 'a vision of things.' Do you know how great it is, Dad, to find someone who *thinks*, and believes in the meaning of things?"

"Anyone, anyone but Michael, Marianne."

"That's what you've said about every boyfriend I've ever had!" She went into her juvenile pouting.

"I know that's partially true, but can't you see *why* in this case?"

"You'll get used to the idea, Dad."

At the thought of this, I tried to find the courage to love my daughter in the face of what seemed at that moment about the worst thing imaginable. "You're serious about him?"

"It's intense."

I gave her a wounded and spiteful look.

"Don't worry, your sheets are undisturbed. Michael's old-fashioned in that way. I mean, I think I want to marry him."

"I find your images appalling. He's mentioned marriage?"

"We haven't talked about it that way, exactly. But he does hint, and he's old-fashioned but not cold."

"I could comment about the short time you've known each other, but I understand how it can be. It does make me feel like a jackass, though. I don't know how I can be reconciled to this. I've always given you what you wanted. I've spoiled you. And now when I need some sense of judgment, being a curmudgeon about it looks like a bad reflection on my character, and giving in looks like the final event in a history of folly. I don't know."

"He hasn't even asked me yet. And you'd have time to work out your differences."

"Spare me. Just this one thing, please, Marianne, spare me."

"He's a minister, Dad. My marrying any other minister would have you shouting hallelujah."

I looked across the room and through the glass doors I saw the backyard foliage wagging and wild in a sudden summer breeze.

Death

The secretary in charge of projects in Los Angeles for the home-missions board contacted me by letter in the middle of the next week (my trial had convened on a Thursday), saying that he had heard through Paul Corwin of my interest in the board's chaplaincy position. He asked me to make an appointment with him at my earliest convenience, which sounded awfully formal.

As it happened, I saw him the next day. I left his office with a job that actually paid more than any of my pastorates, churches being even slower than bureaucracies to make adjustments for inflation. Also, in the secretary's words, it took a man with "an unusual temperament" to find fulfillment in the position, and so they tried to make the remuneration, as they put it, attractive—meaning that few wanted such a job and when they did find someone he usually quit.

My hazardous duty pay made it possible for me to keep the house a while longer, until I knew what Constance wanted to do with it. We had exchanged by now only two letters. Concerned with business matters exclusively—car insurance payments and the like—they conveyed about as much of our life together and apart as cuneiform tablets with their lists of barley purchases convey the social life of ancient cultures.

My history in relation to hospitals, including recent history, should give an idea of how I felt about the new job. That I sought the position didn't lessen my fear in the least. In hospitals I had been the victim of suffering and the recipient of miraculous grace. When it came down to it, however, I didn't want my life to be filled with the high drama of the holiest mysteries; I didn't want to stare death in the face as the church fathers did, by keeping a skull on their desks, or stare into the heart of the divine light without the sunglasses of worldly circumstance, like a contemplative monk. I wanted my ego intact, functioning nicely, thank you.

Why then this suicide? Perhaps only because I had not found relief from this world's pain except in abandonment, as Martin Luther never accepted the fact of his salvation until he valued it above the opinion of the entire Western world. Some of us must go around to the backside of the moon in order to see the light. I kept a journal of my first months there, from September through June of the next year, excerpts of which follow. I reproduce them here because memory, which is never very trustworthy, deteriorates so rapidly, and the journal account, although it might read at times like a telegram, captures the taste of an experience from which now I might extract only a savor.

9/7

Today, my first, and first days always the lowest. If not, I will have to shelve the job—I couldn't take many more todays.

A nurse—I think she was, she had a uniform on, but maybe the clerical help wears them, too?—showed me to my office, explained how requests by patients to be visited will be forwarded to me through in-house hospital mail, and how to respond to an emergency call over the intercom.

My office is small, a cubicle painted in a color that is meant to be a deep sky-blue but is somehow milky and institutional. No place for a couch, just a metal desk, with a fake wood-grain surface. I will hang up the parchment reproduction of the Gutenberg Bible I have and Cranach's portrait of Luther and the brass rubbing of the knight Marianne brought back from her trip to England; and that ought to make it comfortably enough Methodist-Episcopalian for everybody.

All the Baptists will care about is that I don't wear a collar.

I asked the nurse before she left if I should sit there and wait. She told me I could, but the gerontology patients missed my predecessor and they would like to meet me. Seventh floor.

First patient, a man named Gene in his robe and pajamas sitting in a wheelchair before his TV, the sound turned up on the game show, "The Price Is Right." Beside him, the tray-table from which he eats his meals in bed. One of those old men who looks almost faceless, the features disappearing into smooth folds of babylike skin.

I introduced myself. He asked me if I could help him light his cigarette. I told him again I was Rev. March, as if my clerical status should make it clear that I didn't light cigarettes, especially for patients with emphysema, which his difficulty in breathing told me he had. He swore at me. Said he was blind and that he couldn't find his lighter.

I saw it had fallen off his tray and rested to one side of the wheelchair. I lit his cigarette.

I asked him why he had "The Price Is Right" on, did he enjoy it? He told me, yes, he did. He loved to hear women scream and they screamed a lot on "The Price Is Right."

I asked him whether he would like me to pray with him before I left. He said he didn't go in for that kind of thing.

He asked me why I was in the hospital. I told him I worked there. He said I was a fool. No one in his right mind would stay in a hospital more than two minutes, unless he was cleaning up like the docs, or had no place to go except six feet under, like him.

I told him he was probably right and walked out.

In the next room, two old women lay in their beds, one fast asleep and the other moaning and rocking herself from side to side. I looked on the moaner's chart and saw that she had a broken hip and high blood pressure. I later found that her blood pressure made it impossible to operate on the hip and broken hips on the mend are painful, particularly if the patient won't stay still. She was obese, with double-chin after double-chin forming a bib under her face. Together with the moaning she was calling on Jesus. Dear Jesus, she kept saying, dear Jesus help me. Dear Jesus, I just want to die. Let me die and be with you. Oh, dear Jesus.

I put my hand on her shoulder and she opened her eyes; they focused and I could see she knew I was there and I could also see that she was still delirious. She asked me who I was, and I told her I was a minister come to pray to Jesus with her. She asked me if I was a priest. I told her, no, a minister. Her next words came out as if we were having a nice talk over a cup of coffee, very matter-of-fact. "It's no good if you're not the priest," she said. "I keep telling them." She closed her eyes and recommenced her moaning and calling on Jesus.

I hurried back to my office and sat there undisturbed for the rest of the day. Have mercy.

9/8

Ventured back to the gerontology ward today and found I should have kept at it yesterday; there turns out to be a conclave of Protestants up there after all.

In one room two women from The Church of the Open Door, a downtown congregation with a glorious past. Moody preached there, and Machen as well, I think. The one woman, Carlotta, was feeding lunch to the other, Elsie, who lay in bed. As we talked, Carlotta continued her ministrations, turning the spoon under and up quickly and smoothly, each bite the same size as the last, the portions diminishing without the grains of rice being scattered, the trick performed over and over again with the showy finesse of a barber about his task.

Carlotta gave me a little nod when I introduced myself, a Victorian welcoming me into her parlor. She had a maroon house-coat on and moccasin slippers with beadwork on the uppers. Also a turquoise necklace.

Carlotta told me that she had had gall bladder surgery and was about recovered when Elsie had been admitted after a stroke. Carlotta persuaded Elsie's family and the doctors that, once she was out of intensive care, she should be put in a room with her. They had been long-time (if never best) friends at the church, ever since Carlotta had returned from the mission field in Mexico in 1955, when her husband had gone to be with the Lord.

Something about Carlotta is very moving, not the exotic grace notes, the slippers and the turquoise necklace, no, these only adorn and heighten by contrast the strict plainness of her person and character, the roast-beef-on-Sunday and Wednesday-night-prayer-meeting nature of her soul. Behold, an Israelite indeed, in whom is no guile! She's so simple as to be mysterious, a woman who, for her whole life, has taken the Bible as the Word of God and followed the dictates of her heavenly Father in the same way, I'm sure, that she obeyed her parents.

While I was in the room I looked over to her bedside table and saw pill bottles standing in what looked like a circle, and I asked her about it. She told me that she had so many pills to take they confused her and she worried constantly about not following her doctor's instructions. She didn't trust the nurses because, although they were sweet to her, they appeared who knew when and for what reason and she was sure they were getting things wrong. Her doctor was very cross about all this, and came in one day and gave her a real bawling out. She was so worried! She prayed and asked for deliverance, and the Lord answered her prayer with the happy inspiration that if she arranged the bottles in the shape of a clock she would know just when to take the next pill. She had to have dummy bottles for some of the clock's numerals and duplicates for the medicines she took more than once a day, but the doctor let her have these, and complimented her the last few times he was by. Spoke right up and told him, I can do all things through Christ which strengtheneth me!

Whew! I shied away from talking about it today, but soon I'll be regaled with hours of stories about Mexico.

Elsie, the stroke victim, has had a long career of good looks and appears the more pathetic for that. Her right side is paralyzed and that side of her face has fallen and looks wrong, dislocated, in the way of a hill out here after a mud slide. She can only say a few words, and these come out swathed in cotton—the way a deaf mute, who has been taught to speak, sounds.

When I prayed with her before I left, tears stood in her eyes and fell onto her cheeks. She reached out to me with her good left arm, clasped me about the neck and kissed me, although she could only pucker half her mouth.

All told there are about a dozen churchgoers up there, and this afternoon I talked with my superior, Mrs. Robertson, in the hospital administration office, about preaching for them on Sunday. We can't use the hospital chapel; it has to be open at all times for prayer and meditation. (I went in there later, and I wouldn't want to use it anyway; it has the atmosphere if not the reliquaries of a Shinto shrine.) But we can use the large lounge on the gerontology floor.

9/11

At the end of my first week I have a bad case of relevance. If, as the old saying goes, there are no atheists in fox holes, there are no academic questions in hospitals.

Children become ill and die. Their parents want to know if God pays any attention to this fact. Yes, I say. It's a fallen and broken world, I say.

Yes *but*, they say. Jennifer was such a good child. You expect that they won't share their toys at a certain age, but she did. She loved her playmates and cried when she had to leave them.

Perhaps God, I offer, wanted her for himself, to spare her what she might have suffered later. You really think that? they ask. It's more something to *think about*, than think, I say.

Yes but, they say, and I keep quiet and listen.

9/16

A shaky day, haunted by old ghosts.

A patient, Dave Redding, with whom I've had two friendly chats before, underwent a cerebral angiogram this morning. A form of X-ray, this test uses chalk for dye. It's injected through a catheter into the circulatory system of the head and neck via the femoral artery in the groin. Late in the afternoon, when my nerves are shot anyway, he described how the procedure made his neck and head feel like a bonfire that would explode from internal heat and pressure. The pain was so great he had no idea how he had behaved—what he might have screamed—during the course of the test, but afterwards found himself on the table shaking and whimpering like a baby. They had given him a barbiturate, and he had slept through the early afternoon.

He needed to talk about it, and I tried to remain in his room for the length of a normal visit. Sitting straight-backed in the chair, my hands went dead cold, and then the top of my head started to burn. The next moment it achieved liftoff, and the room started to fade.

I fainted. Not for a long time, I suppose, but a nurse stood beside me when I awoke, asking me to make sure there wasn't any pain in my limbs, no bones broken, before she lifted me back into the chair.

Then she called for an orderly, who appeared with a wheelchair, and I had to go through the emergency room rigamarole. That had me peeved. But worse, my fainting unnerved Dave, although he was nice about it. I'm ashamed of myself.

Doctors claim that medical and nursing students either grow used to the pain, or their reactions grow until they find the work intolerable. Somehow this doesn't apply in my case. I wake up each morning with an equivalent quotient of dread. Each patient gives me the willies or not, according to the pain they experience and their proximity to death.

10/4

Carlotta is going home tomorrow, so I finally let myself in for her stories about Mexico—a going-away present.

Carlotta is certainly a simple soul but also a greater and more supple one than I had thought. In the kingdom's reckoning, I'm sure she's worth ten of me.

I can see that in the way Elsie has improved. Rehabilitation for those who have suffered strokes has come a long way, it seems. She can speak now, with a slowed halting, and has regained the use of her right hand and arm. They tell me she has started to exercise the leg and will soon be walking with the help of crutches.

Still, losing Carlotta will be a blow to her I'm sure. She has a way of sitting up straight in bed or in her wheelchair when I walk into the room, and then putting her hand to her hair. She values her dignity. The doctors are worried that once Carlotta leaves she will stop the "resocializing process," because she has asked for a private room. She told me today that they needn't worry, although she was clearly worried about something herself, and wouldn't explain what was wrong. She did make a weak joke about not having any plans to go South of the Border, meaning death, before her time.

10/17

I preached today at the hospital—for the fifth or sixth time. I've lost count. It's a unique congregation up there in the lounge on the gerontology ward. The members hobble or roll in well before the hour. We warm up by singing the old favorites, "The Old Rugged Cross," "Oh For A Thousand Tongues To Sing," and "Amazing Grace." The poignancy of these old weasels singing never fails to affect me, although the congregation's vibrato sometimes wavers far above or below the tune and we have to start over again. Not only the old come, though; sometimes I'll see others. The most faithful ones are usually terminal.

I always use my Billy Graham voice now. Otherwise everyone can't hear, and the partially deaf sometimes play taps on their hearing aids to signal for an increase in volume. The service also takes a Romish cast, with its own incense. Gene (the blind man) smokes right through it, and others have followed his lead.

I talk about heaven a lot and say things which in any other context I would find maudlin. Not that it's not hard for me to do; it's hard because, frankly, I hadn't thought much about heaven before, and it's hard because I never really know what they are thinking. But I've seen much more death in these last weeks than ever before and overstepping the boundaries of good taste is a hazard that one has to take, if only to spare the dying a bit of death's loneliness.

11/3

Elsie and I had a wonderful talk today. As her vocabulary has returned, I've watched an extremely intelligent woman come back to life.

I don't think I've recorded this yet, but when I finally asked her why she insisted on a private room after Carlotta left, she looked at me (bugging out her eyes for effect) and said, "Wouldn't you?" And I saw what a dolt I had been. (I have to get over this prejudice that old people are dim-witted. I'm well along that way myself, yet often wish I had another chance at my exams in school.)

She asked me what theologians I read in particular. I told her of my passion for Martin Luther. She said she'd always thought Erasmus had been right, even if Luther did have the best of the argument. She thought the trouble with much of Protestantism was that, like Luther, it found logic easier to trust than God.

That's why I'm interested in Luther's life, I said.

She saw what I meant right away: yes, she said, he found his wife and children his best teachers in the end.

11/7

I ended up telling Elsie about my experience recovering from the auto accident and compared notes on the state of being mindless.

For her, it had been a particularly insidious form of torment. She lived in a "permanent state of premonition, my life a thought which petrified in the womb." She explained that, in rare instances, women have not miscarried when their fetuses have ceased to grow; autopsies have delivered such freaks after forty or more years in limbo. She had been that petrified child.

"I think the thought waiting to come forth," she said, "was that I would die. Life was going on and I was in it, though hidden from everyone, including myself. I was terribly afraid. Now I'm grateful God has given me this reprieve, this time to prepare myself." She tucked her chin in and folded her arms, pulling them tight against her chest, but I could still see that her whole body was shaking. "You will help me, won't you?" she asked.

Elsie must have been a "looker" most of her life. Her recovery has restored the evidence of this; her wide-set eyes, blue and lustrous, the thin nose with its crescent nostrils, her round chin— these features fly her flag still. But one corner of her mouth turns down whatever her expression, caught, anchored by her illness, and there the floodtide has its purchase, threatens to make a breach, and will finally claim her.

I tell her we will talk about why she is afraid. Every day if she likes.

11/8

Elsie and I talked today again, throwing the names of theologians at each other and calling one another heretics—good naturedly, of course. For all that, we were avoiding what she wanted to say to me, and our mutual discontent went weaving through the conversation.

Then she said. "I don't have the deep, dark secret of Southern novels. Are you disappointed?"

"Yes," I said.

"When I look back at my life," she said, "I find the memories that give me pleasure, those of my reverie, if you understand such an old-fashioned word, are things I felt to be unimportantly worldly at the moment. Like the time I publicly insulted the head of the garden committee and was applauded for having done so. Or the time I went out with the best friend of the young man I was supposed to be in love with that season. Petty things. Ones I might judge harmless in themselves. But I cannot find any delight in the 'things of God.' I have always enjoyed talking about theology and taken pleasure in attending church services, but my moments of ecstasy have been exclusively personal, and now I see them as mean-spirited and yet I can't vanquish their attraction for me. So how will I enjoy heaven? I won't fit in. In other words, I can't help thinking that I'm damned. I'm frightened and I've prayed for God's peace and I cannot find it. Or he doesn't seem inclined to give it to me. Putting it one way or another makes no difference. But do you understand?"

I told Elsie there were many things I might say, but she had too quick a mind for platitudes.

11/10

Returned to Elsie today to tell her that those who most scrupulously examine their motives are often the most insistent that the work of salvation is grace from first to last.

She said her thoughts on that score were the most troubling of all, for she found she didn't care for the economy of grace. She *wanted* to play a part in it; so much so that the whole issue of grace made her feel rebellious.

I mentioned, half-jokingly, trying to cheer her, that Christ said certain devils required more prayer and fasting than others.

She didn't laugh, or reply, but looked straight out at me from her troubled eyes.

11/11

Elsie informed me today that the doctors think she'll be far enough along in her rehabilitation program to return home by next week. That gives us a deadline to meet, she said.

11/16

Elsie's homecoming day.

Her family made much over her, Elsie's daughter arriving early to dress her and fix her hair, the son-in-law coming in later with his daughters, two of Elsie's ten grandchildren. They wore matching outfits and patent-leather shoes and each had a present for their Nanna. The whole family looked like something out of an Oldsmobile commercial, good looks and clothes made out of the best fabrics. And that was fine—why shouldn't Elsie have such a button-down family? But of course I resented them, and not only because of my own situation; they were taking her away, and that made them appear shallow to me. Being Elsie's family, I bet, in truth, they aren't.

Also, I was entertained as long as I remained a part of the commercial, the kind padre who had taken a fancy, as anyone would, to their prize possession. Elsie's daughter detected something more in her mother's eagerness for them to meet me; she insisted that I need not accompany Elsie out to their car.

And so we had our awkward moment of parting there in the room; I would have liked to pray with her; I wanted so much to say the healing words that I have been unable to say; but we were left with social smiles and my kissing her cheek. Damn.

Early in the Christmas season, only days after Thanksgiving, Constance telephoned and told me that her father had died the night before. Eating their dinner alone together (Ben was staying overnight at a friend's house), the old gentleman had suffered a massive coronary. Her voice sounded calm, if distant, and when I asked her about how she was bearing up she said the doctor had given her a prescription. "It happened very quickly," she said. "For him."

Throughout our married life I had worried about how

Constance would take the death of her father. He was for her a world she needed to believe in, and to see as an alternative to mine; her father, as that world's god, sustained it by his very existence and could be loved and cherished through his immanence in Constance's memories: he was coffee after dinner in a demitasse and seeing pictures of one's friends in the papers as a matter of course. He was, preeminently, money, its power and trustworthiness, and not in a crude or bold sense at all but one so finely gauged that only medieval theologians would have been able to classify its ramifying divisions with their piano-wire minds. And he was also her father in the most common and simple and painful sense.

I must admit that, hearing Rome had fallen, I couldn't repress my hope that she might fall back to me, the local bishop. She had a handy check to these hopes. She wanted Marianne to fly out for the funeral. No, I shouldn't come. In reply I suggested that she and Marianne and Ben should fly back after a suitable interval and spend Christmas with me. She promised to think about it, she said, although she suspected she would probably send both children back alone.

With that much of an opening, I put a bee in Marianne's bonnet before she left; I said her mother should get to know Michael over the holidays. Fight fire with fire, one woman's persistence with another's, I thought.

It worked. I claimed my family once again at the Los Angeles airport. I vowed, during Constance's visit, that I would not importune her to return to me; I would let my new job, my influence with Marianne, and Ben's delight at seeing his father, speak for me. So as I walked through the long, white terrazzo corridor to the gate and kept reminding myself to stay calm (I shoved my hands into my pockets; there was, of course, really no hope of remaining calm), I wondered what kind of kiss I should give Constance.

Mercifully, Ben broke away from Constance and Marianne, ran around the others walking through the ramp, and got to me first. I saw he looked the same at first glance, except that Constance had put him in what was to me a new suit: brown tweed, a very 1950's Ivy League sort of thing. He threw his arms around me and I heaved him up into the air, once, finding he had put on weight and would have been too much for me, were it not for the adrenalin-assisted occasion. "Hey, tiger," I said, "I really missed you."

"Hey!" he said, full of life.

I about lost it, as Marianne would say; went to pieces, in my parlance. But Marianne came along and gave me a kiss and a hug, embraced me with the familiar, and that set me back on my pins. And then Constance, whose hands I took in mine, looking her over like a young man assessing his wife's dress, as well as her other merits. I gave her a peck on the mouth. She had been drinking whiskey on the plane.

"You look in fine fettle," she said.

"So do you."

Los Angeles was having one of its rainstorms, those deluges which last from three days to two weeks running and which mark the winter season, although they produce brief springs for the flora in our canyons. With the wet weather, the skies hanging ominously low, the whole family, including Michael, in whose company Marianne spent all of her time, took its ease at home.

Michael and I had not talked about what had happened since the day I visited him in the hospital. Our lawyers had resolved the civil suit amicably; the church's liability covered his hospital bills and I paid the deductible, plus a small sum for mental anguish. Marianne and he had been seeing each other openly for months now, but after I had greeted him at the door the first time, friendly if tight-lipped, he had taken my acquiescence for granted, and I had regarded him as a fact of life, neither of us exchanging more than pleasantries.

During Constance's visit, though, Michael spent more time in the house, talking with Constance, for the most part. She adopted an indulgent attitude toward him, for Marianne's sake, and also because Michael had the good sense to respond to Constance as a woman, not as a future mother-in-law. Constance warmed to him and he let himself be charmed by her and acted the knight in return. While this was going on, these talks in the kitchen or in Constance's old office (to which my wife went frequently as a place of retreat and solitude), I felt Michael being drawn into my orbit, and felt that his meteoric and tangential relation to my life would soon give to the gravity of Constance and Marianne in a way that would land him on my turf.

I expected an explosion, because when merely standing

near him I was charged with a destructive energy—reacting to him like one rod of uranium does to another. This force would either dissipate slowly, as nuclear fuels do in a power plant, or quickly. I would not disgrace myself with him again, I thought; I would speak to him. However, he had kept his distance until this rainy afternoon. I heard his conversation in the kitchen with Constance wane, and wondered, as he must have, when Marianne would reappear from her bedroom, where she'd gone to change her clothes after she and Michael had returned from shopping and tramping around in the rain, and, at last, knew he had been unable to avoid me any longer when he came into the living room and sat down in front of the TV with Ben and me. We were watching a pro football game.

The announcer's voice, the crowd noise, and the popping and grunting coming from the field washed against the rocks of our silence. When we spoke, finally, we kept our eyes on the TV and made sure to keep Ben close to us by including him in the conversation.

"Oakland and who else?" Michael asked.

"Miami," Ben said. "At Miami. The Dolphins are ahead fourteen to three."

"What quarter?" Michael asked.

"Second," I said.

The Dolphin quarterback, Bob Griese, faded back to pass, couldn't find a receiver, and dumped the ball off to Csonka, his running back, in the flat. The fullback turned up field, but was stopped short of the first-down marker and the Dolphins had to kick the ball away.

"What's happened over at the church with the search committee?" I asked Michael.

"I've been appointed the interim pastor, you know," Michael said.

"Right."

"They had me in the other day, talking with me about making the arrangement permanent."

Baffled by how my casual comments when under pressure always seemed to betray me, I tried to treat the topic lightly. "You never know what's permanent." And that, of course, just made it worse.

But Michael got us clear. "Look at that," he said, quite

pointedly to Ben. "Did you see that? Stabler threw that ball on a line about fifty yards. I don't see how Oakland ever loses."

"Turnovers," Ben said.

"How's your work?" Michael asked me. "Marianne says you're raking it in."

"The money's better. The work? It's hard. You know what it's like. You make hospital calls."

"Only when I can't avoid it," he said. He turned and stared at me until I looked up. "I respect what you're doing," he said.

"Thanks."

The crowd screamed. "What happened?" Me.

"Watch the instant replay," Ben said.

The Dolphins blitzed, chasing Stabler thirty yards behind his line of scrimmage, and then sacking him.

"You see," Ben said. "Turnovers, mistakes, penalties. Oakland always beats itself against the Dolphins. Everybody does against that team. I hate the Dolphins."

"Why?" I asked

"They play a boring game," Ben said.

"But they win," Michael said.

"Winning isn't everything," Ben said, parroting some adult. I decided I should test him. "What else is there?"

He gave me a puzzled look, since fathers are the source, not the skeptics, of platitudes. "Fun," Ben said.

"Meaning?" I said.

"This is football, not school," Ben said.

"OK. Sorry." I turned to Michael. "What do they, the committee, think of you going out with Marianne? Has there been any reaction?"

"It didn't come up. They're still reviewing names of possible candidates."

"What reaction have you had from the church, then?"

"Good. You know, people are glad to see her."

"I'm sure they see her more now than during my tenure."

"No."

"No? I can't remember her ever coming two Sundays back to back."

He didn't reply.

"I'm glad, too," I said. "You'll be her salvation." If ever I have performed one, this was an act of faith.

"You're the prophet, not me," he said, timidly.

I was about to say that he could be my Elisha, or that they couldn't handle their children, either, most of the prophets, but then Oakland scored and Ben's jubilation distracted us altogether, for which we were both, I think, grateful.

Constance and Marianne joined us then. Entering the room first, Marianne, the village's fair damsel, her beauty hidden in her woodcutter's outfit of flannel shirt and jeans, stopped at the threshold, her eyes quick and wary, her expression purposefully blank, or more exactly, *absent*. I said, "There you are," and Michael called out something, and from the harmony, or paired tones of our voices, Marianne must have sensed our new accord. She came across the room with her usual long strides. She sat by Michael on the couch but didn't permit herself any of the small intimacies that by then must have been habitual with them.

Constance, in turn, came in and sat down by me on the love seat. Tepid irony. She asked Marianne what plans she and Michael had for dinner. They were going out, they said. We sat a while longer, everyone but Constance pretending interest in the game, and then finally Ben said, "I'm going to go read in my room," snapped off the set, and deserted us.

For a hellishly long time the need to say something, anything, suggested to me a number of thoughts, but each, like a film image stuck before the projector light, burned up. I felt rooted where I sat, by the situation—the screen, so to speak, maddeningly illuminated but blank.

"What will you do now, Constance?" Michael asked, assuring me that any question, in that context, was bound to be loaded. "Will you stay in Philadelphia?"

"I'm not sure," she said, "but then I don't see why not." I tried to catch her eye, but she was intent on staring at the toe of her black pump, her legs crossed and her elevated foot arched back towards her.

We waited and waited and waited. "There are four people in this room," Marianne said. She drew her hair back into a pony tail, then twisted it so that it fell, a heavy cord, in front of her shoulder. "Each person loves the other three; each person hates the other three. Or maybe the hating has a couple exceptions. I'm trying to say that we shouldn't let the hatred get in the way. Life is bad enough, and we're all struggling to cope and we're not going to let go of each other, so why don't we concentrate on the love?"

I did not feel qualified to reply. No one else seemed to either.

Not until Constance's motherhood arose. "Marianne, you can be sure that your father and I won't stand in Michael's or your way." Constance looked at me. "We haven't discussed it, really, but that's the way you feel, isn't it? I've been the grudge-holder, not you."

"No," I said quietly to Constance, meaning that I didn't think she had held any grudges she didn't have a perfect right to hold. And then I turned to Marianne and Michael. "Michael knows that I regret what I did. The trial and the suit are over, and if anybody should understand acting in anger, it's me. I'm just afraid for you. Mostly for Marianne, but also for Michael. The ministry is so hard. It's hard on the man and it's hard on his wife." I found myself lifting both hands and slapping my knees, a gesture my father used to make when he encountered something ineffable and wanted to stop talking about it.

"You don't hate me?" Michael asked, his face slightly up-turned, because he was resting his head in his hands and his elbows on his knees; and his robin's-egg eyes looked focused and full of light in a way I had never seen them, wholly transparent to my presence, without any shading of reserve or of his own dignity. I confess that only Ben had looked at me in this way before, and I realized then that Michael might become my son-in-law, an insight I could acknowledge only with great ruefulness.

"Michael," I said, "do you love Marianne?"

"Yes."

"Do you want my permission to marry her?"

"We still need more time together." And here he did take Marianne's hand in his. They looked at each other shyly, which I liked, since Marianne had rarely displayed such a courtly disposition in her past.

"When you're sure you want to get married, come and ask me. If you know Marianne, you know she'll marry you without any of the courtesies. But come and ask me. I'd like that."

Marianne stepped over and gave me a big kiss on the cheek. "Why do you have to insult me," she asked, "before you feel it's all right to be nice?"

"Where are you eating?" I asked.

"I'm not sure. Do you and Mom want to come?"

"No. I've had enough reconciliation for one day." I waited a moment and no one moved. But a preacher knows how to dismiss a crowd. "Go on, leave, so Ben and I can finish watching the football game."

"Yeah," Ben said, and walked into the room. I'm sure he'd caught every word, sitting quite still on his bed.

Constance's sojourn passed with the two of us acting much as we usually had, though with more success toward Ben and Marianne and her suitor of the moment, now Michael. We even threw two small dinner parties—once again, we wanted to see people, and our second thoughts about our marital status didn't seen so ominous once we found ourselves able to act in concert toward our children. And yet I was constantly aware (and I'm sure Constance was, too) that these roles, these emanations from the source, no longer signified a true marriage. Paradoxically, this made them easier to fulfill but much less powerful. We were that contradiction in terms of the firmament: a dead star. For a time it remains visible, its light traveling on, declaring what no longer exists.

Or so I thought each night lying on the daybed in my study, too exhausted and depressed to sleep.

During the day, I held myself in check as much as possible, never presuming on Constance's time or presuming that tasks like cooking and washing the dishes were hers. My attention to her pleasure and comfort had the air of courtship; she enjoyed this at times and found herself nettled by it at others. Finding ourselves both in the kitchen ready to fill the dishwasher, our good intentions sometimes wore to an irritation that about had us throwing the china at each other.

At other times, of course, we were simply together, and this simulacrum of our real life approximated that life so nearly it seemed a space which might again become our home. I wanted Constance back. And, saying goodnight after the dinner party with the Hinsdales, having laden our guests with the presents of food and talk and humor, we closed the door and I had that old feeling of being secure in the storehouse, pleased at the wealth we held in one another's arms. Then I kissed her cheek, and we found our different ways to bed.

After Christmas, two days before New Year's Eve, we appeared in the kitchen at the same time after our second dinner party; she to have a cup of tea, and I for milk and chocolate-covered marshmallow cookies. We had talked about everything but our marriage and the death of her father, the two meaningful subjects, although unacknowledged, of every glance and light remark. I had, I thought, done an admirable job of being as reasonable as a CPA, never for a minute succumbing to my slobbering humanity or my hunger for the Word. But that night I knew I might starve if I didn't ask for a bite. Under the circular flourescent light in the kitchen, at the wrought-iron and glass-top breakfast table, Constance looked wan. "Are you tired?" I asked.

"I'm not used to people anymore," she said.

"You haven't been entertaining in that great big old house?"

"Daddy and I lived very quietly. And then, with Daddy's death . . ." she let this trail where it might and gave a grimace.

"We haven't talked about that. Do you want to?"

She took a meditative draft of her tea; the cup clattered against the saucer before it found home. "What about it, exactly?" she asked.

"That it happened."

"Yes, it did."

"All right. But does that change any of your thinking, your plans?"

"Ted, you know, you really are a very nice man. I'm glad I married you."

"You are?"

"I mean, with a little distance I can see why I found you attractive."

"A very great distance."

"We're neither of us young anymore. That's not what I mean. You can be kind. Few men are."

"If you were saying all this in a different tone of voice, I'd ask you to come back."

"I don't miss you, Ted."

"I miss you."

"I know. It's not that I'm glad about it or anything of the sort. I think maybe I haven't had enough time to miss you yet. It's like a cloudy day. You don't miss the clear sky for a while." She clasped her hands, and set them beside her teacup.

"I'm good weather, not foul?"

"I went out once, on a date," she said, and I popped a marshmallow cookie into my mouth, whole, to keep from speaking. "He kissed me at the door and asked if he could come in." She shook her head. "No wonder people get married—how awful."

I swallowed at last. "Constance," I said, "come back, stay."

"I'm going back to wind up Daddy's affairs."

"Then?"

"I don't know. I'll wait and see." She looked up at me, and suddenly her eyes glistened. "I've lost too much to understand anything." She looked back down, wiped her eyes with the back of her hand, and I tore off a paper towel and handed it to her. "Thanks." She took a great breath and let it out slowly. "Why is it like this? It's too much, and I can't help feeling it's unfair. I wanted to be a fine lady like my grandmother, declining into old age in the knowledge of the perfect choices she'd made."

"Constance, I have sinned against you in many ways, but I *have* loved you. When you mentioned going out on a date, I felt like a teenager whose girl has deserted him for his friend's new car. I mean, you weren't wrong about what I felt and still feel. My love has not been a sin."

"I was wrong about who you were."

"Every lover is. Love would be impossible otherwise."

"I don't know. With Daddy gone, and the situation with you, I'm having to battle to keep from hating myself." I made a move toward her but she said, "No. I'm all right. I'm going to go back to Philadelphia and I'm going to be all right."

We continued talking, well into the early morning, about Ben, and Michael and Marianne, and nothing more, really, about ourselves. But I understood that I had to let her return to Philadelphia. It was apparent that she needed that much distance.

So again I was at the airport. I saw Constance and Ben off for Philadelphia less than a week after New Year's Eve.

I was propositioned today. A fine-looking woman, Mrs. Hart—who is tall and thin and at forty still able to wear her hair long (it is dark with red highlights)—came into my office and asked me out to dinner. "I know you're separated from your wife," she said, and lit a cigarette in front of Martin Luther, with a kind of playful vampishness.

I've known Shelly Hart through my dealings with the hospital administration office where she works as an administrator—a thoroughly professional one—in her businesslike but nicely-tailored suits. She wore a charcoal grey version today, with black trim at the lapels and a satiny blouse, several buttons undone, showing a necklace of pearls—to which I'm partial: does she know this?—and the ample promise of her breasts. Our friendship has included a lot of teasing—her kidding me about being a holy man, me her about how impossible it was to be one with her around. So I acted as if her invitation were another piece of raillery, mainly trying to insure that comedy would take the day. "Are your intentions honorable?" I asked.

"Not in the least," she said. "I'm out to have you. I've wanted you for a long time, but you're slow to catch on."

"I don't think you'd find me much fun, someone as young as you."

"Look," she said and glanced about, tilting her cigarette up so that the ashes wouldn't fall before she found an ashtray. I lent her the use of one of my two coffee mugs, the one I don't care for. "Ted," she said, in the courteous way she has of beginning each thing anew. "Look, I'm old enough to know what's important for me. Someone who is, well, a man of integrity and warmth. You are."

"I'm hoping that my wife will come back," I said.

She gave her head a little shake and combed her hair back from the sides of her face with the long fingernails of her free hand. As she did, I noticed how her neck looked thin, the skin no longer supple, but dry. "I'm just suggesting one night," she said. "Then if we did start seeing each other, we could still part as friends if your wife changed her mind. I loved my husband. He died. I *know*."

I thought of Constance having dated someone, and I confess the desire to pay her back added to Shelly's allure. But then I am a bumbling, fifty-five year old conservative Protestant minister, who loves his wife and children, and is enough of an old-fashioned gentleman to find such an interview out of kilter—even, in a private way, chaotic.

"Not right now, Shelly," I said, wondering if I'd ever accomplish this seemingly impossible task of phrasing a friendly rebuff. "If Constance and I divorce, then I'll get down on bended knees, begging for the pleasure of your company."

She looked miffed.

"Please," I said. "I'm just an old bag of bones anyway."

She recovered somewhat, her good humor struggling to overcome the drawn expression my refusal had produced.

"This might be a once-in-a-lifetime offer. And if you're happy about *that*, your religion really has made you deadwood," she said, somewhat proudly, partially restoring our byplay.

So tonight I miss Constance more than ever. Her absence leaves me open to life's siren song in a way that makes me feel a ridiculous adolescent. I'll admit that tonight I miss being twenty— hearing the overture has me wanting a music that has passed and can never return again. Has me almost willing to settle for farce, or the pleased chump I would be lying in Shelly's arms tonight. Heavens.

3/21

Today the hardest part of any job: monotony. And tonight I'm exhausted in an impatient and barely tolerable way, which I would simply call "fatigue," if that didn't smack of the medicinal euphemisms I hear *ad infinitum.* Also (and this qualifies what I'm feeling in a singular way), my job doesn't grant me the prerequisite of mindlessness, that best form of relaxation. Making rounds today, I visited patients, prayed with them, and found them to various degrees repulsive because they were suffering and I don't wish to suffer. Constance partly holds the reins to that. It's my state of fear and my agitation that are wearing. I must have the most protracted illness on record, and perhaps that's why I belong where I am.

Doc, I'm in pain!

When did you first notice this discomfort?

At birth.

Ah, well, then it's a congenital condition.

3/28

The pleasure in my work is in being wanted. I'm sure generals enjoy war, Civil-Defense Marshals natural disasters, and in that way I enjoy my work, sometimes. I'm wanted and needed by so many that it bucks me up. But in the face of their need my inadequacy often feels like a form of betrayal. I find myself wishing I were one of the doctors, particularly a young resident who will do so much good, heal hundreds of bodies in his years of practice ahead. Or a nurse. Or even the Catholic chaplain—in his own way he has things *to do*: kiss his stole, make the sign of the cross, and place the communion wafer on a patient's tongue. And I? I only think and pray with people. My presence, my being with them, helps at times, I feel. But that's too indefinite. I can't get over the feeling of being an impostor. Shelly seems to see through me.

3/29

Another weary day.

Dear Jesus Christ, name my illness, fill out a prescription and heal me, or if I require surgery, let it be under local anesthetic so that I can watch and find out how things are supposed to work. Create in me a new heart, oh God. Make this stony thing pump.

In April, on a Saturday night, when I was in my high, narrow office at home, preparing a message for the service on the gerontology ward, I heard the muffled sound of the front door opening and then the voices of Michael and Marianne. I thought I would continue making notes for my message and leave them to each other, but Michael's steps came down the hall and his sure knuckles struck my door. He stepped in and sat on my daybed. My study seemed small at that moment, close—I hadn't been with Michael in such a small space since our fight in the church anteroom. He leaned over, his elbows on his thighs, and clasped his hands together: a posture of both deliberation and power. He stayed in the position long enough for me to observe again that he has good hands for a preacher, large and regularly formed, not bony but thin enough to be capable of gestures that would carry, like a good actor's. His blunt-cut hair always seemed the same length—not a young man indifferent to style but with a vanity that might have been called womanish in another day.

"You asked me," he said." I mean, you said to come and see you when I was certain I wanted to marry Marianne. So I've come. She loves me. I love her." He looked up for the first time since he'd entered, and straight at me, as he had that day in the living room. "Is it OK, the marriage, I mean, with you?" His jaw shut tight, his compressed lips, the vertical line between his eyebrows—in all this there was not only determination and resolve but a bit of rancor or resentment.

"We've never talked about what happened since you were in the hospital," I said. "Marianne told me you were going to call off the trial—or did, in fact, in a sense. I'm wondering what you think about me as a father-in-law."

"We might not be close," he said. "But that's no reason to call off a marriage."

"No, Michael, I'm not thinking of the marriage right now. What I should have said is, What do you think of me, period."

"I'm still angry at you," he said, and I saw the knuckles of his clasped hands tightening. "I've prayed about it, and I've said before God that I forgive you. But I'll admit I'm just barely capable of saying the words, no more. And maybe able to say them only because of what I feel for Marianne. You are her dad. I don't see why you expect perfect sanctity from me."

"Oh, I don't."

"What is that supposed to mean?"

"You see, that's what I'm afraid of. That what is still between us will make us see each other in the worst possible light. What I meant to say was that I think you've done all that you can, spiritually and personally. I want you to know that—before the tensions of marriage pit us against one another, as they often do a father-in-law and a daughter's husband."

"OK, well, hey look," he said, a bit of the hipster again showing through. "I'll try to relate to you like I once did. We got along, or I thought we did. I know this will be harder in ways, but hey, I love Marianne, and, you know, I want this to work."

"What do you think about Constance?"

"Why?"

"I'm just wondering. Simple as that."

"I *like* Constance," he said, and then colored at the force of his emphasis. "I mean, we started fresh. And, I don't know, I've always found it easier to talk with women. Is that strange?"

"No."

"Whatever. I'm trying to say that I like Constance, and I think she likes me, so I see no problems there." He turned his face away, his tone once more utterly candid, if a bit desperate. "Man, I didn't think this was going to be so hard." He looked back at me. "You asked me to come and talk and I did. OK?"

"I'm giving you my consent, Michael. But we have to talk these things over before we find ourselves in church together. You know what I mean? This is going to be quite a little tempest in a teacup."

"I've thought about that."

"We can deal with it, though, I believe, if we know what the other's thinking. And there's another thing I want to mention. It may seem a strange topic under the circumstances, but believe me, I have your ministry at heart in this. Marianne is not exactly the most steadfast believer."

"Oh, about that . . . Say, what do I call you now? I can't use 'pastor' anymore, can I?" he said, and had to grin, one corner of his mouth pulling up.

"Ted. Not Father. Never. Please."

"Sure," he said. "I was going to say that you shouldn't worry about Marianne in that way anymore. We've spent months talking about her faith. She had a lot of questions, which she knew most answers to, but the whole thing had never become clear for her. But about two weeks ago, she gave her life totally to Christ. We prayed together. People talk about getting such a kick out of witnessing, but that was the first time in my life it was real for me. She didn't tell you?"

"No."

"But I'm sure. I wouldn't be here if I thought we were going to be 'unequally yoked.' "

How to tell him: And maybe Marianne wouldn't follow Constance's example. But I did know that Marianne would realize later the conditions under which she had had another conversion experience (she had walked down the aisle at twelve), and once the usual marital problems came up, a thousand devils would be at her. So I tried: "Michael, the ministry puts a couple under great stress, as I said before. It's hard—"

"I know that already. A lot of couples broke up while I was at seminary. I had one friend, he was devastated."

"And Marianne has never been very disciplined, as you know; she's been rather wild. When she starts getting the criticism you can expect from a congregation, I don't know how she'll handle it. She's seen it with me, of course, but that's not the same. Maybe you've already sensed how bitter Constance is. Well, Constance isn't with me anymore."

"I know all that, but I'm sure this is what God wants for us." We stared at each other, with all the memories of what we had been through and confessed to travelling over our expressions. "I really have my faith back now," he said. "What I went through in the hospital, what I told you about my feelings the night it happened, that was an unreal time for me. I mean, it was too much. It had me flipped out. But not anymore. I know this is the Lord's will for our lives. Check out Hosea and Gomer. You know what I mean."

I didn't relish his comparing my daughter to a whore, and almost said as much. Promiscuity is not quite whoredom, I wanted to say. "Right, right. I'm happy that you feel renewed in your faith. With all that's happened to me, my inclination is to question and worry. My ministry— She's my daughter, Michael. I hope you'll make her happy. You'll probably have a time doing it."

He stood up, and we shook hands, still uneasy with one another, the stains of our history still visible on this new, flimsy costume of friendship. No, family relationship, rather. Michael Dennis was as good as being my son-in-law.

4/10

Elsie Mayfield was readmitted today. She had another stroke; in medical lingo, a "cerebrovascular accident"—as if her arteriosclerotic artery didn't *mean* to deprive her brain of its blood supply. Doctors excuse the inevitable, and even stand behind it, I've found, in their dealings with patients, as if the body makes all the decisions and for a patient to adopt another view is willful and childish. Perhaps that's what I really am, an advocate of the soul in its struggle with the body. I realize that I shouldn't engage in this kind of dualistic thinking, which is an affront to the age; it knows nothing of the "sullied flesh," but then I don't give a fig for the age. Christianity, however, isn't dualistic, and that's the danger. The greatest holistic doctor, resurrected, said, 'Handle me, and see; for a spirit has not flesh and bones, as you see I have.'

I saw Elsie in intensive care, two heart attack victims on either side; for the most part they were screened from view by the partitioning curtains, which always strike me, in their skim-milk whiteness, as partaking of their guests' pallor. I could hear their heart monitors beeping, Elsie's regular if fast, another almost normal, and the third so irregular it was almost like a hiccup. Naked under the sheet, she looked half submerged, the tubes like eels draining her anemic and bloated body of its last life, rather than being lifelines. She lay with her arms slightly out to the side to accommodate the IV's, her legs apart and feet splayed—not a posture of sleep or comfort, but like something washed up by the sea, without the tension and torque of the truly alive. She would have, I suppose, been the image of a corpse if she hadn't been snoring.

The I-C nurse moved about her, checking the monitoring systems with the deftness of a geisha conducting a ceremonial tea. I asked her what the doctors were saying. She said they weren't (which is a bad sign). I worked up my courage and laid a hand on Elsie's forehead. The nurse looked at me as if to decide in her own mind whether touching the patient was part of a minister's function, whether I might be performing some kind of a rite, or perhaps had enough medical knowledge to raise Elsie's eyelids and check her pupils. I simply touched her forehead with my palm, perhaps because checking the children's temperature in that way was about all I have ever known how to do for them medically. My mother did that, too, and I liked it.

Elsie was very hot. The heat of her forehead remained over my palm after I had lifted it off in such a noticeable way that it felt as if I had taken an impression of her broad and flat forehead. I looked around for a paper towel, but saw only a pitcher of water and a glass—there on all occasions, like a Gideon Bible in a hotel room. I poured a few drops into my cupped hand and let the water trickle onto Elsie's forehead at the hairline, then wiped the excess away.

The nurse promptly told me that the patient received sponge baths every hour. What I had done had been awkward, maladroit, foolish, so I stood on my dignity. I told the nurse that I was baptizing Elsie. She apologized. I reassured her.

I just wanted *to do something*, I might as well have said.

4/11

Visited Elsie again today. She has come out of the coma, and, if this stroke has produced its own disabilities, at least she is alive.

Still in intensive care, she was sitting up with the aid of the metal sides of her bed, looking straight ahead. Her eyes were open wide: too wide. I thought at first her look was the sign of her having gone blind. But she can see; swiveling her head around, she followed me from the foot of the bed to her side. It seems her eyeballs are paralyzed, and until they are freed she will have that poached look.

She is also able to speak. With a verbal tic, however. She said, "Oh, you son of a bitch, you've come." Biting and then pursing her lips as if to pull the string of words back into her mouth, the skin around her eyes tightened and she looked pained. "Profanity," she said, and closed her lips tight. I saw her take a deep breath before beginning with great restraint to try again. "When I speak . . . oh damn, you son of a bitch," she said, shaking her head even as the last expletives rattled their way out. "I can't control." She paused. "Sentences," she said. "Impossible." She took another breath. "Questions. OK?"

We talked for about fifteen minutes. I asked her as many questions as I could which required only one-word answers. The more we talked, the more I wished I could have asked her about the state of her soul, but I knew this would have provoked her demon, and while it didn't matter to me, I understood how upsetting the breach of decorum was to Elsie.

Why have you brought her into this valley of humiliation? You have not made our palates for herbs this bitter. How can there be laughter in heaven after we have wept such tears as these on earth?

4/12

Elsie was transferred from intensive care to a private room on the gerontology ward today.

Her daughter was with her most of the day. We met several times in the hall on the way to and from wherever, until we finally stopped to talk.

She asked me, standing there in her light strawberry sweater, as if we had by chance become detached from the rest at a garden party, what could have gotten into her mother? She angled the question in a slightly rhetorical and fully quizzical way, which let me know I had the liberty to extend my answer as far as I liked.

I got to the point. I said that during Elsie's earlier hospital stay, I discovered that she feared death. Elsie believed, in one way, I said, very deeply in the truth of her faith. And yet a host of scruples made her feel that she hadn't appropriated the salvation Christ offers.

Staring at me with her chin lowered, from beneath her shapely eyebrows, the daughter, Jill, told me that this had to stop. It would impede her mother's recovery for her to fret, she said.

A stern performance: her kids must know where the lines are drawn.

I said I would keep trying, but the speech impediment had so far prevented me from taking up where Elsie and I had left off. The daughter wanted to be reassured that I would try again, remarkably maternal, with an instinct for ending each turn of talk on a chord of resolution.

I promised her I would.

And then she did something that marked her as Elsie's daughter. We turned to go back into the room, and she took my arm and let herself lean against me as we took those few steps. Elsie's daughter in a gesture at once cultured and at the edge of the conventions of propriety: her daughter in manners, where at last feeling may dwell.

4/13

Elsie, today, was wearing makeup. Rouge on her cheekbones, blue eye shadow, pencil, and even delicately applied eyeliner. She has the complexion of a lifelong blonde, like good vellum paper that yellows with a deepening quality through the years. Her natural color was in such contrast to the paint that she looked like a character, a Mrs. Malaprop, in the nineteenth-century comedy. Her hair, usually in disarray, had been combed, showing more clearly her bald patches.

But her preparation, or her daughter's work, was a gift—a way of giving her into my hands. And though her appearance was all but grotesque, her charm neared nobility. She is still a great woman, as a city whose statues are crumbling, and whose stone houses are merely gutted scenery or facades for museums, can remain great.

I told her she looked beautiful, and she swore eloquently, whether on purpose this time I couldn't be sure. I asked her whether she had found peace about God's love for her. She didn't or couldn't speak right away, and when I took her hand, I found she was shaking. What I meant to say, I said, was that God did love her and always would and she should expect nothing but love from him.

She looked not at me but directly above her. "Dear Jesus," she said, and followed that with a string of, in her situation, not entirely inappropriate oaths, ending with "I'm still scared."

Her chest began to heave with the violence of her feeling or the physiological state into which those feelings had pitched her. I hit her nurse's button, and asked whether she was in pain, having another attack. She gripped my hand with prodigious strength. "No, no," she said. "I'm facing it. I won't, dammit, escape."

Those words, so painful to her, seemed not to have been said so much as brought into being, born. She was calm once again. When the nurse came I told her that I'd accidently pushed the button, and she shook her finger at me and said, "Wolf."

As soon as she cleared out, Elsie said, "I damn, damn, I, damn, I am going to . . . son of a bitch, die. I know it. He's shown me. I'm . . . waiting. But Jesus. Jesus, he will be there."

She closed her fixed eyes, and I continued holding her hand until her grip relaxed. She was asleep.

So Elsie has gone beyond me, and I'm glad. I think the final humiliations of her illness, not being able to control her speech, her poached eyes, the curses which have lashed her pride, must be the way through which God is accomplishing the final purification of whatever dross remains in her. There's a poetry in it that makes a terrible but unconditional sense. Whatever negotiations are being conducted, I know I'm not needed as an arbiter. God has offered his peace.

4/14

Elsie relapsed into a coma today, and they have her back in intensive care. When I went up to see her, the doctors were attending to her or ordering the nurses to—actually, when I peeked in, the three doctors looked like white pillars about an altar, erect and impassive, watching another doctor, the priest, elevate a hypodermic. I called the nurses' station several times and tests were being performed or about to be. That means complications have developed.

4/15

I looked in on Elsie today. That's all I could do; she's still unconscious. Holding her hand for a minute or two, I breathed a bitter, burned scent: urine, which I'm all too familiar with now, and looked to see if the catheter was in place and functioning. It looked all right. Still, intermittently, I smelled it. I had been rubbing the back of her hand, and as I left off with this I noticed that a fine white powder had rubbed off. Thinking it talcum, I sniffed it: the urinous odor. And then I saw that every exposed portion of Elsie's body was covered with this dew, like talcum, but reflecting the light as fine sugar does. And yet, and yet, although this rime might be composed of urine, I didn't feel it could be responsible for the odor, which came in drafts. I was puzzled, lingering beyond mere curiosity, and then Elsie began again to snore. The next draft was fuller and more pungent, and then I knew. Her breath. Her breath carried the scent.

I didn't know why, and asked a nurse.

Her kidneys have stopped functioning over the last two days. She will die of uremia, if another stroke doesn't take her more quickly.

I've been looking at my book of symptoms tonight. Please

let her die quickly, O Lord. Deliver her in your mercy from this corruption and let her put on the incorruptible. For the sake of your Son, please.

4/16

I spent the day, canceling my worship service (this is Sunday), with Elsie in the room where they have her. She's been spared any further treatment—since that would only mean worse pain and longer suffering—except for periodic shots of morphine. Her daughter was there, too. We didn't do anything but read and talk quietly now and then and make sure the nurses arrived at three-hour intervals with the shot. The drug works, at least. Her breathing becomes more relaxed, although it remains shallow. And the sudden, uncontrollable movements of her limbs, which are accompanied by cries that reach back to my mother's own, don't appear until she's almost due for another hypo.

Somehow it's easier being in the room with her than out in the hall getting coffee or, what has become impossible, continuing with my other duties. It's horrible being with her, but I'd rather see how badly she's suffering than imagine it. Of course, who knows, really, what she feels or doesn't, whether her mind functions, records the pain, or has recognized its own superfluity and lets the death go on unacknowledged? When I'm with her, my presence says that this shall pass. That's probably why I'm there, to receive the benefit of this knowledge. Maybe she knows I'm there too, occasionally.

There appear to be two places, in the fiery furnace and out, and I believe I know at long last that there's no getting out of it prior to death. Seeing the fourth presence, then, is the only way to bear the flames.

4/17

Her convulsions were nearly continuous today. The shots no longer prevail against it. Jill and I took turns at her bedside, holding onto her when her muscles went into spasms. She's unbelievably strong. Her elbow hit my jaw so hard it popped it out of place, and I thought I'd have to go down to the emergency room, but the nurse knew how to unhinge the ungainly device and set it back in place—a relief to have such a petty crisis. In fact, I'm pretty banged up, bruises all over my body. And each one, as our most bloody poet, Crashaw, had it, is a kiss.

4/18

Jill was out of the room; I was beside Elsie's bed. Her breathing had been slow and shallow for hours, and her back arched every time she inhaled. Another spasm came, and she reached out as if to take someone in her arms. I caught her and held her, supporting her weight just off the mattress. She gripped my arms tightly, holding onto me and whatever power I had to relieve the pain. I supported her head in the crook of my arm and heard her take another breath; with the fluid in her lungs, it had the sound of water sucking down a drain. All she could expel was a faint cry.

I kissed her cheek and lowered her back onto the bed. She had suffered so horribly in the last few days that her head looked shrunken—black shadows around her eyes, her cheeks drawn and scored with lines, her lips parched, white, and her skin layers of flaky crust. Except for her yellowed complexion, which hadn't yet undergone the waxy composition of the mortician's portrait, her body had rendered up what had made her Elsie. There was one more rasping intake of breath and then she lay still.

She had done the last thing she would ever have to do as a Christian: die.

I sat back in my chair by the side of the bed. I was tired with a fatigue that I knew would dog the next weeks and months. But looking at Elsie, I didn't feel particularly sad—not, surely, the eloquent upheaval of grief, which would come later in my missing her in an absolutely hopeless way. Elsie had done what she had to do; she had "finished her course." And she had done it well.

Then I thought how strange it was for me to be there. Gideon again. The last man in the world. You have such a strange sense of humor, Lord. But the last shall be first, and the first shall be last, I thought, as I shook my head and almost laughed.

But that was it: how else become the supernatural creatures God intends us to be? How else but at some point to find ourselves doing and thinking what before would have been impossible. For with God, all things *are*. They are, indeed. I felt satisfied that I had done the best thing I had ever done in my life.

Elsie looked so small where she lay, as if her soul, in leaving, had left behind nothing but worn-out clothes. I thought about her ascent to God. I thought of the chariot of fire which ushered Elijah into the kingdom, and glancing up at the flourescent light on the ceiling, imagining Elijah and wishing I could have been there, I heard that chariot. Or heard the whirlwind following it. I heard it by the tone it struck in my heart, as if I were a stand of trees in a mountain pass that sets the wind to making such a sound. *Swing low sweet chariot.* The melody and words rose up inside me. *Swing low* . . . And it did; it brushed over me as Elsie was gathered up.

The sound can only be described in other terms, mostly as mirth—the holy laughter of a God who seizes everything wrong and assures that it all turns out right.

It was what I heard when the woman named her baby after me, it was present at the births of my own children, it was at the end of my last revival message—there all the time, but never heard unless it's attended to. I hadn't been silent enough. I hadn't learned to *wait*. It was the sound of my name in God's mouth, the word that I was created and chosen to be, the part that I have been given in the chorus to shape into song.

I looked back at Elsie once more. Her hand had fallen so that a finger pointed between the bars on her hospital bed toward me. This benedictory gesture seemed to confirm my oldest fear and my greatest longing. I have been chosen to see people into heaven. I am a metaphysical midwife—this man beside Elsie Mayfield's bundle of dry bones—or, to use the older term, a spiritual doctor.

What my degrees say I am, I should have been all along.

Heaven and Earth

"Wilt thou have this Man to be thy wedded husband, to live together after God's ordinance in the holy estate of Matrimony? Wilt thou love him, comfort him, honour and keep him in sickness and in health; and, forsaking all others, keep thee only unto him, so long as ye both shall live?"

Marianne stands before me in white, her almond eyes on me aslant, for her head is turned mostly toward Michael. She sees that I have indeed finished speaking, and responds, "I will." She takes Michael's hand in hers, as he is supposed to do later, not she, now or then. The wrists of her gown are lace, and a flowering vine traces its way through the material, blooming into rosebuds. Not the demure bride concealing her hidden joy, Marianne rubs the back of Michael's hand in her ardent yearning. With her looks and smiles, she fashions a hedge of intimacy around them; inside, the collusion of their wills seems to begin—all that they share, apart from their appearance to the world. And I wonder why she, Eve, should insist upon her perfection as a sanctuary, and have to take Adam captive. No, she has not been listening to the vows, but there in the handclasp the same promises form. And yet, too, it's only Marianne eager to possess this latter-day surfer, with his unaccountable scruples about the flesh. Still, hers, rose-tinted, fresh and highlighted, especially at her pillowy cheeks and within the shining arc of her collar, looks to me transfigured— the bright presence I have always seen arrayed, even when disguised in pauper's clothes, for the bridal of her father's heart. It will cushion the flesh of this man I have bruised and wounded (Christ's body eventually assuages us all).

Her self-willed epiphany is for Michael, of course. I have already given her to him earlier in the service, holding her arm while Michael's new assistant, Roger Forster, asked me the question. The assistant now stands beside me in his academic robe, as I am in mine, a tall fellow with a heavy beard and heavy disposition, from what I could tell during the wedding rehearsal—far more reticent and scholarly than Michael. Which makes me think that Michael may do better by my old church, and in the future of his ministry, than I had thought. Is the church, in its staid purification, at last coming into its own?

So I lead Michael and Marianne through the choreography of their double-ring ceremony. "With this ring, I thee wed." The band distracts Marianne a moment; she waggles their joined hands as if to see how the band affects the way her diamond takes the light. She is pleased. Michael prompts her to take his band from me by tapping her hand with his yet unadorned fingers. She slides the ring on, and her free hand grasps Michael's forearm, slipping his sleeve up, sheathing its underside.

They kneel on the white cushions of the gilded prie-dieu while a friend sings a Renaissance ballad from the balcony. It's an appeal by the Lover to his Lady to let him worship at her shrine, and I actually enjoy the music at a wedding for once, in its contrast to the usual warble through "O Promise Me." The woman's voice, the harp and viola accompanying her, repeat the chantlike melody; its simple notes seem to rub against each other and set vibrating the deep-registered chords of prayer.

The candlelabras at my sides shed their light upon the bridesmaids and groomsmen, animating their fresh faces. Each young god in his ancient place, they compose a firmament, which, aligned as it was in the beginning, starts another cycle—for them, and somehow for the rest of us, too, the first. The half-lit church simulates dawn, a darkness that is not blind, a light which is general and filled with promise.

A white runner leads back down the center aisle. Every fourth pew has a stand of flowers attached to a makeshift trellis. I look again at Constance in the front row, wearing a light-blue chiffon dress with a large bow at the collar and a plush, dark

beret back from her face and to one side of her head. She sees
me looking and makes a show of wiping away a tear. I nod.

Beyond her the pews are filled almost to the very back.
Cecil and Patti and Jerry and Allen—they've all come; Michael
gave an open invitation to the church members from his pulpit.
I, of course, haven't stood here before them since the night of my
dismissal. I don't feel as I did about them then; although I recognize the individual faces, in a greater sense they have merged
back into a crowd: not being under my care, they are a landscape
in which I have no habitation, no position which orders all in
relationship to it. The time in the hospital has already done this
and made today a reunion, an event that in deference to a real
past will overshadow memory and remain at a double remove
from life. It's not as if I do not care what they are making of this
spectacle; but I believe I shall quit caring rather quickly after we
say our good-byes.

Ben stands as the last groomsman, to my far left. His neck
is longer, his features out of alignment, his nose too long and his
ears shifting outward, as adolescence starts to play its joke on his
perfect boyhood. Cruel humor. A cruelty that has begun to make
him react in kind. When he arrived with his mother he wanted
to show his loyalty to me, but showed instead that he was learning
to hurt her, when I said something about Constance looking like
a bride herself, and he said, "Yeah, in a horror film." He's standing still, now. Very grown up and solemn, there on the end, but
with his fingers in his pockets and his arms slammed to his
sides—probably thinking of having his counterpart, Michael's
cousin, Laura, on his arm again.

The music ends and I pray. Then Michael helps Marianne
rise, as her maid of honor, Jennifer, adjusts her train for the
descent down the platform steps and the aisle.

"I pronounce that Michael and Marianne are man and wife.
God the Father, God the Son, God the Holy Ghost bless, preserve,
and keep you; the Lord mercifully with his favour look upon you,
and fill you with all spiritual benediction and grace; that ye may
so live together in this life, that in the world to come ye may have
life everlasting."

They kiss. Standing two feet away, Marianne demonstrates
emphatically to me that she knows how. Michael breaks their
clench, but Marianne adds another peck for good measure, and

then, seeing that her lipstick has marked the side of his mouth, she touches his cheek and wipes away the offending smear with her thumb.

As we recess, I stop by the first pew and take Constance on my arm and her hold, light yet secure, disdains any appeal for physical assistance, and in its pure pomp makes the gesture one by which she seems to be choosing, step by step, to be at my side: each pace self-contained, the joy enacted anew again and again anew. I remember our wedding, this walk, and how stunned I was; we were now man and wife. My wonder at her love for me began then and has never ceased. And, passing the middle pews, at this juncture in our progress, I come to understand that perhaps it is this very bewilderment at her love that has finally led me to forfeit it. Her being by my side might now signify nothing.

Before we reach the foyer, in the privacy of public view, she whispers to me under the recessional music, "What was it that they played for us? Bach?"

"I don't remember the music," I whisper back. "I remember you." I bend down and kiss her cheek, which she suffers me to do. And expecting to see my perfect felicity in her expression, I see instead the crosshatch lines at her eyes, and she looks as she does when awakened from a dream, lost for a moment between worlds.

Today our marriages couple for me like lovers. I only hope that Constance has something of the same feeling, despite our separation and impending divorce.

In the hall, I step to the left, out of the way of the other party members, and Constance withdraws her arm but follows. We stand together watching the bridesmaids lean across the barriers of their satiny dresses to kiss Marianne. Michael is standing with his fellows, where Ben, looking at ease for the first time in his tuxedo, waits his turn to shake the groom's hand. When it comes, Michael gives him a great hug. I hear Ben say quickly yet distinctly, "We're brothers now!"

Usually the embarrassed one, Ben sees how affected Michael is by this; he can only respond by putting his hand on Ben's shoulder. Then Michael's best man, his brother John, says, "Yeah, and if you act like a squirrel, we'll come stomp you."

"Sit on it!" Ben replies, overjoyed at the attention.

They jostle him among them, pushing him from one to the other.

Someone announces that the cars are waiting, and Michael takes Marianne's hand.

I walk out with Constance. The second car is reserved for our use, but I want to drive myself to the house where the reception is being held in order to escape early, if I find the celebrating unendurable.

I tell Constance I'm driving my car.

"Oh, no," she says, genuinely hurt.

"Come with me," I say. Her look seems to indicate our reserved car. "Let someone else use it," I say.

"Ben!" Constance calls. He was running a few strides after the limousine as it took off with Michael and Marianne. "Ben, come here. Laura, you too, come here for a minute, please."

Constance bends to Ben and adjusts his bow tie. "Dad and I are going to drive over in the family car. Why don't you go with Laura in the limousine?" Constance turns to his partner. "Your mother will pick you up there, Laura. I'll tell her."

Ben looks at the sharklike black car, a newly-minted Cadillac. He takes Laura's hand. "Come on," he says, rather too simply. I cannot decide whether the chance to ride in the Cadillac has overcome Ben's timidity, whether he has grown up this much in the last months, or whether he'll be lucky—his mother's social grace prevailing—and not have trouble courting.

They hop in, Ben first, and though he has committed this initial *faux pas*, they do look like a couple: the figurine which tops the wedding cake. Laura will be a beauty; her eventual growth will alone subdue her large front teeth, and her round face will be someone's world, her long-lashed eyes his seas. Ben shouts at the driver as they take off, something with James in it, and Laura, who knows her part, acknowledges his daring with a look, and laughs.

Constance returns from talking with Laura's mother, and by this time the crowd is milling around us. I lead Constance out through the parking lot, the asphalt field I used to think of as my pasture (from here I saw the heavens as a mosiac of the Pantocrator's vault, holding Ben's hand, now eons ago) and we drive onto the freeway. At four o'clock the sun has started its arc down, but the day still appears full, eternal; the light has become more substantial and golden. Golden California. The freeway sends us along, with a roof-view of the passing communities, like a checkerboard tilting up toward the haze of the horizon above the surrounding mountains.

Constance checks her makeup, returns her compact and its mirror to her purse and snaps it shut. "The service was lovely" she says. "Your sermon was perfect. I liked that about marriage being 'an earthly place for heavenly exercises.' "

"Thank you."

"And the other part about harmony. A good way to answer the questions about you and Michael, I thought."

"You picked that up. I'm sure most people didn't—that's why I wanted a getaway car."

"Michael. If we didn't know Marianne, we'd wonder how it could possibly work out, too, I suppose."

"But I don't think it is the same. I think she loves him. I pray that she does."

"When she was dressing, she was talking about divorce. She said she thought it gave their marriage a better chance, that he doesn't believe in it. So I asked her if she believed in it, thinking of us, you know, and she said that she thought she'd already been through it several times. But then she became more serious. She confessed to me that she had been very afraid of being unable to know whether Michael was any different. And then she decided he was. I realized, she said, that I would want to kill myself, and him, if it didn't work out. She says you call it, 'loving too much.' I was proud of her. And then she had to say, 'I hope I think the same *after* I get his gorgeous bod into bed.' "

"Well, he better be good, to avoid unfavorable comparisons."

"Jealous?"

"Think about it. He's inexperienced, and Marianne, well, it's a lot rougher than in the days when they used to hang the sheet out for the neighbors approval."

"This is embarrassing, but now that we are talking about it, I told her the same thing. Not to worry. She's ready to be his teacher."

"Constance, listen to us. We're getting along."

"Yes."

"So?"

"So the past week has been good," she said. "And, well, I've missed you. While I was back this time, I missed you." I glance

over at her. She has her fingertips to her mouth and is looking
out the window. She seems to take several deep breaths. "I can't
get it right in my mind, though."

"What?"

"What was supposed to happen. Something was supposed
to happen, and now it seems too late. It makes getting back
together seem preprosterous. Not bad or painful, but silly. I
would be disappointed in myself, or else I'm admitting I already
am."

"Success, fulfillment, those things?" I keep to the expected,
knowing we're on the edge.

"Yes."

"They have happened. Off and on."

"Off and on," she says, and gives a sharp, ironic laugh. "I'm
almost fifty years old, mister." She shakes her head ruefully. "Off
and on."

"I love you," I say. I see the expression she wears now from
the past, our courting days: the chin lifted, her face set, imperi-
ous, but those eyes intercsted, flicking once and then twice on me.

"I love *you*," she says. Looking straight ahead, she adds in
a sly voice, "Off and on." She turns on me, the woman of the
world, and we laugh together.

I reach out and take her hand. She slides over a bit so that
I won't have to keep reaching. We sit with our hands clasped
through the last of the ride, in silence.

The reception is being given at the Beverly Hills home of
Constance's friend, Marietta. The place has been used for a
movie set—the exterior—several times. It's the colonial manse at
the beginning of the movie, and in its circular drive the up-and-
coming young man or detective can be seen parking his car. I
park ours. Constance and I walk through the house to the garden
in back, where tables are laden with food, and the reception line
will empty from the library.

Beyond the pool, Marietta's backyard becomes the side of
a hill which has been terraced. A switchback walk rises from one
plateau to another, and the levels are demarcated by objects
made of stone: a bench, a fountain, a piece of statuary—among
them a modern mother and child in such abstracted shapes they
melt into one another, a cherub face on a wall disgorging a trickle
of water. Ice plant covers the hill, but the plateaus are marked

also by plantings which tend to be horticultural curiosities, night-blooming tulips and bonzai trees (their tags tell the guest what he is appreciating), and although Constance will soon be taken up with the reception line and helping prepare Marianne for her rice-strewn departure, I know that after this she will have to wander up to see all of this, and the view from the top of the hill, with her designer's eye.

The line is organized in the library, a book-lined and wainscotted room with an oriental rug and a desk at one end with its legs bowed like the legs of a deer, and I step lightly. I shake hands with everyone. People keep telling me I look well, as if I have been suffering from an illness too terrible to mention. The line ends. I'm standing in the corner reading the spines of the volumes on the shelves when Marianne comes up to me.

"What kind of bride do I make?" she says, and steps back and spreads one hand as in a low bow, all peacock.

"A happy one. You're enjoying this, aren't you?"

"I never thought I'd have a wedding. Not even as a little girl, and all little girls do. I woke up today and I was having a nice dream, but it was even better to be awake. Do you know what that's like? What I'm saying?"

"Yes."

"I understand now about 'loving too much.' "

"Your mother told me."

"You know what I've been thinking? If you had never hit Michael, I wouldn't be here now. It's frightening."

"You might have met and talked eventually, dear. You needn't lay all the praise and blame at my feet."

"I would have been afraid of him, I think. I needed to see him when he was hurt. Is this you and Mother all over again?"

"Always."

"Oh, God."

"Don't think about that now. The reverse is equally true. It could never be like us, never in this world."

We stand together for a moment more. "I don't know what else to say, Daddy. I don't want to leave you, though, I know that."

"Give me a hug and then go get dressed. A bride shouldn't *linger* at her party."

Michael comes up to us just as she slides her arms from my shoulders, a timing that I'm pleased to see.

I call to Constance and then send them away to get Marianne dressed in her traveling clothes. The honeymoon will be spent in a resort hotel near Big Sur.

"Thank you," Michael says. "For the service, everything."

"I want to talk with your folks before they get away. Your mother will make a good in-law for Marianne."

"Well, Christian Scientists may be heretics, as they say, or cultists, but they don't pamper their children. Mom never did me."

"Did she take you to the doctor when you were growing up?"

"Oh, for sure. They only take it seriously when it suits them, usually around the time of the yearly conventions." He looks back over his shoulder. "How is the old flock treating you?"

"With more respect than formerly."

"I'm going to preach on forgiveness when I get back. It might bend them out of shape, but in the right way, you know."

"Michael," I say, "pray for us. We can't be allowed to forget what this day has been like."

"You gave me your daughter today, Ted. And I love her. What's gone before, well, it's being redeemed, don't you think?"

"The creation groans."

"The heavens declare the glory."

I put my arm around him. "One rooster to a henhouse, as they used to say in Texas. Go tell your family good-bye. Marianne will be down soon."

The party gathers in the circular drive. The car, a Grand Prix—Michael has borrowed it to fool his prankster groomsmen—waits purring. Abashed, I peer through the corridor of people and see the two in the grand hall, Marianne wearing a cocktail dress, low-cut and with a slit up the side which—as she runs forward, the dress whipped about her—seems even less of an encumbrance than it's designed to be. The rice explodes into the air, some of it getting into my left eye. I can't see anything until they are invisible behind the distant, tinted windshield.

I walk back in and through the house. I see Constance by the pool, talking with one of the caterers. She soon takes to the hill, fulfilling my quotidian prophecy, and I follow.

I go up to the third plateau, and then back down one, not seeing her, thinking she may have turned off onto a side path there, and then go up again. I walk all the way to the top before I see her already sitting serenely on the promontory's bench. Hardly looking at me, she pats the place beside her. And sitting, recovering my breath, I notice that Constance is winded herself. In fact, she works to get her breath long after I do.

"You saw me coming after you," I say.

"Up the primrose path," she says, as if proud.

We look out over the tops of the trees where the hills, gouged and brown where the rains have cut out the scrub foliage, fall away to the valley, a maze of different greys in the early-evening light. The moon is up already, although no stars have appeared. The sky looks opalescent, its first darkening only a loss of transparency.

"Look," she says, "See Ben down there. Ben and Laura."

"Where?"

"Not by the pool, that cul-de-sac about half way up."

Ben sits kissing Laura. They are so stilled, their heads tilted, their hands on one another's shoulders, that they could be a piece of the statuary. Then they pause, look at one another, and resume, assuming the same reverent attitude.

"He has grown up these past months," I say.

"He's ready to fly," Constance says approvingly. "Once he gets through his ugly duckling period."

"Don't be so happy. It feels like we're losing them both today."

"You wouldn't think that if you'd been living with him the last few months. He's been fishing around for a way out of the family womb."

The late afternoon haze has begun to settle on the valley below us, and, mingling with the brown smog, makes the city look flooded, as if it were being washed away by the night.

After a time, she says, "You have me thinking about you and your work. That new job."

"I noticed. I mean, I noticed you thinking."

"Why are you there? I wouldn't have thought you'd ever take work like that."

"I couldn't get another job."

She frowns.

"The job involves everything else," I say.

"I'm willing to believe that."

"It's inevitable. Whatever you run away from looms into view around the last turn. You can't escape the Promised Land. It's here. You can't sail away from Ninevah."

"I suspect that's so if you've got them in your head like you do," she says.

I shrug my shoulders.

"But you are coping with it all. You seem happy, dear. Explain it, I really am ready to listen."

"I've learned a lot."

"How to live? Those doctors must be testing a final wonder drug on you."

"How to die."

"That's a brave thing to say when you're still healthy."

"I'm not saying I'm not afraid of the pain."

Ben and Laura have disappeared, I notice.

Constance shakes her head and smooths her hair back, in profile to me, and I see the failing light remove years from her face. "I hate your perverse logic," she says, and bites a knuckle, then rests her chin on her fist, that crimp of anger in her lower lip. "The whole deathly Christian thing."

She turns toward me, and suddenly she looks as calm and noble as a renaissance lady in her most luminous portrait. "But it's real for you," she says. "I knew that absolutely when you were up on the platform as the church was voting. It's taken me this long to understand what it means to you. And I don't like it. It's not my way. But I am still in love with you. There's a part of me that's like you. I can love you, I do love you, and probably wouldn't if you weren't so, dammit, *impossible*."

As I take her into my arms, she's laughing and crying at the same time. I hold her until she stops shaking and brush her tears away, realizing how my ministrations to Elsie have gentled my touch. We press our cheeks together and then kiss with a desire that returns slowly, like hunger after a long fast, while she puts a hand to the back of my neck, and scratches at the line where my apron of hair leaves off. We stop and gaze at each other, and this is the only constraint on our felicity, that we cannot behold one another and devour one another at the same time.

"Oh, how I've missed you," I say. And we both laugh at how unspeakable the truth is.

"What shall we do about Ben?" she asks.

"So that we can be alone?"

"Yes."

"Marietta."

"She's done an awfully lot today."

"Please ask."

"All right."

I take her hand and stand up. But she remains seated, looking down toward the valley, where the lights of the city are beginning to shine. "I'm not sure I want to leave here," she says. I'm not sure I want to go back down."

"Let us build three tabernacles."

"Oh, all right. Lead on."

We hurry down the hill, giddy young lambs again, and there Constance makes arrangements with Marietta at a speed which, as much as anything else, confirms how eager she is to come back to me.

In the car, she asks, "Shall we treat ourselves to a hotel?"

"No, no, at home."

She scoots over to me, hugs my side and leans against me. "Are you sure? Home?"

"We've never been there before," I say, and she looks up at me with a puzzled skepticism. "I'm sure we haven't, Constance. Isn't your name Constance? I'll carry you over the threshold."

"No grand gestures, please."

We arrive. The wedding presents brought to the ceremony have been delivered back to our place by a groomsman, and their clutter in the living room makes Constance remark that it looks like someone is moving in.

In the bedroom, we slip beneath the covers and bury ourselves, our pain and our sorrow, in one another's arms, turning from darkness to light, until the morning when we shall arise.